D1579397

MAGGIE SHAYNE

BLUE TWILIGHT

MILLS & BOON

All the characters in this book have no existence outside the imagination of
the author, and have no relation whatsoever to anyone bearing the same name
or names. They are not even distantly inspired by any individual known or
unknown to the author, and all the incidents are pure invention.

First published in Great Britain 2011
by Mills & Boon, an imprint of Harlequin (UK) Limited,
Eton House, 18-24 Paradise Road, Richmond, Surrey TW9 1SR

© Margaret Benson 2005

ISBN: 978 0 263 88012 0

089-0811

Harlequin (UK) policy is to use papers that are natural, renewable and
recyclable products and made from wood grown in sustainable forests. The
logging and manufacturing processes conform to the legal environmental
regulations of the country of origin.

Printed in the UK
by CPI Mackays, Chatham, ME5 8TD

Multiple *New York Times* bestseller **Maggie Shayne** is one of the hottest authors currently writing paranormal romance.

Her works are fresh and sexy, carrying the reader into a darkly compelling and fully realised world where vampires are creatures of the heart, not just the night.

To all of you fans of WINGS IN THE NIGHT who've been
following this series since the first "Twilight" book in 1993.
And to all of you more recent readers we've picked up along
the way, who've gone above and beyond in your journey to
collect the entire series. And to all you brand new readers who
are just discovering this collection for the very first time.
Thank you, thank you, thank you! I truly hope you
enjoy the ride as much as I have.

Maggie Shayne

Prologue

The woman cowered on the brown velvet chaise in his parlor, her eyes wide with fear. Blue eyes. Flaming red hair. He would have preferred a blonde with eyes as black as coal—that stunning contrast in a female's coloring never failed to stir his passion. Or his memory. But so long as they were in the parlor, in view of the portrait, any female would do. It had to be the parlor. He always took his victims there.

Fieldner had brought him a lovely morsel tonight. She was, perhaps, close to her thirtieth year of mortal life. Though she was lean and tall, and he preferred them petite, she was trembling in a way that aroused him. Her pale-skinned face was finely made, her lips a bit on the thin side, nose a hint too straight, but the cheekbones were high and prominent. He loved good cheekbones in a woman. Yes, his drone had done well this day. The fear in the woman's eyes, though, that would have to go.

It would be no trouble, he thought as he moved toward her, mustering a smile and hoping he appeared attractive to her. Women held less fear of attractive men. Foolish, of course, but true. It was difficult not being able to look into a mirror to judge his appearance and its impact on a woman. He knew his hair was long and dark, and that his eyes were deeply set and brown. But it was difficult to remember the precise structure of his own face, or to guess how much he could smile without revealing the unnatural length and razor sharpness of his incisors.

Even if he were frightening to behold, however, he could ease the fear from her mind. He held an entire town in his thrall—day and night. Asleep or awake. One frightened woman was hardly a challenge.

"You have nothing to fear," he told her, moving slowly closer, infusing his words with power even while keeping his voice soft. "This is nothing more than a dream. A fantasy. Nothing can harm you here."

Her wide eyes flickered. She drew a stuttering breath.

"Look into my eyes, lovely one. Hear my words. Feel them. You are not afraid. You are safe, and warm, and completely relaxed."

He watched as some of the tension left her body. Her eyes were no longer wide but becoming heavy-lidded. He moved a little closer, reached out and touched her cheek. "Your mind is completely at ease now. You've relinquished all control, all responsibility—released it to me. You know only what I tell you. You feel only what I make you feel. You want only what I tell you that you want."

Her eyes fell closed; a slow, deep sigh whispered from her lips. The tension eased from her shoulders. That was much, much better.

"Right now, what you want, my precious, is me. My touch. My caress. You want it more than you want to live. More than you've ever wanted anything. Don't you?"

"Yes," she whispered, rubbing her cheek against his hand.

"You will know the most exquisite pleasure you have ever known this night. Perhaps for another night, as well, or maybe several more. Do you want that?"

"Yes," she whispered.

"Very good." To reward her, he let his hand drift across her cheek, over her jaw and neck, and down to brush across her breast. She shivered in reaction, and he smiled. It would be good for her. He would make sure it was good for her. He would plumb her mind, find her deepest fantasies and fulfill them all. And she would remember nothing when it was over. She would be returned to her home with no harm done to her. And he would be sated. At least for a little while.

She rose to her feet and unbuttoned the dress she wore, then slid it from her shoulders and let it lie on the floor. He watched her as she removed her bra and panties without a hint of inhibition, and he was careful to keep his attention on her body, not her face. The only face he wanted to see was above and behind her, gazing down at him with love in her eyes.

He drew the woman to him, touched and caressed her, using his mind as much as his hands to make her feel sensations everywhere at once. And he probed inside her mind to hear every desire. When she wished he would touch her breasts he did so, caressing until she wanted more, then tugging the responsive nipples, pinching and rolling them between his fingers. When she wanted his mouth, he kissed her, then eased her backward onto the chaise. When she parted her legs to him, he moved his hand between them, every touch infused with his power. He could make her climax without even touching her, but he preferred it this way.

When she was twisting and writhing against him, he lay atop her. He hadn't undressed. He didn't need to. She would feel him penetrating her even though he had no intention of doing so. She would experience him deep inside her, and he would take the satisfaction he so needed in his own manner.

From her throat.

"Call me 'My Prince,'" he instructed.

"Yes, you are my prince."

He tipped her head back, gently moved her hair away from her neck. She was moving now, her hips rocking to take him, even though he wasn't there. Humping air and a fantasy he'd implanted in her mind. "Say it in my tongue, pretty one. Say *'prinţ meu.'*"

She repeated the phrase, even as he gathered her upper body, lifting her slightly, so that he could keep his gaze on the portrait above. And then he lowered his head, pressed his mouth to the tender skin of her neck. She whimpered and clutched the back of his head, straining to reach her peak. But he wouldn't allow that, not until he was ready. "Tell me to take you. To drink you into me."

"Yes, *prinţ meu*. Take me. Drink me. I need you to. You must!"

"Then I shall." He parted his lips, closed his teeth over her throat and pierced her jugular, his eyes riveted to the ebony eyes of the portrait as the elixir, the stuff of life, flowed into him. He drank, and as he did, the woman shrieked and shuddered as the orgasm rocked her body.

Still staring at the portrait, he lifted his head, sated. The woman reached for him, but at a wave of his hand, she relaxed back against the cushions, her eyes falling closed. He curled up on the chaise and wrapped her in his arms, holding her gently against his chest. Gazing up at the portrait, he whispered, "Can you feel my love, where you are? I hope you can, my heart. It was you, you know that. It was you. They all are."

1

White Plains, New York

"He'll be here," Maxine Stuart said as she smoothed packing tape over the flaps of a cardboard box. "There's no way he'll let me leave without coming to say goodbye. He's nuts about me."

Stormy leaned over the box with her black marker and scrawled Kitchen Stuff across the top. Then she capped the pen and put it back into her pocket. "That's it," she said. "That's the last of it." She picked up the box and started for the door.

Max snatched it from her hands. "I told you, no heavy lifting."

"Knock it off, Max. The doctors say I'm fine."

Subconsciously, perhaps, Stormy ran a hand over her short hair. It had grown back by now, short, spiky, platinum blond and overly moussed, just as it had always been. Her hair covered the scar where the bullet had rocketed through her skull only a few months ago, plunging Stormy into a coma and nearly killing her. But though Max couldn't see it, she was acutely aware that the scar remained. She would never forget how close she had come to losing her best friend. It shook her still, to remember.

"Stop looking at me like that," Stormy said.

"Like what?"

"Like those coppery curls of yours are going to catch fire from the intensity. I really am fine."

"You'd better be." Max shook off the melodrama, knowing Stormy hated it. "Get the door, would you? My arms are breaking here."

Stormy opened the door, and the two walked out of the cozy white Cape Cod, down the concrete front steps and around to the back of the bright yellow rental van that waited in the driveway. Its back doors were open. Max climbed aboard and crammed the final box into the one remaining spot, near the top of the pile. Her whole life, she thought, was in that van. Sighing, she jumped down and closed the doors.

"Excited?" Stormy asked.

"To be starting a whole new life, yeah. I am. Are you?"

"If I wasn't, I wouldn't have agreed to come with you. Besides, what's not to be excited about? We're moving into a restored mansion, for crying out loud. Hanging up our shingle. Starting a new business."

"Think it will succeed?"

"I think it will kick ass," Stormy said. "What with those flyers we sent out with both our pics on them, full color, no less? They made us sound like the best detective agency since Sam Spade's. And besides, we're hot."

"We *are* hot," Max said.

Stormy pursed her lips. "You don't look very excited, Maxie. You look as if your heart's breaking."

Max leaned back against the van and eyed the house where she'd grown up, its neatly trimmed hedges and freshly mown lawn. "I'm a little bummed we're going to have to make two trips. I mean, if I trusted myself to drive this van with the car behind it, I'd use the tow bar that came with the thing. But I'm not that confident."

"Uh-huh." Stormy crossed her arms and tapped her foot, giving Max a look that said she knew perfectly well that was not what was bothering her.

Max nodded and gave in. "I really thought Lou would agree to go into business with us. I mean, you and I have two P.I. licenses and some pretty powerful contacts—"

"Even if they are mostly dead," Stormy put in with a wink.

"But none of that adds up to a retired cop with twenty years under his belt."

"I think there's other stuff under his belt that interests you more."

"Yeah, well, short of bashing him over the head and attacking him, I don't think I'm going to get within a mile of his belt. Much less what's under it."

Stormy tipped her head to one side. The sun caught the rhinestone in her nostril and winked. She'd given up the eyebrow ring. During her coma they removed it and the hole had closed up. But to celebrate her recovery she'd added the nose stud. Personally, Max liked it better. It was petite and daring, just like Stormy.

"Are you telling me," she asked Max in a tone of disbelief, "that during the whole time I was in the coma, and you two were up in Maine saving your sister from notorious vampire hunters and tracking down the bastard who shot me, that you never once—"

"Like you don't think I'd have told you if we had?"

"You'd have rented a billboard," Stormy said with a sigh. "So now you're giving up?"

Max pursed her lips. "If I'm living in Maine and Lou insists on staying here in White Plains, I don't see what choice I have."

Stormy looked at her, a mix of pity and skepticism in her vivid sapphire eyes.

Slowly, Maxine straightened off the van, looked down toward the road and smiled. "I'm not beaten yet, though. Here he comes." She nodded toward the oversize rustmobile that was pulling up to the curb, since there was no room in the driveway. The small square of blacktop held the rental van on one side and Stormy's little red Miata on the other. Max's green VW Bug was in the garage.

The noise level dropped to zero when Lou shut off his engine; then the heavy driver's door swung open. Lou got out, and Max drank in the sight of him. God, he was something. Oh, he tried real hard, especially for her, she thought, to pull off the saggy, burned-out ex-cop routine. With his loose-fitting suits and always crooked ties, and slow-talking, slow-walking ways, he tried to be the living proof that forty-four was over the hill. And *way* too old for a twenty-six-year-old. But she saw through the act. He wasn't too old; he was just too damn wary. The only thing burned out about Lou Malone was his heart, though she didn't know why. She'd always intended to fix it, whether he liked it or not. Now, she thought she was about to run out of time.

He came across the driveway to where she stood, glancing at the van, then at her. His eyes met hers, held them, and she thought she saw something sad in them before he covered it with a smile. Could he be sorry to see her go?

He broke eye contact and nodded hello to Stormy.

"Hey, Lou," Stormy called. "We'd just about decided you weren't coming to see us off."

"Wouldn't miss it. How are you feeling, Stormy?"

"Fine, except for being sick of everyone asking how I'm feeling." She softened the words with a smile. "You?"

"Can't complain." He eyed the van, his glance tripping over Max's tummy on the way. Good, she thought. It would have been a waste of good low-rise jeans and a cropped-short T-shirt if he hadn't even noticed the bared section of skin in between.

He cleared his throat, nodded at the van. "Are you going to have to make a few trips with that thing, Max?"

"Nope. Everything that's going is packed up and ready. Except my car, anyway. I'll have to come back for that."

"Everything?" He lifted his brows. "You couldn't have fit furniture in there."

"You've been to my sister's house, Lou. Morgan's will left me everything, furniture included."

"Still, seems like you'd want some of your own."

"Most of the stuff in this house isn't my own, anyway. It's nearly all hand-me-downs from my parents." She never qualified the word *parents* with the word adoptive, even though it was true. "Besides, what do I have here that would fit there? That place is…opulent."

"Yeah, but it's not *you*."

She planted her hands on her hips and frowned at him. "What's *that* supposed to mean? I'm not opulent?"

He lifted his brows. "It wasn't an insult, Maxie, just an observation. Morgan's house is—hell, it's Morgan. Dramatic, dark, *rich*. You should be in a place that's…I don't know. Cute, quirky, fun."

"Sexy?"

He sent her a quelling look.

Maxie sent him back a wink. "That's what you meant, and you know it. But don't worry, Lou. Once I get settled in, I'm going to redecorate a suite of rooms just for me. I can't exactly do the whole place, though. It's not like Morgan's really dead, after all."

"No, I suppose not." He lowered his head, shaking it slowly.

"What?" she asked.

"We talk so matter-of-factly about it. Like it's nothing. And then every once in a while it hits me. Everything that happened. Everything we saw. Stuff I thought was nothing but superstition, turning out to be real. The fact that one of Mad Maxie Stuart's conspiracy theories turned out to be dead on target."

He said it with a teasing smile that made her want to lean up and kiss it right off his face. Instead, she only shrugged. "I wish you were coming with me."

"Yeah, well, I told you, I didn't retire from the force with the goal of going back to work full-time."

"Right. Instead you're going to buy a fishing boat and spend your time lying around, smelling like bait and growing a beer belly."

"Sounds like paradise, doesn't it?"

"Yeah, for a seventy-year-old in failing health, maybe. Not for you."

He eyed her, maybe seeing a little beyond the words she said out loud, so she averted her eyes. She hadn't meant to sound petulant or pouty. Childish was the last way she wanted him to think of her.

"I'll visit, I promise."

She shot her eyes back to his. "When?"

"When? Well...I don't know."

"How about now?"

"Now?"

"Today."

"Maxie, sometimes I don't even know how to follow your conversations."

She rolled her eyes. "Hell, you're going to make me admit it, aren't you?"

He held up both hands, shaking his head, as if she'd lost him.

"I'm not sure I can drive that...thing." She nodded toward the van. "It's huge, and I can hardly see over the steering wheel. It steers like a truck, shifts like a tank, catches every breeze like a sailboat. It wobbles and rocks, and I can't see behind me with those stupid mirrors."

He looked again at the van, then at her. Stormy

said, "I'm going back inside, make sure everything's locked up, shut down, turned off, you know."

"You drove it here from the rental place," Lou said, as if he hadn't even heard Stormy's announcement. Stormy shook her head, sent Max a surreptitious thumbs-up and hurried back into the house.

"Of course I did," Max admitted. "How do you think I know how hard it is to drive?"

"I think you're trying to twist my arm to get me up there."

"I can think of a lot of men whose arms wouldn't require any twisting at all," she said.

"Then have one of them drive you."

"I don't want one of them. I want you." She let the double entendre hang there.

He pretended not to notice. It was damned infuriating. He responded to all her flirting that way, either pretending it sailed over his head—when she knew damn well it hadn't by the flash of fire it sometimes evoked in his eyes—or by changing the subject. She was beginning to think he didn't take her efforts at all seriously.

"I'm going fishing for the weekend," he said. "Leaving from here, in fact. Got my bag all packed in the car, and a friend with a big boat waiting for me at the pier."

"God forbid I interfere with that," she said.

"You'll do fine on your own, Maxie. You're the most capable woman I know."

She drew a breath, sighed. "Fine. Just fine. Will you at least hang around until I get the beast backed out of the driveway? You can pretend you're a traffic cop again."

"Aah, the good old days." He looked toward the house. "You gonna wait for Stormy?"

"She's driving her car up. And she knows the way." She dug in her jeans pocket for the key, then climbed up into the van and cranked the engine. Through the windshield, she saw Stormy step out of the house and close the door. She sent her friend a secret smile. Stormy frowned, looking worried.

Max shifted the van into Reverse and looked in the side mirrors. She saw Lou standing in the road, making hand motions at her, probably to tell her to back out. She popped the clutch. The van bucked and then stalled.

She started it again, and this time backed up a little before the bucking and heaving began. She kept that up—start, stop, start, stop, jerk, cough, sputter, start—until a car came along the road and Lou changed his hands to a "stop" position. Then and only then did she back up smoothly and quickly, over the mailbox, aiming dead into the path of the oncoming car.

A horn blasted. Tires squealed. Stormy shrieked, and Lou shouted.

Max stalled the van again and got out, leaving it sitting there, with its ass-end poking out into the road. The car had skidded to a stop five feet short of the van, and the driver, a neighbor she recognized, got out, looking scared half to death.

"Sorry about that, Mr. Robbins," Max called, sending the man a sheepish wave and walking behind the van. Lou and Stormy joined her there. She looked sadly at the crushed mailbox and shook her head. "Okay, this isn't so bad," she said. "I'll just pull in and start over." She looked ahead at the driveway, where Stormy's car was parked. "Um, you might want to move that."

Mr. Robbins was muttering, shaking his head and stomping back to his car. He got in, pulled a K-turn and drove away. Stormy went to move her car.

Lou said, "Didn't you hear me tell you to stop?"

"I did. I just hit the wrong pedal. I'll do better this time, promise." She went to the driver's door, reached up and put her foot on the step.

Lou's hands closed around her waist, picked her up off the step and set her back down on the driveway.

She had to forcibly resist the urge to moan in pleasure, because she loved his hands on her. Anywhere, anytime. She really hadn't tried hard enough with him, she thought. Flirting was flirting. But men could be awfully bad at picking up hints. Maybe she should have set him down and told him flat out. She visualized it in her mind. Her looking him in the eyes and saying, "Lou, I want you. I want you in my life and in my bed and in every other way that matters. What do you say?"

He probably wouldn't say anything, she thought. He would probably go speechless with shock. No, she really hadn't tried hard enough. And now it was pretty much too late—unless her hastily devised plan worked the way she intended.

She just blinked up at Lou, her eyes wide with innocence and questions.

He sighed, lowered his head. "You win, Maxie. I'll drive."

Ye-e-es!

"Don't be silly, Lou. You don't have to do that."

"Yeah. I do."

"But your fishing trip…"

"Will wait for another time."

She flung her arms around his neck and hugged him. Lou put his hands on her waist after a moment, though instead of pulling her closer he seemed more interested in keeping her hips a safe distance from his. She didn't resist, because she needed to take things slowly and carefully this time. This was a second chance—she couldn't blow it.

Demurely, she said, "Thank you, Lou."

"I'm not staying, Max."

God, how did he manage to see right through her like that?

He took her arms from around his neck, held her wrists in his hands as if to keep some distance between them and looked her squarely in the eye. "I'll drive the van up there, help you unload, and then I'm coming right back. Understood?"

"Well of course it is." She nodded toward his car. "You can leave your car in the garage. I'll drive you back whenever you're ready. Better bring that weekend bag you have packed, though."

He blinked at her as if she were speaking a foreign language. "Honey, I just told you, I'm not staying."

"I know that. But hell, Lou, it's an eight-hour drive. At the very least you're gonna want a shower and a change of clothes before you head back."

He watched her through narrow eyes. "I won't need the bag," he said. "I'm not staying."

"All right, all right. Whatever you say."

She walked up the driveway, hauling open the garage door. "Hey, if you're driving, then we can use the tow bar and bring my car along, can't we?" she called, as if she'd just had a brilliant idea.

He looked at her car. "There's a tow bar?"

"Yeah, mounted underneath the van."

He nodded, went back to the van, got in and moved it out of its precarious position, parking it safely along the shoulder of the road, on the opposite side of her driveway from where he'd parked his car. He left room behind the van for Maxie's Bug. When he got out, he moved behind it to mess around with the tow bar.

Stormy came walking over to join Max in the garage. "He's coming with us, isn't he?" she asked.

Max smiled. "Well, he couldn't very well let me drive, once he saw how likely I was to get killed on the way. Could he?"

"That was pretty risky, Max. Suppose Mr. Robbins had smashed into you?"

"He had plenty of room to stop. I'm not stupid."

"No, no, you're far from stupid," Stormy said, shaking her head.

Max tossed her a set of keys. "Do me a favor and pull my car out of the garage and around behind the van, so Lou can hook it to the tow bar?"

"Sure." Stormy got into Maxine's car and pulled it carefully out of the garage, past her own and into the road. Then she pulled it along the shoulder, behind the van.

Max went out to where Lou's car was parked and saw that the keys were still in the switch. She started it up and drove it into the now-empty spot in the garage. When she got out, she glanced into the back seat. There was a big satchel there, stuffed to bursting, along with a cooler of beer and plenty of fishing gear. She glanced outside.

Stormy and Lou were busy behind the van, hitching up Max's car.

Licking her lips, Maxine reached into the back seat and snatched the satchel. She took it into the driveway and tucked it into Stormy's car. "Quick and sly as a fox on a caffeine high," she muttered. Then she went back to the garage to close it up. By the time she finished, Lou had her car ready to go. She waltzed out to the van and handed him his keys.

"Your Buick is in my garage, Lou. It'll be safe and sound there until you get back."

He looked at her suspiciously.

Stormy tapped him on the shoulder. "Don't lose me. I'll be right behind you guys, okay?"

"Okay."

"Keep the cell phones turned on."

"Will do," Maxie said, wondering why Stormy seemed nervous about the trip. "Honey, are you worried about something?"

Stormy denied it a little too quickly. "I have the directions and everything, I'm just worried I'll get lost. So don't drive too fast." She hurried to her car and started the engine. As far as Max could tell, she didn't even notice the extra bag behind the passenger seat. Not that she would say anything if she did. Storm was on her side in this.

In everything. She was Max's best friend—which was why Max knew her well enough to be worried about the drive. Storm was *not* herself, and hadn't been, not since the coma.

Max reached for Lou, deciding to take advantage of another opportunity for physical contact. "Help me into this thing?" she asked, standing next to the passenger door.

He pursed his lips, but she didn't care, because he put his hands on her again to do as she asked.

"I'm not staying, Maxie," he said, one hand on the small of her back, the other bracing her forearm as she climbed into the truck.

"Quit saying that, Lou. I got it already."

Lou walked around to the driver's side and

climbed in. Maxie fastened her seat belt, settled in for the long ride, and told herself she had the next eight hours to figure out how she was going to convince Lou to stay with her in Maine.

Failure was not an option she even bothered to consider.

2

Stormy drove along behind the yellow van and told herself everything was going to be fine. She visualized a bright future, she and Max with their own private investigations agency: SIS. Supernatural Investigations Services—because that would be their specialty. Max had assured her, though, that they wouldn't turn down ordinary types of cases. The acronym "sis" was, Max said, as much in honor of her own newfound twin sister, Morgan, as it was in honor of her relationship with Stormy. The two were far more than best friends—always had been.

God, it would be just like the old days, just like when they'd been in their teens and snooping into things that didn't concern them. They'd been kids then, amateurs, usually digging for proof of one or another of Max's far-fetched conspiracy theories and most often finding none.

Until that day when the "research lab" in White Plains had burned to the ground. Max had always insisted there was something more going on in that place than met the eye. And that time, for once, she'd been right.

The building had housed the headquarters of the DPI—the Division of Paranormal Investigations—a super-secret government agency dedicated to the study and elimination of vampires. The repercussions of what Max had learned while snooping through the debris that night almost six years ago were still reverberating through their lives. She had found proof of the existence of vampires. It still rattled Storm's brain when she tried to process everything that had happened since. But it had all been leading up to this. Max and Stormy, professional snoops now. *Licensed* professional snoops, specializing in things beyond what most considered "normal."

But it wasn't quite the same, was it? Back in the old days, there had been three of them. Stormy, Max and Jason. Gorgeous, chocolate-skinned, studious, conservative Jason Beck. He'd provided a counterbalance to Storm's fearlessness and Maxie's impulsiveness. But he'd moved away, never knowing what Max had found in the rubble that night. Hell, she hadn't even told Stormy until a few months ago.

Stormy often wondered what might have happened if she hadn't turned Jason down when he'd asked her out back in college. Or if he'd stayed, instead of moving away, going to law school. She missed Jason.

Jason.

Pain. A red-hot blade plunged deep into her head. White light blinded her, and noise—radio static like a thousand stations fighting for a frequency—exploded inside her mind.

She pressed a hand to her head and jammed both feet on the brake pedal, since she could no longer see the road.

Jason.

The light in her mind took form, and she saw his familiar profile in her inner vision. Harder, more angular than she remembered him. Older. Brown eyes, shaved head, drop-dead handsome as he'd always been.

Facing him, also in profile, was another man's face. A chiseled face with full dark lips and deep brown luminescent eyes with paintbrush lashes and brows so full they nearly met. His hair was long, perfectly straight and raven-wing black. And he was as familiar to her as her own reflection in the mirror. And yet a total stranger.

Dragostea cea veche îti sopteste la ureche, a woman's voice, strange and exotic, whispered. And though the words were in some language she didn't know, Stormy realized that the voice she had heard was her own. Only...not.

It frightened her that she understood those words she had uttered. "Old love will not be forgotten," she whispered.

The pain faded. The light dimmed. The noise went silent. She opened her eyes. Her car was sitting cock-eyed on the shoulder of the road in a cloud of dust. A glimpse behind showed black skid marks on the pavement. A look ahead told her the van had pulled over, as well. Max and Lou were getting out, running toward her.

Stormy closed her eyes. Yes, things were different now. *She* was different now. Had been, ever since she'd come out of the coma.

She hadn't stayed in that hospital bed the whole time. She'd left the hospital. She'd left her body. She'd gone somewhere...else.

And she couldn't shake the feeling that when she'd come back, she hadn't come alone. Something had hitched a ride. The owner of that voice that didn't even speak her own language, perhaps. She didn't live alone in her body anymore.

Max was tapping on the glass of the driver's side window, and Stormy rolled it down. "I'm okay," she said.

"What happened? Stormy, you just went out of control for no reason! What is it?"

"Nothing. Really, I...I fell asleep. That's all."

Max wasn't buying it. She searched Stormy's face, then paused, and her eyes widened. "Stormy, your eyes!"

"What? What about them?" Stormy reached for the rearview mirror and stared into it. An ebony-eyed stranger stared back at her. But even as she looked, the color changed from ebony back to their normal vivid blue. She quelled the full body shiver that moved through her and turned back to Max again, schooling her expression to a picture of calm. "There's nothing wrong with my eyes, Max. Must have been the way the sun was hitting me," she said.

Max squinted at her. "But..."

Lou put a hand on Maxine's shoulder. "There's a diner up ahead. Maybe we need to stop for a rest."

"Good idea," Max said. She nodded to Stormy. "Shove over. I'm driving."

Stormy knew better than to argue. Max was worried. And she'd seen something. Hell, Stormy was surprised she'd been able to keep her strange symptoms to herself for as long as she had—keeping secrets from Mad Maxie was not easily done. She'd had a few episodes similar to this one: blacking out, seeing strange flashes, hearing incoherent murmurs. But never before had an image come clear, the way this one had, nor had any of the murmurs taken on the form of words, foreign or otherwise. Whatever it was, it was getting worse. But dammit, she couldn't tell anyone about this, not even Maxie. Not until she knew what it was—what it meant.

She flipped down the visor, looked in the makeup mirror there, and was relieved to see her own eyes looking back at her.

Maxine was pulling her car into motion. "So you gonna tell me what's up?"

"Honestly, Max, I don't know. I was tired, and I guess I nodded off."

"That's all?"

"That's all."

Max thinned her lips. Time to change the subject.

"Hey, Max, you remember those flyers we had made up, announcing the new business?"

"Sure do."

"Did you send one to Jason Beck?"

Max frowned at her. "Yeah, I did. A business card, too. I sent them to everyone I could think of. Why?"

"I don't know. I've just been thinking about him lately."

"Yeah?"

Storm nodded, then pointed ahead. "There's the diner. Lou's pulling around back."

"Probably more room to park that tank back there. We'll pull around, too." She drove Stormy's car into the parking lot.

Subject successfully changed, Stormy thought slowly. She wanted to rub her head—it didn't hurt, exactly, just felt tender. Sensitive, or something. But she didn't dare. If she gave Max any sign she was in less-than-perfect health, Max would hover like a first-time mother.

"I really am starved," she said. Max always saw an appetite as a sign of good health.

"Me, too." Max pulled Stormy's car to a stop next to the van.

"How's the ride going?" Stormy asked. "Any progress with Lou?"

"Hell, no. He put the radio on some country music channel to limit opportunities for conversation."

"You sure you don't want to ride the rest of the way with me?" She tapped her CD collection. "I have *Disturbed*."

"You *are* disturbed," Max told her with a wink. Then she frowned as she looked at Stormy again. "Despite that, I think I will ride with you for a while. Give you a break from driving for the next couple of hours."

"I was kidding, Max. You need to ride with Lou. Maybe he'll hit a bump and you'll wind up in his lap. You can't miss an opportunity like that."

"Hell, I'll have plenty of opportunities once we get him installed in the mansion."

"But I thought he wasn't staying," Stormy said.

"So does he," Max replied. "But I stashed his bag in your car, just in case."

Stormy looked behind her seat and saw the black leather satchel that she hadn't put there or even noticed up until now. "How observant am I?" she asked. "Could have been a serial killer squatting back there for all I noticed."

"No room for a whole serial killer," Max observed.

"Hey!" Lou tapped on the roof of the little car. "You two getting out or what?"

Grinning, Max opened her door and got out of the car.

Stormy did, too, but her legs felt oddly weak and her muscles, shaky. As if she'd worked out to the point of muscle fatigue. Only she hadn't.

When it had happened before, the weakness had soon passed. But it had never been this clear or this powerful before, nor had it ever left her this shaken. She'd asked her doctor about it after the first attack, but though he had run a battery of tests, nothing abnormal had shown up.

Whatever it was, Stormy was convinced it wasn't physical. It didn't *feel* physical. She couldn't describe why, exactly, or what it did feel like.

They walked into the diner, Max watching her every move.

3

"Here they are, my lord."

He stepped through the open doors into his parlor. It had been weeks since he'd fed. He'd learned to do without for long periods, and Fieldner had been whining that no woman had passed through Endover in all that time.

But tonight, *tonight,* he would feed his body and, more important, his soul with the memory of his beloved.

He looked at the female Fieldner had brought to him. Mocha skin, brown eyes, hair like mink that curled to her shoulders. Beautiful. She stood trembling and wide-eyed at his approach. "You needn't be afraid," he said, staring deeply into her eyes, working to ease her mind with the power of his own.

He frowned and moved closer, and when she backed away, he said two words. "Be still." And he waved his hand to direct his power more fully.

She didn't move again. Just stood there, still afraid. He could hear her heart fluttering as madly as the wings of a trapped dove.

No matter. He would calm her soon enough. He moved nearer, and when he was right in front of her, he touched her chin with one hand and studied her face.

Anger flooded him, though he was careful to keep his voice gentle. "How old are you, child?"

"S-s-seventeen."

He lowered his hand and turned away from her, disappointment washing through him as his hunger stabbed more deeply. Free from the hold of his mind, the girl stumbled backward as if suddenly released from a powerful grip.

"A child?" His eyes sought out those of his servant. Fieldner stood in the shadows, cowering now. "You've brought me a child, Fieldner?"

The man cringed into himself but didn't back away. "Seventeen is hardly a child. And I brought two of them, master."

"Two?" He turned again, noticing the second girl. Caucasian, blond and apparently unconscious on the chaise. He moved to her side, bending over her, touching her, his long fingers sending messages to his keen mind. Then he shot another look at Fieldner. "You've *drugged* her?"

"B-both of us," the other girl said.

He shot her a look, turned to face the girl again. "What is your name, child?"

"D-Delia. Delia Beck. She's Janie." Her lip trembled. "Is she going to be all right?"

"Yes, I promise you she's fine. Don't be afraid, Delia Beck. You have nothing to fear from me." He took a moment to ease her mind, reaching out to it with his own until she relaxed visibly. "Sit there with your friend," he told her. "While I deal with this."

She went to the chaise and sat upon it, taking her friend's hand in her own, speaking softly to her.

He walked across the room to Fieldner, who started babbling at his approach. "I—I *had* to drug them. I did! There are two of them, and they would have fought me. I didn't want to have to hurt one of them. You got angry the last time I hurt one of them."

"And what good did you think it would do to bring

me tainted blood, you idiot?" He looked back at the girls.

The one called Delia was staring at him as if she couldn't look away, her heart still racing, though she wasn't as afraid as she had been. She was mesmerized and terrified all at once. The other one, Janie, moaned, shifting restlessly on the chaise.

"I cannot feed on tainted blood," he said to Fieldner. "And I *will not* feed on children."

"I'm sorry, master."

"The damage is done. There's nothing for it but to keep it from getting worse. They will be missed, surely."

"No! They were traveling alone."

That, at least, was a point in his favor. "Good. I'll command them to forget and send them on their way. But I need sustenance, Fieldner. And I won't take it from them."

"The emergency stores, sir?"

"I don't think so."

Bowing his head, the drone—who was also the police chief of Endover—moved across the room to the hardwood bar, a modern contrivance but one he liked. Fieldner removed a velvet case and set it on top. Opening the lid, he extracted a beautiful cut-crystal wineglass and then a jeweled, razor-sharp dagger.

"I apologize for the girls, sir. But there is something else. Something you should know before I proceed."

"You wouldn't be trying to stall, would you, Fieldner?"

"No, master." He held his wrist over the wineglass and, clasping the dagger in his other hand, laid the blade against his own skin. He would do as commanded. But his blood would be gamey. Male blood always was. And the blood of a man as weak-minded as Fieldner would lack spark and power.

The vampire sighed. "Go on, then. Tell me what it is I should know."

"That one. The dark one," the chief said with a nod of his head toward Delia. "She managed to make a call on her cell phone."

He lifted his brows. "And how did she manage that?" he asked.

"Cowering in the back of my car. I didn't realize what she was doing." He swallowed, his Adam's apple swelling and receding like a wave. "Her brother is in town."

The girl gasped. "Jason?"

Fieldner sent her a quelling look. "You shouldn't

ought to have made that phone call, girl. What happens to him now will be on your shoulders."

The vampire felt her panic returning, and glanced again at the child. "No harm will befall your brother, Delia. Trust me."

"But what about *him?*" she cried. She pointed a finger at Fieldner. "He kept us locked up in the bottom of some lighthouse for hours! It was dark and we—"

"Calm," the vampire said. He drew the word out, aiming more power at the girl. Teenagers—God, but their minds were so much more difficult to control than those of adults. "Relax, child. Everything is fine."

She gulped back a sob and sat on the chaise once more.

Turning to Fieldner again, he said, "Perhaps you'd better begin at the beginning."

The other man nodded. "The two girls were passing through town. Stopped at the old visitor center. While they were looking for rest rooms, I pulled a couple of the plug wires, so their car wouldn't start. Then I offered them a ride to the nearest diner, where they could wait for a tow truck to arrive. They trusted me."

Of course they had, he thought. Fieldner was a

policeman. He wore a uniform and drove a marked cruiser. Any woman would trust him.

"That was this morning. I couldn't very well bring them out here then, so I locked them up in the lighthouse. But on the way there, that one caught on that something wasn't right and called her brother. I don't know how she even got through, with the reception being as bad as it is. There must be a hot spot on the highway somewhere."

"And why didn't you hear the phone call?"

"By then they were making a fuss, demanding I stop the car, let them out. I...I put on the radio to drown out the noise."

Disgusted, the vampire rolled his eyes.

"So she told her brother where she was."

Fieldner nodded. "He was in my office not an hour ago, asking if I had seen her."

"Her car?"

"I'd already hidden it."

The vampire nodded slowly. "That makes one smart move you've made this week," he told Fieldner. "Where is he now?"

"He's staying at the North Star. I think he suspects something."

"Of course he suspects something, if he's less than a complete moron." The vampire heaved a deep sigh. Complications. God, how he hated them. He'd created an idyllic life for himself here, one where he was in complete control. Anytime unexpected complications crept in, they put his entire lifestyle at risk.

He would have to deal with this as quickly and cleanly as possible. "I'll speak with these children, and then you may return them and their car. Leave them far from the shores of Endover. They will remember nothing, of course. This brother of hers will not find them here, and he'll go on his way to discover them safe and sound." He nodded at the man's wrist. "Proceed."

"There's more."

Closing his eyes slowly, the vampire sighed. "What more?"

"This," Fieldner said. He took a paper from his pocket, unfolded it and handed it over.

He took it, skimming the glossy flyer, which advertised some sort of detective agency. But then he went as still as if he'd suddenly turned to stone. His eyes were riveted to the photographs of the women on the front. One of the women, to be more precise. It was impossible. Impossible.

"What is the meaning of this?" he asked, and his voice was no more than a whisper.

"The resemblance is amazing, isn't it, master? I thought the same."

As he said it, the police chief looked up. So did the vampire. He looked up at the portrait of the woman with the delicate facial features of a porcelain doll and beautiful blond hair flowing over her shoulders. She wore a gown from an era long, long ago, and her wide, expressive eyes were as black as the night.

He kept looking from the face on the flyer to the face on the wall. "Tell me what you know of these two women," he whispered.

"The girl's brother—Jason Beck—he had this flyer in his wallet. It fell out when he took out his sister's photo to show it to me. As to the women, I know only what's on the flyer, sir. Their names are Maxine Stuart and Tempest Jones. They're some kind of investigators for hire, who work, apparently, out of an office in Maine. When I asked who they were, Beck said they were old friends of his."

Another good move on the chief's part. One that might keep him alive a little bit longer, the vampire thought. He paced closer, removed the blade from the police chief's hand and returned it to the case. "I'll need you at full strength, Fieldner."

"I await your command, my lord."

He drew a deep breath, moving back to the girls.

The second girl, Janie, was sitting up now, watching the men with unfocused eyes. She was confused and frightened.

"I'm afraid you two will have to be my guests for a short while."

The blonde found both her voice and her courage. "Don't put us back in that cell. Please. We haven't done anything to you."

He pursed his lips, shook his head. "No, no cells for you. My servant has treated you grievously, but I will make up for that. You are my guests, my cherished and honored guests. No harm will come to you in my care. You have my promise."

They seemed to absorb the mental commands he was sending. Delia had already relaxed to a great degree, and Janie's fear began to ease, as well. He leaned closer to Fieldner, spoke softly. "Take them up to the guest rooms. Lock them in." Then he turned to the girls again. "My man here knows now that he was mistaken in his treatment of you. You have no more to fear from him, I promise. And if all goes well, you'll be home with your families in a day. Two, at most."

He nodded to Fieldner, again lowering his voice. "Photograph them, and then hurry back here, Fieldner. There is work to be done."

4

Maxie couldn't hide her excitement from Lou—he thought there wasn't a hell of a lot she *could* hide from him—when she jumped out of Stormy's car in the curving, white gravel driveway and stared at the beautiful house. He didn't blame her. The place was a freaking dream house, a pristine white mansion resting on the rugged coast of Easton, Maine. She was racing up the white flagstone walk to the front door with its tall, oval stained-glass inset even as he parked the van. He smiled as she used her new key to let herself in.

Then he shut the van off and sent a look back at Stormy. She was fiddling with some things in the trunk of her car, obviously not as eager as Max was to rush inside. Preoccupied, perhaps. Maybe Max's worry about her wasn't as overblown as Lou wanted to think.

He climbed out of the van and joined Max in the house. She stood in the great room, taking it in. The chandelier in the domed ceiling above. The gleaming hardwood floors and the rugged, almost Norse-looking furniture. The way the stairs widened at the bottom so that they seemed to spill down from above, like a waterfall flowing into the room. She loved this place—it practically glowed from her eyes. Mostly, Lou thought, she loved it because it was her sister's. It seemed filled with Morgan's presence, her touches, even when she wasn't here.

"Aren't Morgan and Dante here to greet you?" Lou asked.

"No. They're traveling. A delayed honeymoon, I guess." She smiled up at him. That smile hit him in the solar plexus every time she flashed it, and this time was no different. "Besides, I think Morgan wanted to make sure I understood the place was really mine now. Give me time to settle in, get comfortable here. You know?"

He nodded, looking around. "So where's the office going to be?"

"Oh, we already started setting up—took a drive up here last weekend. It's the room Morgan used for her writing when she was here. I think it was originally a den." She walked as she spoke, glancing over her shoulder once. "Stormy...?"

"She's going through some stuff in her car," he said. He saw the way Max's eyes clouded with worry. "Was she okay the rest of the way here?"

"Seemed to be."

"But you're still worried."

She sighed. "You think I'm being dumb."

"I think it's great the way you worry about her, Max. You're the most loyal person I know."

"Yeah?" She smiled again. "That's sweet, coming from a guy who's as miserly with compliments as you are."

"Am I?"

"You'd think they were an endangered species." She looked toward the door again. "Lou, something's wrong with Stormy."

He frowned, a little shiver tingling up the back of his neck. "She said she fell asleep."

"She lied." Max shook her head and paced back to the entryway to stare out at Stormy, who was still picking through the luggage in her trunk. "I think she's been keeping something from me for a while now. Since the coma."

"Any idea what it's about?"

Max shook her head. "Back there, when she went off the road, I could have sworn for just a second that her eyes were jet-black."

Lou frowned at her. "What color are they usually?"

"Blue," she said. "You telling me you never noticed the color of Stormy's eyes?"

"It's not the kind of thing I notice. So shoot me."

"You're a cop. You notice everything."

"Ex-cop," he corrected.

Max flattened a palm over her eyes. "What color are mine?"

They were green, he thought. Huge, sparkling green eyes like a pair of emeralds in the sunlight. Aloud, he said, "I haven't got a clue."

She lowered her hand, looking partly hurt and partly skeptical.

"So you're saying Storm's eyes changed color?"

"It was more than just the color, Lou. It was like— like they weren't even her eyes." She rubbed her outer arms as if she were suddenly cold.

"You wanna know what I think?"

"Of course I do."

He nodded. "Good, because I was going to tell you, anyway. I think you're overly worried about her. And you're overwhelmed with this move, the new business, the new house."

"In a good way, though."

"Doesn't matter. Max, it was only a few months ago you found out your birth mother was a reformed prostitute and that you had a twin sister. You located Morgan, only to learn she was terminally ill and apparently being stalked—by a freakin' vampire, of all things. Then you found out the vamp was the good guy, after damn near getting him killed."

Max shrugged and averted her eyes. "So shoot me for thinking *undead* meant *evil*. It seemed like a logical assumption. Besides, it all worked out okay. He changed her. She won't die now. Ever."

"Still and all," Lou said. "You've barely had time to digest all that. You're suddenly unsure about everything you ever believed. What's real and what's not. The lines that used to be clear are all blurry in your mind."

Max looked at him intently. "That's pretty good."

"I know it is. Don't think I haven't been going through a lot of the same stuff, Max. But here's the thing. With all that fueling it, your imagination is bound to be stuck in high gear. Even more so than usual." She sent him a smirk but he kept on talking. "So Stormy—after damn near dying on you a few months ago—goes off the road, scares the hell out of you, and you rush back there, your emotions heightened to the breaking point, and the sun hits her eyes in a certain way, and bam! There you have it."

She tilted her head. Her copper-red curls brushed past her shoulder on one side, fell behind her neck on the other. He tried not to notice, and noticed, anyway. "You really think that's all it is?" she asked.

"I really do."

Max sighed, nodding slowly. "I suppose you could be right."

He almost gaped in surprise, until she added, "But I doubt it."

Yep, that was the reaction he'd expected. The two of them were so opposite it was predictable. "I suppose you have a theory of your own?"

"I'm working on one."

"And I suppose it's something flaky."

"By flaky you mean...?"

"Paranormal. Supernatural. Otherworldly. Extra—"

"Yeah, something flaky."

He sighed, disliking the way this conversation was going. Now that one of her far-fetched theories had been proved correct, there would be no talking her down from the next one. "I'm afraid to ask."

"Then don't. It's still in development." She shrugged, dropping the subject. "I'm really sorry I made you miss your fishing trip."

"No you're not." Hell, he wasn't, either. He would rather spend time with Max, far-fetched theories and outrageous flirting and all, than in a boat with a fishing pole. But he would be damned if he'd admit it. It would only encourage her.

"You're right, I'm not."

At least she was honest. For the most part, though he had no doubt she was even now plotting ways to get him to stay longer than he intended.

Stormy came in then, a suitcase in each hand. "Isn't this the best place in the universe?" She dropped the cases inside the door. "Are the phones turned on yet? We're supposed to call my parents when we arrive."

"I haven't checked," Max said. Then the two of them headed across the great room and through the double doors off the right of it, into the office.

Lou watched them go. Watched Max, mostly. The girl was hell on wheels. If he thought for one minute her constant flirting was a sign of serious interest he would…

He would what? he asked himself. He wouldn't do anything but brush her off as gently as possible and head for home. He liked Max too much to subject her to a relationship with him. He was hell on women, and he knew it. A miserable failure at that sort of thing. Every woman he'd dated in the past decade had dumped him in short order, most of them accusing him of being about as emotional and romantic as a dying trout. Then again, he hadn't really tried with any of them. Hadn't ever tried since his divorce.

He hadn't wanted to. He still didn't. And Max deserved better.

Sighing, Lou followed them into the office. It was pretty much as Morgan had left it, furnished in her elegant style. A computer was already set up on the antique mahogany desk. Stormy was replacing the telephone receiver on its hook when he came in. "Got a dial tone. Phones are up and running." Then she frowned at the telephone's base. "Hey, the message light is blinking. Think we got a customer already?"

"No way, not yet," Max said. "We haven't even unpacked."

"Maybe all those flyers announcing our grand opening are already paying off." Stormy hit the Play button and sank into a chair to listen. The voice that came from the answering machine was male, and her eyes widened a little when she heard it.

"Max, Storm, it's Jason. Jason Beck. I know it's been a long time, and now I'm only calling because I need your help. I feel like a jerk, but—look, something's going on—I think my sister's missing."

Stormy shot Max a horrified look.

"There's something wrong," Jason's voice went on. "She was on a trip with her best friend. Spring break, her senior year. I got this odd phone call. Really broken up—bad connection. But I know she's in trouble. There's just—there's something off about this whole thing. I need you guys. So call me back. Uh, the cell phone won't work out here, but I have a motel room. Call me, okay?" He gave the number. There was a distinct clicking sound as Jason hung up, and then another. The machine beeped to signal the end of the message.

"Jason Beck—hell, I remember him," Lou said. "Third part of the gang of three, wasn't he?"

Max nodded. "He moved away, went to law school. What time did he leave that message?" she asked Stormy.

Stormy looked at the machine. "At 7:10 p.m. Less than an hour ago."

"Play it again," Lou said.

"Lou?" Max must have seen something in his eyes, because she leaned closer to look into them. "What is it? What are you—"

"Just play it once more."

Stormy hit the Play button, and they listened to their old friend's worried voice. When the message ended, Lou said, "Did you hear that? That extra clicking sound?"

Max nodded. "What is it, Lou?"

"I can't be sure, but it sure as hell sounded fishy to me."

"Fishy how?"

"Fishy like someone was listening in."

Stormy jumped out of her chair. "You think his phone is bugged?"

"I don't know. Maybe." Lou shrugged. "Or maybe it was just a glitch in the line."

The vampire sat comfortably in the overstuffed chair in the cheap motel room's darkest corner. Jason Beck, standing near the bed, hung up the telephone; then Fieldner hung up the extension on the other side of the room.

Jason turned to face him. His lip was split, but it had stopped bleeding. The eye, on the other hand, was already beginning to darken. It would be purple by morning. He was still angry with Fieldner for that. The man had become carried away when young Jason Beck decided to fight rather than comply. A foolish decision. Fieldner might look as if a stiff wind would blow him over, but occasional sips of vampiric blood made him strong. And utterly obedient.

It was a shame the man was also an imbecile.

"I did what you asked. I called them," Beck said. "I want to see my sister now."

"You left a message on an answering machine," the vampire said slowly. "That's not precisely what I told you to do, now is it?"

"They'll call back. When they do, I'll get them down here. I swear."

"How can you be so certain they will come?"

"They will," Beck said, lowering his head to stare at the photograph that lay on the bedside stand beside the telephone. "They're my friends. They'll come."

"They'd better. And when they do, you would do well to follow my instructions to the letter. Do you understand, Mr. Beck?"

Jason met his eyes. "No. I don't understand any of this. Who the hell are you? What do you want with Storm and Maxie? If you're going to hurt them—"

"I'm not. Not that you could stop me if I were.

You have one mission here, Beck, and that is to do as you're told. So long as you obey, there will be no harm done—to the women or to your sister. Or to you."

Jason's eyes lowered beneath the vampire's steady, penetrating gaze. He had a brilliant mind, this young man. His intelligence was great, his love for his sister even greater. But he had a deep affection for the two female detectives, as well. It could prove to be a problem if not properly controlled.

"Since you've acted in good faith," the vampire said slowly, "I will take you to see your sister now."

Stormy dialed the number, was connected to Jason's room and waited. Then she slowly shook her head. "No answer."

As she put the phone down, Max frowned at her, recalling their earlier conversation, right after she'd gone off the road. "You were thinking about Jason on the way here," she said.

Stormy nodded. "Yeah. Odd, isn't it?" She didn't meet Max's eyes.

"What was it, some kind of premonition?"

"Please," Stormy said, loading the word with sarcasm. Then she turned the subject right back to the telephone call. "No answer, and no voice mail. Must be one nice hotel."

"Motel," Lou corrected. "He said motel, not hotel. It's probably nothing fancy."

"We should go there," Stormy said, and now she did meet Max's eyes, her own imploring.

Stormy *did* have a feeling about all this; Max was convinced of it. "Go where?" she asked. "We don't even know where Jason is."

"We could run some kind of trace on the call." Stormy shot her gaze to Lou's. "You still have friends on the force. You could do that, couldn't you?"

Lou nodded. "Yeah, but there are easier ways. You got the phones here turned on, how about the Internet?"

"It's ready to go," Max said.

"We can do it online, then."

Maxie moved behind the computer to make sure the cable was plugged in, while Lou took the chair in front of it.

His cop juices were flowing; Max could tell by the light in his eyes. He had a real passion for his work. And when he immersed himself in it, he forgot to play the worn-out, burned-out role he seemed determined to play for her benefit. The mask fell away, revealing him as he truly was. A man in his prime, with a sharp, determined mind and a keen sense of justice. This was the Lou Malone who turned her on like no one else ever had. She watched his long, powerful fingers move over the keyboard, licked her lips at the way his strong hand cupped the mouse.

Several keystrokes later, he looked up. "The call came from a town called Endover, in New Hampshire."

Max held his eyes. "You're gonna have to show me how you did that."

"What, you weren't paying attention?"

"Sure I was. Just not to the right things." She winked at him and saw him squirm. It was his usual reaction to her flirting, and far from the one she wanted.

"We should go," Stormy said softly.

Lou seemed to have trouble breaking the hold Max's eyes had on his, but he finally did, and focused instead on Stormy. "Look, he said we should call him back. Let's wait it out. He can tell us what he wants us to do when we get him on the phone."

Max hid a secret smile at his use of the words "we" and "us." He might think he was still planning to hightail it back to White Plains, but deep down, Max thought, he already knew better.

"Lou's right," she said. "Besides, it'll give us time to unload the van."

"How old would Delia be now?" Stormy asked. "What was she last time we saw her. Ten? Twelve?"

Max nodded. "She must be all grown up. Sixteen, seventeen by now. He did say she was in her senior year."

"Hard to imagine," Stormy said. "God, where did all the time go? He didn't mention his older brother, did he? Mike?"

"Last I knew, Mike had a wife and kids and was living somewhere in California," Max said. She put a hand on Stormy's shoulder. "We'll keep calling until we get him. Then we'll take it from there, okay?"

Stormy closed her eyes, sighing deeply. "Okay, we'll wait."

5

He hadn't left, Lou told himself a few hours later. He kept telling himself he was going to, right after the next little job, or the one after that. But he hadn't left.

Of course he hadn't left. He'd been fooling himself to think he was going to get out of this place if Maxie wanted to keep him here. There wasn't much he wouldn't do for her—and no, that had nothing to do with anything other than the fact that he liked her and seemed to have developed a soft spot for her, despite her being his polar opposite in every way.

She was also his biggest pain in the ass, and he personally thought she ought to be voted the girl

most likely to get herself dead before her time.
Which was a large part of the reason why, when she
got into trouble, he tended to want to stick around
and help her out of it.

So he'd said he would hang around to help her unload, and he did. And then she declared they needed
to eat, so they ordered pizza from a place in town
and ate it on the patio outside the office. It was nice.
Three friends, munching pizza and ignoring the herd
of elephants currently dancing in the parlor.

Stormy's odd symptoms. Max's worry for her.
Max's mad theories. Lou's skepticism about them.
Max's constant flirting. Lou's phony don't-care at-
titude toward it. His lie about wanting to get home.
Max's lie about intending to let him go. And the fear
for an old friend that hovered over all of them.

Yep. A herd of elephants.

But the patio was nice, white fieldstones smooth
as glass, wicker furniture, glass-topped table, an um-
brella for shade, white with a pattern of green ivy,
like the cushions on the chairs. It was a warm evening. Sitting out there in the starlight, smelling the
sea breeze, citronella torches ablaze, it felt just fine.

When it got too cool to remain, Lou decided to
make coffee, which meant unpacking cups and
things. And that task turned into unpacking nearly

every box marked Kitchen. The three worked in synch and had the job done in under an hour. Max's blender and toaster and coffeepot were on the counter—the pot half-full. All the dishes were put away except the cups they'd been drinking from. Those he stacked in the dishwasher.

He liked the kitchen here. Of the entire place, he thought he liked it best. It was clean, efficient, not overly fancy. And the pink-and-gray marble was perfect. Tiny squares of it covered the walls, and a huge chunk formed the surface of the island in the middle of the room. Now, that, he thought, was Max. Pink swirls. Soft on the surface, but tough as rock underneath.

Fortified with caffeine, kitchen unpacking all done, Lou next carried some boxes up the stairs to the bedrooms the girls would be using.

Maxie's room—formerly Morgan's—was huge, with an attached bathroom that included a sunken tub and a shower with multiple heads. It had a balcony with French doors, and filmy white curtains, and it was fully furnished.

He set Max's boxes of clothes and toiletries in the bedroom and took a look around. The room was dark and dramatic. It wasn't Maxie. But when he tossed her ladybug-patterned beanbag chair into a corner, he thought that she might transform it, given time.

"There are a half dozen other bedrooms, besides mine and Stormy's," Max said.

He turned to see her standing in the doorway. She moved into the room past him, scooped a box off the floor and set it on the huge bed. "Yeah, I know," he said. "I've been here before, too, you know."

She nodded. She was pulling items out of the box now. Nightgowns. Underthings. She held each one up as if to inspect it before folding it and dropping it into the top drawer of the bureau beside the bed. "So which room do you want to use?"

"Max, hon, I told you, I'm not staying over."

"Oh, come on, you don't still mean to leave. If you did, you'd be gone by now. At this point, you'd have to drive all night." The item she was holding up now was a sheer black teddy. He looked at it, then at her, and then he was imagining her wearing it, which was a stupid thing to think about. And yet he couldn't shake the image from sneaking through his mind. The nightie was short, and her legs were long. He'd seen her in shorts in the summer, so he knew about her legs. Hell, she'd made sure he knew. Maxie seemed to live for teasing him, though most of the time he managed to believe she didn't mean anything by it. She was young, probably thought it was safe to flirt with him. He was too much older than her to take her seriously, and too good a friend to be dangerous. She thought he was safe. Comfortable.

She ought to be right. He felt like a pig for the images of her prancing around in that skimpy teddy that were currently filling every corner of his mind.

"Lou?"

He shook himself, snapped out of it, looked at her again.

She smiled at him. "You like this one, huh?"

"What?"

"The teddy. You were kind of staring at it."

He shook his head. "No, I wasn't."

"Sure you were."

"I was lost in thought, that's all."

"It's okay. I don't mind."

"You damn well should," he muttered, turning away to leave the room.

"What?" she asked.

"Nothing. Back on topic, kid. I can't stay the night. Plain and simple. I'll stay until you get hold of your friend Jason, just so I know what you're up to, but then—"

"Will you be reasonable, already?"

He knew she was right. He was being utterly unreasonable. Why drive all night when there were vacant bedrooms for the taking and an open invitation?

Because he didn't trust himself to spend the night under the same roof with Maxie, that was why. He searched his mind for a reasonable argument and latched on to the first one he found. "I didn't bring anything with me," he said.

There. She couldn't very well argue with that. He kept walking along the hall toward the stairs.

She popped into the hallway behind him. "Yes, you did."

Lou stopped and turned slowly to face her.

She was standing with one hand braced on the door frame of her bedroom, and she turned her green eyes up to their most innocent setting. "You were being stubborn. I was afraid you'd end up stranded here with none of your stuff, so…I tossed your overnight bag into Stormy's car before we left White Plains."

"You…?" He couldn't even form a sentence, he was so stunned.

"You can use this room here," she said, striding down the hall toward him and flinging open a door. "This is a *nice* room. One of my favorites. I think it's the one Morgan's godfather, David Sumner, used when he came out here to visit. It's all earth tones, greens and browns. Very masculine."

It was also, he realized, the room right beside her own.

She read that observation on his face and said, "Besides, you'll be close to me. In case I need you."

He stared at her. God, why wouldn't she lay off him with this constant flirting and teasing? He was human. He was not a gelding. He was a red-blooded man, and he could only take so much. And it didn't matter to his libido that she was his opposite in every imaginable way from personality to phase in life. She was just starting out, ready to take on the world and whip it into submission. He was ready to slow down, lie back, relax a little. She wanted marriage, long-term commitment—kids, for crying out loud. And she deserved those things. He wanted none of the above. Wasn't capable of any of them even if he did want them.

"Maxie, maybe you and I need to sit down and have a talk."

"It's about time," she said. "My room or yours?"

He opened his mouth, but before he got a word

out, Stormy was calling to them from the bottom of the stairs. Max clenched her fist. "Curses, foiled again!" Then she started down the stairs. "What's wrong, hon?"

"I've got Jason on the phone."

Max glanced at Lou, and he got the distinct feeling he'd just had a narrow escape—he couldn't be exactly sure what from. More of her teasing, more than likely. Sure as hell wouldn't have been anything more. But damn, if he ever slipped up—lost the iron grip he held on his self-control…

Showed her I'm not a gelding after all…

He slammed the door on that kind of thinking. "On our way, Storm."

He walked behind Max down the broad, curving staircase that belonged in lifestyles of the richer than he'd ever be, and tried not to notice the curve of Maxie's butt in the tight little jeans she wore. Her butt was none of his business.

They hit the ground floor, and she practically ran into the office. He took his time, just to give himself a second. He had to shake off the entire past ten minutes, everything about Maxie, her cute ass, her sexy teddy and her big bedroom. All of it. Wipe it out. Zip. Done.

God, he was getting good at it.

* * *

The vampire watched and listened as Jason Beck made the phone call.

The young man's reunion with his sister had been exactly what had been needed, he decided. He'd stood just inside the closed door of his mansion's most opulent bedroom suite as Beck's little sister rushed into her brother's arms. The young man held her, then opened his arms to include the other girl. After a moment, he held them away from himself and looked them over. "Are you all right? Have you been hurt?"

"We're okay," Delia said. "But God, look at you. Look at your face. Jason, what happened? Did they—was it…?"

"It was an accident. Honestly, it's fine." He ran a hand over his injured face. Black eye. Split lip. Silently, the vampire cursed Fieldner for his over-developed violent streak.

Delia didn't look convinced, but she wanted to be. She said, "We're fine, too. This guy—he's been… decent."

"That other one wasn't," Janie muttered.

Beck looked at her sharply. "You mean the police chief? Fieldner? Did he hurt you?"

"No." Delia put a hand on her brother's arm and

shot Janie a dirty look. "He was gruff and bossy, and he kept us in a—a cell of some kind for a while. But now that we're here, we're fine. Honestly, Jay. I don't want you to worry. We're okay. Besides, you're here now. It's over. We can go home with you."

Jason licked his lips.

"Jay? We *can* go with you, can't we? You did come here to take us home…."

Lowering his head, Beck said, "Not just yet. But it won't be long."

Delia's face fell, until the vampire thought she would cry. Janie pouted, looking petulant. "What is it the bastard wants you to do?" she asked.

"What do you mean?" Jason asked, giving nothing away.

Smart, the vampire thought. The boy didn't want to upset the girls with any details. He only wanted to protect them and get them out of here safely. He was as intelligent as the vampire had taken him to be, then.

"He wants something," Janie said. "He's holding us to force you to do something or give him something. What is it? Money? Help with some legal problem? You are studying for the bar after all."

Delia caught her breath. "I hadn't thought of

that. Jay, don't do anything that would ruin your chances—your future—"

"It's nothing like that. I promise you. I'm going to have you out of here in a day or two. I swear." He looked back toward where the vampire stood. "He's given me his word on that."

"Indeed," said the vampire. "And my word is my bond."

"Nothing's going to happen to you," Jason promised. "You'll be safe here until this is over."

"Time is short. You have that phone call you're expecting, Mr. Beck," the vampire said.

Jason nodded, but Delia snapped her arms around his neck. "He *is* making you do something. I know he is. What is it, Jay?"

"It'll be over soon." He gently took her arms from his neck. "It'll be done before you know it, and you'll be home with me, hon. I promise. You've gotta trust me on this."

She let him untangle her arms, but her tears were flowing. The vampire found himself actually touched by the obvious affection between the two, the heartbreak this separation was causing them. He felt it, of course. Every bit of it, every emotion, from the fear to the sadness to the stubborn determination on the part of the young man to do whatever it took to save his sister. *Whatever* it took.

He almost regretted having to put them through this.

And yet, he had to see the woman for himself. He had to know...

"Come, Jason," he said. "We have to get you back to the mainland now."

The young man obeyed, hating to, hating the vampire with everything in him. The only emotion stronger than his hatred was his love for his sister. The vampire was counting on that.

He took Jason back through the halls of his home and outside into the beauty of the night. But all the way along the paths of his island, he was acutely aware of the soft crying coming from that bedroom, the tearful sobs of those two young girls.

He could easily kill Fieldner for getting him into this. And yet now that he'd seen that face—he had no choice but to follow through.

Soon they were back in Beck's motel room. And he was, at last, on the telephone with the girl-detectives, rather than their answering machine. Fieldner was listening on the other line, but the vampire had no patience for that. He crossed the room, held out a hand, his command unspoken but clearly understood.

Fieldner handed him the receiver and backed away, stationing himself near the door without being told.

The vampire brought the telephone to his ear and closed his eyes in a mingling of hope and despair at the sound of the woman's voice. It wasn't the same.

"Jason, thank God. We've been trying to call you for hours."

"I had to go out," he replied. "Sorry about that."

The vampire sighed. The voice was not the same, but that didn't mean he could let this go. He looked at Jason Beck and sent his words directly into the young man's mind, without ever parting his lips to speak them aloud.

You will tell them to come here. Immediately.

Jason Beck's eyes widened as he stared at the vampire.

Do it! Need I remind you what will happen to your sister if you disobey?

Beck closed his eyes slowly, nodded to tell the vampire he understood, and turned his attention to the woman on the telephone.

By the time Lou joined them in the office, Stormy was hitting the speaker button and setting the receiver down. He found himself a chair and waited, listening to the conversation.

"Jay? I put you on speakerphone, hon, so we can all get the full scoop. Now, just be calm. We're here for you. Tell us what the hell is going on."

She listened. So did Lou. He came up out of his chair when Jason spoke, because he could have sworn there was a thickness to the other man's voice. As if his throat were tight, the way it would be if he'd been crying.

"I don't know exactly, Storm. But damn, it's good to hear your voice."

"Yours, too." She sent Max a searching look. "Are you okay, Jason? You sound—"

"Fine. I'm…" He sniffed. "Is Max with you?"

"I'm here, Jay," Maxie called. "And so is Lou. You remember Lou Malone?"

"Your cop?"

Lou shot Max a look. Since when had he been considered *her* cop?

"Jason, what's happened to Delia?" Maxie asked quickly.

"I don't know. That's just it. She was on a trip with her best friend, Janie. Headed up the coast to celebrate spring break. Senior year, you know? Then I got this call from her. She sounded terrified, Storm. Said she was in trouble. We got cut off after that. And to be honest, the entire call was broken, full of static, I could barely hear her most of the time. But I'm sure she said the name of a town—Endover, New Hampshire."

"And that's where you are now?" Stormy asked.

"Yeah. It's like a freakin' ghost town here."

"You've tried to call her back?" Max asked.

"That was the first thing I did. First through hundredth. No luck. It's freaking weird, Max." He sighed, a broken sound. "But I believe she's here—I think they both are."

"When did you get that phone call, Jay?"

"Earlier today," he told her.

"And you haven't heard from her since?"

There was the slightest delay before he said, "No. Not a word."

Stormy looked up at Max. Lou saw that they'd both heard the hesitation. Jason had started to say something else, then thought better of it.

"I need you guys to come down here. Immediately."

Stormy opened her mouth, but Lou spoke first.

"Have you called the police?"

"Hell, Lou, you know as well as I do they wouldn't take this seriously. Not when she was out on a road trip with a friend. They'd think I was being overprotective, melodramatic, alarmist."

"Are you sure you aren't?" Lou asked.

Max sent him a furious scowl and mouthed "Knock it off."

"It's all right, Jason," Stormy said. "Look, this is what we do for a living now. Right, Max?"

"Right," Max said. "Jason, you're in Endover now, correct?"

"Yeah. The motel where I'm staying is at the north edge of town on 1-A, on the right. The North Star Motor Lodge. You can't miss it."

"All right."

Stormy had turned to the computer and was typing rapidly as Jason spoke. Lou looked at the monitor over her shoulder to see she had punched the information into an online map-making program. She hit Enter. About three seconds later the driving directions appeared, and she hit the print button. "Jay, it looks like it's about four and a half hours from here. Allowing time for us to pack a bag or two, we can be there by 5:00 a.m."

"Wait a minute, wait a minute," Lou said. "Jason, these two have already driven close to eight hours today. And not without incident," he said with a sharp look at Stormy and Max when he sensed they were about to object.

Max sighed. "He's right. We shouldn't be driving without a few hours' sleep."

She didn't surprise him. He knew her concern for Stormy would be the one thing that would outweigh her rush to help out an old friend.

"How about we get a decent night's sleep and leave first thing in the morning? We could still make it by noon."

Lou hadn't realized he'd said "we" until he felt Max's eyes on him, and by then it was too late. Then Jason voiced the question he was already asking himself.

"What do you mean, 'we'? Look, Lou, I don't want the police involved in this."

"I'm not the police. Not anymore. Retired a few months ago, kid. Any other reason you don't want me in on this thing?"

The suspicion and the hint of inexplicable animosity in his tone were not entirely unintended. He couldn't seem to keep them out, and he didn't particularly want to. This guy on the phone was sending up so many red flags, Lou could hear them flapping in the breeze.

"Of course not," Jason said. "The more help I have on this thing, the better. Noon tomorrow will be fine. Thank you, guys."

"You're welcome, Jason," Maxie said.

"We'll see you tomorrow," Stormy added.

Jason hung up without a goodbye. Stormy reached to hit the disconnect button, but Lou held up a hand. Sure enough, the second click came, just as it had before. They both heard it, and he saw their eyes widen. Then he nodded, and Stormy hung up.

Stormy looked at Max, then at Lou. "Something is wrong with him."

"His sister's missing," Max said. "It's like he said, it's amazing he can form a coherent sentence. You know how he adores her." She snatched the pages off the printer and took a look at the driving directions.

"Seemed like more than that," Lou said.

"Hell, Lou, you barely know him."

"That makes me more objective. Besides, I'm a cop, remember?"

"Ex-cop," she corrected.

"Once a cop, always a cop. And I'll tell you, kid, after twenty years, you get to know when something's off, and something about your friend Jason is definitely off. Way off. And then there are the monitored phone calls."

"You can't be sure that's what that extra click was," Max said.

He nodded, conceding that. "Can't be sure it wasn't, either."

She shrugged. "I can be sure of one thing, though."

"Yeah? What's that, Nancy Drew?"

She met his eyes and smiled the most triumphant, smug little smile he'd ever seen her wear. "You're planning to come with us."

He couldn't even argue with her. Instead, he sighed and lowered his head.

"I need more pizza," Maxie said. She walked out of the office, a little bounce to her step on her way to the kitchen, where they'd left the extra slices in a box on the island.

Lou watched her go and tried to quell the little voice that told him it was a mistake to give in to her yet again. But there was an even bigger feeling, one that was far more important. It sat like a brick in the pit of his stomach, and it told him that something very bad was waiting for Mad Maxie Stuart in Endover.

6

Lou didn't follow Max to the kitchen right away. He didn't like the way Stormy looked: pale, shaky, shielding her eyes with a hand, as if the light of the computer monitor was too bright to bear.

Except for the kitchen, every other room in the place was cluttered with still-packed boxes and crates. Not this one, though. It was huge, fireplace on the far wall, French doors with the small patio just beyond, overlooking the rolling lawn all the way to the cliffs and the sea far below. It held two desks, though they'd all been gathered around one. The second one faced it from the opposite side of the fireplace. Its surface was still empty. No computer, no phone.

On the wall was a large oil painting of Max's twin sister, Morgan, and her beloved Dante. She wore a scrap of gossamer with thin straps, and sat in a fur-covered chair with her legs folded beneath her. He stood behind her, hands on her shoulders. Lou got lost while staring at the portrait for just a moment. Morgan's facial structure, her deep-set green eyes, coppery-red hair and her smile—so much like Maxie's. And yet she was pale, had been even before the change. Skin like porcelain. Hair straight and sleek. A body so waif-thin he wondered if she actually cast a shadow. Not that she would be spending any time in the sun from now on. She was frail. A hothouse orchid. Max was a wild rose. Tough, thorny, strong.

"Hard to believe they're twins, isn't it? I can't think of two women more different," Stormy said, looking over his shoulder.

"I was thinking the same." He dragged his gaze from the portrait to Stormy. "You all right?"

"I'll be fine. I just…I hate waiting."

"You're exhausted. Why don't you get some sleep? Give yourself a break."

She nodded. "Yeah. I will." She hit the keys that

would shut down the computer, then slid out of her chair as the machine whirred and clicked and finally went dark. "So I take it you're staying over?"

"Max isn't giving me much choice." He drew a breath, sighed deep and long. "My bag still in your car?"

"Nope. I brought it in." She reached under the desk and hauled out the black satchel. "Are you mad?"

"Hell, what's to be mad about? Even smuggling my bag couldn't force me to stick around with you two if I didn't want to." He shook his head. "Max thinks she's playing me, but I'm only here because I want to be."

"She'd sure love to hear that."

"No way. I'm not giving her any more ammo to fire at my head."

"I've got news for you, Lou. It's not your head she's firing at." She studied him, tilted her head to one side. "How do you feel about her, anyway?"

"How do I...*feel* about her?" He shrugged, averting his eyes. "I like her. I've always liked her."

"As a friend?"

He shrugged. "More like a guardian." Stormy's eyebrows shot up so high he thought he must have shocked her, so he tried to explain. "I always feel as if she needs looking after, you know? She tends to just charge headlong, straight into trouble, without thinking first."

"So you see yourself as her...protector."

"That's one way to put it. Sure."

"Like a big brother," Stormy said.

"More like an uncle. I'm too old to be her brother."

Stormy put a hand on his shoulder. "Lou, she doesn't want you to be her uncle. You do realize that, don't you?"

He frowned at her. "Oh, come on. You're not telling me you take all her teasing and flirting seriously, are you?"

"Don't you?"

"Not on your life. She's half my age."

"Twenty-six is not half of forty-four."

"Close enough."

"That's bullshit. What's the real issue here, Lou?"

He met her eyes, then had to avert his because she was probing a little too deeply. "This is getting kind of personal, Stormy. If you don't mind..."

"Nope. Don't mind a bit. I'm going up to bed, but I'm setting my alarm. I want us to get an early start." She picked up his bag and swung it into his chest. "And just in case you didn't notice, Lou, there's room in this office for another desk. Hell, that spot over there almost looks bare without one. Don't you think?"

He looked where she was looking, at a large, vacant section of the room. "You'll find something to put there."

"Or some*one*. 'Night, Lou."

"Good night."

She left. Lou didn't waste a hell of a lot of time wondering where she got her crazy ideas. Instead, he wandered through the vast house, crossing the dramatic formal dining room, heading all the way to the kitchen in the rear of the mansion. Maxie was sitting on a stool at the pink marble island, scarfing down a slice of cold pizza. For a second he marveled that anyone could look as good as she did while chewing. And then he stared a little longer, mentally contrasting her with her wisp of a sister. Where Morgan was whisper-thin, Max was curvy. He didn't often allow himself to think about her breasts, but they were nice ones. Full, rounded, bouncy. Her waist was little, and the curve of her hips just right. She had a round backside that filled out a pair of jeans in the nicest possible way. Her skin was pink, and her hair thick and riotously curly.

Her attitude matched her looks. She was feisty, impulsive, fun-loving, restless.

Stormy was right. Two women couldn't be more different.

She turned and caught him looking, swallowed her latest mouthful and sent him a smile.

"I'm going to get some sleep," he said. "I'll check the locks before I go up, make sure the place is all buttoned up. Thought I'd say good night."

She eyed the bag in his hand. "So you meant what you said to Jason on the phone? You're sticking with us for this one?"

"Looks like."

"I'm so glad." She hooked her foot around the stool next to her own and pulled it out. "Sit. You want a piece?"

"No thanks, I've had enough pizza."

"Who said I was talking about pizza?" She sent him her trademark smile, full of mischief and danger.

He sighed, nodded. "Fine. I'll sit. I need to talk to you, anyway."

"'Bout what?" she asked.

He sighed as he lowered himself onto the stool. "The truth is, kid, I want to go with you to Endover. I like working with you, and I'm scared shitless to think what kind of trouble you might get yourself into without me."

She rolled her eyes. "Your faith in me is overwhelming."

He lowered his head, searching for the right words. "The thing is, while I like working with you and I want to watch out for you, I don't like some of the things you do."

She lifted her eyebrows. "You don't?"

"No. Now, don't go getting all hurt and wounded on me, hon, but—"

"Ooooh," she said, drawing the sound out into a sexy purr. "I just love when you call me 'hon.'" As she said it, she leaned closer, so her breath warmed his neck.

Lou shot to his feet, slammed his palms on the marble. "Goddammit, Max, that's exactly the kind of thing I'm talking about."

She jumped and stared at him, wide-eyed.

"Look, this isn't easy for me. It's goddamn embarrassing, as a matter of fact, but I don't know how to do this except to just come right out with it. I'm not a gelding, Maxie. I'm not a monk. When you play those games with me, I react, okay? My body—reacts. I'm a healthy, red-blooded man. I'm not too old to feel…" He let his words trail off, unable to finish the sentence.

"Lou?"

"I need you to stop, Max."

She blinked at him.

He was sure he'd just fallen off whatever pedestal she'd placed him on. God, to confess to having sexual thoughts about her—sexual desire for her—it was mortifying. He wouldn't blame her if she threw him out of here once she had time to digest his words, to understand what they implied. "I'm going to bed," he told her. "I just…had to get that said." He turned and walked away. "If you still want me to come with you in the morning, I will."

"Lou?"

He stopped, but he didn't turn to face her.

"You've got it all wrong, you know."

"No, I don't. Good night, Max."

Maxie paced her bedroom most of the night. Hell, she'd been nuts about Lou since her first year of college, when she'd taken a self-defense class he'd taught. But she'd kept her flirting minimal back then. Since he'd come back into her life, she'd turned it up several notches.

But she hadn't realized until now how her efforts were being received.

There was a tap on her door. She hurried to yank it open, half expecting to find Lou there, ready to admit defeat and sweep her into his arms for a passionate kiss.

Instead Stormy was standing on the other side, framed by an elaborately tooled, walnut-stained casing.

She took one long look at Max's face and said, "Lou talked to you, didn't he?"

"How did you know?"

"Told me he was going to. Then I heard you pacing. Slamming doors or drawers or whatever. Figured I'd better come in before you broke something." She smiled, a teasing sort of almost-grin. "So what did he say?"

Max pursed her lips. "He *claims* to think I've just been teasing him, that I see him as harmless. A *gelding*. He actually used that word."

Stormy sighed, crossing the room and hopping onto the foot of the giant four-poster bed, where she folded her legs underneath her and sank into the softness of high-piled mattresses and bedding. "So, did you set him straight?"

"I was just so stunned. I mean, he caught me off

guard. I didn't know what to say. Hell, I still don't." Max padded across the thick carpet to stand at the French doors, where she stared outside at the stars, twinkling from a velvet canopy of midnight-blue sky.

"Well, clearly you have to tell him you've never thought of him as a gelding. I mean, if he really believes that, it can't be good for his ego."

Max gnawed her lip for several seconds. "I know what I ought to do. I ought to put on that black teddy and march right into his bedroom and show him just how serious I am."

She strode away from the gorgeous view, yanked open the top drawer of the dresser that took up fully half of one wall and pulled out the teddy. A crescent-shaped mirror framed in scrolled wood was mounted to the dresser, and she held the teddy to her chest and stared at her reflection.

"You sure that won't send him running back to White Plains at the speed of sound, Max?"

Max frowned and licked her lips. "I can't have him thinking what he's thinking."

Stormy slid off the bed, came behind her and put a firm hand on her shoulder. "I have my doubts he really believes any of that crap, anyway. Deep down, I mean."

"Then why would he…?"

"Maybe it's just easier that way," Stormy said. "Telling you to stop teasing him is way easier than telling you to stop wanting him, don't you think?"

Max turned slowly. "You think he knows I'm serious, and just…isn't interested?"

"I know it's a possibility you've never considered, hon, but don't you think you have to?"

"But…but how could he not want me?" She blinked away the stupid, ridiculous moisture that had gathered in her eyes.

Stormy squeezed her shoulder. "Might not be about you. Might be about him."

"Now you sound like a goddamn man." Maxie crammed the teddy back into the drawer, then slammed it closed.

"Look, Max, you know the age difference bugs him."

"That's an excuse, not a reason. It's only eighteen years."

Stormy shrugged. "He's been married before. Maybe he was burned so bad he's sworn off women forever."

Max paced the bedroom. "Okay, that could be a possibility. At least that's within the realm of reason."

Stormy nodded. "You know anything about the wife? What went wrong?"

Max shook her head. "He never talks about it. If I ask, he changes the subject."

"See? Doesn't that sort of prove it was bad?"

"Maybe it just proves he doesn't want to talk about it. The question is, what am I supposed to do next?" Max stopped pacing, spun to face Stormy. "How can I overcome whatever it is that's keeping him from even thinking about me as a—a love interest?"

Stormy blinked slowly. "Because giving up is not an option, right, Max?"

"Of course it's not an option. Lou is mine." Max paced across the room in one direction, then turned and started back again. "He's meant for me. I'm certainly not going to let a little thing like his unwillingness to cooperate get in the way of that." She stood still and smiled then. "Now that I think about it, he basically admitted to wanting me, too. He said I had to stop because he was a normal red-blooded man, and that his body reacts to my flirting."

Stormy sighed. "I suppose he might really believe you aren't serious about him, and that would make him feel guilty for having feelings for you."

"Well, I'll get that out of the way first and proceed from there."

"Have you decided *how* you're going to get it out of the way?"

Max eyed the dresser drawer. "I suppose the teddy's out of the question?"

"I think if you show up in his bedroom wearing that teddy, he'll be gone when we get up in the morning. The man's gun-shy."

Max sighed. "I suppose I could just tell him."

"That might be best."

The vampire's mind was his most powerful tool. He knew that others of his kind shared many of the same abilities—to control the mind of another, to communicate without speaking, to hear private thoughts, to invade dreams, to enslave. But none, to his knowledge, had honed those skills to the degree he had.

The woman, for example.

She wasn't even here, not yet. She was somewhere to the north, asleep in her bed. But he could reach her, even there. He *would* reach her....

He stared at the photograph on the glossy flyer. Stared into the eyes that were, he reminded himself, the wrong color. He probed and sought, and, eventually, he felt her. She was there, far away, but he could touch her.

He slipped inside her mind. She felt him there, stirred in her sleep.

Who are you? he whispered, and his mind searched hers for answers. *Tell me who you are.*

He didn't expect the question to generate the violent response it did. He felt a struggle as she searched her mind for the correct reply. There was a tearing, a tug-of-war going on, as if for control.

I am—

No! I am—

Get out. Leave me alone, dammit!

Never!

Help me. God, Jesus, help me—what's happening to me?

Tears. He heard and felt them. Racking her. Quaking through her.

Just let go. Let go and let me—

"Nooooooo!"

The shriek was so pain-filled, so desperate, he withdrew immediately, then sat very still, holding his head in his hands. Maybe he had made a terrible mistake in seeing to it the woman came to him here. She was not, he realized, entirely sane.

Lou felt like slime. He'd hurt Max's feelings, he knew that. And he'd probably convinced her he was just like every other man she'd ever known in the process. He'd always loved that she saw him differently. That she trusted him when she didn't trust many of the others. That she felt safe around him.

He hoped he hadn't blown that.

He couldn't sleep. He'd tried a cold shower, then a hot one. He'd stripped down to his shorts and T-shirt, and pulled on a robe over them just in case she came wandering in wanting to talk to him. Though he doubted she would. He didn't want to sleep. He wanted to make things okay between them again.

He was still pacing the floor when he heard the scream.

Max!

He flung his bedroom door open and ran to hers, whipped it open as well without knocking, and strode inside, ready to do battle.

Max wasn't in her bed. The bathroom door was open, and a light shone and music wafted from within, so he lunged inside.

Maxine lay in the giant sunken tub that sat at the top of a dais in the room's center, with three ceramic-tiled steps going up to it on each of the four sides. He'd come to a stop on the second step, his eyes riveted to the tub. It was full of steaming water. And Max was sound asleep inside. The water was clear.

Not cloudy, no bubbles. She lay there, knees bent slightly and rocked over to one side. He couldn't stop his eyes from drinking their fill. Her breasts, small, round, perfect, just beneath the water. Her smooth torso and soft belly, and the sleek curve of her hip and rounded buttocks.

The sight of her crawled into every crevice of his mind, burning her image there. He felt as if his muscles had turned molten. God, she was beautiful.

Then the scream came again, louder this time, jerking him out of his trancelike state. *Not Max,* his mind told him. *Stormy.*

Max's eyes flew open at the sound, met his, widened.

He ran down the steps, snatched the robe that hung from the back of the door and tossed it in her direction. "It's Stormy. Something's wrong." Then he turned and ran from the room and down the hall to Stormy's.

Max sprinted down the hall, damn near slipping because of her wet feet. She tied the robe as she ran and burst into Stormy's room to see Lou leaning over her bed, his hands on her shoulders.

"What happened? What's wrong?" Max shouted.

Both Lou and Stormy looked at her. Stormy said, "Bad dream."

"About what?"

"I don't know. It didn't make any sense." She sat up in the bed, pushed her hands through her short blond hair. "There were all these voices, one asking me who I was. Another trying to answer for me. I felt like my head was going to split open."

"Are you okay?" Max moved to the other side of the bed and stroked Stormy's hair.

"I'm fine. But it hurt so much in the dream. And once it started, the splitting just kept going—tearing my body in half, splitting my head down the middle, and then my chest, my heart, my belly. I couldn't stop it. It was so real, Max, this sense of being torn in half."

Max frowned at her. "Are you in any pain now? Your head, is it…?"

"No, no pain. It was all part of the dream, I swear. I'm fine."

Max took her hands. "I don't think you're being honest with me."

Stormy's eyes widened and met hers.

"Something's different—since the coma. Something's wrong, Storm, and it's about time you come clean about it."

Stormy shook her head slowly. "Never could fool you, could I?"

"So what is it?"

"I don't know. I just know I don't feel the same."

"That's not an answer," Max said.

Stormy rolled onto her side and closed her eyes. "It's the only one you're getting tonight. I'll be okay. Go back to bed."

"Are you sure? I can sit with you if you—"

"Lou, make her go to bed, will you?" Stormy muttered, snuggling more deeply into her pillows.

She looked fine, Max had to admit. And it didn't seem there was a damn thing she could do for her friend, anyway. She sent Lou a helpless look. He only shrugged, then leaned over to pull Stormy's blanket up over her shoulder. "Call if you need us," he said.

"I will."

He nodded at Max, and they both left the room. In the hallway, she looked up at him. He licked his lips and averted his eyes. "I'm sorry about busting into your room. When I heard her scream, I thought—"

"It's okay."

"It's really not."

She reached out to him, closed her hand around one of his and then studied it as her thumb ran over his knuckles. "I gotta tell you, Lou, it does me a world of good to know you'd come on a dead run if I were to cry out in the night."

"I know."

She nodded. "I'm scared to death there's something wrong with Stormy. Something big. Major, you know? And no matter what you say, I know I'm right about that. That's topmost on my mind right now. You catching a glimpse of me in the bathtub is barely a blip on my radar compared to my worry about her."

He nodded. "I think you're overreacting."

"So what's new? You always think I'm overreacting."

He sighed, lowering his head.

"Even so, Lou, the only thing keeping me from going off the deep end over this is having you here. Knowing you've got my back even if you don't agree with me. You'll hold me together if I start to fall apart. I trust you like no one else. I trust you with my life. And with Stormy's. And I can't even tell you how glad I am that you're coming with us tomorrow. Because I've got a bad, bad feeling about all this."

He turned his hand in hers and squeezed. "You, too, huh?"

She met his eyes. "Yeah. Why? Don't you feel good about it, either?"

"I don't know why, but my gut's telling me we're walking into the lion's den."

He sighed. "If I thought I had a snowball's chance in hell of talking you out of going down there, I'd try. But I know you too well."

She nodded.

He released her hand. "We should get some sleep. Get an early start."

"Yeah. Just...one more thing first."

He looked down at her. She swallowed hard and gathered up her courage—drew it straight up from her ovaries, she thought. "I never thought of you as a gelding, Lou. I don't believe for one minute you're too old to react to a little flirting."

She watched his brows go up. He seemed to be searching for words, so she shook her head. "I'm not trying to put you on the spot for a response to any of that. I just—I thought you needed to know."

With a firm nod, she turned and walked down the hall to her bedroom and just left him standing there.

7

One vehicle seemed more practical than two, so Stormy left her Miata safely at the house in Maine, and Lou drove Maxie's Bug. Not because he was the man, Stormy supposed, but because he was still pretending Maxie's lousy driving was the reason he'd come along in the first place. She knew better and, personally, thought the two of them were pretty pathetic. Meanwhile, though, they were both still way too overprotective of her. God, it was getting old fast. She could only imagine how much worse that would be if they knew what was really going on with her.

Hell, how could they? She didn't even know.

Either way, the upshot of it was that Lou drove,

Maxie sat in the front of her own car, beside him, and Stormy had the small but comfy back seat all to herself.

Not that she minded all that much. She leaned with her back against the side of the car, and her legs on the seat, knees bent. She'd rolled up Maxie's ever-present car blanket to use as a cushion. The position gave her a chance to observe the two of them. Much more pleasant, she thought, speculating on the state of their issues than wondering about her own.

Lou seemed stiff, guarded, as he drove. He must feel the tension—it was emanating from Max in waves a dead man couldn't have missed. Not anger, not exactly. Or not purely anger, anyway. She was pissed off, sure, but mostly, Stormy thought, she was frustrated and impatient with him for so thoroughly misreading her for the past six months. She must feel like all that flirting had been totally wasted. And she'd done some class-A flirting!

Lou didn't talk much, except about where they were going, driving directions or when to stop. Stormy didn't blame him. He was a male, which meant Max's mood was likely confusing him. He had no idea what he'd done wrong, so he didn't dare say much, in case he made things worse.

Poor clueless man.

Max was off her game this morning, too. A little awkward, unsure of herself, and probably resenting the hell out of him for making her feel that way. She couldn't relate to him as she usually did, with teasing, flirting and baiting, because he'd called a halt to that, and she hadn't yet figured out the next best way to talk to him, so she didn't talk at all. It wouldn't be long, though, before Max had a brand-new approach. In the meantime, she was unnaturally quiet. Someone who didn't know her as well as Stormy might think she was brooding, but Stormy knew better. Maxie was regrouping, working out a new plan of attack.

Meanwhile, though, the usual teasing banter between them was gone. Stormy found herself missing it.

She leaned back in her seat, bored with pondering her two hardheaded friends. Instead she wondered what it would be like to see Jason Beck again after all this time. He would be older, more experienced, maybe harder than he'd been before. Life seemed to have that effect on people. She wondered if he would look drastically different—whether he'd let himself go, grown a beard or put on a ton of weight. Whether he'd let his hair grow back or kept his head shaved, the way he used to. She wondered if he would still be the conservative 'fraidy cat he'd been before.

What if he wasn't? What if he'd opened his mind, grown a little more outgoing over the years? Stormy swallowed and closed her eyes, told herself she wasn't going to New Hampshire to audition Jason as her new love interest—she was going to help him find his sister. Period.

Besides, she'd agonized over her decision not to pursue more than friendship with him in the first place. He was too buttoned-up, too tight-assed. He wasn't for her. She would have driven him crazy, or he would have clipped her wings. Neither was a happy outcome.

Whatever she might have expected of Jason, though, it couldn't have prepared her for the reality she faced four hours later.

They drove into town a little after noon, rolling past a green sign that read Welcome to Endover, followed by another that read Curfew Enforced. Stormy frowned and wondered about that, but she wasn't sure if either Lou or Max had noticed. They were both focused on the opposite side of the road, where a brick building stood at the rear of an empty blacktop parking lot. The letters attached to the red brick face spelled out Visitor Center.

Stormy felt a cold shiver go up her spine. She rubbed her arms, and the motion drew Max's attention. "What's wrong, hon?" she asked, turning to look over the seat at her.

"Just a chill." Max narrowed her eyes, and Stormy hurried on. "That would be a likely place for a stranger in town to stop, don't you think?"

The visitor center was behind them now, but Max looked back at it. "Good point. We should check it out."

Stormy nodded, glad that Max was now distracted from worrying over her. She watched as Max rummaged in her shoulder bag for a notepad and jotted something on it. Probably a reminder to snoop around that visitor center.

They drove on through the town, which seemed to be little more than a few houses, leading up to a strip that apparently comprised the "business district." They drove by a gas station/convenience store, a doughnut shop, a hardware store, a small grocery, a pharmacy and a post office. Lots of brick buildings—nearly all of them were brick, in fact. It made for a neat, orderly facade, even if there were weeds and grass sprouting between the sections of sidewalk. One of those brick buildings seemed to house several offices, including the one that had Endover

Police Department painted on the pebbled glass in the door.

There was little traffic, only one light. A handful of people walked along the sidewalks in groups of two or three.

The short strip of businesses came to an abrupt end, with a handful of homes, the elementary school and a long, winding strip of nothing. Trees lined the road, and now and then she caught glimpses of the ocean beyond them.

She glanced down at her driving directions. "That motel should be coming up in a couple of miles. I'll call Jay and tell him we're nearly there."

"No you won't," Max said. She held up her cell phone, to show her the screen. "No reception. Hasn't been since we got into town."

"Makes you wonder," Lou said, "how Jason's sister managed to call him from here."

Max tipped her head to one side. "There could be spotty reception somewhere. Or maybe she has a different company or a more powerful phone than any of ours."

"Or maybe she was never here."

Max was already a little irritated with him, and by the way her face darkened, Stormy knew she'd just shifted that up a notch. He should have stuck to his policy of keeping quiet.

"What are you saying, Lou?" Max asked. "That Jason made it up?"

At her tone, Lou shot her a sideways look. "I'm not calling him a liar. He might just be mistaken."

"Not likely. He's got an IQ that falls somewhere between genius and freak. And he wouldn't lie to me, Lou. He's one of my dearest friends."

"*Was* one of your dearest friends. You haven't seen or heard from him in, what? Five years now?" He sighed. "People change, Maxie."

"Not Jason."

He pursed his lips, sent her a lingering look. "Maybe not. I hope not. I just want you to be careful."

That was better, Stormy thought. If Max thought he was only being protective of her, she would let just about anything slide.

Then the idiot added, "Don't go charging in half-cocked the way you usually do."

Max's jaw went tight, and she faced front, not saying a word.

Damn, Stormy thought. He blew it.

They parked the car in the lot of the North Star Motor Lodge. The L-shaped building that housed the guest rooms was tan with brown trim and seemed well kept. A concrete sidewalk unrolled in front of it, and each door had a gold number on the front. The motel office was a small square structure that stood apart from the rest. A freshly mown lawn spread out around the blacktop and held a handful of picnic tables. Behind the motel, she glimpsed a shaggy meadow backed by woods. But when she got out of the car, she could smell the ocean and knew it must be close.

The three of them strode up to room number two and knocked on the door.

Jason opened it, and Stormy sucked in a breath and then pressed a hand to her mouth. He sported a deep purple half moon under one swollen eye. His lower lip was split. A bruise on his cheekbone stood out darker than the rest of his skin.

"What the hell happened to you?" Maxie blurted. "You look like you went ten rounds with a bear."

He lifted his brows, opened his arms. "Not even a hello before you start with the questions, Mad Maxie?"

Max hugged him briefly. Then she stepped back, and he turned to Stormy. "Long time, huh?"

"Too long," she said. He embraced her—more tentatively than he had embraced Max, though. But suddenly white light blasted the center of Stormy's brain—blinding and hot. She jerked her arms tightly around Jason in reaction and slammed her eyes closed against the flash, but the images came anyway. Fists pounded her face. She felt the blows, and the sharp toe of a booted foot in her rib cage. And then it was gone.

She released Jason, only to find him staring at her oddly. Sure he was—he couldn't know why she'd hugged him as if trying to break him in two just now. She stepped awkwardly out of his arms. Lou extended a hand.

"Beck."

"Hello, Lou. It's good to see you."

"I wish it were under more pleasant circumstances," Lou said.

"So what happened to you?" Max asked.

Jason ran a hand over his nape. "Idiocy, that's all. I was out in the woods, looking for Delia," he said. "Not a real bright idea in the dark. I took a bad fall."

Lou frowned, shooting a quick look at Max, his lips thin. Stormy didn't think he believed Jason had gotten those bruises from a fall, and she knew damn well she didn't. She didn't know what was happening to her, but she was pretty sure that flash she'd just experienced had been a look at what had really happened to him.

"Why were you looking for her in the woods?" Lou asked.

"It seemed like as good a place to look as any." He opened the door wider, stepping aside. "Come on in. Now that you're here, maybe you'll come up with a better idea."

"Does that mean you want us on the case, Jay?" Max asked.

"That's why I called you, Maxie. And I don't expect a free ride, either. I'll pay whatever you charge."

"I'd do it for free."

"I wouldn't ask you to do that. I couldn't, Max."

"Then we'll give you our special rate—for old friends and former members," Max said with a wink. "Don't worry, Jason. We're here now, and we'll find Delia. Doesn't matter that we're new to this— 'cause we aren't. Not really. Just new to doing it on an official level. And it doesn't matter that a missing teenager isn't our area of expertise. We'll find her, because we care more than anyone else would. And that's gonna make all the difference."

Jason met Maxie's eyes, but he couldn't seem to hold her gaze for more than a beat or two. He quickly lowered his, then stepped aside so they could troop into his motel room. It was tiny, with a queen-size bed, TV stand and bathroom. Not a hell of a lot more. Jason had a map laid out on the bed, hand-drawn on a large sheet of white paper that might once have been a take-out food bag.

As they gathered around it, Jason leaned down and pointed. "This is the road into town. There's an information center right here."

Stormy nodded. "We saw it on the way here."

Lou said, "Jason, what makes you think your sister is here, in Endover?"

He frowned as he looked up at Lou. "I…it's where she was when she called."

"Are you sure? We haven't been able to pick up any reception for a couple of miles now."

Jason nodded firmly. "I'm sure."

"Why? What makes you so sure?"

Max sent Lou a quelling look. "If he says he's sure, he's sure, Lou."

"He said her message was broken up, full of static."

"Still—"

"It's okay, Max." Jason put a hand on her shoulder. "I did hear her pretty clearly when she said 'Endover, New Hampshire,' Lou. And the bad reception here is probably why the call was so choppy, and why we got cut off. If anything, it makes me even more certain I heard her correctly." He shrugged. "Since she hasn't called again, I'm assuming she's still someplace where she can't call out. Still here, in Endover."

"How could she call again? Your cell phone isn't working here, is it?" Lou asked.

Jason's gaze shifted from the bed, to the dresser, to the window. "I…no. It's not. But she hasn't called home, either. I've been checking the machine."

"Have you asked anyone around town about her?"

"I, uh—I talked with the police chief."

Lou frowned. "When was that?"

"Right after I arrived here."

Nodding slowly, Lou said, "Before you called us?"

"Right."

"Then why did you say you didn't want the police involved?"

"Lou, that's *enough*." Max barked the words at him. He sent her a look of impatience, but he stopped grilling Jason.

Jason lowered his head, pushed his hands through his hair. "Look, I barely know if I'm coming or going here. I went to the Endover police because it seemed like the thing to do. It was a waste of time, though. There's only one cop in town and he was no help at all. I figured I'd have to do this on my own." He looked from one face to the next, as if trying to read them.

Stormy thought Lou was suspicious as hell of Jason. And she wasn't entirely sure she didn't agree with him. Max, on the other hand, seemed to believe him—clearly she wanted to. She kept touching his arm, his shoulder, as if to comfort him.

Stormy turned to the other two. "Where do you want to start?"

"I'd like to see that visitor center," Max said. "I think you were right, Storm. She could have stopped there for directions or something."

"The visitor center is closed," Jay said. "I stopped there on the way into town. The place is abandoned."

"Then we can case the town, check for any other place where she might have stopped. Diners, gas stations, that sort of thing."

Lou nodded. "I'd like to talk to the local police chief myself, see what he has to offer. Helpful or not, it's a good idea to let him know we're here and we're looking for her, put him on alert to keep an eye out and contact us if anything turns up."

"There's no point, Lou," Jason said. "The local cop doesn't even believe she was ever here," Jason said.

"It won't hurt anything to talk to him," Lou said. "What was she driving?"

"Little red Neon," Jason said. "Only two years old." He swallowed hard. "She works part-time wait-ing tables to make her payments."

"You have the plate number?" Lou asked.

He nodded. "Yeah."

"So we can have the local cop keep an eye out for the car, too. Like I said, it can't hurt."

Max stroked Jason's upper arm. "Lou's right, hon. We should use every resource we can, even if it does seem unlikely to pan out." She glanced at Stormy. "I think we should run a check on this town. See if anything like this has happened before."

"I'll get the laptop out of the car," Stormy replied.

Lou put a hand on her shoulder, stopping her even as she turned to go. "Let's book ourselves some rooms first, huh? Set the computer up in one of them?"

Stormy heard it in his voice, loud and clear. He

didn't trust Jason. He wanted a place where they could talk without him hearing every word. "All right."

"I'll take care of the rooms," Max said.

Lou shot her a look and seemed about to say something, then bit it back. Maxie rolled her eyes at him. "A double for me and Stormy, and a single for you," she told him. "That suit you, Lou?"

"Fine." He pulled out a wallet, reached for a credit card.

Max put a hand over his. "This is going on the company card," she said. "It's our first official case." She headed off to book the rooms.

Lou sighed, turned and went after her. Stormy didn't blame him. She was liable to have him sharing a bed with her if he didn't keep an eye on things. And he'd pissed her off all morning without even meaning to.

Once they had gone and she found herself alone in the room with Jason, she cleared her throat. He walked to the bed, folded up his map.

"Is it going to be hard, working with me?" she asked.

He looked up at her, sent her a sad smile. "If I have trouble working with every girl who ever turned me down, Stormy, I'm in for a pretty tough existence. No. It'll be fine."

She thinned her lips.

"I heard you'd been in the hospital," he said. "Nothing serious, I hope."

She shrugged. "Bullet to the head, a few days in a coma, no big deal."

He swung around to face her, his features expressionless. "Tell me you're kidding."

"'Fraid not," she said. "But it's okay, really. I'm fine now." Shc wasn't. Far from it, in fact, but that wasn't anything he needed to know.

"Someone *shot* you?"

She nodded.

"Who, for God's sake?"

"The bad guy." She rolled her eyes. "Sheesh, who did you think?"

"Jesus, Storm, how can you joke about something like this?"

"Because it doesn't matter, that's how. It's over. History. Gone." God, she wished that were true.

Jason came closer to her, reached up a hand to brush it lightly through her hair. She lifted one of her own to cover it, guided it to the spot where he could feel the misshapen bump, the scar. When he did, his eyes fell closed. "I'd have come if I'd known."

"Max was there. Until she had to go after the jerk who did it, at least."

"Did she get him?"

"Not entirely. She fucked up his plans, saved some people he'd intended to hurt as much as he hurt me, set him back a whole lot, but in the end, he got away." She shrugged. "Someone will put him in the ground sooner or later."

Jason let his hand remain in her hair a moment longer than he needed to, but then he lowered it slowly. "It means a lot to me, your coming down here like this," he said.

"We couldn't not come."

"I know." He lowered his head, paced away from her. "I knew that when I called you. I'm not going to let anything hurt you, I want you to know that."

"That's an odd thing to say. No one here has any reason to want to hurt me. Do they, Jason?"

"No. Of course not, it's just—well, hell, you got hurt on your last case, didn't you?"

She frowned, searching his face, wondering why the stupid flashes that came at the most inopportune times weren't coming now, when she would have liked them to. If they turned out to be some sort of... of psychism, she would have liked a clue about what-ever it was Jason *wasn't* saying.

But then Max and Lou were back. "Lou's in four and we're in three," Max called, holding up a diamond-shape plastic key ring with a worn-out numeral on its face and a copper-colored key dangling from the end. "Got you an extra key, Storm, but the pimply-faced adolescent in the office says we're dead meat if we lose it."

"That would be Gary," Jason said.

"I didn't like him," Max informed him.

"I guessed that already." Jason smiled at her. "You haven't changed a bit, Max. God, it's good to see you."

"You, too," she replied with a smile. Then she hugged him, more firmly than she had before. "It's gonna be okay, Jay."

Lou cleared his throat. "Let's go visit with the local police chief. Best to coordinate with him from the get-go. Even if he isn't any help."

Jason seemed to want to argue, but he changed his mind.

Max nodded. "Maybe we can get some lunch while we're at it? My belly button is touching my backbone."

"There's a diner across the road, just a little ways up. And another near the police station in town,"

Jason said. "I'll give the chief a call and let him know we're coming."

"If it's okay with you guys, I'm gonna stay here," Stormy said. "I can get settled into our room and maybe catch a nap."

Max frowned at her. Stormy told her with a swift glance not to start in with the "Are you okay?" refrain, and Max, reading that look, kept quiet. "I'll bring you back a sandwich," she said instead.

"Thanks."

Chief Fieldner had red, scraped knuckles. Maxie noticed it right off the bat. She also noticed his pale skin, gaunt face, beady eyes and the mustache that cried out to be trimmed. It hung, white and gray, like a walrus's whiskers, drooping to his chin on either side of his mouth. She didn't like him. And she told Lou so the first time the man left their presence, ostensibly to go look through some files or something.

"I don't like him," she whispered. Short and to the point.

She was sitting in one of two chairs in front of Fieldner's spotless, tiger-maple desk. Jason sat beside Max, and Lou stood, his eyes working the room like hawks at a pigeon farm. Though there wasn't a hell of a lot to see. Couple of phones, a bulletin board with six layers of posters and memos pinned to it. A wall's worth of filing cabinets and a coffeepot.

His busy eyes slid to hers then. "What's not to like? He's no prime hunk of youth," he said with a pointed look toward Jason, "but—"

"Jesus, Lou, *look* at him." Max pretended not to notice the look he sent Jason. If he was a little jealous, fine. Better than fine. But she seriously doubted it was anything like that. He didn't like Jason. Hadn't from the moment he'd heard his voice on the phone, and his dislike and distrust seemed to be growing with every minute he spent in Jason's presence. She couldn't do anything about that right now, so she kept her focus on the matter at hand. The only cop in Endover. "If it wasn't daylight outside, I'd peg him for a vamp, no question. And I don't mean the good kind. Lily-white skin just hanging off his bones like sheets on a clothesline. Nothing underneath. No fat or muscle or…soul. And those eyes."

"Vamp?" Jason stared at her, his eyes widening.

"As in *vampire*," Max whispered.

Lou glanced toward the door through which the cop had gone. The only thing visible back there were file boxes stacked high.

"You don't suppose he's found some way to overcome the natural aversion to daylight, do you?" Maxie whispered.

"Jesus, Max, you don't actually believe in that sort of thing. Do you?" Jason asked.

Maxie and Lou both looked at him. Max said, "You've missed a lot since you've been gone, pal."

"I hope you're planning to fill me in."

Lou jumped in before Max could answer, steering her back to their conversation. "You're jumping to conclusions, Max. You've got no evidence that Fieldner's a vamp. You're just wrought up about Stormy begging off the way she did."

Max had to look away, because he was dead right on that score. Stormy, claiming to be tired and wanting to hang out in her motel room and maybe take a nap—that was totally off. "It's not like her to admit to needing a rest—even when she does."

"I know."

"You're worried about her, too, then?"

Lou nodded.

Jason said, "Do you…have some reason to worry?" When they both looked at him, he went on. "She told me about the shooting. Is she really all right?"

"That's what the doctors keep telling us," Max said.

"But you don't believe it?"

Chief Fieldner came back into the room, moving on legs that seemed too thin to carry a normal-size torso around. Yet despite his gauntness, he seemed strong. Almost unnaturally so. He had a map in his hand and was unfolding it even as he worked his way across the room to the desk, to lay it out.

"Here we go," he said. A skinny finger with a cracked, chipped nail pointed to the map. "This is a map of the entire town. Here's that visitor center you were asking about." He lifted his dead, pale blue gaze to each of theirs in turn—they lingered longest on Jason's face. "You have some basis for being curious about that particular spot?"

Yeah, Max thought. Stormy got an odd feeling about it. She hadn't said so, but Max had seen her reaction. It wasn't something she was willing to ignore. But she kept all of that to herself. Lou would think it was foolish, and it wasn't anything the others needed to know.

"Just seemed a likely place to start," Lou said.

"It's closed, you know. Been closed for years."

Lou nodded. "We passed it on the way into town.

Wouldn't have known it was closed to look at it. Maybe the girls didn't, either."

The chief sighed and returned his attention to the map. "Well, there's not much out there. Parkin' lot. Woods out back. You can see, those woods spread out some. Run right down to the coast. But I did a walk through myself, last night. Didn't find a thing."

"You searched the woods?" Lou sounded surprised.

"Well, sure. I took a look around after this young fellow told me about his sister and her friend vanishing like they did. I couldn't do anything official, them bein' gone only a matter of hours at the time. No sign of foul play. No basis for a case. But that doesn't mean I didn't want to help out if I could."

Lou sent Max a look, almost as if he were saying "See? I told you he was an all-right guy." She rolled her eyes, because she didn't agree. Lou turned his attention to the cop again. "How thoroughly did you search them?"

"As good as you could. Probably better, bein' I know my way around out there."

Lou nodded.

"You won't mind if we take a look ourselves all

the same, will you?" Max asked. "Just for my peace of mind?"

"You wanna waste your time, be my guest," the chief said. "Fact is, even if they did run off, I don't think two girls slipping away from their families to raise some hell would go into the woods to do it. No, I expect they'll turn up anytime now. You'll see."

"Still, I'd like to go out there," Lou said.

The chief nodded. "Fine by me. Just make sure it's before dark."

Max went silent, turning wide eyes on Lou. His were just as startled, and then they both turned to stare at the chief. "Why's that?" Lou asked.

"This town has a dusk-to-dawn curfew in effect," he said. "Didn't you see the sign?"

"A little town like this?" Max asked. Her voice had gone soft. She didn't want to start thinking what she was thinking. But damn. Vanishing girls. No one allowed out after dark. Scrawny pale guys? What was she *supposed* to think? "Mind if I ask why?"

The chief shrugged. "Aah, we had some trouble a few years back. Kids coming down from bigger towns, raising hell. It was starting to turn into party central for the college crowd. Beer bottles all over the beaches. Goddamn metal music blasting from their car radios." He shook his head. "It was a nuisance. So we instituted a curfew."

It was not, Max decided, a very logical reason.

Lou sighed. "As a professional courtesy," Lou said, "one cop to another—"

"You're a cop?" Fieldner asked.

"Yeah. Twenty years on the force in White Plains. I'm retired now."

"I see." He seemed to mull that over and looked not at Lou, but at Jason.

"So as a favor to a fellow officer, would you give us permission to be out after dark if we need to?" Lou smiled his friendliest smile. "After all, it's not like we're going to have a beer party on the beach."

Fieldner held Jason's gaze until Jason looked away, then slid his cold eyes back to Lou. He said, "Last thing I need is for more of you to come up missing. Those woods are dangerous in the dark. I prefer you honor the curfew."

Lou sighed but nodded his acceptance of that edict. Max had no intention of obeying.

"If you don't mind my asking," she said, "is it true you're the only cop in town?"

He smiled at her, though it, like every other expression, never reached his eyes. Behind the mustache, his teeth were big and yellow. "Have been for twenty years."

"You're shitting me."

His grin widened. "How many men do you think are needed to tend to a handful of retirees and a few families? Heck, that's all the more reason for the curfew. I have to sleep sometime." He got up from behind his desk, walked toward the door. Clearly, he'd had enough of them for one morning. "I'll tell you, I seriously doubt those girls are really missing at all. They're safe and sound someplace, probably out raising hell somewhere."

Max shot Jason a look, half expecting him to rise to his sister's defense. Instead he only shrugged. "It's possible. Delia's been...a little on the wild side lately."

Max got to her feet. "Guess we'll head over to that visitor center now. Check out those woods."

Lou shook the other man's hand, then followed Max out to the waiting car. Glancing her way, he said, "His hand was warm. He's got body heat."

"He probably had a hot pack tucked in his pocket."

She got in the front passenger side. Jason got in the back, shaking his head. "Just as suspicious as you always were, aren't you, Maxie?"

"Not as suspicious as *I* am," Lou said as he got behind the wheel. "What were you thinking in there?"

"Excuse me?" Jason looked confused.

"Why did you agree with that cop that Delia probably just ran off?" He turned in his seat as he spoke.

"Why wouldn't I agree with him? It's possible, isn't it?"

"You aren't going to get any help from him if he thinks she's a runaway. And I don't think you'd be out here looking for her, much less that you would have dragged private detectives down here to look for her, if you really believed that," Lou said.

"He's upset, that's all, Lou. Go easy on him. His sister's missing." Max sent Jason a reassuring smile, then faced Lou again. "Shouldn't we insist on an Amber Alert or something?"

Lou shook his head. "Delia and Janie don't meet the requirements. You have to know for sure a child's been abducted, and you need a description of the perp or at least his vehicle."

"That's asinine."

"That keeps kids who are lost or who've run away from clogging up the system—so the ones who really need help get it faster."

"And what about the ones who slip through the cracks?"

He shrugged. "I didn't say it was perfect. I happen to think it's the best system it can possibly be, flaws and all." Then he shrugged. "Besides, officially, she's not even missing."

She could have growled at him but didn't.

Lou looked at her. "Where to, Max? This is your game, your call."

Hell, he was the one with all the cop-sense, not to mention experience. His giving her the upper hand was a means to placate her, to skirt around her irritation with him for his treatment of Jason, and she knew it. But she would take it all the same.

Sighing, she said, "I want to check around town, like we discussed. The gas stations, diners, convenience stores. But I really want to check on Stormy first. Let's grab some take-out and head back. I don't like this town. I don't like that pimply-faced kid at the Bates Motel back there, either."

"If we do all that first, that will make it heading for sundown by the time we get to the visitor center," Lou said.

She nodded. "Yeah. That's another reason. I want to see what goes on around this place after the sun goes down. Just what is it that creepy cop doesn't want us to see?"

"Oh, don't even start with the paranormal theories, Max. You've got no basis—"

"Don't start. We both know you're too skeptical to be objective." She sighed and changed the subject. "Did we bring flashlights?"

"Just one," Lou said. "I think I saw a hardware store up here just…right there." He pointed to it just before pulling the car into the tiny square of parking lot in front of the store. The place was no bigger than a shack, but the sign on the door read Open.

Max got out of the car and hurried into the store at Lou's side.

For a small place, it held a lot of goods. The shelves were set close together, making narrow aisles. Not a shopping cart in sight. Every shelf was stacked with goods clear to the ceiling. Tools everywhere, a row for plumbing supplies, another for electrical, two rows devoted to gardening needs, with everything from soil, fertilizer and seeds, to hoes, rakes and shovels. A silver-haired woman was picking through the mesh sacks of flower bulbs when Max and Lou walked past her. She looked up, met their eyes and held them for an elastic moment, her own utterly blank, before finally returning her attention to the bulbs. Other customers wandered about, everyone placid-faced, calm.

Max fought down an insistent shiver. Something was just *wrong* with this place. With these people.

"Found 'em," Jason called.

He came around the corner bearing several flash-lights—the big Maglite brand, with their bright colors. He'd grabbed two blues, a red and a black. "One for each of us?"

"Fine," she said. "We'll need batteries." She took one of the lights from him. "Sixteen of them. D-size."

"I've got those up front," a male voice said.

She damn near dropped the flashlight as she spun to see a tiny, bent-over man who reminded her of something from a Tolkien novel. He smiled up at her. Well, his eyes aimed upward. His head remained bent. The man had the worst case of what her mother had called "bend-over disease" that Maxie had ever seen.

"Uh. Thanks."

He turned stiffly and walked to the front of the store, leaving the three of them to follow. Max took out her wallet, ready to give her biz-only credit card its second workout.

"I should pay for this stuff," Jason said.

"Don't worry, you will. It'll all be in your bill." She sent him a wink. The old Jason would at least have pretended to get the humor in her remark. This one just blinked at her.

Max rolled her eyes and followed the old man to the counter.

"You folks are new in town, eh? Just visiting?" the proprietor asked.

"We're here to search for two missing girls," Max said. "In fact, maybe you can help. Have you noticed any teenage girls who shouldn't be here? They would have been driving a small red car." As she spoke, Jason pulled a photo from his wallet and handed it to her. She showed it to the man.

The man looked at the photo, then at her, meanwhile taking one flashlight from her and slowly punching numbers into his cash register. "Can't say that I have. Though I'm sure they'll turn up. Girls, you say? How old?"

"Seventeen," Jason answered. "The one in the photo is my sister."

The man set the first flashlight down, picked up the second, peered at it and again began punching numbers. Good God, couldn't he just ring one of them up and multiply by four? "Well, you'll find her. Chief Fieldner, he's a good man. A good man."

He rang up the third light and started on the fourth.

"Has he handled this sort of thing before?" Lou asked. "Missing-persons cases, I mean?"

"Oh, sure. It happens now and again. Hasn't lost one yet." He reached beneath the counter and began setting four packs of D-cell batteries on the counter.

"So this has happened before, then?" Max asked. "When?"

He peered at her, worry in his eyes. "I was speakin' in generalizations, missy. I can't think of a specific case. But you know, there's not much hasn't happened in a town as old as this one at one time or another." He rang up the batteries with fingers that suddenly moved efficiently—and quickly. Before she knew what happened, the items were bagged and he was swiping her credit card.

"Is there anyone else in charge around here? Besides Chief Fieldner, I mean?" Max asked.

"I don't know who would be." He drummed his fingers, waiting for the credit machine to work.

"Don't you have a mayor? A town supervisor? Anything like that?"

"No one but the prince."

"You have a *prince?*"

He grinned. "It's just a nickname."

The old woman stepped up behind Max with her arms full of bulbs. "Sam!" she snapped. "You mind picking up the pace a bit? I don't have all day."

Max sent her a frown, but even as she did, she heard the credit-card machine whirring to life as it spat out her receipt. Sam shoved it across the counter with a pen, and Max signed it.

"You have a nice day now. Good luck tracking down those girls."

"But you didn't answer my—"

"Honestly, some people." The old woman shouldered Max out of the way to lay her piles of bulbs on the counter. "Now, one of these has a split bulb in it, Sam. I don't expect to be paying full price for that."

"I'll take care of it, Maddy."

Lou took Max's arm about a half second before she bit the old lady's head off. She shot him a look. He advised caution with his eyes and pulled gently, so she gave in and let him lead her out of the store.

"Jesus," Max said as soon as they were outside. "Are they *all* fucking vampires around here?"

"Nope," Lou said. "Still daylight."

"But what the hell? And who is this goddamn prince person, anyway? Was Gollum back there hallucinating or what?"

"His name was Sam. And just be patient. We'll find out." He popped the trunk at the VW's front end. She dropped the bag inside and got into the car. Jason said nothing, maybe afraid to get between them at that moment.

"I'd have made him talk," Max said.

"And if that's what you want to do, you can go right back in there and do it."

Lou sat there, maddening in his patience. A boy rode past on a red bicycle, a sack of newspapers over his shoulder. "Fine," Max said at length. "I'll bite. What's the 'but'?"

"But," Lou said, smiling because he had made her ask, "you'll make enemies of everyone in this town if you do it your way. You're an outsider. You get pushy and unpleasant, it's gonna burn through the Endover grapevine like a brushfire. If you're nice, on the other hand, people start wanting to help you out."

She pursed her lips. "I hate when you're right."

"No you don't," he said. "You hate when you're wrong. Which is why I usually don't point it out."

"Hey!"

He smiled at her. A real smile. She hadn't been on the receiving end of one of those since their conversation the night before, and seeing one now made her melt. Hell, Lou could correct her all day, and she'd still want him. He could treat her dearest old friend like a murder suspect, and even then, she still wanted him. She had it bad.

8

Stormy waited until everyone had left, then walked around to the back of the motel. She followed a strip of blacktop, probably there to grant a garbage truck access to the large Dumpster out back. Beyond it, there was just the weed- and wildflower-strewn field. She walked to the window of Jason's motel room. She'd flipped the lock during an idle moment when they'd all been gathered in his room earlier. No one had noticed a thing. Well, she had trouble believing Max hadn't noticed. Max noticed everything, though she seemed pretty distracted lately. Still, if she *had* noticed, she hadn't mentioned it. And Jay hadn't noticed, or he would certainly have locked it back up.

Stormy was convinced her old friend was hiding something, and she intended to find out what it was, so she slipped into the room through the window. No one was around to see. No one was around, period. This place was deader than a cemetery at midnight.

A shiver raced up her spine, and she shook it off, slid the window back down and faced the bland room that looked just like her own. Shouldn't take long to toss it. She was so tired, though. Listless—as if she'd been up all night or something. But she ignored the feeling and got on with her mission. She went first to the desk, checked the drawers, found a telephone directory and an out-of-date TV listing guide. Then she tried the dresser. Nothing. No clothes, socks, underwear. Apparently Jay hadn't taken time to pack before charging down here to search for his sister. That, at least, made sense. The closet held a coat, ironing board, extra pillow. The bathroom had the usual motel-provided, eye-dropper-size shampoo, conditioner, bar of soap.

There was just nothing.

Dammit!

She checked the pockets of the coat as a last resort, and then she stopped dead.

There, in the pocket, she felt something. She pulled it out: a Polaroid photo, in which two young girls stared, wide-eyed with fear, at the camera. "Jesus," she whispered.

She flipped it over and read the words scrawled on the back. "Do as you're told, or they both die."

Cold chills rippled down her spine. She ran a hand over the scrawled lines—and they hit her like a sledgehammer. Stormy staggered backward, one hand pressed to her head, eyes squeezed tight. Her legs hit something, and she fell to the floor. A man's face hovered in her mind, behind her tightly closed eyelids—the face of a fallen angel. The same dark, haunting face she'd seen beside Jason's when she'd gone off the road on the way to Maine.

She hit the floor and her hand went limp. She dropped the photo and passed out cold.

"Stormy? Honey? Come on, wake up, babe."

Stormy blinked her eyes open. Max was leaning over her, looking worried. Oh hell, they were back. The realization that she'd been caught red-handed in Jay's room hit her like an electric shock, and she sat up fast—too fast. Dizziness washed over her brain, and she held her head, blinked a few times to let it pass. When it did, she tried to get her bearings and then frowned. "How the hell did I get into the bed?"

"I don't know," Max said. "It's where I found you."

"Where's Jay? Is he back?" She swung her feet to the floor. "Let's get the hell out of his room before he—"

"Honey, we're in *our* room."

Stormy went still, her eyes fixing on Max's. *"What?"*

"Look, you're disoriented. You came in here to lie down while Lou and Jay and I went to grab some lunch and visit the local cop-shop. Remember?"

"Yes, but—"

"You must have fallen asleep. I got worried when I couldn't wake you."

Stormy fixed her friend with an earnest stare. "I was in Jay's room. I passed out in Jason's motel room."

Max frowned.

"I unhooked a window when we were there earlier. I didn't really want to stay behind to rest, I wanted to poke around his room a little while you were gone. And I did."

"You did?"

"Yes. Jesus, Maxie, don't look like that."

"I guess I just don't follow. Why are you suspicious of Jason?"

"You telling me you're not?"

"Of course not." She frowned, shrugged. "Maybe he's acting a little...off-kilter, but hell, given what he's been through... Besides, he's our friend, and he's in trouble. That's all that matters."

"Some detective you are. You're right, he's in trouble. So might we be."

"I'm not following."

"I found—"

Nothing. You found nothing.

Stormy frowned at the deep, oddly familiar voice in her mind. "I found...something." She pressed her hands to her head, squinted her eyes, but all she conjured up was a deep black hole. "I know I did."

"Well? What?"

"I...I don't remember."

"Honey, are you sure you didn't just dream the whole thing?"

"Of course I'm sure! I just—"

That's what it was. A dream, all just a dream.

"I don't know. Maybe."

Max sat on the bed beside her, reached up to stroke a hand through her hair. "Honey, are you sure you're okay?"

"Of course I am."

"No you're not. Look, we've been friends too long

for this. Something's going on, and I know it. When are you gonna come clean with me, Stormy? Don't you trust me anymore?"

Stormy lifted her head to stare right into Max's green eyes. "You know me too well, don't you?"

"Yeah. As well as you know me. So what is it, Storm? What's going on?"

Stormy drew a deep breath, held it a moment, then nodded once. "Okay. It's probably nothing, anyway. But...sometimes I get...pain."

"In your head?"

"Yeah. And there...are these flashes."

Max's brows came together. "Like, light? Colors? What?"

"Images. Pictures, faces. Voices, sometimes. Stuff that doesn't make any sense." She sighed. "It all comes at once, and I can hardly...it's just a jumbled mess. Most of the time."

"Is that what happened on the road, on the way to Maine?"

Stormy nodded. "Yeah."

"And what did you see?"

She shrugged, shook her head. "Jason. And another man, a man I don't know. But...I do. It's like when the word you want is on the tip of your tongue and you can't quite make it come out, you know?"

"I…guess so."

"It's like a strobe effect, too many things, too fast to make any sense or even try. But I know there was something about Jay. And it happened again, when we first got here, when he hugged me. And that time I think I saw him being beaten, kicked. I think that's how he got those bruises. Not from some accidental fall in the woods."

She chanced a look at Max's eyes, and saw them wide and riveted.

"Don't. Don't look at me like I'm insane."

"You're not insane, Stormy. Maybe…do you think you might be psychic?"

Stormy rolled her eyes, got to her feet, paced the room. "It could just as easily be imagination running amok. Delusion. Hallucination. I had a whopper of a head injury, right? So who's to say something didn't get knocked off-kilter?" She pressed her lips tight. "I think maybe I have to face the fact that there could be some brain damage after all, pal."

Max closed her eyes, shook her head firmly. "No. Look, you said you saw Jason in that first flash. On the way to the house. And when we got there, he'd left a message for us. He was in trouble, and you knew it. You picked up on it. It was precognitive."

"You can't know that."

"The hell I can't."

Sighing, Stormy went back to the bed, put a hand on Max's shoulder. "You want to believe it because it's easier to deal with than the other option. I know you pretty well, too, don't forget."

Again, Max shook her head. "I won't believe it's brain damage. Do you know how many people experience the onset of this kind of ability after a near-death experience or a coma?"

"Yeah. And ten thousand times more people experience permanent brain damage instead."

Max narrowed her eyes on Stormy. Then she surged to her feet and stomped to the door. Stormy didn't know what she was up to and hurried after her. She marched along the sidewalk to the room next door and pounded on the door.

"Jesus, Maxie, don't tell Lou about this. He'll have me in the nearest hospital for a round of CAT scans—"

"I'm not going to tell him." She pounded again.

The door was flung open, and Lou stood there with a towel anchored around his hips. Stormy had to fight a grin when she saw the look on Max's face. She wondered if her friend had ever seen Lou Malone's chest before. 'Cuz damn, it was quite the specimen. Apparently Max thought so, too, because her eyes were ravaging it.

"What?" Lou asked.

Max blinked, forcing her eyes to meet his, and said, "Uh—yeah, I…uh…" She caught herself, cleared her throat, seeming to have forgotten why she'd come over, but only briefly. "Tell Storm what you told me about Jason's bruises."

Frowning, Lou gave a quick glance up and down the sidewalk, then gripped her arm and pulled her inside, jerking his head to tell Stormy to follow. She did, and he closed the door.

"Jesus, Max, why not announce it to the world?"

"Just tell her, Lou." Her eyes were on his chest again.

He frowned, snatched a plaid flannel bathrobe from where he'd flung it over his duffel bag and pulled it on. While he tied the sash, he said, "I thought you wanted me to put a lid on my suspicions of your boyfriend, Max?"

"Just freaking tell her."

He sighed, his eyes probing Max's before he turned to face Stormy. "I've seen a lot of accidents. And a lot of beatings. And I think Jason's bruises came from the latter."

Stormy stopped watching Max, turned to watch him instead. "You think he was beaten?"

"Yeah."

"Are you sure?"

Lou shrugged. "No. Not a hundred percent. But if I were a betting man, I'd put a lot of money on it."

Max managed to turn her attention back to Stormy. "See?"

Lou looked at her with his brows raised. "What? You got a suspicious feeling about him too, Storm?"

"Just an inkling."

Lou nodded, then shifted his gaze to Max. "You?"

She pursed her lips, sighing. "Hell, I don't know. I could argue with one of you, but if you both think something's wrong, I guess I have to acknowledge the possibility. But hell, I don't want to. I love Jay, and my natural instinct is to trust him. And besides, even if he did lie about how he got those bruises, that doesn't mean he's up to anything sinister."

"Bullshit," Lou muttered.

Stormy cleared her throat, deciding to change the subject before the two of them got too bristly with each other again. "What did you guys find out at the visitor center?" Stormy asked.

"Haven't been yet," Lou said. "Max wanted to get back here to check on you first. You were sleeping so soundly she wanted to give you a little more time, so we agreed to unpack, catch a shower and meet Jason outside about twenty minutes from now."

He glanced at Max. "We still on for that?"

"Yeah. I'm ready when you are."

"I'm coming with you this time." Stormy added, "I just…I need to run a comb through my hair first."

"And eat the sandwich I brought you," Max said. "Turkey with the works, and extra mayo. Just the way you like it."

"That'll give me time to throw on some clothes," Lou said.

With a nod, Stormy left the room. She noticed, though, that Max didn't.

Max stood there, near the door, watching him.

Lou looked at her, met her eyes. "What?"

She shrugged, lowered her head.

He moved closer, caught her chin and tipped it up so he could see her face. "What's wrong?"

She wanted to lean up and kiss him. She wanted it so much she barely restrained herself. But hell, he'd all but warned her he would be history if she kept pushing. She'd made up her mind to change tactics, but damn, it was tough. "You're a liar, that's what."

He looked at her as if she were speaking a foreign language. "I haven't lied to you about anything, Max."

"No? You go around in those baggy suits of yours, playing the tired-out, worn-out, burned-out cop to the hilt. But underneath it, you've got…" She let her eyes slide lower, over his chest, his belly, even though he'd hidden them behind that stupid robe. She wanted to rip it off him. She wanted to touch him.

She swallowed the impulse and almost choked on it. "You've been hiding behind an image that's a big fat lie."

"Why? Because I don't parade around naked?" He held up a hand. "Don't."

She closed her eyes briefly. "You work out, huh?"

"Have to. It's necessity, not vanity. It was, anyway, and I can't seem to break the habit just because I've retired. You can't be mad at me for that, Max."

She let herself look at him again, couldn't help licking her lips as she did. "Mad at you? For having a belly I could bounce a quarter off? No, I don't think *mad* is the word I would use. You're a beautiful man, Lou. Inside and out. I'm not mad, I'm…" The word *horny* crossed her mind, but she decided not to say it. She couldn't hide the secret smile, though, that came when she thought of the look that would doubtless appear on his face if she were to say it. "Never mind," she told him at last. "Get dressed. We'll be ready to go in a few minutes. I'll get Jay."

He nodded, and Max left the room.

"This would have been preferable in the daylight," Lou muttered as the four of them marched around the visitor center, aiming for the woods behind it. Max was walking beside him, Jason and Stormy behind them. They all had flashlights, and the moon was full. It could have been worse, Lou figured, but not by much.

He was still puzzled over Max's reaction to walking in and catching him half naked. He'd expected her to revert to shameless teasing and outrageous flirting. She hadn't. Oh, she'd made it clear she liked what she saw—and he was human enough to feel good about that. Hell, every man had an ego. She'd given his a boost and then some. But no flirting. No "accidental" touching. No sexual remarks. Maybe she really was going to knock it off. And that was a good thing. That was what he wanted.

Which didn't explain the slightly disappointed

feeling that had hit him when she'd left. Almost as if he missed it.

And he couldn't help but wonder if she'd dropped her constant flirting because he'd asked her to, or because she'd found a more interesting and appreciative target. He hadn't missed her tenderness toward Jason Beck. The hugs, the touches—she touched the guy a lot. And if anyone else were acting the way Jason had been, Max would have been questioning his motives in less than a minute. With Jason, she defended him instead.

It shouldn't bother him. He told himself the only reason it did was because he sensed the man posed a threat to her. He sensed it in that deep, hidden part of him that had kept him alive for the past twenty years. And if she didn't wake up, she was going to be a sitting duck.

The visitor center was a single-story brick rectangle with a soft-drink machine in front of it and rest rooms at the rear. It sat at the back side of a wide strip of pavement. Shaggy grass grew on all sides. There wasn't much else.

"Now, remember, we're breaking Fieldner's curfew in express violation of his orders," Lou said. "And we're in plain sight. We should make this fast and get out of here."

Everyone nodded in agreement. Everyone but Jason. He was looking around them as if certain a bogeyman was going to jump out of the shadows and grab him at any moment.

They checked the parking lot first, spreading out, their flashlights sweeping the blacktop, finding nothing. At first. Then Max knelt, picked something up.

"What have you got?" Lou asked.

"It's a receipt from an ATM." She looked up at him, then shifted her gaze to Jason. "Albany, New York. Your hometown, Jay. Dated two days ago."

Jason held out his hand. "Let me see that."

As he scanned the tiny slip of paper, Stormy said, "The last four digits of the account number should be on there. Do you know if they match hers?"

Jay closed his eyes. "I haven't got it memorized."

"Doesn't matter," Lou said. "After all, how many people from Albany do you figure have been here in the last two days?"

"Not very damn many," Max said. "So we know she was here."

Jason nodded. "But her car's not here. She must have gone on—"

"Anyone could have moved the car. I say it's time we take a look around those woods." Max put her hand on Jason's arm. "Just as a precaution. Okay?"

"Okay."

They walked behind the visitor center. The place looked neat, until they traipsed along what looked like a well-worn path that wound from the rear of the building into the woods behind it. There things got messy.

Soft-drink cans, fast-food and candy-bar wrappers, and crumpled cellophane potato chip bags littered the ground. Decomposing cigarette butts, discarded paper towels and tissues…

"Jesus, people are slobs," Lou muttered.

Max shot Lou a look that said she agreed and trudged on along the path. She slowed her pace, moving her flashlight beam carefully over the ground. "Most of this litter looks like it's been here awhile. Colors are faded, papers are soggy."

"Mother Earth's in the process of turning garbage into mulch and fertilizer," Stormy said, bending to pick up a molded foam cup that was so covered in dirt it had probably been lying there for months. "She won't have much luck with some of this, though. Not for several centuries, anyway." She didn't put the cup back; instead she stuck it into her backpack.

"Like that helps," Jason said.

"Every little bit helps, Jay. If everyone who came

out here picked something up instead of throwing something down, the place would be pristine."

"This is getting us nowhere," Lou said. "Not in the dark without some idea where to look. I hate to say it, but Fieldner might have been right about this being a waste of time."

"We got the ATM receipt," Max said. "That's something, anyway." She narrowed her eyes. "Fieldner said he'd taken a look around out here. Kind of surprising he didn't find it."

She shot a look at Stormy, who shot one right back. And when they both looked at Lou, he had to agree with what he knew they were thinking. Fieldner was a cop. He would have found the slip if he'd been out here looking at all. But why would he lie?

"This is useless," Max said. The four of them had moved off in separate directions, using a large boulder as their hub. Their hope was that in searching in an ever-widening circle, one of them might stumble upon a clue to which direction the girls had gone. Or had been taken. If they'd even been in the woods at all.

Max took the east, with Lou on her left, heading north. Stormy was on her right, heading south and deeper into the woods. Jason had the west, which basically covered the area between the boulder and the vacant brick building. It hadn't been an organized plan; it had just worked out that way, though Max was certain none of them trusted Jay quite as much as she would have liked. She kept telling herself that she *did* trust him, that she knew him, had known him forever, and that his odd behavior was just due to stress and worry over his sister. But all the while she felt a niggling doubt gnawing away at her loyalty to her friend. Something was off about Jay, and she could deny it, but that wouldn't make it right.

She was, Lou had often told her, the queen of denial.

Hell, maybe she was. She'd certainly been in denial where Lou was concerned.

"It's too dark," she muttered as she swept the beam of her light over the moss-and-twig littered ground amid a patchwork of moonlight and shadow. She raised her voice a bit, making it loud enough to carry to the others, who were beyond her range of sight now. "We should give this up and come back tomorrow."

The breeze picked up, making the leaves rustle and whisper through the trees.

"I agree with Max," Lou called.

It gave her a start when she heard how far away he

seemed to be. She hadn't realized she'd ventured this far—that any of them had ventured so far—from the boulder. "Let's meet back in the middle," she called, a little louder this time. No point in risking any of them getting lost. God, she would hate like hell to prove that creepy Fieldner right. "Okay?"

"Works for me," Lou called.

"Me, too." Jason's voice seemed even more distant than Lou's.

Max turned toward the south. But no confirmation rang out from that direction. "Stormy?" she called. "Hey, Storm, are you there?"

Nothing. No answer. Max's heart beat faster. "Storm?"

Something came crashing through the trees from behind her, and she spun around, half expecting to have to fend off an attack. Suddenly something very dark seemed to permeate these woods. She raised her fists, poised to kick the stuffing out of whoever—whatever—appeared.

But it was only Lou who emerged from the dark foliage, his face bathed in moonlight, creased with worry.

"Something's wrong. Storm's not answering," she told him.

He nodded, never slowing his pace, just coming

up beside her, sliding a hand around her waist and propelling her forward, toward where they both knew Stormy was supposed to be. "Dammit, Stormy, where the hell are you?" Lou called.

He didn't sound as frightened as Max felt. That was comforting—almost as much as his broad hand against her waist, resting just above her hip where her shirt had ridden up to bare the skin. He didn't pull away or try to correct it, and she was grateful, but too worried about her best friend to enjoy his touch as much as she normally would have.

She would just file that bit of pleasure away to be recalled and relived later.

"Storm?" She tugged Lou to a stop and tilted her head to one side. "Wait, listen…what is that?"

The sound grew clearer, slowly wending its way amid the trees and darkness. A low, deep growl that vibrated to the core of Max's soul. "Jesus." Her eyes shot to Lou's. Then she lunged into a run, her flashlight beam bounding uselessly ahead of her.

Lou was on her heels. She heard him there, felt him close, knew he had her back. "Storm!" she shouted.

The growl was closer, louder. She had to be almost upon it, whatever the hell it was. She stumbled to a halt, dragging in breath after ragged breath, lifting her flashlight, which all but pulsed in time with her heart as she fought to hold it still, steady the beam, aim it in the direction of that sound.

It caught on eyes that glowed back at her. Stormy's eyes. But not.

Stormy was backed up against a gnarled tree, silent, motionless, maybe dazed or in shock, and no wonder. For there were huge paws braced on her chest and bared teeth in front of her face. The dog—no, sweet Jesus, it was a wolf—the wolf leaned so close to her that she had to feel its breath on her face. Its lips curled, baring teeth that dripped saliva. The low growl kept coming, and the creature never blinked.

9

Lou's heavy tread stopped right beside Maxie. He saw what she did: the wolf braced against Stormy. Max felt him there, though she couldn't take her eyes away. She knew when Lou drew his gun, could see him peripherally, his steady hands and outstretched arms, when he leveled the weapon on the wolf.

"Don't move, Stormy. Just stay perfectly still," Max said. She tried to make her voice loud enough for Stormy to hear her, while keeping it steady and even enough not to startle the wild animal into action. God, it could rip out Stormy's throat in the next heartbeat.

She knew Stormy heard her, saw her friend's

strange eyes shift from the wolf's toward her and Lou. And then those eyes widened, and Stormy shouted in a voice that was very different from her own.

"Nu! Cine scoate sabia de sabia va pieri!"

"What the hell?" Lou asked.

Stormy lifted a hand. It trembled as she stroked the fierce animal's neck, sinking her fingers into its fur. *"El nu e asa de negru cum îl zugrãvesc oamenii,"* she murmured.

The wolf dropped down onto all fours, turned and loped away into the forest, but Stormy remained where she was, eyes eerily wide. She watched Max as if she were as afraid of her as she had been of the wolf.

Lou lowered the gun, and Maxie started forward slowly, holding one hand out in front of her, keeping the flashlight's beam slightly to the left of Stormy's face. It was hard to tell, even in the beam of the flashlight, but she was certain Stormy's eyes had changed, darkened. They were no longer her own.

"Storm? Honey? It's me, Max. Are you all right?"

The perfectly arched brows drew together in a puzzled frown. Stormy lifted a hand as if reaching out to Max, and then she collapsed to the ground.

"Hell!" Max fell to her knees beside her best friend, gently touching her face, her hair.

Lou joined her there in the next breath. "Is she hurt? Do you see any bleeding or—"

"Nothing. I don't think the wolf hurt her."

"Jesus, Max, there must be something. She's out cold." He was kneeling, too, now, tracing Stormy's limbs in the beam of the flashlight, searching desperately for injuries.

"I think it's…I think it's her head. Not an injury, not the wolf."

"What do you…?"

"It's happened before, Lou."

He stopped feeling for wounds and looked at Max sharply. "On the way up to Maine, when she went off the road?"

Max nodded. "And again, back at the motel. She's hearing voices, seeing flashes of light and sometimes images. I think it's precognition, but she's not so sure. And now this."

"Come on, Max, precognition? She's fresh out of a coma. She had a bullet in her brain a few months ago, and you're writing this off to some kind of ES-freaking-P?"

She closed her eyes, lowered her head.

"She belongs in a hospital, Max."

"No." Her head came up sharply. "It's not brain damage, Lou. It's something else."

Lou rolled his eyes, shook his head and scooped Stormy up into his arms. "This isn't about you, Max. This is about her. It's about Storm."

"You think I don't know that?" She ran to keep up as he strode through the woods back toward the boulder, carrying Stormy as easily as if she were a small child.

"If you know it, then stop thinking about yourself. Stop focusing on how bad it's gonna be for you if something's wrong with her, and start thinking about what's best for her. She's fucked up. We need to get her well again."

"I'm telling you, it's not denial this time! I know this thing isn't physical."

"You don't know shit. You might think it, you might feel it, sense it, intuit it, but you don't *know* it. You *won't* know until you have proof, and you won't have proof until she gets a once-over from a qualified doctor. Maybe another set of head shots, just to be sure."

They emerged onto the knoll where the boulder was. Jason was sitting on the rock, but he leaped off when he saw them, his face twisting at the sight of Stormy. "What happened?"

"She was attacked by a wolf. I don't think it hurt her, but she passed out," Max began.

Lou cut in. "We need to get her to a hospital, Jason."

Nodding, Jason turned and used his light to lead them back along the path. "The back seat folds down in the Jeep," Jason said. "You can lay her down in there. I'll drive."

"Do you know where the nearest hospital is?" Max asked.

"No idea."

"There was a sign five miles back on the highway," Lou said. "The exit right before Endover, remember?"

Max nodded as they rounded the brick building and headed into the parking lot. Jason raced ahead to open the back of the Jeep and lower the seat. Then Lou slid Stormy inside. He was as gentle with her as he would have been with an injured child.

"I've got this," Jason said, sliding behind the wheel.

Lou shot Max a look.

She read it, gave him a nod. "I'm riding with her, Jason."

"There's not room—"

"Then I'll make room." She barked the words,

causing Jason to snap his head around and stare at her oddly. "She's my best friend, and I'm damn well staying with her. Got it?"

"Sure. Jesus, Max, I'm on your side here."

"Are you?"

Jason frowned, but looked away. He did wait for her to get in the passenger side, because he was correct: there wasn't room for her in the back with Stormy. Max could lean over the seat, though, stroke Stormy's hair, her face, talk to her.

Lou pulled Maxine's forest-green VW Bug into motion and led the way.

Oddly, Max felt some kind of odd weight lift off her mind as soon as they left the town of Endover behind them.

The vampire was watching. He was always watching. He'd watched through the eyes of the wolf, possessing the animal, living within its mind as he stalked the strange woman, eager to get a closer look at her, to feel her. But he'd learned nothing.

Except that she spoke in his own language. Defended the wolf when the man, Lou Malone, threatened it, telling him if he lived by violence he would surely die that way. A threat.

And then she'd touched the wolf, looking deeply

into its eyes—*his* eyes—whispering in *his* tongue. "He is not so black as he is painted."

As if she knew.

And now Jason Beck was driving her away, taking her beyond his reach—outside the town he controlled.

Where the hell do you think you are taking her?

Jason's head jerked up sharply and he jerked the wheel, startled, no doubt, by the voice in his head. He'd obeyed well thus far. He'd brought them here. All this searching, the questioning of Fieldner, plotting with the maps—it had all been an act. Beck was going through the motions, playing the part. Just enough to keep his friends here, long enough to placate the vampire who held his sister.

"To the hospital," he said. He answered aloud, because he didn't know how else to reply to a voice that echoed inside his head.

It was fine, the vampire thought. So long as he didn't give anything away.

The redhead called Max shot him a look and said, "What?"

"How far did Lou say it was to the hospital?" Beck said quickly, covering. And sweating. He was sweating bullets.

The vampire knew he hated lying to his friends.

To Max and even more to the one who called herself Stormy, an insult to her true name. Tempest. It suited her. The vampire was certain Lou Malone saw through Beck's act. Beck no doubt knew it, told himself it would be all right. That he wasn't going to let any harm come to his friends. That he could both get his sister back and protect Storm and Max from harm.

He was little more than a boy, however, up against a man more powerful than any he would ever encounter. Malone…that one might prove to be a worthy adversary. Beck was nothing but a tool, and the vampire would use him in any way necessary.

"Lou said the exit was five miles back," Max told him.

But Jason didn't hear her, for the vampire was speaking to him again, making his voice ring in the young man's head like the bells of Notre Dame, maddening, deafening. *Do not take her to the hospital. Bring her to me, instead.*

"Why?"

"Why, what, Jason?" Max asked.

Fool! Do you not know better than to question me? I rule this place! I hold the life of your own sister in my hands, and I will not hesitate to crush it to dust. Do as I say!

"I can't."

"Jason, who the hell are you talking to?"

"I'm not alone," he said.

Max slammed him in the shoulder. He struggled to shake his thoughts free of the vampire's grip and faced Maxie. "I can't stand this. First my sister, and now Stormy. But at least I'm not alone," he said.

She looked at him oddly, her eyes narrow, probing, as if she thought maybe he was cracking up. He asked himself if maybe he was. Hearing voices in his head—how real could that be? Then again, he didn't imagine people being mauled by wolves was exactly a commonplace occurrence in twenty-first century New England.

Not for the first time, he thought maybe he should just come clean and tell Max the truth, all of it.

Do not even think of doing that, Jason Beck. If you do, your sister will pay the price.

Beck nodded, acknowledging inside his mind that he had to do what that voice bade him. Even if he was putting his old friends at risk in the process. Delia's life was at stake. He was her brother. He had to take care of her; it was his job.

But he hadn't anticipated that voice demanding Stormy. Stormy. He'd thought himself in love with her once. Maybe still.

In love with her, the vampire thought, hearing every whisper that passed through the young man's mind. So that was the shape of things.

What is wrong with her? the vampire asked.

"I wish I knew," Jason said. Then he glanced sideways at Max. "What's wrong with her, I mean."

Max nodded.

The vampire knew they were rapidly moving farther away than his power could reach. He could stop them, but there was no need. He'd seen inside Beck's mind. He would come back. He would bring Tempest back, because he loved his sister above all else.

See her to the hospital, then. But she must not remain! I will have her returned to Endover before this night is out. Is that understood?

"Yeah," he said. "I understand." His head was clearing, he thought. He rolled down the window to breathe in the fresh air. He felt the rush of it rejuvenating him.

In the back of the Jeep, Stormy moaned.

By the time Lou pulled into the hospital parking lot and got out, Stormy was awake and arguing. He could tell by the way her mouth was moving and the angry expression on her face in the glow of his headlights, when Max and Jason tugged her out of the Jeep and herded her toward the entrance.

It didn't look like much fun, but Lou opted to join the party, anyway. He walked up to them somewhere in between "Come on, Storm, it's only common sense to get it checked out" and "If I have to see one more fucking doctor I'm going to need a shrink instead!"

He smiled in spite of himself as he joined them, and his mere presence earned him a scowl from Stormy that should have wilted him. "Hey, don't look at me. I'm just along for the ride."

"Oh, thanks, Lou," Max snapped. "Don't let him kid you, Stormy. He's the one who talked me into this."

"I'm fine." She said it with her jaw clenched.

"You're probably right," Lou said. "Maybe there's nothing wrong at all. Tell you what, you tell me what it was you said back there, and no one will make you see a doc tonight, okay, kid?"

Her brows rose, but then she smelled a rat and lowered them. "What do you mean, what I said back there?"

"Wait a second, I jotted it down on the way over." He dug in his pockets, his face all innocence. Max was watching him, he noticed, curiosity in her eyes.

Maybe a hint of awe at his tactics. Hell, he wasn't that good. He was mighty relieved, though, at the way she'd snapped at Beck just before they'd all left the visitor center. Maybe she wasn't as unequivocally trusting of her old friend as she'd been pretending to be. He finally found the slip of paper, the back of a gas receipt. "I wrote it phonetically, of course." He cleared his throat. "New! Keen-ay sko-ah-tay sah-be-ah, de sah-be-ah va pi-ere-ay." He glanced at Max. "That was it, wasn't it?"

"More like, 'keen-eh sko-uh-tay,'" she said. "Other than that, you nailed it. Well, you butchered it, but you got the gist." Her eyes touched his, just briefly. Gratitude, a little humor, some of the affection he was used to seeing there.

He'd missed it during her recent snit. He didn't know what the hell he would do if he screwed up his oddball friendship with Mad Maxie. He'd been afraid he'd damaged things beyond repair, but the look they'd exchanged just then gave him hope that maybe their friendship could still be saved.

Max turned her gaze to Stormy, who was looking from one of them to the other, suspicion oozing from her eyes.

Lou thought the four of them must look pretty conspicuous, standing huddled in a hospital parking lot, under the streetlights, talking gibberish to one another.

"What are you talking about?" Stormy demanded. "When did I say anything like that?"

"You said that and a lot more. But I was scribbling in the dark," Lou told her. "I don't think I even want to attempt to repeat the rest of it. It was when that wolf had you backed up against the tree in the woods back there."

"Wolf? There was a wolf?"

"Actually, Lou, she didn't say any of it, until you drew down on the wolf," Max clarified. "I almost got the feeling she was protecting it, telling you not to shoot."

"You guys are making this up."

Max moved closer to her, her expression serious and concerned. "Look at your blouse, Stormy."

Stormy looked down at the front of herself, seeing the slight tears in the fabric of her blouse and the distinct paw print atop one breast. Her brows drew together. Her lips trembled. "Oh, my God."

"You...you reached out. You petted the wolf," Max told her. "It was the damnedest thing I ever saw. You petted it, and it stopped growling. It dropped to the ground and ran away."

Stormy's eyes, wet now, met Maxie's. "Why don't I remember?"

"I don't know, baby. I don't know. That's what we're here to find out." Max slid her arms around the other woman, held her for a second. "It'll be okay, though. We're here for you."

Stormy straightened, but the defiance was long gone from her face and her stance. There was stark fear in her baby blues now. Fear and confusion.

"I wonder what language that was?" Max asked as they moved toward the emergency room entrance.

Lou shrugged. "I don't think it was any language at all. Just gibberish. Does Storm even speak a foreign language?"

"Nope," Max said.

"I do so," Stormy said, a hint of weak humor in her tone. "I speak Spanish." They all knew her grasp of Spanish was pitiful, at best.

"Was that Spanish, Storm?" Max asked.

Sighing, she lowered her head. "No. It's nothing I ever heard before. And I don't remember saying it, or anything about any wolf. Jesus, you'd think I would remember a wolf."

Max nodded. "You passed out cold right after. Stayed out almost all the way here. That would account for being disoriented."

"Just get checked out, huh, Storm?" Lou asked. "For our sakes, if not your own."

"I agree with them," Jason added. "It's only logical to make sure you haven't developed some side effect from the bullet or the coma. A blood clot or a hemorrhage or whatever."

She closed her eyes, nodded once. "All right. We're here, we might as well. I'll get a quick X ray. Have them send the films back to my doc in White Plains, just in case. Okay? Will that get you all off my case?"

"It sure will," Lou said. Then he moved past her and opened one of the double doors, held it wide as Stormy and Max walked inside, with Jason bringing up the rear.

The place wasn't busy. Five minutes in the waiting area and Stormy was ushered into a treatment room, while Max continued filling out forms in the waiting area. She'd just finished with the forms when Jason appeared with three cups of hospital-stale coffee. He handed one to Lou, took another to Max.

Max accepted it and looked up at him. "I'm sorry I snapped at you back there, Jay. I was shaken up, that's all."

"I understand. I've been pretty shaken up myself the past couple of days. It's forgotten, okay?"

She clutched his hand in one of hers, squeezed it. "Okay."

Lou tried to pretend his grimace was due to the taste of the coffee, even though he had yet to take a sip.

Two hours and several cups of mud later, Stormy returned, with a forced-in-place smile and a clean bill of health. Max seemed relieved but not surprised. Lou couldn't believe it.

As they all trooped out to the waiting vehicles, Max walked close to him, and, leaning up, she whispered, "I told you it wasn't physical."

"You can't be a hundred-percent sure of that. Not until her head doctor in White Plains reviews the tests."

Max shrugged. "That phrase she muttered back there. The one you jotted down. You still got that?"

He sent her a narrow-eyed glance. "Yeah. Why?"

"Can I have it?"

He dug the scrap of paper from his pocket. She took it from his hand and jammed it into her own pocket with a quick glance at Jason and Stormy, who were walking a few feet ahead.

"What are you up to, Maxie?" Lou asked.

"Gonna try to get it translated."

He shook his head. "It's gibberish."

"Maybe. But what if it's not?"

"How could it be anything else? You said it yourself, Max. She doesn't speak a foreign language. Even her high school Spanish is a running joke. There's no way she could just start spouting sentences in a language she doesn't know. It's not possible."

She looked up into his eyes and shook her head slowly. "Lou, haven't you learned by now that anything is possible?"

10

Even as they reached the vehicles, Max's cell phone bleated.

She frowned as she dug in her purse for it. "What do you know? It's working again. I didn't even realize it was still turned on." She hit a button and brought it to her ear. "Maxine Stuart," she said.

Brisk and businesslike—if the person on the other end had never met her, he would never realize he was talking to an impulsive hellion with a huge imagination, Lou thought.

Stormy and Jason stopped walking and turned around. "Guess we have reception again, huh?" Jason asked, while Max covered her free ear and hunched over the phone as if she were having trouble hearing.

"Maybe it's only inside Endover the reception dies completely," Stormy said, and the look she sent Lou told him she was starting to adopt Max's penchant for conspiracy theories. Hell, it was bound to happen sooner or later.

"Do I need to come back there, Officer Gray?" Max was asking.

Lou looked at her sharply. "What's going on, Max?"

She held up a hand. "All right. Thank you. Yes, I'll check in as soon as possible." She hit the cutoff and dropped the phone back into her purse, lifting her head to meet his eyes. "There was a break-in at the house."

Lou swore softly. "Someone probably saw you moving out and wanted to look for any valuables you might have left behind," he said.

"No, not that house. The house in Maine. The mansion. The alarm system Morgan had installed alerted the Easton PD, and an Officer Sandy Gray went out to investigate. The front door had been forced open—that gorgeous stained-glass oval broken all to hell and gone. The place was rifled. Computer's missing. They're not sure what else.

They want me to come back and take inventory as soon as possible."

Lou frowned, a million questions running through his mind. "Why would someone go after your computer, Max?"

She shrugged. "I don't know. To sell it, I guess."

"Good thing I had the laptop with us," Stormy said. "Don't worry, Max, there's nothing on your hard drive that we don't have backed up."

"Gimme the phone." Lou held out a hand.

Max handed it over, and he hit the incoming calls log button to get the number, then pressed Send.

"Easton Police, Officer Gray speaking."

Lou introduced himself as a fellow cop and a friend of Maxine's, and proceeded to fire questions at the cop. By the time he hung up he had a better handle on things. "The televisions, VCRs and jewelry were undisturbed, as far as Gray can tell," he said. "They left the computer monitor, the scanner, printer, all that. All they took was the tower. The break-in happened earlier today—they've been trying your cell every couple of hours since. Got the cell number off your business cards. The files were rifled. Not much else. Whoever did this was after something specific. Something they thought they would find in your files."

Max frowned. "Well, it's not like I have any top-secret information in there, aside from the..."

She stopped there, her eyes widening. "The DPI files," she said. "The CD I stole five years ago from the burned-out ruins of that so-called research lab in White Plains. It had the case files of hundreds of vampires on it."

"You never copied that onto your hard drive," Stormy said.

"No, but there were copies packed in our stuff. I never took the time to put them in the safe. We...we barely unpacked. What if someone got it?"

"You think it was Frank Stiles, that bastard who shot me and tried to murder Dante?" Stormy asked.

Jason was staring from one of them to the next, his eyes wide. "Wait a minute, wait a minute. Vampire files? DPI? Who the hell is Frank Stiles?"

Max sighed, lowering her head. Lou could see the worry in her eyes, the regret. Hell, he didn't blame her for it. If those details about the undead fell into the wrong hands, a lot of innocent vampires might die.

Innocent vampires. Hell, life since Max came into it was freaking surreal.

"Let's get back to the motel," Max said. "Lou,

you drive Stormy. I'll ride with Jay. He's got a lot of catching up to do."

Lou nodded. "Okay. Fine by me." He reached for Max and snagged one arm around her waist, tugging her against him. It was the only way he could think of to get her close enough to warn her. Bending his head until his mouth was close to her ear, he whispered, "Be careful what you tell him, Max. I don't trust him."

"Damn," she whispered back. "And here I thought you just wanted to hold me." When she said it, her lips moved so close to his neck that they brushed his skin, her breath caressing, warm. It heated his blood. He felt a pulse in his throat beating harder. He *did* want to hold her, goddammit. What the hell was the matter with him?

"I don't want to leave this case to go back there, Lou," she whispered, successfully changing the subject.

He looked down into her face, her sincere, frustrated eyes, so wide and green. Her perfect, round cheekbones that always seemed to be begging to be touched. Traced. Kissed. He realized belatedly that his arm was still wrapped around her waist. He liked it there. She fit in the curve of his embrace.

With no small surge of regret, he let his arm fall

to his side. "You don't have to go back. Call Lydia. She'd be glad to drive up there and take care of this until we can get back. You tell her where you left the CDs, and she can check to see if they're still there."

She lowered her eyes. "Lydia. I don't know, it seems like a huge favor to ask."

He nodded. "Look, I know you haven't known her that long. But she's your birth mother, Max. She's nuts about you. And she's a good friend of mine, has been for years. Believe me, it wouldn't be overstepping the bounds of your brand-new relationship with her. It really wouldn't." He shrugged. "I tend to think she'd move up there with you if you asked her."

"Really?"

He nodded. "She loves you, Max." And damn, he thought, what was not to love?

She nodded slowly. "Short of calling Morgan back from her honeymoon, I guess I don't have anyone else I can ask."

"I'll call her on the way back, before we lose cell reception again."

"Thanks, Lou. You always know what to do." She slipped her arms around his neck, pulled his body close and brushed her lips over his jaw. Then she lowered herself and hurried over to Jason's Jeep.

He watched her go, wondering why he was such

a confused mess where she was concerned. At least she didn't seem angry at him anymore. But just when he thought their friendship was safe, she went and pushed it a little further, leaving him turned on and ready to run, all at once.

He turned and started for the Bug. Stormy caught up before he reached it. "Looks like you're finally falling for her, huh?"

"For who?"

"Max. That hug you gave her before she left—" She broke off, probably because he winced a little when she said it. He'd only hugged her so he could whisper his warning without Jason Beck overhearing it. He supposed that quick kiss she'd given him in return was her idea of payback.

"Don't tell me," she said. "It wasn't a real hug."

"It was real enough." Even though he hadn't meant it to be, it had certainly *felt* real. A little too real, he thought.

"Don't play with her, Lou. Not unless you mean it. She couldn't take it."

He frowned at Stormy, but she only turned and opened the passenger door to get into the car. What the hell was she talking about? Maxie was the toughest female he'd ever met. He couldn't think of anything she couldn't take. Besides, she'd given up on trying to seduce him despite that little display a moment ago. She was glad he was around. He understood that, because the feeling was mutual. No big deal.

A little voice inside reminded him that he'd been starting to doubt that was all there was to it. Ever since her passionate claim that she had never seen him as too old or worn-out to respond to her teasing, he'd been wondering, what if it wasn't teasing at all? What if it was for real?

Hell, he couldn't deal with that possibility, because he didn't know how. Truth was, he was afraid of her. Imagine that. A veteran cop who'd seen just about everything there was to see, afraid of a pretty, spunky sprite like Maxie.

Well, stranger things had happened.

Max was still warm all over from Lou's embrace—and still stinging with disappointment that it hadn't meant a damn thing. Not that she'd thought for one instant that it had. Okay, maybe just for one *brief* instant—that moment when he pulled her hard against him, and her heart reared up on its hind legs and took off at a full gallop.

God, if she closed her eyes she could still feel him, holding her to him, hard and tight, as if—

"So the research lab in White Plains wasn't really a research lab," Jason said. "I got that much."

His voice reined her ecstasy to a halt, and she forced herself to pay attention to him as he drove. "Actually, it was. Just not for cancer. It was the headquarters of a government organization called the Division of Paranormal Investigations."

"DPI," he said, nodding. "And they researched… vampires?"

She nodded. "Sounds insane. But it's not. It's real, Jay. When you and Stormy and I sneaked in there to check out the place, right after the fire, I found a CD. It was full of information, case histories of vampires. How old they were, who sired them, where they'd last been seen. Some had been captives in that place, used as guinea pigs for their research."

He shook his head. "You know, when I got that flyer, saw that you were investigating supernatural-type stuff, I thought—hell, I don't know what I thought. Goth kids playing dress-up and drinking blood for kicks, I guess. Maybe a little ghost-busting on the side." He sent her a brief, probing look. "But this stuff can't be real, Max. I mean…vampires?"

"I've met them. I've seen them. Hell, some of them are my friends." She didn't tell him one of them was her own sister. She might want to trust Jason, but wanting to trust wasn't trust itself, and she knew Lou had a point in advising caution.

"It's hard to believe. What are they…what are they like?"

She sent him a look, sensing more to his question than what rested on the surface. "Just like anyone else, I guess. Some are good, some are bad. Some are freaking insane."

He licked his lips. "But not *just* like anyone else. Not really. I mean, they're different. Physically, right?"

She tipped her head to one side. "They can't go out in the daylight. They need blood to survive."

"What do they look like?"

She fixed him with a steady gaze. "Why? You think you've seen one?"

He laughed at that, but it was a nervous laugh. "No way. But I'd like to know if I did."

Max shrugged. "Paler than we are. Otherwise, not much different."

He nodded. "What about…powers?"

"What about them?" She was none too comfortable discussing this with him, all of a sudden.

"You know, the stuff you see in the movies. Changing into bats. Talking to people inside their heads." He sent her a sideways glance. "Any of that for real?"

She nodded slowly. "They're pretty good at the mental conversations. I've heard some can shape-shift, but I've never seen it happen."

"Unbelievable," he said, shaking his head slowly. "So how do you kill them?"

Max didn't gasp, but it was close. She didn't know how to answer, and while she was searching her mind, he went on.

"Crucifixes? A wooden stake?"

"It's, um…it's never come up."

"Do you think—" He stopped himself. "No. It's crazy."

"Do I think what's going on in this town is connected to the undead? That's what you were going to ask, isn't it, Jay?"

He thinned his lips, nodded once.

"I don't know. I didn't think so, but now…hell, whoever broke into the house was after those files. That's my gut feeling, anyway. And if they knew I was away, it might be because they knew I was here." She paused, drew a breath, decided to plunge ahead. "I might be able to figure this out, Jason, if you would tell me everything."

He swung his head toward her fast. "What do you mean?"

"Why all the questions about vampires? Do you have some reason to think one is involved in this?"

"No. Of course not. I was curious. Hell, Max, it's not every day you talk to someone who claims to have personal experience with something like that."

She sighed. "I think you're holding something back, Jason. I think you know more than you're saying."

He faced front again, his jawline seeming to harden. "I've told you everything I know."

"Including how you got those bruises?"

He said nothing.

"It wasn't from a fall. Those came from a beating, Jay. Someone attacked you."

He licked his lips, nervous, trying hard not to appear to be. "All right. I was upset. I was in a bar asking the locals if they'd seen Delia, and I had a few too many. Ended up in a brawl. It was nothing."

"So why did you lie about it?"

"I got my ass kicked. I was embarrassed, okay?"

"And that's all? There's nothing else?"

"There's nothing else."

"Chief Fieldner had skinned-up knuckles, Jay. How do you explain that?"

He slanted her a quick look. Barely missing a beat, he said, "He landed a few blows when he came to break up the fight. That's all."

She sighed, certain she would get no more out of him, hoping that was because there was nothing more to get.

Jason cleared his throat. "He's strong, Max."

"Who is?" She frowned at him. "Chief Fieldner?"

He nodded. "He looks scrawny. Like a scarecrow. But he's strong. Almost...unnaturally strong."

It was a warning. She didn't mistake it for anything else. "I'll keep that in mind," she told him.

"Take a look at your cell phone," he said. "See if there's a signal. We're getting close to Endover."

She took out the phone. "Three bars." Then she watched the signal bars vanish, one by one. "Two," she said. "One. Nothing. Damn."

"The motel's a mile ahead. At least we know how far we have to drive to get a signal."

He had changed the subject, she realized, and wondered if it had been deliberate. "I'll plug it in tonight, charge it up just in case."

He nodded. "So what do we do next?"

"Research," she said. "I want to know if anything

like this has ever happened before. Maybe missing girls aren't an unusual occurrence in Endover, New Hampshire."

It was close to midnight when someone pounded on her door. Max came awake with a start that set her heart hammering in her chest. Her first glance was at the clock. Her heart jumped, and fear sang in her veins. Then she heard Lou on the other side. "Open up, Maxie, it's me."

Sighing in relief, she flipped on the light and slid out of bed, then padded to the door and undid the chain. When she flung it open, Lou looked at her. His eyes betrayed him, lowering to take her in from her bare toes up, and she smiled to herself, glad she was wearing nothing more than a baby-doll T-shirt that didn't even cover her waist, and a pair of bikini panties.

"You want to put on a robe or something?"

"I didn't bring a robe or something."

He closed his eyes, as if that were the only way he could stop looking at her, and when he opened them again and came the rest of the way inside, his gaze shot straight to the empty bed on the far side of the room. "Where's Stormy?"

"The couple next door left while we were gone.

She took their room. Said she needed some space."
The truth, Max suspected, was that Stormy had only
moved out to give Max some space—just in case
things heated up with Lou. But she wasn't about to
tell Lou that.

"I'm not altogether comfortable with her being
alone."

"Neither was I," Max said. But she pointed to the
door in the wall, opposite the twin beds. "There's a
connecting door. I told her to leave it unlocked so I
could check on her at will. It's not even closed all the
way, so I can hear her. She's fine."

Lou nodded. "Good."

"So what's up?"

"Put on some pants, Max."

She rolled her eyes. "I can't believe any man finds
the sight of a half-dressed female as upsetting as you
do."

"Who said I found it upsetting?" he asked. "We're
going for a walk, and it's chilly outside."

She frowned at him, then shrugged and turned
to the suitcase that was sitting open on the dresser,
tugged out a pair of jeans and pulled them on. She
noticed that Lou didn't turn away as she did. Well,
that was progress, wasn't it? She pulled the jeans
up slowly, not slowly enough so he'd know it was

deliberate, but slowly enough to turn him on—she hoped. It was cruel to tease him, but dammit, old habits were hard to break.

She zipped, snapped, then stepped into her scuffy slippers. "Ready."

"Jacket," he said.

"Nah. I like to feel the night air on my skin."

He sighed but didn't argue, just stood there in the open doorway waiting for her to join him outside. "Where are we going?"

"Out here." He walked her across the parking lot, toward the place where the motel's grassy lawn met the pavement. There were a couple of picnic tables there, and he walked right up to one of them, took something out of his pocket and dropped it onto the redwood-stained surface.

Max took a seat atop the table, picked the thing up. "What is it?"

"It's a bug."

Max looked up fast.

"I found it in the phone in my room. Ten to one there's one in yours, too."

"Jesus." She reached out for the tiny electronic button, turned it in her fingers, then shot a look at Lou. "Is it still—"

"No. It's dead. But near as I could tell, it was working right up until I found it."

"God, Lou, how did you even know to check?"

He shook his head. "I couldn't stop thinking about that extra click on the phone line when Jason spoke to us from the phone in his room. It sounded more like someone on an extension but...I don't know, you get an instinct about shit like this after a while. Something told me to check, so I checked." He shrugged. "We ought to go back—check your room. Storm's and Jay's, as well."

Sighing, she nodded. "Okay."

"What's wrong?" he asked.

She looked up, caught him searching her eyes. "Nothing."

"Something is. This place is getting to you. The town. The missing girls. The goddamn eerie feeling that seems to permeate this freaking place."

She met his eyes. "You feel it, too?"

"Yeah. I feel it. As if I'm walking around under an anesthesia cloud or something."

Max nodded hard. "It's like my senses are dulling by degrees. I feel slow, heavy. It seems better when we're outside of Endover, but then it comes right back as soon as we return. It's subtle."

"Maybe we should do a little extra research. See

if there's any history of chemical pollution near here. Or radon or…hell, I don't know. A natural gas leak?"

"You'd smell natural gas, wouldn't you?"

"I don't think so."

"I do. And radon wouldn't have any effect for years."

"I don't like it," he said. "What do you say tomorrow we drive a few miles away from Endover, find ourselves another place to stay?"

"I don't know. I feel like we need to be here, you know?"

"Well, think it over, at least."

"Okay." She slid off the picnic table, taking the listening device with her, and started walking back toward the parking lot and the motel.

Lou was quick to catch up.

"You were right before," she said. "Something was bothering me, but it wasn't this town. It wasn't the case. It wasn't the bad air in Endover."

She kept walking, right up to her motel room door, then stopped there to look at Lou. "I can see in your eyes that you already know what I'm going to say—and you're praying I won't say it."

He held her eyes for a long moment. "You promised you'd knock it off with this kind of shit, Max."

"Yeah, well, you're not making it easy. Not when you yank me into your arms the way you did tonight at the hospital, just as some kind of ruse." She probed his eyes. "You know, for one insane moment, I thought you meant it. I thought you were going to kiss me."

He lowered his eyes, dodging the intensity in hers. Damn, he made her angry.

"And then, when you came to my room just now—"

"Jesus, Max, stop it already. We're working a case together. Even if something was going to— this isn't the time."

She nodded. "I know you're right. But if you expect me to keep my end of the bargain, Lou, the least you can do is stop jerking me around like this."

"Jerking you—"

"I almost get the feeling you're enjoying it. Dangling the bait just to see if I'll still jump."

Sighing, she turned from him, thrusting her key into the lock.

Lou's hands came to her shoulders, turning her to face him. "Max, I would never—please don't think that's what I'm doing. Hell, I wouldn't even have thought..." He pushed a hand through his hair, maybe giving up on trying to express his confusion.

"I know. You would never have thought you had it in you to hurt me. Because you've never once taken me or my feelings seriously."

"Max, I wouldn't hurt you for the world."

He looked as if he meant it. And maybe he did. Max turned the lock, opened the door. "But you did. And my feelings *are* serious. If you want me to keep them to myself, fine. I said I would do that, and I will. But you've got to do your share, too."

He nodded. "I'm sorry. I mean it. I'm really sorry. I won't…let it happen again. I promise. No more hugs or showing up at your door in the dead of night, okay?"

She sighed deeply. No more hugs. Hell, that was the last thing she wanted to hear from him. "Just don't hug me unless you mean it," she said. She shrugged. "And until this case is over, I suppose you might have to show up at my door in the dead of night for reasons that have nothing to do with crawling into my bed, so we probably shouldn't rule that out. Actually, let's not rule out the alternative, either." She let him off the hook with a smile over her shoulder as she stepped into her room.

He seemed relieved. Maybe he really hadn't been playing games with her feelings. Hell, how could he have been? He'd never believed for a minute she had any real feelings for him. He'd always chalked her behavior up to a flirtatious nature, blithely refusing to notice that she didn't flirt with any other man but him.

He came into the room and walked past her to the bedside stand, picked up the telephone handset, removed the mouthpiece and neatly plucked another listening device from amid the tangled nest of bright-colored wires inside.

She opened her mouth, but he held a finger up to his, then flipped the back off the tiny button-shaped bug, did something to its innards, then snapped the back on again. "Safe now. Unless there are others."

She looked around the room, suddenly feeling exposed, watched, as if a hundred unseen eyes were looking in on her. She rubbed her arms against the chill that feeling evoked. "I'll never be able to sleep in here."

"Yeah, you will," Lou said. And then he began searching. He started on one wall and checked every surface, every baseboard, the curtains and the rods that held them, the window casing. He worked his way around the room, even running his hands over the carpet to check for lumps, and using a pocket knife as a screwdriver to remove the switch plates and plug covers to check behind them. He searched the closets, removed the dresser drawers, took the clock radio apart. He checked the bathroom, the faucets and light fixtures. He left the bed for last, stripping it bare, then lifting the mattress to check under it, before searching the area under the bed itself.

Finally he nodded, satisfied. "It's okay. The only bug was in the phone. The room is clean."

"Odd choice of words," she said. She stood in the center, hands on her hips, surveying the mess he'd made.

Lou slid the mattress back into place, then began putting on the sheets, making the bed. Max picked up the drawers and slid them back into their places.

"So what about the other rooms?"

"We'll check them tomorrow. No sense waking everyone."

"How could anyone have known we were coming, Lou? Much less which rooms we'd be in?"

He shook his head. "If Jason's phone is bugged, and he phoned us from that room, then someone—whoever is listening—might have known we were coming. But why was his phone bugged in the first place?"

Max frowned. "Maybe every room in the motel is bugged." She lifted her head and eyebrows. "And there's no cell phone reception around here. Lou, maybe that's no coincidence. And maybe it's not us—maybe someone is keeping close tabs on all visitors to this town."

Lou narrowed his eyes as if in thought, but then shook his head. "That wouldn't make any sense, Max."

"None of this makes any sense, Lou." She shook her own head slowly. "I'm going to bed. Either come with me, or go back to your own room."

He shot her a look.

Max shrugged and sent him back a sheepish smile. "Sorry. Force of habit."

He sighed and turned to walk toward the door. She said, "Lou?"

"Yeah?" His hand was on the knob.

"What happened between you and your wife?"

Lou went still. He lifted his head and turned back toward her very slowly. "I think I told you already, didn't I?"

"You said you were a lousy husband. That didn't really tell me a thing."

He sighed, lowering his head. "Hell, maybe you need to hear it. Maybe that'll—" He stopped there, lifted his head again, met her eyes, and then slowly came back across the room.

Max thought that he was going to talk to

her—really talk to her. She hoped it, at least. She quickly climbed onto the bed he'd made so neatly, her back to the headboard, legs curled beneath her, and she patted a spot beside her.

Lou didn't even argue. He sat, but only on the edge of the mattress, his feet remaining on the floor. "We had a kid, you know."

Max felt her jaw drop.

"A boy."

"Jesus, Lou, how the hell did you manage to forget to mention that in all the time we've known each other?"

He shrugged. His broad back was toward her. She wanted to turn him, to see his face. "It's not something I talk about. He, uh…he was only with us for three years."

11

Max's heart twisted hard and tight. She slid across the bed until she sat beside him, legs still under her, one hand on his shoulder. "He...died?"

Lou nodded. "Leukemia."

"Oh, my God."

He shook his head. "I couldn't handle it. I was no good to anyone, not my wife, not myself. I threw myself into my work. She fell apart. She wanted another child. I couldn't even bear the thought of going through what we'd gone through with Jimmy again. So she found someone else. End of story."

"End of story?" She was shaking all over. My God, she hadn't so much as had a clue, and if she found just hearing about it this devastating, how must Lou feel? "End of story, Lou? I don't think so."

"Well, it is. There's no more to tell."

"How long ago was this?"

He nodded. "Jimmy would have been fifteen this year."

She closed her eyes. "I'm sorry. I'm so sorry."

"I know you are, Max. It's okay. It was a long time ago."

"It's not okay. Hell, something like that is *never* okay. No wonder you're…the way you are."

He looked sideways at her. "How am I?"

She couldn't take her eyes off his face. Everything in her wanted to hold him, comfort him, take away the old, deep shadow of pain in his eyes. But she couldn't do that, because he wouldn't let her. "You're…solitary and kind of shielded. You never go too deep, never get too close. Sometimes I get the feeling you keep the truest part of yourself locked away in a dungeon somewhere deep inside you. And now I know why."

He pursed his lips as if considering those words, and then he dismissed them with a shake of his head. "I'm just who I am. No deep, dark psychological knots to untangle. Nothing locked away or hidden. It's more like I've been worn down until everything in me is callused and tough, like old leather." He shrugged. "It's a good way to be."

"I'll bet. Nothing can hurt old leather."

He smirked at her. She lifted a hand to his cheek, staring into his eyes. "I am so sorry you lost your little boy, Lou. You must have been a wonderful dad."

He got to his feet rather abruptly. "Go to sleep, Max. Get some rest. We have a lot to do tomorrow."

She nodded. "Good night, Lou."

"'Night. Lock up behind me."

He walked out of her room.

Max slid out of bed to go to the door and turned the dead bolt, because she knew he would be listening for that on the other side. Then she waited, to give him time to get back to his own room. Five minutes, she figured, ought to be plenty.

She used that time to ponder her new knowledge about Lou. No wonder he was afraid of relationships. He hadn't healed from his failed marriage, from his lost little boy. He hadn't let himself heal.

She knew Lou. Everything he did, he either did very well or he gave up. She'd joked with him once about how he'd tried golf and was lousy at it. So he'd never played the game again.

He was a good cop. Hell, he was a great cop. If

he hadn't been, she thought, he would have quit as a rookie and looked for a different profession.

So he'd been married. And his marriage had failed. He'd had a child and lost him. He'd made up his mind those things were things he wasn't meant to do, wasn't any good at and would never do again.

She closed her eyes. God, it was going to be harder to get through to him than she had even imagined.

Forcibly, she tugged her mind back to the task at hand. She glanced at the clock but wasn't sure Lou had put it back together in a way that was entirely reliable, so she counted off time in her head, even as she gathered up a credit card, notepad, pen and her trusty penlight. When enough time had passed, she unlocked the door, opened it and peered outside.

She saw no one. Crickets chirped and sang in the distance. She smelled night air, sea-smells. They were not far from the shore. It was light outside; the light of the now-lopsided waning moon beamed brightly, bathing everything in a soft glow. It made up for the broken streetlight that stood like a crippled sentry over the parking lot.

Slipping outside, Max walked quickly, quietly, in her bare feet to the motel office, then cupped her hands around her eyes to peer through the window.

No lights were on. No one seemed to be around.

She tried the door, but it was locked. Didn't matter. She'd scoped it out earlier. Now she headed around to the side, where there was a window. It was an old window, and she flipped the lock around easily by sliding a credit card between the panes. Then she opened it wide and climbed inside.

The office was tiny. There was a four-foot length of counter, a small workspace behind it, and a door behind that. That door was closed now. She hadn't been able to see enough last time she'd been in here to decide whether that door led to a large office or a small apartment. If the latter, that creepy young clerk might be lurking back there even now.

She moved silently, slipping behind the counter, sliding the penlight from her jeans pocket, glancing behind her over and over. She bent to the shelves under the counter and slid out the guest registry. Setting it on the counter, she opened it and found her own registration. Then she started copying down the names, addresses, license plate numbers and telephone numbers of the people who had been there prior to her. She decided to get as many names and addresses as time allowed.

She stood there, flipping pages and scribbling down names—hell, there weren't very many.

A noise—so soft it might have been her own pulse

beating in her throat—made her pen go still. She looked behind her. The door was still closed.

Carefully she tore the top page from her notepad, folded it small and slipped it into her jeans pocket. Then she bent over the registry to begin filling a second page.

She was jotting the third entry on that page when the back of her head exploded in pain. White light flashed like lightning in her mind, and then she was pitched into darkness.

Lou didn't go back to sleep. Of course he didn't go back to sleep.

How the hell did Max manage to get to him the way she did? How did she get him to talk about things he had lived more than a decade without sharing with anyone else?

Hell, how did she manage to do any of the things she did to him? Ever since he'd known her—on and off for close to ten years now—he'd taken her flirting as playful teasing and nothing more. Of course, they'd never been more than mere acquaintances— until the Frank Stiles case.

It was only then, when they'd been thrown together on a daily basis in the height of a life-and-death situation, that he'd begun to suspect her play-ful flirting might be something more.

And now he was sure of it. At least, he was sure she thought it was. And he was damned if he knew what to do about it.

She was wrong about him. He *hadn't* been a wonderful father. Hadn't been much of a husband, either. He'd spent far too much time working, always assuming there would be time for his family later. It was only when Jimmy was diagnosed that he'd real-ized there might not be a later. And sure, he'd taken time off then, tried to make up for his lack of atten-tion. But it was too little too late. He hadn't blamed Barbara for leaving him. He'd expected it. And he'd managed to go twelve years without feeling anything more than a slight attraction toward any woman.

He felt something for Max, though. Hell, he had a pulse. Naturally he felt something for her. Who wouldn't? The thing was, it went way beyond attrac-tion. But dammit, he just wasn't ready—didn't think he would ever be ready—for a relationship like one with her would have to be.

And she was too special for a fling. A fling would destroy what they had, and maybe destroy her, too. He didn't see that there were any options other than those two—a serious, passionate, long-term relationship, or a fling—except for keeping what they currently had. A growing and genuine friendship. Mutual respect. Admiration. He liked her, and she liked him.

Yet more than ever, he feared Max wasn't going to settle for that.

He needed to take a walk. Walk her off. Hell, being friends was great, in theory. But when she looked up at him with those big green eyes of hers, and he looked back down at her wearing a tiny T-shirt with no bra underneath, with her smooth, taut belly showing above her jeans, and her bare feet so goddamn cute he wanted to kiss them…hell.

Yep, a walk. Clear his head.

He opened his door, stepped outside and saw a car in front of the motel office. Taillights lit briefly. Then the trunk popped open. He glimpsed the form then, lying on the ground in front of the building.

Max!

He dove for his gun, lunged back outside in time to see a dark form bending over her and ran full bore. He saw something like surprise in the man's eyes— as if the woman he was about to scoop up was not the one he'd expected—but then that vanished when he swung his head toward Lou just in time to meet the butt end of Lou's handgun.

The stranger went down hard, landing flat on his back, but he sprang up again, hissing, teeth bared.

And that was it. There was no longer any doubt about what this guy was.

Lou pointed the gun at him. "Stay the fuck away from her, you bloodsucking bastard!" He crouched between the immortal and Max.

The vamp's eyes, feral and almost glowing, narrowed on him. "You can't kill me with that toy."

"I know what I can do with this toy, pal. I can make you hurt like you never hurt in your life. And if I place the bullet right, I can make sure you bleed out before sunup."

Surprise registered in the vampire's eyes. "You know more than any mortal ought to know."

"I know enough to hold my own against you. Get the hell out of here."

The vampire lunged. Lou fired the gun once—a warning shot—and the dark creature froze in place. He was tall, powerfully built, with long black hair that moved in the night breeze as if with a life of its own. His black eyes held Lou's for a long moment. "You have something that belongs to me, mortal. And I will have it from you."

"If you're talking about Max, it'll have to be over

my dead body, mister. And even then, I might give you a run for your money."

With one lingering look, the vampire turned on his heel and became no more than a blur. Vanished. Those goddamn vamps gave him a headache when they decided to move at speeds too fast for the human eye to follow, Lou thought. No time passed between that last lingering look and the car speeding away into the night. None.

He thought he moved almost as fast himself, because a heartbeat later he was gathering Max to him, pushing her hair away from her face to search for signs of life. "Maxie? Come on, baby, talk to me."

He heard motel room doors opening, heard people asking what was happening, heard Stormy cry out as she and Jason came racing forward. Lou cradled Max's head with one hand, searching her slender neck for a pulse with the other. He found one, steady and strong, and at the same instant he felt sticky warmth coating his palm where he cradled her head. "Oh, hell. Max."

"What happened?" Stormy asked when she got to his side. "I heard a shot."

"That was me, chasing off the bad guy. She's hurt. I need a light."

Jason produced one, kneeling low and aiming

it at Max's head. The manager was coming out of the motel office now, blinking sleep from his eyes. "What happened?"

"Oh, God, she's bleeding," Stormy said.

Lou scooped her off the pavement. "Let's get her back to the room. You. Motel-guy."

"It's Gary."

"Call the police, Gary. And if you have a doctor in this town, get him out here, too. Can you handle that?"

The young man nodded, and Lou carried Max back—not to her room, but to his own. He laid her on the bed, rolling her gently onto one side. Jason flipped on lights. Stormy brought a wet cloth, and Lou took it from her, dabbing the blood away until he finally managed to find the small cut in Max's scalp.

Not a crushed skull. Not a bullet hole. Not a life-threatening injury. Jesus, he'd been sick, physically sick, close to vomiting, with fear for her. The relief that washed through him now made his knees weak.

He pressed the cloth to the wound, using pressure to stop the bleeding and letting her body lie flat.

Max squinted and frowned and puckered her face

almost comically, all without opening her eyes. "Ow. Damn, that hurts."

"I'll bet it does. Open your eyes, honey."

She opened them slowly, and only to mere slits. "The light's too bright. My head hurts."

"That's because somebody hit you with something." Lou snagged a shirt off the back of a chair and draped it over the bedside lamp. "That better?"

She peered out again. "Yeah."

"What happened, Max? You remember anything?"

Her brows drew closer, and she shifted her eyes past him, almost as if checking out who else was in the room. "Give me some time, my head's spinning."

Lou nodded.

"How did you know I was in trouble?" she asked.

"Couldn't sleep. Went out for some air and saw you lying in the parking lot behind a car. Some guy popped the trunk and looked to be about to toss you into it."

Her eyes opened wider. "Someone was trying to kidnap me?"

Lou nodded. "Looked like. I fired a warning shot and he took off." He licked his lips. "He took off...fast."

Max blinked. "How fast?"

Lou shrugged, but held her eyes. "Beck, go see where that goddamn clerk is with getting us a doctor out here. She needs a couple of stitches."

"I'm on it," Jason said, running from the room.

Lou caught Stormy's eye, nodded toward the door. She went to it and closed it. Lou said, "If there's a 'prince' in charge of Endover, I just met him, and there's no doubt in my mind, the guy's a vamp," he said.

"Yeah, well, just to placate my skeptical nature, Lou, can you tell me what you're basing this on?" Max asked.

"The fangs, mostly."

"Oh, hell." Max looked at Stormy. "Did Lou tell you our rooms are all bugged?"

"No."

"I figured it could wait until morning," Lou said.

Stormy threw up her hands and paced the room. "What the hell is going on here? Bugged rooms? Midnight visitors? Why would some vamp want to kidnap Max?"

"Maybe the same reason he kidnapped Delia and her friend?" Lou suggested.

Stormy swore softly. "I'm going back outside to keep an eye on things. See if anyone saw anything."

"Watch your back," Max called.

She gave a nod, then headed out the door.

Max looked at Lou, smiled a little. "You saved my ass."

"Your ass shouldn't have been out there in the first place. What happened, Max?"

She shrugged. "I broke into the motel office. Thought I'd get the names of some former guests here over the past few months, see if anything interesting showed up."

He closed his eyes, shook his head slowly.

"Someone clocked me on the head from behind. I didn't see who, but I'd bet dollars to doughnuts it was that Gary."

"What makes you think so?"

"Like I said, it was from behind. The only thing behind me was the door that leads from the motel office into—into whatever it leads into. Probably his apartment."

"And no one else was around?"

"Whoever it was came from beyond that closed door."

"Unless it was someone who moves too fast to be seen."

"A vampire wouldn't need to bash me on the head to knock me out," she reminded him.

Lou pursed his lips. "Did you get any information out of this expedition, or just risk your life for kicks?"

"Kicks, mostly," she said. "I had a notepad, but I don't suppose it was lying out there next to me."

"No."

She sighed, then seemed to brighten. "Wanna see what's in my pants?"

He shot her a look even as her words heated his blood and sped up his pulse. "You haven't even got the hole in your head stitched up yet."

She smiled slowly, shifting her position.

Lou pressed a hand to her shoulder. "Lie still. Every time you move, the bleeding starts to get worse."

"Then I guess you get to put your hand in my jeans. Not that I mind."

What the hell was she up to? he wondered, searching her eyes as the brief, forbidden image of him sliding his hand where it should never be sliding crossed his mind and slithered through his groin.

"Front pocket, my right, your left."

Lou slid his hand into the pocket she indicated and knew she was loving this. Hell, he was loving it, too, as much as he hated to admit it.

So then, what's your problem?

The little voice in his head sounded a lot like Max's. He ignored it and thrust his hand a little deeper, then pulled out a folded piece of notepaper. Unfolding it, he read the words there, partly out of curiosity and partly because he didn't want to look at Max's eyes right then. They would either be full of mischief or full of heat. Of the two, the heat scared him more.

The paper held a list of names and contact info. He lifted his brows, forgot his caution, met her eyes.

"There were more. Get a fresh pad and pen, and I'll tell you what I can remember."

Someone knocked. "Too late. Try to hold on to them, Max." He got up, started for the door, pocketing her notes on the way. Before he opened it, he looked back at her. "That was good work. Quick thinking."

"Thanks."

"I didn't say I approved of the way you went about it, kid. No information is worth risking your life."

"If I'd known I was risking my life, I might have thought twice," she told him.

He opened the door to the police chief and a frail-looking man with less pigment than an albino, who had to be the doctor.

* * *

"Three stitches," Stormy said. "Shoot, girl, you're gonna have to do a lot better than that to catch up to me."

"Give me time. I'm still young yet," Max said. She was sitting up now, still in Lou's bed. The police chief and the doctor had gone. Jason stood. He'd barely sat down since he'd come in. And now he was on his feet again almost before his rear end had time to settle in the chair.

Max heaved a sigh and turned to lower her feet to the floor. "It's time we all went to bed. We won't be worth a damn tomorrow without some sleep."

"I think you and Storm should stay here," Lou said. "Share the bed. I'll take the chair."

Stormy held up a hand. "No way, Lou. I'm going to my own room. Don't worry, I'll lock up. Believe me, if anyone tries to get in, you'll hear me. I'm only two doors down. 'Night, Maxie. See you in the morning."

"'Night."

Stormy and Jason left them then. Lou sighed, not liking it a bit, Max knew, but he also knew better than to argue with Stormy. You couldn't win. Then he turned to Max. "How about you?"

"What kind of a question is that?"

He actually smiled, just a little. She saw it, before he moved to the closet for the extra blanket and pillow tucked inside on a shelf.

"Lou, don't sleep in the chair. Come on, I promise your virtue will be safe. You'll be miserable in that little chair all night."

"I'll be fine."

She sighed. "You don't trust me. Do you honestly think I'm so damn desperate for you that I'd attack you in your sleep, even though I just got my head bashed in? Jesus, Lou, is that what you really think of me?"

"I don't think that at all."

"No? Then prove it." She slid underneath the covers and patted the spot beside her.

He stood there, blanket and pillow under one arm, halfway between the chair and the bed.

"Maybe it's not me you don't trust? Maybe it's yourself."

"Don't be ridiculous."

She shrugged. "Well, if you trust me, and you trust yourself..." She patted the bed again.

Lou sighed and came to the bed. "Fine. If it'll make you settle down and go to sleep." He sat down, tossed the pillow behind him and lay back on it. On top of the covers.

Man, he just wasn't taking any chances, was he? she thought. He shook the extra blanket out and laid it over him, closed his eyes.

Max wriggled underneath the covers, maneuvering her jeans off, then tossed them onto the floor. "You gonna sleep in your clothes, Lou?"

"Yep." He reached out for the lamp beside the bed and snapped it off. "'Night, Maxie."

"'Night, Lou."

The vampire knew when they returned to his domain. He felt their presence, sensed it as clearly as he could sense the sunrise. And hers most of all.

It's good that you returned, he told Jason Beck, invading the man's mind as easily as he could stroll through a moonlit garden. *I would not have been pleased had you broken your word to me.*

Beck sat up in his bed, looking around his darkened motel room. But the vampire wasn't there. He relaxed slightly when he realized that. "How much longer do you think I can keep them here? They're getting suspicious of me."

The vampire knew it was true. But mostly the young man was impatient to have his sister back. Too bad. He wasn't ready yet. He needed to know more about the woman. There was something terribly wrong—with her, with his own feelings, with this entire situation. And he hadn't lived for centuries by rushing into situations without first knowing all the risks.

Be patient, he told Beck. *It won't be much longer.*

"I want my sister back," the man said. "I want her back soon."

The vampire didn't reply.

Beck went on. "You said you wouldn't hurt my friends. But you hurt Max last night."

Not me. One of my henchmen. It was a mistake, and one for which he will be punished.

"I can't betray them unless I know they won't be harmed," Jason Beck said.

So the young man had a hint of honor, of nobility. Not one strong enough that he would risk his sister's life, however. Best to reassure him, ensure his continued cooperation, the vampire decided. *It won't happen again. I give you my word.*

And then, before Beck could reply, he retreated from the man's mind to focus on the myriad things plaguing his own.

Lou knew damn well that he was taking a huge risk. Lately, he'd been thinking about Max in ways he'd managed to avoid until now. Getting into bed with her was going to make things far worse. And damn, he didn't want her to know how attracted to her he was. She would never let up if she knew—not until he gave in. And giving in would end up ruining them both. She would build up romantic fantasies, while he fought to keep things purely physical. She would get hurt, and she would end up hating him. Hell, if he hurt her, he'd end up hating himself.

He couldn't give her what she wanted: a deep, abiding, romantic kind of love. He didn't have it left in him. His heart had been emptied a long time ago. There was nothing inside it to give to her.

It wasn't worth it. *He* wasn't worth it.

And yet he let her twist him around her little finger, just like he always had. He got into that bed knowing damn well it was a bad idea, partly because there had been a hint of hurt in her eyes when he said no, and partly because he wanted to be there as badly as she wanted him there.

So when he woke the next morning, he was not surprised to find Max's little body wrapped around him like a spider monkey. She'd kicked off her covers and rolled onto her side, facing him. Her head lay on his chest, so that the mingled scents of her hair and the antiseptic the doctor had applied surrounded him. Her arm lay across him, hand resting on his shoulder. He lifted his head just slightly to look down at her. And, hell, her thigh was across his body— across his pelvis. And it was firm, and naked, and way too damn delectable.

He felt a stirring in his groin and realized he had to ease out from under her before she woke, because in a minute more, she would know beyond any doubt that he wanted her. But even as he started to shift, she sighed softly, squeezed his shoulder and lifted her head to blink at him with sexy, sleepy eyes. "'Morning, Lou."

"'Morning."

She smiled slowly, and her hand moved to his face, palm rubbing his cheek. "Stubbly. I like it."

"Max…"

She moved a little closer, then ran her cheek across his.

Jesus, he was going to catch fire if she didn't get off him soon. "Time to get up, honey. How's your head?"

"Achy. Sore. And the pain med the doc gave me is still making me a little loopy, I think. At least, that's what I'll say when you yell at me later."

"Why will I yell at you later?"

"'Cause I'm going to kiss you good morning."

She turned as she said it, so her face was very, very close to his. Her mouth, her lips, no more than a breath away. "Don't worry, you won't even enjoy it. Morning breath and all."

He hadn't slept. Had been up pacing three different times and had brushed his teeth the last time—mortified at the prospect that he would have offensive breath and she would be close enough to notice.

She moved closer. She smelled like peppermint. He could have turned his head away. Yeah, he could have—if he were made of stone, maybe. But he wasn't made of stone, and he didn't turn his head. He stayed still, and hated her for moving so slowly that he had plenty of time to avoid her. Hated that she was going to know, no matter what kind of spin he might try to put on this later—she was going to *know*—he'd wanted this.

And then some.

Her lips pressed to his, soft and moist, and her eyes fell closed, lashes sweeping downward to rest on her cheeks. Her breath stuttered out of her as her mouth locked to his with gentle suction, and one of her hands slid along the side of his face and upward, into his hair, while the other moved in tiny circles, fingers kneading, on his chest.

Every practical, logical thought process came to a grinding halt as Lou's insides melted like butter in the sun. He lost every sense except that of *feeling*. Her mouth on his, moving, hungry. Her body, stretched over his, and the almost imperceptible movements of her hips—so slight, so subtle. And her thigh over his groin, pressing, moving. Oh, God. His palm was skimming over that smooth, taut thigh now, and he didn't remember moving it. He was kissing her back. Jesus, he was kissing her back.

He slid his hand into her hair, to hold her head just right…but his fingers touched the edges of the bandage at the back of her head. And that reminded him of the sight of her lying there, on the pavement. His fear. The creature bending over her. His own fury. Then gathering her up into his arms, every protective instinct on high beam.

This was Maxie. This was his adorable, intrepid, pain-in-the-ass best friend. What the hell was he *doing?*

He opened his eyes, gently cupped her face and pulled back, breaking the kiss. Her eyes opened, sexy and full of green fire. "Oh, Lou…"

"Don't, Max. This is…a bad idea."

She pouted, but rolled off him. "At least I know the truth now."

"What truth is that?" He sat up in the bed, turning his back to her to put his feet on the floor.

"That it's mutual. You feel it, too."

"I tried to explain this to you before, kid. I'm human, and I'm male. A pretty girl kisses me, there are certain reactions that are going to happen. The body takes over, and the mind kind of shuts down. It's a guy thing."

"And that's all it was. Physical."

"That's all it was."

She sighed. "I think you're a liar."

"Well, I think *you* are," he shot back, eager to change the subject. He got to his feet, hard as hell and determined to keep his back to her, so he only looked over his shoulder as he said it, and kept walking toward the bathroom.

"I'm a liar? What did I lie about?"

"The morning breath."

She smiled slowly. "I found one of those mints they leave on the pillows."

"You're sneaky as hell."

"But I taste like heaven."

Her eyes burned into his, and he had to force himself to turn away, open the bathroom door and step inside for a brisk, frigid shower.

Forty-four years old, he told himself. He felt about seventeen when he was around her, and randy as a billy goat on the Fourth of July. Damn.

12
_____

Someone tapped on the door while Lou was in the shower and Max was still hugging the pillow to her chest and grinning like a loon. Despite her lingering headache, she floated off the bed and danced to the door to peer through the peephole. Stormy stood on the other side, laptop under her arm, a fistful of tangled cords and cables. Behind her, Jason balanced a tray of foam coffee cups on top of a large white box that looked for all the world as if it had come from a bakery. Hot damn, she sure hoped so.

"One sec," she called. Then she pulled on her jeans and opened the door.

"Since I don't know jack about debugging my

room or Jay's," Stormy said, traipsing inside to set the laptop on the nearest surface, a round table against one wall, "we're having our breakfast meeting here." She scooped up the magazines and motel pamphlets, and tossed them onto the nightstand. Jason came in, and set the bakery box and the coffee on the table, as well.

"We're pretty sure it's only the phones that are bugged," Max said. "Still, better safe than sorry."

Stormy paused in plugging in cables, straightened and looked around. "We need more chairs. Jay, go get the ones out of our rooms, will you?"

She tossed him a key, and he hurried away even as she plugged in the power cord, then the telephone line for the modem. Stormy gave a glance toward the door as if to be sure he was gone, then another toward the bathroom, where she could hear the shower running, then another toward the rumpled bed, and finally she met Max's eyes. "Any luck?"

"A little. I kissed him."

Stormy grinned. "He didn't run for the hills?"

"Nope. He kissed me back."

"Details, kid. I want details."

Max reached for a coffee cup, pulled up a chair and tried to keep the triumphant grin off her face as she filled Stormy in on every intimate second of it.

She was just getting to the part where Lou ruined it all by trying to explain it away with his version of an anatomy lesson when the shower shut off. At the same moment, Jason arrived with two desk chairs.

"Later," Max mouthed. "So what did you bring?"

"Pastries. There's a bakery in town—opened at 5:00 a.m. I borrowed the Bug, went for a drive to clear my head," Stormy said.

They had keys to each other's vehicles. In fact, there was very little she and Stormy didn't share.

"Next time you do that," Max said, "try driving in the other direction."

"Huh?"

"The air outside Endover is much more conducive to head-clearing," she explained.

Stormy nodded. "Yeah, I noticed that, too."

Max opened the box, eyed the selection of muffins, Danishes, turnovers.

"I ordered a breakfast pizza, too," Storm said. "It'll be here in ten minutes."

"Damn, you must be hungry."

"I was up most of the night."

Max frowned. Jason was situating the chairs around the table. There were three desk chairs now, and one easy chair. Lou came out of the bathroom, his hair wet, jeans and T-shirt looking sinfully good.

He wore forty-four the way Harrison Ford had worn forty-four. It ought to be illegal to look that good. At any age.

She dragged her attention back to Stormy. "Why were you up all night? You okay?"

"Fine, just wide awake. Couldn't sleep."

No wonder she couldn't sleep, Max thought, given what she'd been going through lately. Those flashes and lapses in her memory. An attack by a wolf and maybe some kind of newly developed psychic ability. Not to mention speaking in tongues.

"I spent the night doing research," Stormy went on. She looked fine, Max thought. Not tired or run-down. She was already tapping the keyboard. The modem screamed like a cat with someone standing on its tail. "I ran a search on missing persons and on Endover, New Hampshire. What I found was... interesting."

She waited for a page to load, reached into the box for a Danish and handed it to Max. Then she held her open hand out, and Max reached for the coffee. "Which cup is yours?"

"It has an *S* on the lid." Stormy said it without looking up.

Max nodded, took the cup from the cardboard tray and put it into Stormy's hand.

"Here, here's the list of hits. I sorted it by limiting it to newspaper articles containing both those phrases."

"Lots of Endover folk tend to vanish?" Max asked.

Lou was pulling up a chair and settling into it, so Max spotted the cup with the *L* on the lid and handed it to him. His fingers brushed hers when he took it from her, drawing her eyes to his. They met and held just for a second; then he looked away.

Was he regretting that kiss? Probably. But she was damn sure he'd enjoyed it.

"That's just it," Stormy said. "Not a lot of Endover people vanish, but a lot of people seem to vanish *in* Endover. Take a look."

Max got up and leaned over Lou, her head close to his. The screen showed a list of sites that had articles including the search phrases, each one highlighting the related sentence. "Last seen in Endover, New Hampshire" was the common theme.

"Looks to me," Lou said, "as if strangers who pass through Endover tend to vanish without a trace."

"My God," Jason said. "How long has this been going on?" He had come closer, too, leaning over the others to get a look at the computer screen.

"Three years, near as I can tell," Stormy said.

Lou nodded firmly. "This is excellent work, Storm. Have you read the articles?"

"Yeah." She clicked the address-book button, and it opened to reveal a list of Web site URLs. "These are the ones that were pertinent. All female. All attractive. And all fairly young, though none as young as Delia and Janie."

"But...but what happened to them? To the others?" Jason asked.

"I don't know yet. It took me a while to get this far. Now we need to search for follow-up articles. And that's going to generate a ton of hits—so many people with the same names, you know? It's going to take some time to sort them all, figure out what's relevant and what's not."

"That's your plan for this morning, then," Max said. "Stay on this, Storm. Jason, stay with her. Make sure no one gets near her, understand? That attempt on me last night was no accident."

Stormy nodded. "What are you going to do?"

"First, Lou's going to debug your phones. Then he and I are going to find a print shop and get a few hundred posters of the girls made up, and post them around town and interview as many of the locals as we can manage."

Jason got up, taking out his wallet and tugging out a photo. "You can use this."

He handed her a snapshot of Janie and Delia in evening gowns. Probably at a prom. It made Max's throat tighten up to see it.

Stormy nodded. "Great. Sounds like a plan. While you're out, Max, see if you can find us some decent maps of this place."

"What kind? Road maps? Or topographic?"

"Either. Actually, both. The more the better."

There was a knock on the door. Everyone looked up, but it was Lou who went to open it.

A young boy stood on the other side with a pizza box and a bicycle. He smiled broadly—big gums, unnaturally small, unevenly spaced teeth, almond eyes and a rounded face. "I brought your pizza," he said, his voice as thick as the mop of black hair atop his head.

"You sure are a busy kid," Lou said. "Didn't I see you delivering newspapers earlier?"

"Need money so I can go to school."

"Oh, yeah? You don't go to public school here in Endover?"

"Yeah, but I don't like it here."

"Why not?"

The boy shrugged. "Ten-fifty," he said.

Lou tugged out his wallet. "What's your name, son?"

"Sid."

"And how old are you, Sid?"

"I'm ten. Almost 'leven."

"I'm surprised the pizza place would hire such a young delivery man."

Sid flashed a grin. "It's my uncle's pizza place," he explained.

"So you're saving up to go to a private school?"

"A special school. Away from here."

Lou knelt down to bring himself eye level with the boy. "Why do you want to go away from here, Sid?"

He pursed his lips. "Bad air," he said. "Can't you tell?"

Lou frowned, then sent a quick look behind him at Max. She barely restrained herself from gasping at those words. So close to the way she'd described the feeling she got here. "Yeah. I thought there was something wrong with it."

"Most grown-ups don't notice till too late."

"Too late?"

He nodded. "Makes 'em stupid. It'll make you stupid, too, you stay long enough."

"What about you, Sid? Does the bad air get to you, too?"

He shook his head from side to side, rapidly.

Lou took out two tens and two quarters. He took the pizza box and handed the boy one of the tens and the two quarters. "This is for the pizza," he told Sid. "And this—" he handed him the other ten "—is for you."

"Thanks!"

"That's okay. You know, if you want another job, I might be able to find you something."

"Really?"

"Sure. I need a guide. I don't know my way around here yet."

The boy's wide smile grew even wider. "I finish with the pizzas at two o'clock."

"Will you meet me back here then?"

"I sure will." The boy looked up at the door. "Room four. I'll be here."

"I'll see you then."

"Bye!"

Lou closed the door and turned, pizza box in hand. "That was freaking surreal."

"Something's wrong here," Max said. "There's something contaminating this place. Affecting our minds, dulling us."

"Making us stupid," Lou added with a frown. "Listen, right now, right here, we need to agree to spend a few hours outside this town every day. See if it helps with this thing—whatever the hell it is."

"You think Sid's immune?" Jason asked.

"Maybe. I don't know. Hell, I don't even know if there's really anything to this 'bad air' theory. Maybe we can learn more from our new friend Sid this afternoon," Lou said. He set down the pizza box. "Let's chow down and head out. We need to get moving."

Stormy had put up with Jason's hovering, pacing and reading over her shoulder just about as long as she could stand it. It was too damn distracting, the way he kept looking at her. She found an article, a follow-up piece on one of the missing women saying that she had been found alive and well a week after her disappearance. Her eyes skimmed the lines as she sought details. Where the woman was found, and how and by whom, and—

"So you're feeling all right today?"

His voice intruded on her focus. She shifted her attention away from the computer and onto Jason. He'd finally stopped pacing and settled down in one of the chairs, where he had a clear view of the computer screen.

"So far," she said. "You don't need to worry that I'm going to pass out on your watch, Jay. I'm actually feeling pretty good this morning."

He nodded. She went back to reading. There it was.

Theresa Mulroy, 24, a woman reported missing by her Maryland family more than a week ago, has been found. Mulroy turned up sleeping in her car along the side of a gravel road in Culliver County, some fifty miles inland from the coastal New Hampshire town where she was reportedly last seen. A county sheriff's deputy, checking out what looked like an abandoned vehicle, found her instead....

"It gave me a real scare, seeing you like that."

She turned again, a frown etching itself between her eyebrows at Jason's tone. It was...a little on the tender side.

"I mean, it's been a long time, Storm, but you know I still care about you."

"That's sweet, Jay. When you're as close as you and Max and I were, I don't think it changes just because of time and distance. I think you always care about one another."

He nodded.

"I mean, that's why we came rushing out here when you needed us, right?" she went on. "And I know if it had been the other way around, if it had been me or Max needing help, you'd have come running."

"I would," he said. "I really would."

"I know."

He sighed. "I always hoped...there could be more between you and me than, you know, friendship."

She lowered her head. "I know you wanted there to be."

"Have you ever wondered what might have happened if you had given me a chance, Storm?"

She turned her chair around to face him. "I have. I've wondered about that a lot of times."

"Really?"

She gave a small smile, nodded once. "But I figure there's not much use dwelling on it. It's in the past."

"That doesn't mean it has to stay there."

Stormy let her gaze slide over Jason's face. She had always found him attractive. He had great bone structure, and that milk-chocolate skin begged to be kissed. His lashes had always struck her, thick and dark around velvet-brown eyes.

"Jay, I know what you're saying. But...look, I've got a lot going on right now. A lot...happening in my head. Things I don't even understand. And you've got issues now, too, with Delia missing." He lowered his eyes. "Have you called your brother yet?"

"No. I can't. I can't do that until I have something more solid to tell him."

"How about Janie's parents?"

He shook his head. "They're in Europe. I tried, but I couldn't find a way to reach them." He swallowed hard. "I hope I won't have to."

She nodded. "What if we table this discussion about us, hmm? Just for now."

"Then...you're not ruling it out?"

She met his eyes, felt them pulling at her just as they always had. "I'm just saying now is not the time. We need to focus on the girls." And frankly, she thought, she was surprised Jason wasn't. He should be champing at the bit, pushing harder for action, pacing the floor in frustration. But he wasn't. It was as if he were just...waiting.

But for what?

Jason smiled, leaned down and pressed his mouth to hers, a hand sliding around to cup the back of her head. He kissed her tenderly, gently, very briefly. Her eyes fell closed and...

Traitor!

Stormy jerked her head back, and her eyes flew

open. She looked frantically around the room while Jason searched her eyes.

"What's wrong, Storm?"

She swung her gaze back to his. "Didn't you hear that?"

"Hear what?"

"A voice—a woman's voice, I think." She looked around some more, saw no one.

"No," Jason said. "I didn't hear a thing. Maybe because my heart was pounding so hard." He smiled at her, but worry lingered behind his eyes.

Stormy understood then. The sound—the single, shouted, accusatory word—hadn't come from outside her but from within. And she needed to smooth this over. She didn't want anyone to start questioning her sanity, because, God knew, that would be the next leap of logic. If odd things kept happening to her and a physical cause had been ruled out, that only left a mental one.

She smiled back at him a little. "Maybe that's what I heard. But I think more likely it was the old woman in room twelve. She's been yelling a lot at that young man who's staying with her."

"Her son?" Jason asked.

"I don't think so." She smiled and wiggled her eyebrows. Then she turned back to the computer, fought to find her place in the article again. There it was.

The missing woman had no explanation for where she had been. She claimed to have no memory at all of the days since she was reported missing. Deputy Welsh refused to speculate, though his official report made mention of empty bottles and the smell of alcohol permeating the vehicle.

"Storm, would you like some more coffee?" Jason had come to stand behind her chair, his hands closing on her shoulders in a gentle massage. "I could run over to the diner."

Yanked out of her concentration yet again, she tried not to let the irritation show on her face as she turned and looked up at him. After all, the guy was being as attentive as he could, and it was kind of flattering. "You know what I really need, Jay?"

"What?"

"A printer. I can save all this information on the hard drive, but a printer would let me put it right at our fingertips."

"A printer."

"You can buy cheap printers for thirty bucks these days. Isn't there a Kmart or anything around here?"

"Well, I could ask Gary, I suppose."

"That would be great. Get an extra ink cartridge,

too—the ones that come with the printers never hold very much. And some paper, and don't forget the cable. Wait, I'll make you a list."

She got up and moved across the room to the nightstand, snatched up the complimentary pad and pen, and started scribbling her list. "While you're out, you might as well pick up some snacks."

He nodded.

"Here, take my card." She rummaged in her purse for the business credit card that had her name on it.

"I'll use my own," he said. "I ought to pick myself up a change of clothes and stuff while I'm at it. I didn't bring a damn thing. Had to get a complimentary toothbrush from the motel office this morning."

She was surprised this motel office even had them.

"I'll bring you the receipt, and you can deduct the applicable things from my bill when this is over," Jason said.

"Okay."

"Okay." He hovered for a moment, but finally turned and left.

She sighed, wondering how she should handle his attraction. She wondered if it was mutual. It always had been. She'd been attracted to him in the past. That had never been an issue. But she'd decided, as a barely twenty-year-old, that he was too staid for her, too conservative, too practical. She was older now— old enough to know that dependability was not a bad thing. But she couldn't tell how she felt. There were too many things twisting around in her head—too many emotions, thoughts, feelings. Sometimes they seemed almost foreign. She didn't know how the hell she felt about anything right now.

She returned her attention to the computer screen, reread the implication that the missing woman had been on a drinking binge. She'd been taken to a hospital, checked out and deemed unharmed.

"Hey, Storm?"

She snapped her head up to see Jason poking his head back through the motel room door. She pasted a smile in place and forced her voice to be kind when she asked, "What is it, Jay?"

"Gary says it's a good ninety minutes to the nearest store that might carry printers. You sure you want me to go?"

Thank God.

She frowned and silenced the foreign voice in her head. "Yes, I still want you to go. In fact, it's vital."

"But are you sure you'll be okay here alone?"

"Don't worry, Jay. This thing is looking more and more like one of those 'things-that-go-bump-in-the-night' cases. And so far, all those things tend to go bump *only* in the night. I'll be fine."

"What if it's a thing that goes bump by day?" he asked.

She smiled, lifted up her shirt, and patted the pancake holster that rested snugly against her side and the .38 revolver it held. Lou had insisted on leaving his spare gun with her. "Then I'm gonna bump back," she said.

He nodded, seemed reassured.

"You have your list?"

"Got it," he said. "I'll see you in a few hours."

"Bye, Jay."

He backed out and closed the door. She made sure it was locked this time, chided herself for being irrationally eager to be rid of him, then went back to the Internet, relieved that she would be able to proceed uninterrupted.

Max stapled the poster to a telephone pole. She'd stapled so many now that her hand was sore. And Lou had managed to put up twice as many. They'd covered the surrounding towns first, stapling the posters up on every corner and stopping at every place of business along the way to ask if anyone had seen the girls. And maybe it was nothing more than the power of suggestion, but she swore her head had cleared and her energy was restored by the time away from Endover.

When they returned to town and began hanging up posters, the streets were quiet. A few people walked past but didn't seem the least bit interested in what they were doing. Just kept walking, not even looking twice. The people they questioned didn't seem surprised or troubled when Max and Lou showed them the posters, the way those in the neighboring towns had.

The fifth person who passed by her while she was stapling up a poster was a middle-aged man walking a scrawny Chihuahua. Max stopped stapling and stepped into his path.

"Hi, there. I'm Maxine. And you are?"

The man looked surprised. She saw Lou glance her way from across the street, saw him stop what he was doing and frown.

"I'm...Hadden Stoddard," the man said. He sidestepped, as if to go around her. She sidestepped, too.

"Mr. Stoddard, aren't you even curious about what I'm doing here? Why I'm hanging up these posters?"

He glanced up at the poster she had just hung.

"Looks like you're lookin' for those girls." Then he shrugged. "None of my concern."

"But they vanished from right here in this town. You live here. It's your town. Don't you think that makes it your concern?"

"It's not my town. It's his."

She frowned. "Whose?"

The man blinked, shook his head, sidestepped again. Again she moved with him.

"Whose town is it, Mr. Stoddard?"

"You should go home. Those girls will show up again."

"So I've been told. Tell me, why is everyone in this town so sure of that?"

He shrugged. "I have to go."

"You're not going anywhere until you tell me what you know about their disappearance," she said. She saw, from the corner of her eye, Lou hurrying across the street. She would have to make it fast.

Stoddard looked her in the eyes. His seemed dull, lifeless, almost as if a thin film were lying over the blue. "You shouldn't ought to be poking around here, young lady. You ought to just wait. Be smart."

"Who's really in charge around here, Mr. Stoddard?"

"You ought to talk to the chief."

"I've talked to the chief. He's no help. But he's not the top dog in this town, is he? Who does he work for? The man they call 'the prince'?"

Stoddard lowered his head. "Let me be, woman."

"Jesus, don't you want to help us? Don't you care what's happened to Delia and Janie? They're only seventeen. Just a couple of innocent girls who—"

"Leave him be, Max." Lou put a hand on her shoulder. "Sorry, mister. She's just upset. I'm sure you understand."

The man gave Lou a glance, a nod, then walked past Max and continued on his way. She turned to glare up at Lou. "Why didn't you let me grill him?"

"Because you catch more flies with honey. Besides, how do you know he knows anything?"

"Because he mentioned this town being 'his.'"

Lou's brows went up. "His?"

"Just 'his.' Couldn't get him to elaborate. Might have, if you hadn't butted in just now."

"Hell, Max, I could see by your eyes you were getting ready to break out the bamboo for his fingernails, and I just couldn't watch."

"Next time, cover your eyes." She knew he wasn't being entirely honest. As a cop, he couldn't be squeamish about the occasional "hard interview." He was protecting her again, probably afraid she would piss off some local who might decide to retaliate.

He grinned. She smiled back, but it wasn't heart-felt. It went like that for the rest of the morning. People passed but didn't ask. Didn't seem to care. If she called them on it, she was advised to go home and wait for the girls to return.

As if they all knew something she didn't.

Just what the hell was up with this place?

It was after one o'clock, and she was starved, by the time they hung the last of their posters and hopped in her VW to head back to the motel. She let Lou drive because she was feeling unreasonably tired, and rested her head against the seat.

"I managed to question dozens of locals. But I feel as if I was talking to the same one, over and over again. Just with a different face and body."

Lou glanced her way, flipped on the AC and drove out of town. "Glazed eyes, kind of unfocused, sort of a monotone voice that just drones on."

"That's the one," she said.

He nodded. "I think I met several versions of him myself."

"Hell."

He kept driving, past the motel, taking her out

on the highway another five miles, before pulling over along the roadside, in a spot that looked out on the rocky shore below. He opened his door and got out. She couldn't seem to drum up the energy, but it didn't matter. A second later he was opening her door, tugging her arms until she was on her feet. He walked beside her, a hand draped casually over her shoulders, and led her to the wooden rail that had been placed along the very edge, where the pull off became a drop-off. Then he stood there, holding her up, more or less. The ocean breeze washed over her face. She closed her eyes and sucked it into her, blew out the bad air of Endover and sucked in some more of the good.

"Better?" Lou asked.

"Yeah."

"It's getting worse, isn't it?"

She nodded. "Whatever *it* is. Yeah. Or maybe it just seems worse 'cause we were in the middle of Endover proper most of the day. Maybe it's…denser there. Or more potent or something."

"I've got a call in to a friend of mine who works for the EPA. He hasn't returned it yet, but I'm gonna give him another call before we head back into the dead zone."

"Dead Zone," she said. "Good name for it. Creepy, but good. What can your friend do?"

Lou shrugged. "I don't know. Tell me if the Environmental Protection Agency is aware of any known leaks or contamination issues in the area. Maybe come out here and take an air sample or something."

She nodded. "Hell, it can't hurt."

He reached for his cell phone, placed the call. Max sat down on top of one of the squat fence posts that held the barrier, watched the rolling waves below, the entire ocean seemed to undulate, to heave and relax again. Almost as if it were breathing. Then she spotted something and frowned.

"Lou?"

"Just a second, hon."

She glanced at him because of the "hon" part of the sentence, though she was getting used to him dropping endearments he didn't mean. Or maybe he did mean them—given that kiss this morning.

He finished his conversation and hit the power button, then turned his full attention to her. "I'm all yours."

"Liar."

"You know what I meant."

"Unfortunately, I do. What did your friend say?"

"He checked. There's no history of any contamination of the air or water in Endover. Nothing on the books that he could find. He can come out, but it will be a few days. He's swamped."

She listened, watching him, the way the sea breeze ruffled his hair and the sun hit his face. Finally, remembering her train of thought, she nodded toward the ocean. "What is that?"

"What is what?" He shielded his eyes and looked.

She pointed, her arm angling back toward the Endover coast. "That."

Frowning, he looked, then looked some more. "I don't know. An island?"

"Does it look to you like there's a house on it?"

"Can't tell from here. You have binoculars?"

"Not on me."

"Hell of a P.I. you are. You aren't supposed to leave home without 'em."

"So yank my license." She squinted harder but couldn't see any better. "Why haven't we noticed it from Endover?"

"Probably there's a bend in the shoreline, maybe

some woods or a hill that blocks it from view. Or something."

"Yeah. It's the 'or something' part that worries me."

13

"Look over there," Lou said when they pulled the VW into a parking space at the motel late that afternoon.

Max looked where he indicated. A little boy was stationed outside Lou's motel room as if he were standing sentry duty.

"It's Sid. Wonder why he's outside?" She frowned. "You think Storm and Jay took off?"

"Jason's Jeep is still here."

They got out of the Bug and started across the parking lot. As they did, a car pulled in and moved in their direction, and suddenly Lou snapped his arm around Max's waist and propelled her quickly off the pavement as he kept a wary eye on the vehicle.

They stopped on the sidewalk that ran past the room doors. She put a hand over his on her waist, so he wouldn't take it away too soon, and looked up at him. "What was that about?"

"Just being careful."

She smiled a little, her heart going warm and gooey. The car, meanwhile, pulled harmlessly into a parking spot. "I like you this way. All protective and watchful."

"Someone made a try for you last night. We can't be sure he won't try again."

"A vampire made a try for me last night," she reminded him. "He won't try again during broad daylight."

Lou shrugged and averted his eyes. "I'm just making sure he doesn't get the chance."

"Because you care about me."

"Of course I care, Max. You're one of my best friends. Maybe the *very* best, you know?"

"I know." She held his gaze, wishing he could see that there was a lot more than friendship flowing back and forth between them. But he knew that. He might deny it, but he knew. He had to know.

She could see the knowledge right now, in his eyes.

"Hey, mister."

Lou jerked his gaze from hers, and Max felt lonely without it. But she turned with him to face the little boy who stood near Lou's door.

"Hi, Sid." Lou glanced at his watch. "Sorry I'm late."

"It's okay. I waited."

"I see you did. Why didn't you go inside?"

The boy frowned. "You said meet you here. At the door."

Lou nodded, as if that made perfect sense. "That's right, I did, didn't I? Well, I'm here now, so you can come on inside."

The boy looked a bit hesitant. Max said, "Normally, you shouldn't talk to strangers, of course. But Mr. Malone is a policeman. A real one. So it's okay this one time."

Sid looked up at her and smiled his crooked-toothed smile. "It's okay. I know who's good and who's not."

"You do?"

"Uh-huh."

"And how do you know that?"

"By the colors. You have orange, red and yellow. And you're blue and green," he told Lou.

Lou frowned, looking down at his clothes as if in search of the alleged colors.

"I think he's talking about auras."

"Nope. Jus' colors," the boy said.

She smiled at him and tapped on the door. Footsteps crossed the room, then Stormy tugged it open. "You're back," she said.

"And I'm beat. How about you?"

"Exhausted. Found some interesting stuff, though." She smiled down at the boy. "Good to see you again, Sid. You want some junk food?"

He frowned.

"Chips, dip, soda, cheesy poofs?"

"Yeah!"

"Help yourself," she said, stepping aside and pointing to the table, where open bags and crumbs reigned supreme. The boy raced inside and dug in.

Max sank into a chair and leaned her head back against it. Lou went straight to the bathroom and came back with a pair of tablets in his palm, grabbing a diet cola from the ice bucket as he passed. He handed both to Max. "For the head."

"I'm fine."

"Take 'em, anyway. Humor me, huh?"

She nodded and took the pain reliever, washing it down with the soft drink. She thanked him with her eyes, then turned to Stormy. "We talked to people and put posters up in the next towns in three directions, then plastered Endover with them. Funny thing is, around here, no one is the least bit interested in knowing what we're doing or why. They don't ask. And when you tell them, they really don't seem to care."

Stormy nodded thoughtfully.

"The ones who responded at all mostly said the same thing. 'Stop poking around, go home and wait. They'll turn up.'"

Stormy nodded again. "Makes sense."

"How so?"

She reached for a stack of papers, and Max noticed the printer that sat on the table where none had been before. "You two have been busy," she said.

"Yeah, Jason picked us up a printer, along with a full supply of snacks and Coke." She handed the stack of pages to Max. Lou leaned close to read over her shoulder. "A lot of people seem to disappear while passing through or near this place. Every one I've been able to check up on turned up safe and sound within a few days to a week later."

"I'll tell you one thing, it was a huge load off my mind when Stormy told me that," Jason said.

Max flipped through the printouts of news articles Stormy had apparently found online. "Where were they found?"

"Usually within a few miles of their homes. The odd thing is, none of them had any memory of where they'd been."

Max frowned. "Break it down for me, Storm."

"Women, between twenty-two and thirty-eight, not counting our two seventeen-year-olds. Attractive, as I said before. Those seem to be the only common denominators. Other than that, they're all over the map. Married, single, professionals, blue-collar workers, some had kids, some didn't, and they come from a wide range of locations."

"But they were all passing through Endover?"

"Looks like."

"Did you lose somebody, too?" Sid asked.

Max had nearly forgotten the boy was in the room. She turned to look at him, sitting on the foot of the bed, a bowl of cheese curls in his lap, his lips coated in orange powder. Beside him was one of the posters she and Lou had run off at a print shop this morning. It had a photo of Delia and Janie on it. She'd sprung for the extra bucks to have the posters done in color. Grainy black and white just wasn't as effective.

Lou moved to the bed, sat down beside the boy. "That's right, we did. Those girls there in the picture. This one is Delia," he said, putting a finger on Delia's face. "And that's her friend Janie."

The boy looked around the room, his gaze halting on Jason. "Don't worry," he said. "They'll come back."

"How do you know that, Sid?" Lou asked.

The boy shrugged. "I don' know. I jus' do."

"Sid," Max said, moving closer. "Have other people come here looking for people they've lost?"

"Sure," he said with a nod. "But they don't find 'em here."

"They don't?"

"Nope. They find 'em home." He looked again at Jason. "You should go home. That's where she's gonna be."

"I'm not so sure about that, kid," Jason said.

"Is that why you're so spotty?"

"Spotty?"

"Are you talking about his colors, Sid?" Maxie asked. Sid nodded, and she looked at Jason. "You know I can't see them, like you can."

"Nobody can." He lowered his eyes, looking a little sad.

"What do Jason's colors look like?"

"Not good," he said. "Can't even see the real colors—got a dark cloud over 'em. Like everybody else around here. An' black spots, too."

"Everybody in this town has a dark cloud over their colors?" Max asked.

He looked at her, then at Lou. "My mama says it's all in my head. Same as the night man."

"The night man?"

He nodded, his eyes big, searching, fearful. Until Lou said, "I think I saw the night man, too, Sid. I saw him last night."

Sid blinked, looking as if he didn't quite believe it. "Grown-ups never see him."

"Maybe some grown-ups can," Lou said. "I sure saw someone. Someone with long dark hair. And he was in dark colors." Lou lifted his brows. "I mean, his clothes were dark-colored. I don't know what his other colors were like."

"He don't have any. I thought maybe 'cause he wasn't real, like Mama said." Sid lifted his gaze to Lou's. "But he does have long black hair and black clothes."

"And you're the only one who's ever seen him?" Lou asked.

"I don't know. Maybe."

"Do you know where he lives?"

Sid averted his eyes quickly, swiping them with the back of his hand.

Lou leaned closer. "Hey, it's okay. Don't be afraid."

"I'm not. It's just—nobody ever believed me before."

Max glimpsed a tenderness in Lou's eyes she had never seen there. A moment later, he was hugging the boy close, patting his back.

"I believe you," he said. "We all do. And I think your mama would, too, if the bad air wasn't putting that dark cloud over her colors."

The boy's arms locked around Lou's neck, and he held on tight. When he finally released his grip, he sat back and looked up into Lou's eyes.

Lou blinked down at him, then averted his gaze. "Excuse me a minute. I, uh…left something in the car." He got to his feet and left without a word or a glance back.

Stormy sent Max a questioning look. Max said, "Have some more snacks, Sid. I'll be right back." Then she went outside to find Lou.

* * *

God, it hurt to hold that little guy in his arms. Brought it all rushing back as if he'd only lost his precious Jimmy yesterday. He'd grown hard over the years. He'd locked the pain away in a dark corner of his mind and, for the most part, managed to keep it there. Incapacitated and impotent. But lately—Jesus, lately it was leaking out like battery acid. Burning through his veins at the most inexplicable moments.

Something was softening his hard shell, and he had a feeling he knew what it was. Max. Keeping that damn shell in place required not caring too much about anything. He'd managed to cultivate his "don't care" attitude to perfection over the years. He was laid back, never got too wound up. Took life as it came to him and rolled with the punches. Nothing could hurt you if you didn't care.

Maxie made him care. She'd grabbed him by the scruff of his neck and dragged him into her misadventures and her crazy life. And even though he thought all he wanted was peace and quiet, she made him want to stay right there, in the midst of her chaos.

She stepped up behind him then. He recognized the pattern of her footsteps. Felt the warmth of her presence, and then of her hand sliding up his back to his shoulder. She said, "I know it hurts, Lou. It must hurt like nothing I could even imagine."

He thought about denying it, telling her he just needed some air, but hell, this was Maxie. She *knew*. "He's nothing like Jimmy was. Not even the right age. Just…something about that hug back there…hit me like a sledgehammer."

"I know." She moved around in front of him. "You miss him."

"Like I'd miss my limbs."

She nodded. "I got a taste of that when I thought I was going to lose Stormy. And even that can't really compare. Not with losing a child." She slid her arms around his waist and hugged him. "I'm here for you, Lou. As your friend, if that's all I can be, but I'm here. I always will be."

Lou closed his eyes tight and wrapped his arms around her, held her to him for a moment. "I know you will. I know."

They stood there like that for an extended moment. Then, finally, he gripped her shoulders and set her away from him. "We should get back inside. Storm probably thinks I've lost it by now."

"You've got her wondering, that's for sure." She smiled gently at him. "Don't worry, Lou, I'm not going to tell her about Jimmy. I wouldn't do that to you."

He knew she wouldn't. It amazed him sometimes how much he trusted this crazy redhead. "You know something, Max?" he asked, taking her by the hand to lead her back to the door.

"Hmm?"

"I'm glad you're around."

"I know you are." The mischievous grin she sent him then made him wish to hell he could be more than a friend to her. Made him wish he were capable of the kind of loving she deserved. There was a pang of longing in the region of his chest. He squelched it, and they walked back into the room together.

Sid looked up as soon as they entered. He said, "I know where the night man lives—but you better not go there."

Lou went closer, hunkered down to put himself at the boy's level. "Now, Sid, if I don't know where he lives, how can I be sure I won't go there? You know, by mistake."

The boy frowned, considering that. Then he pressed his lips tight and nodded. "It's on the island. Out in the water. You can't see it except from the lighthouse."

"Aah, right, the lighthouse. And the lighthouse is…?"

"You gotta walk. It's down that dirt road out past town."

Lou ruffled Sid's hair. "Thank you, son. You've been a big help to us."

"Yeah?"

"Yeah." Lou dug out a twenty and gave it to him. "This is for you. You put it in your piggy bank, okay?"

"Okay." Sid jumped off the bed and raced to the door, but paused there and came back to hug Lou once again. Then he was gone, off like a shot on his bike, sailing at light speed down the street.

Lou turned slowly.

"I think we need to get that kid out of this town," Stormy said softly. "If any part of what he thinks he knows is true—"

"It's ridiculous," Jason said. "He can't know anything. And what's this crap about a 'night man'? Sounds like he's watched too many monster movies to me."

Max sent a look at the others, a question in her eyes. Lou nodded. Stormy did, too. "Jason," she said slowly, "Sid is the only person in this town who isn't acting…dull, almost tranquilized. And I think I know why."

"You think someone's doping the water or something?"

"No. I think this entire town is being held under a vampiric thrall."

"A vam—are we back to vampires again, Max?" Jason started to smile, but it died when he saw the look in her eyes. "You…you think a vampire has taken my sister?"

"I didn't say anything earlier, because I didn't want to frighten you, Jason. But that man who came after me—he was a vamp."

Jason's eyes searched hers. He swallowed hard. "I…I don't know what to say. I don't think I believe you. I don't think I want to."

He paced away, looking shell-shocked.

"Sid's in danger," Max said. "Especially if someone realizes he's immune to whatever kind of power this vampire has over everyone else here."

Stormy lifted her brows. "You think this guy's badass enough that he'd hurt a child?"

"Delia and Janie aren't much older than children," Max said.

Jason spun to face her. "But he hasn't hurt them." When everyone just stared at him, he went on. "I mean, that we know of. He never hurt any of the others. So it makes sense to think—if he were some kind of evil menace, then why were all those other women found unharmed?"

"I don't know," Max said. "But you're right, it's a good point. Hold on to it."

"I agree with Jason, for what it's worth," Stormy said. "I don't think he would hurt anyone."

Lou searched her face. "What are you basing that on?"

Shrugging, Stormy said, "I don't know. Gut feeling, maybe?"

"Sid said he was saving up to go to a private school," Lou said. "How about if he gets an opportunity to visit one, all expenses paid? We fork over a couple hundred bucks for a room at a Holiday Inn, some traveling money, and hook him up."

"If his mom would go for it, it just might work," Max said.

"I can find the right school in a snap online," Stormy said. "Set this whole thing up."

"Make it for at least three days," Lou said. "Maybe some time away from here will clear the mother's head. Maybe she'll think twice about coming back."

"We can give her a call while she's away, see if

she's open to reason after a few days. Maybe suggest she not hurry back."

"Agreed," Lou said. "Meanwhile…"

"Meanwhile," Max said, rubbing her palms together, "we've got an island to visit."

There was precisely one boat-rental place in all of Endover. It was housed in a barnlike building on the water's edge, with the words Endover Boat Rentals painted across the front of the building. There were several docks, numerous boat-hoists, and a half-dozen motorboats of various sizes, some tied to the docks and bobbing serenely in the water; others dangled from their hoists a few feet above the reach of the waves that rolled gentle and steady over the pebble-and-sand shore.

"It's beautiful out here," Stormy said, as they got out of Jason's Jeep. She stood there for a moment, taking in the view: blue-black water speckled with tiny whitecaps as far as the eyes could see.

"It *is* pretty," Max said. "I love the shore." She took a deep breath of the sea air. Rather than invigorating her, it made her want to yawn. Sighing, she followed Lou, who was already making his way to the entrance, a small door situated to the side of a much larger one, with a tiny sign tacked to it that read Office.

Lou knocked twice, then opened the door and stuck his head inside. "Hello? Anyone here?"

A short, wiry man limped into view. Unshaven, dressed in bib overalls, wiping his hands on a rag, he sent them a smile with teeth that were even and white, and gave a tug on the bill of his olive-green cap. "Come on in," he called. "What can I do for you?"

"Stan, is it?" Lou asked, glancing at the patch on the man's overalls and holding out a hand. "Lou Malone."

"Good to meet you. I'm afraid you haven't come at the best of times."

"No?"

"Nah. I haven't got a craft available. I'm guessing you wanted to rent one."

"Yeah, we were hoping to."

The man pushed back his cap and scraped a hand through his hair. "Sorry about that."

Lou frowned. "You telling me every boat here is spoken for?"

"Only those that are running. We been having a rash of engine troubles this past week."

"You have, huh?"

He nodded.

"I don't suppose you know anywhere else we might be able to find a boat around here?"

"I'm the only place there is. You come back in a day or two, though, and I might be able to fix you up. All right?"

"Sure," Lou said. "Not a problem."

The man nodded. Max opened her mouth to argue, but Lou put a hand on her arm and met her eyes. She let it go and joined the others in walking outside, back to the waiting Jeep. Only when they were safely inside and driving away did Lou speak. "Did anyone here believe Stan back there?"

"Those boats all looked sound to me," Max said. "And hell, they can't all be broken down."

"That's what I thought. But he didn't look like he was lying."

Jason frowned at that comment. So Max explained. "Being a cop for twenty years, Lou has a great sense of when he's being lied to. It's more accurate than a lie detector. So you thought he was telling the truth, Lou?"

"As little sense as it makes, yeah. Or at least what he thought was the truth."

Max frowned and tipped her head to one side.

Stormy said, "He had that blank look in his eyes. Like so many of the others in this town."

Lou sighed. "Let's drive up the coast. There's gotta be a boat somewhere we can beg, borrow or steal. It's the freaking ocean, for God's sake."

Within five miles Max thought they had found what they were looking for. A boat, bobbing gently with the waves, tied to a dock without a house in sight. "Stop here," she said. "Pull over, right there."

They stopped the car, all of them looking around.

"What do you think?" she asked.

"What do I think?" Lou looked at her. "I think it's not our boat."

"You said beg, borrow or steal," she reminded him.

"I was kind of hoping for one of the first two."

She shrugged. "This *is* one of the first two. We're borrowing it."

"Without permission. Which makes it stealing."

She sighed. "Once a cop, always a cop."

"How do we even know it's seaworthy?" Jason asked.

They got out of the Jeep and trooped down to the water's edge. Max looked inside the boat, then sighed. "There's no motor. And look at the size of that hole in the bottom. Hell, these ropes aren't keeping it from floating away, they're keeping it from sinking."

"That solves the question of stealing it."

Max frowned, leaning over the small craft. "Look at that hole." As they all did, she said, "Hell, what are the chances of hitting a rock or whatever and causing a hole like that? It's almost perfectly round. Dead center, too."

"It could happen," Lou said.

"Looks like someone took a mallet to it." Max turned to Stormy, fully expecting her to agree. But Stormy was staring down the shore at something in the distance. When Max turned to see what, she saw the top of the lighthouse, just visible around a bend.

"Lou," Max said, "didn't Sid say something about a lighthouse?"

Lou nodded. He was staring as well.

"We should go there," Stormy said.

Max put a hand on Stormy's shoulder. "You okay? You look a little—"

"I'm fine." She blinked, shaking off whatever had been weighing on her. "We need to go there. To the lighthouse."

"Okay. So let's go."

They piled back into Jason's Jeep and drove down the coast road, taking a few wrong turns onto side roads. Stormy pulled out the map of the town, and they located the little finger of a peninsula. It didn't show any lighthouse, but it was the only place on the map that matched the location. And apparently no roads led out there. Very strange. Still, they finally located a barely passable dirt track with a gate across the front and No Trespassing signs posted everywhere. Jason got out to open the gate, then looked back at the Jeep, shaking his head, pointing to a padlock and chain.

"Guess we hoof it from here," Max said.

Lou looked uneasy. "I think maybe you and Storm ought to head on back to the motel. Jay and I can check this out."

"Stop being chivalrous, Lou. We're as capable as you are," she said. "Besides, we've only got one vehicle at the moment. We go together or not at all."

He sighed.

"I'm not giving in," she said. "So you can stop thinking up arguments."

With a nod, Lou got out. The four of them climbed over the gate and hiked along the dirt path. It was a mile if it was a foot, but eventually they started catching glimpses of the lighthouse. Finally they emerged from the tree-lined track onto the clear-cut, crooked finger of land that seemed to be beckoning the sea to come closer. At the tip, the once-white lighthouse stood, leaning slightly, sadly in need of paint. Shingles were missing from the roof here and there, and the upper windows had panes that were missing, others that were cracked or broken. Some were still intact but smudged with the grime of disuse.

"This place doesn't look like it's been used in years," Max whispered, then wondered why she was whispering. The place had that creepy, "someone's listening" feeling that made you automatically lower your voice.

They walked out toward the building then Lou pointed out to sea. "Look, there's that island Sid mentioned. He said it was only visible from the lighthouse."

"You think that's where his night man lives?" Storm asked.

Lou shrugged. "No way to know. First things first. Let's check out this lighthouse."

Jason followed in silence. Max could only imagine how painful this must be for him, not knowing what they might find inside.

They walked beside him up to the only visible entrance, a small, faded red door with chipping paint and a tarnished brass knob. She tried the knob, found it locked.

"That's odd," she said. "Who locks a place with half the windows busted out?"

Lou shrugged. And while he had been averse to stealing, he didn't seem to have any qualms about breaking and entering. He moved her aside, gripped the knob and slammed his shoulder into the door. It popped open without much resistance. Max started inside, and Lou kept pace right beside her, a hand on her arm, eyes watchful, scanning the place.

It was bereft of signs of human presence. Dust and cobwebs coated everything. The floorboards were ancient and unfinished, with wide gaps between them. Lou pointed downward. "Footprints in the dust. Look."

Everyone looked. "Someone's been here—and recently," Max said.

"More than one someone, too."

Max nodded, and they crept along, following the tracks. They led to a rickety door, and when Lou jerked it open, there were stairs leading downward, spiraling to the left.

He looked behind him. "Someone bring a flashlight?"

"I did." Jason came closer, taking out his flashlight.

Then he elbowed Max gently. "Better go back, something's wrong with Stormy. She started acting funny as soon as we got inside. Lou and I will check this out."

Max didn't hesitate. She swung her gaze behind them to see Stormy. She was sitting on the floor underneath a window, her back against the curving outer wall, staring at nothing. Max rushed back to her friend, while Lou and Jason crept down the stairs.

"Stormy? Honey, what is it?"

"I don't know, I don't know. God, there's something…" She pressed her hands to her head, closed her eyes and began rocking slightly.

"Does it hurt? Are you in pain?"

"It's…I…"

"Storm. Talk to me, dammit!"

The rocking stopped. Stormy lifted her head, her eyes furious and blazing—and jet-black. She stared at Max with a withering gaze and whispered, *"Vulpea bãtrânã nu cade în curse."*

14

Lou walked down the stairs, following the beam of light Jason kept aimed at the floor. And then he could go no farther. At the bottom, a barred cell door blocked them from moving any farther.

"Jesus Christ," Jason muttered.

Lou took the light from Jay's hand and aimed it at the door. Then he tugged on it and it opened, its hinges groaning. He pointed the beam at the lock, which looked functional. And the bars were strong enough that he didn't think a normal person would have much luck getting out of here if those locks were engaged.

Stepping inside, he moved the flashlight beam

slowly along the inside of the cell. It was curved, like the lighthouse itself. Small, maybe thirteen feet in diameter, with stacked stone-and-mortar walls, and a dirt floor. He traced it all, then started painting the floor in brushstrokes of light, in search of any clue. Already he was flooded with relief that there were no bodies awaiting them down there. He wouldn't be surprised to find other evidence of violence, though he prayed he wouldn't.

His light beam inched along the floor.

"Stop!" Jason said. "Back up a little—I saw something."

Lou moved the light backward, just a little. It caught on something shiny that gleamed a reflection. Lou narrowed his eyes. It looked like…

Jason rushed forward, fell to his knees and snatched the object up. "It's a hair clip. A butterfly," he said softly.

Lou looked at the man, and Jason turned to meet his eyes.

"It's Delia's." He closed his eyes. "My God, she was held here in this…in this hole. She must have been terrified."

"There's no reason to think she's not still alive, Beck," Lou said. Hell, as much as he disliked and mistrusted Jason, he felt sorry for him in that moment.

"Lou!"

Both men whirled at Maxie's shout from up above. Lou took off at a run, Jason scrambling to his feet and following right on his heels. They emerged from the darkened stairway to find Max backing away from Stormy, who glared at her, her face twisted in a snarl as she rose slowly to her feet from the floor.

"Ce ti-e scris, în frunte ti-e pus!" Stormy shouted the words and flew at Max with a shriek, her hands like raking claws in front of her.

"What the hell?" Jason shouted.

And even as he said it, Lou lunged in front of Max. He gripped Stormy's shoulders as she thrashed, swinging her clawed hands and scratching his face, kicking, shrieking, as he struggled to hold her at arm's length. And then she just stopped. Her body went limp, her eyes rolled back, and she collapsed.

Lou caught her against him, then picked her up in his arms, shocked at how limp, how lifeless, she seemed. She was motionless, dead weight. "We need to get her the hell out of here." He turned as he said it and saw the reaction in Max's eyes the instant they moved over his face.

"What?"

"Oh, God, Lou—she scratched the hell out of you."

"It's okay. I'm okay, Max," he repeated firmly, to snap that look off her face. "Let's get her back to the car."

She nodded, the movement jerky, and led the way to the door. "I don't know what happened. She was sitting on the floor, looking dazed and maybe in pain. I don't know. And then she just got up and came at me, screaming that language she doesn't even know."

"What did you do with the last bunch of gibberish she was spouting—the stuff I wrote down?" Lou asked.

"I e-mailed it to a linguist at the University of PA. Haven't heard back yet, but it's tough to get to the computer without her knowing. She's got it in her room with her."

Lou nodded, carrying Stormy back along the path. Her head lolled like a rag doll's. "Maybe you'd better light a fire under that linguist's ass when we get back. And I think at this point, you might as well feel free to do it right in front of her. If she doesn't like it, too bad."

"I agree. What did you find in the basement?" Max asked.

"A cage," Jason said before Lou could answer. "A small, pitch-dark cage, like a jail cell, with a dirt floor and steel bars. And Delia's barrette."

"Oh, Jesus," Max whispered. "Then she was there."

"She was there," Jason said. He seemed angry, angrier than Max had ever seen him. "I'll kill that son of a bitch."

Max swallowed. "We have to get out to the island. That has to be where the girls are being held."

"Not tonight," Lou said.

"But, Lou—"

"Look, what do we know so far? Huh? We know we're dealing with a vampire who apparently makes a habit of kidnapping women and then wiping their minds clean and setting them free again. We know the chief of police is probably in league with him, and that the rest of the town is either willingly involved or held under some kind of…thrall. We've got to use common sense here. We're outnumbered, and it's getting dark. We do not want to go up against this bastard in the dark, Max. We're at such a huge disadvantage already, we need to use anything we can to gain the upper hand. We need to get back to the motel. Now."

Max didn't want to wait. God only knew what

those poor girls were going through out there—
if indeed that was where they were. If indeed, she
thought grimly, they were even still alive.

"I don't understand," Jason said. "If this guy really
is a…a vampire…what does he *do* with these girls he
takes out there?"

Max met Lou's eyes and saw how dark they were.
He was angry, too, she realized. Angry because she
had been attacked. Angry because two teenage girls
were at some rogue vamp's mercy.

"All we know for sure, Jay, is that he returns them
unharmed."

"But…what does he do with them in the meantime?"

Lou closed his eyes. Max looked away.

"Jesus, do you think he's…feeding from them?"

"That would be my guess," Lou admitted.

Jason swore and looked ready to do murder. Lou
said, "It's not as bad as you're imagining, Jason.
There's no pain. And if he's wiping the memory
from their minds and leaving them unharmed, your
sister is probably not in imminent danger. Less danger, in fact, than Max is right now, from her own
best friend."

Max put a hand on his shoulder. "Stormy would
never have hurt me, Lou."

He glanced at her as if he knew better. "She was as strong as a man, just now. I don't know what the hell is going on, but—I don't think that was Stormy. I don't think it was her at all."

Max held his gaze and silently agreed with him. That person she had just seen, glaring at her, shouting at her in some foreign tongue, had not been Stormy. No way. "Her eyes changed again. They were a different color."

His lips thinned. He said nothing.

Jason said, "Let me carry her for a while. When I get tired, you can take her again."

Lou nodded, stopped walking and carefully placed Stormy into Jason's arms. Then he moved closer to Max and slid an arm around her shoulders.

"You're bleeding," she said.

"Better me than you."

"Thank you, Lou. You're always there for me, you know that? You always have my back."

He met her eyes. "Always will, too." He lifted a hand to touch the scratches on his own face, drew his hand away and looked at the blood on his fingertips.

"I've got some antibiotic ointment back at the motel," she said. "The doc left it for my head.

I'll take care of those scratches as soon as we get back."

He thought about telling her he could manage on his own, but then he thought better of it.

She slid an arm around his waist, leaned her head on his shoulder. "I gotta tell you, Lou, I'm getting scared. I don't know what the hell kind of vamp this is we're dealing with here, but he's got to be incredibly powerful. To be able to hold an entire town under his control... Maybe he's exerting some kind of mind control over Stormy, too."

"The question is, why her and not the rest of us?"

Max shook her head. The gate was coming into sight now, and the sky was growing darker by degrees. Lou took his arm from around her. "My turn."

Jason shifted Stormy back into Lou's arms, but even as he did, she opened her eyes, lifted her head, blinking.

"Storm?"

Stormy frowned at Max, then up at Lou. Her frown vanished, eyes widening. "What the hell happened to you?"

Lou relaxed. It was Stormy's voice, speaking English. And whatever color they'd been before, her eyes were the right color now, though it was rapidly becoming too dark to tell.

"Max, Lou is bleeding," Stormy said. "What happened? Where…where are we? Where's the lighthouse?"

"We're on our way back," Lou said. "You passed out again. And I had a run-in with a…a pissed-off squirrel. Walked right into it. No big deal."

Stormy frowned, shifting her eyes from Lou's to Max's again, clearly not believing him.

"Just relax, Stormy."

"Why are you carrying me?"

Lou sighed. "I told you, you passed out again. I wasn't sure you were strong enough to walk."

"I can walk. Of course I can walk. Put me down, Lou."

Not liking the idea, Lou set her on her feet.

She straightened, but then her knees buckled and she had to catch herself on Lou's shoulders. She steadied herself, then got her footing and let him go. "Damn. Little head rush, there."

"You sure you're all right?" Max asked.

"Sure." She looked at all of them, and while Max and Lou were doing a pretty good job of looking casual, Jason was not. He was watching her as if she were a rabid dog about to spring. Stormy saw it. "Jesus," she whispered. "What happened back there?"

"Come on, let me help you climb the gate, hon," Max said. "We'll talk about it back at the motel. Okay?"

Stormy reached out to grip the gate, then stopped and stared down at her hands. She lifted them, fingers open, then blinked up at Lou. "My nails are broken…. There's…blood. My God, I did that to you, didn't I?"

Lou sighed. "Look, you had a momentary lapse."

"An out-of-body experience or something," Max put in.

"*I* did that. I can't believe…Jesus, why would I…?" She pressed her hands to her head, shaking it side to side. "What the hell is happening to me?"

Stormy had never been so frightened in her life— hell, not even when she'd taken a bullet after being lured to Lou's apartment by someone trying to set him up for her murder. She hadn't had time to be scared then. She'd walked through Lou's door, heard a pop and felt her head jerk back. There had been no pain. That was all of it, nothing else, no time for fear, for panic.

This was entirely different. She felt as if she were

under attack, but not from the outside. This attacker seemed to be hitting from within her, inside her own mind, her own body.

Somehow.

"You don't look so good, honey." Max walked beside her into Lou's motel room. She'd tried to talk her into going back to her own, going to bed, but Stormy knew there was work to be done. And she never would have slept, anyway. "I'm gonna send Jason out to the diner for takeout," Max said. "I'll have him bring you back some herbal tea."

"Thanks, hon. But I'm more in the mood for cheeseburgers, fries, a milkshake and about a six-pack of something carbonated and caffeinated to hell and gone."

Max smiled. Stormy could see the relief in her eyes and vowed to keep trying to act like her old self—even if she was far from feeling it.

"How about the rest of you?" she asked. "Empty calories all around?"

"Sounds good to me, and I'd kill for a beer to go with," Lou said.

"Hang on." Max went to the telephone stand in the room, picked up the pad there and made a short list. "So we need a fresh case of diet Coke, a six pack of Bud, and burgers and fries all around?"

"And a milkshake," Stormy said. "Chocolate." The thought made her stomach churn, but if she admitted to feeling sick, Max would be even more worried than she already was—if that were even possible.

Max scribbled and handed the notepad to Jason. "You willing to make a food run?"

Stormy looked at him. He looked horrible, almost as bad as she probably did. His eyes had rings around them, and he seemed dazed, shell-shocked. She doubted he had any intent of pursuing his interest in dating her after what he'd just seen. Hell, if she were reading him right, he was afraid of her now. And who could blame him?

"I couldn't eat," Jason said. He looked outside the window, unfocused, distracted. "Yeah, I'll go. Not much else I can do right now. For Dee. God, I want her back. This is killing me."

"It's going to be okay, Jason. One more night. That's all. One more. Tomorrow we'll get out to that island, come hell or high water," Max said.

Jason nodded, tore the top sheet off the notepad and headed out.

Max licked her lips. "We also need someone to track down some of those other women. Talk to them, see if we can learn anything."

Stormy nodded slowly. "I could get started on that tonight."

"Storm, tonight you should rest. After what happened—"

"After what happened?" Stormy said, cutting her off. "The problem is, we don't know what happened. Not really." She looked at Lou, who'd walked through into the bathroom and was standing there now, in front of the sink, pressing a wet washcloth to his face. "How could I do that to Lou and not even remember it?"

"I don't know."

Stormy shook her head, paced to the bed and sank onto it. "You guys should lock me up someplace until we figure this out. God only knows what else I might do. I feel like I'm losing control of my own body—like someone else, some stranger, just takes over at will." She closed her eyes. "God, it's a horrible feeling."

"It must be." Max sat down beside her.

"What do you think it is, Max?"

"I don't know."

Stormy stared her friend in the eyes. "You have a theory. Come on, Max, you always have a theory. What do you think is going on here?"

Max pursed her lips, lowered her eyes, cast a

quick look into the bathroom. Lou had closed the door now, and she heard the shower running. She supposed he was beyond overhearing. "It seems to me it's got something to do with the coma."

"I thought of that, too. But I don't understand...."

"You remember how after you came out of it, you said you'd been lost? Wandering around in some dark place, unable to find your way back? And how you met my sister there?"

"Morgan. Yeah, I remember. She helped me find my way back." She lowered her head. "And *she* remembered it, too. She recognized me when she saw me, even though we'd never met before."

"Which means it was real, on some level. That place where you went. You were able to interact with other people, other...beings."

"I guess so. Yeah."

"Do you remember encountering...anyone else while you were there?"

Stormy frowned, thought back, searching her mind. "No...I...no."

"You seem uncertain."

She shrugged. There had been other encounters, but they had been with herself. She'd seen her life unfold before her eyes, scenes of her own childhood. She'd seen her early childhood, happy times with her parents. She'd seen herself finding Jason and Max, way back in the second grade, and how they'd become friends from the start. She'd seen so much.

But none of that counted. "There were others. Flashes, speeding by us so fast. We thought they were people who weren't...stuck or lost like we were. We thought they knew where they were supposed to be—it was like a parade of souls flying past like comets, to the other side, or from it. They went in both directions. It seemed like we were in some kind of...way station. An in-between point. But besides them, I didn't see anyone else," she told Max.

"I think maybe you did. Maybe you don't remember it, or maybe you weren't even aware of it, Stormy, but I think maybe someone...or something...sort of...came back with you."

Stormy's face went utterly lax, and every whisper of breath fled her lungs. Max's theory—it fit what she had been feeling so perfectly that it gave her chills.

"Maybe some kind of...I don't know. Do you think maybe...something walked into your body while you were out of it? Sort of took up residence and now doesn't want to leave?"

Stormy closed her eyes. "Like...some kind of possession?"

"When you blank out, Storm, your eyes change color. Your voice changes. And I can't be sure, but I think you're speaking in a different language. It's like you're someone else."

She couldn't stop the sob that rose up, nearly choking her. She doubled over, clutching her waist, fighting a sense of panic that wouldn't release its grip.

Max stroked her back and shoulders. "I could be wrong, Storm. It could be something else entirely, but—"

"It doesn't feel wrong. Jesus, Max, I just want it out of me. How do I get it out of me?"

"I don't know. But I promise you, we'll find out."

It was dark when Jason Beck pulled up at the diner. He got out of the Jeep and started for the entrance, but the vampire didn't let him go inside. He snapped his powerful arm around the young man's neck from behind. Before Beck could blink, the vampire pulled him into an alley and shoved him up against the cinder-block wall.

"What do you think you're doing, Jason Beck?"

"Ah, Jesus, easy, would you?"

The vampire eased his grip, but didn't release him. "I have no intention of being easy on you. You've been given your orders. I told you to be patient. To wait for further instructions. And yet you let those prying bastards break into my lighthouse."

"It's not like I could stop them! Not without tipping them off. Jesus, will you let me loose? I'm not going anywhere."

The vampire let him go and heard his thoughts. *This is no man,* he was thinking, *but a vampire. The animal who holds my sister's life in his hands.*

Jason's feet settled more firmly on the ground, and he smoothed his jacket where it had bunched around his shoulders.

He lifted his chin. "Is all this cloak-and-dagger crap really necessary? Couldn't we talk over a beer inside the diner? It's not like anyone in this town is going to challenge you."

The vampire made sure his smile was slow and deliberate. "Quite correct. So what is this, an attempt to befriend me? It won't work, Jason Beck. I don't have any friends. And I never drink…beer." His smile faded. "But you already knew that, didn't you? What did they find at the lighthouse?"

"I saw where you were holding my sister. My God, what kind of a monster would put a young girl in a hole like that?"

The vampire felt a twinge of conscience and had to lower his eyes, but only briefly. "The girls were there only for a short time. I assure you, their current accommodations are nothing short of luxurious, as you saw for yourself when you visited them. They have use of a theater, a pool, even a sauna. My house has every convenience. They're getting gourmet meals and the best of care, and they will continue to—as long as you follow my instructions to the letter." He frowned then, staring hard into Jason's eyes and seeing there the man's nightmarish thoughts. "Your fears are unfounded, Beck. I haven't…tasted her. Children are not my preference. Stop torturing yourself with such thoughts and focus on what needs to be done."

Jason Beck didn't know whether to believe that or not, the vampire sensed. But the young man hoped it was the truth.

"I understand the listening devices on the telephones in the motel rooms are no longer functioning."

"That wasn't me. It was the ex-cop, Malone. He found one in his room and then checked all the others. Hell, if I'd stopped him, he'd have known something was wrong."

The vampire searched his eyes, his mind, and then nodded. "It doesn't matter. I can keep tabs on you without the aid of electronics."

Jason swallowed, nodded. "I did what you asked. I got Max and Storm to come here. I don't know what more you want from me."

The vampire lifted his dark brows. "Oh, a good deal more. I've found some of the information this Stuart woman has gathered on…certain matters. But I still don't know all I need to know about her. And far less than I need to know about the other woman. The one you call Storm. She interests me far more."

Jason's head came up sharply. "What interest could you possibly have in her?"

"That, Jason Beck, is none of your concern. She is…ill?"

Jason shook his head. "She took a bullet to the head a few months ago. Spent some time in a coma. Now there seem to be…side effects. Or something."

"Or something?"

Jason shrugged. "She's passed out a couple of times. Seems to have blackouts where she—I don't know, loses it."

The vampire narrowed his eyes but could find no sign in the young man's mind that he was lying. "When you took her to the hospital, what did the doctors find?"

"Nothing. They couldn't find a damn thing. Malone seems to think you might be the one messing with her head."

"I am not. If she is ailing, it's not due to any interference from me. You…you have feelings for this… Storm?"

"We're friends. That's all."

He nodded slowly. "You'd do well to see to it you remain no more than that."

Jason frowned. "What the hell is that supposed to mean?"

"You're not to touch the woman called Storm. Do you understand?"

Jason didn't answer, didn't acknowledge the words. He was angry, fighting angry, but he knew better than to challenge the man who stood in front of him. He didn't stand a chance against him. He was smart.

And it was lucky for him, the vampire thought, that he was.

"I need the women. Both of them. You are to bring them to me, on my island, without the man."

"No. Look, if you want to talk to Max, why don't you just go to the motel and ask her whatever the hell it is you want to know. Jesus, there's no way she'll refuse to tell you if she knows my sister's life depends on it."

He held the young man's eyes. They were intense and determined. "You will bring the women to me, on the island. By night, only by night, and without this Malone. If you do this, I will release your sister and her friend. If you don't…"

"They're my friends," Jason said. His voice broke. "Jesus, I can't just hand them over."

"I do not intend to harm them."

Jason shook his head slowly. "How the hell am I supposed to believe that?"

"I don't really care whether you believe it or not. I need the women. You will deliver them. Find a way."

Jason lowered his head. "I'll try."

"Three nights. Beginning with this one. If, by midnight of the third night, you have not brought them to me, I will come for them. Blood will be spilled. Your blood. Malone's blood. And that of your sister, for good measure. Do you understand?"

Jason nodded, unable to look the man in the eye.

The vampire knew there was no doubt in this young man's mind that he would betray the best friends he'd ever had in order to save his sister.

Jason lifted his head and dashed the moisture from his eyes when the vampire bade him good night. He tried to stop his shaking as he made his way out of the alley and into the diner.

Max watched the page print out and pulled it from the printer tray, eager. "Where the hell is Jason with our food?"

No sooner had she said it than someone knocked on the door. Stormy went to open it and Jason came in, his arms loaded down with bags. Stormy relieved him of one bag, set it on the bed, then took out the six-pack of beer and two six-packs of soft drinks. "We're gonna need some ice."

Jason was already unpacking the other bag, setting their burgers and fries, all wrapped individually, on the paper plates that had been tucked into the bag beside them.

"Any trouble, Jay?" Lou asked.

"Nope. The service was a little slow. This town really needs a fast-food joint or two." His tone was a little too cheerful, a little too light, Max thought. As if it were false, forced. "What have you guys been up to?" Jason asked.

"We went through the list of victims. People who've come up missing only to be found later on. Turns out a couple of them aren't too far away. Or weren't, when the articles were written. Storm's been using the Net to track them down. We thought maybe we could talk to them."

"Good idea," Jason said.

Max set aside the sheet of paper. "I've got some phone numbers. Going to call them after dinner."

"Tonight?" He seemed surprised.

"Sure, Jay. Tonight. Why wait? The sooner we can unravel this thing, the better it'll be for Delia."

He nodded.

"Why? Is there some reason you think we should wait on this?"

"No." The denial was instant. "No, not at all. I'm just surprised. You sure do work fast."

"It's the only speed she knows," Lou said. "Let's at least eat first, though."

Max smiled and moved the computer aside, making room on the table for them to sit around it for their meal. "We got those arrangements made for Sid and his mom. Storm called in a favor from a friend with connections. They'll be getting a call from a private school tomorrow. I think it will work."

"That's good," Jason said. "The quicker the kid gets out of this hellhole, the better."

Several burgers, fries and colas later, Max dialed the telephone, her stomach a little fluttery. She glanced at the clock, just to assure herself it wasn't too late to be phoning people. It wasn't quite nine, so she thought it was safe.

Sitting beside her, Lou looked at the list of names on the printout. "Starting from the top?" he asked.

She nodded. The telephone on the other end was ringing now. As she sat there, Stormy picked up the extension near the bed and curled her legs beneath her to listen in.

"Hello?" It was a woman's voice, deep and soft.

"Hello. I'm trying to reach Lisette Campanelli."

There was a pause. "Who's calling?"

"My name is Maxine Stuart. I'm investigating the disappearance of two young women in or near the town of Endover."

"I'm sorry. She's not available."

Max decided to take a shot and said, "Lisette, please. They're high school girls."

There was silence on the other end. But no telltale click in her ear.

"All I want to do is talk to you. That's all. I'll meet you wherever you say."

There was a sigh. "It won't do you any good. I don't know anything about this."

"That's more than I know," Max said. "I know you were missing for a time under very similar circumstances. I think that whatever happened to you is happening to them."

"I hope you're wrong."

"Then you do remember something?"

Again, silence. A long stretch of it. Max fought to be patient, to give the woman time, when what she wanted to do was reach through the phone lines and shake her. But finally the woman sighed. "I'll meet you. Nowhere near Endover, however."

"I understand."

"Is that where you are now?" the woman asked.

"Yes."

"There's something wrong with that place. You shouldn't stay there." There was a pause. "There's a Starbucks in Manchester."

"Just one?" Max laughed a little. A weak attempt to lighten the conversation.

The woman didn't respond in kind. "There are several. I'll give you directions to the right one, though."

Max looked around the room for a map, only to see that Stormy already had an atlas open on the bed. Stormy put her hand over the mouthpiece and whispered, "That's forty miles away."

"Lisette, Manchester's about forty miles for us."

"Closer to fifty. You're coming just west of it. And

that's as close to Endover as I will ever get. There's an invisible line I've drawn, right down the middle of this state. I won't cross it. Don't ask me to."

"All right. I won't. It's fine, Manchester's fine. I can be there in an hour. Will the coffee shop still be open?"

There was a heavy breath, then, "I don't go out at night anymore, Miss Stuart. But I'll meet you in the morning. Is 10:00 a.m. too early?"

Max wanted to check out the island in the morning. It was vital. "Actually, noon would be better."

"Noon. Are you ready for those directions?"

Stormy had already grabbed a notepad and pencil, and she nodded. Max said, "Ready."

The woman rattled off directions. Max barely listened, because Stormy was scratching them down. "Thank you, Lisette."

"I'll see you tomorrow."

The woman hung up. Max drew a breath, lifted her eyebrows and sent her gaze around the room. "That wasn't easy."

"Did you expect it to be?" Lou asked.

"No. And I don't expect the rest of the people on this list will be any easier." She looked at Stormy. "Do you think I left us enough time to visit that island?"

"Yeah, if we can go out there early enough. Which means we need to find a boat."

"If I can't find one, I fully intend to steal one," Max said. "You should speak to the next person on our list, Storm. She's way down in Massachusetts. And the one after that is north, in Maine. We'll have to split this up if we're going to talk to all of them."

"With any luck, we'll have the girls back before we have to keep any of these appointments."

"Even if we do, I think we should follow up. This bastard needs to be stopped."

Stormy nodded, picked up the phone again. Max dialed, since the list was closest to her. "This one is Mary Ann Prusinski," she said.

When they finished, they had two appointments each for the next day. Max was going to Manchester first, then all the way to Newport, another forty miles inland. Stormy would go south to Boston, then stop at Lowell on the way back. Max had expected that one of them would have to go north, to Maine, to meet the fifth person on her list, but when she phoned, she learned that the woman had committed suicide.

15

He should have waited. Waiting, after all, was
something he'd been doing for centuries. He ought
to be good at it by now.

But he wasn't. And so he found himself at the
small motel, moving slowly through the darkness,
from one door to the next. At each one, he laid his
palm flat against the door, closed his eyes, opened
his mind and searched for her—the one he'd been
feeling ever since she had arrived here. The one
whose photograph had so startled him. Who was
she? Why did her presence distract him to the point
of madness?

"Excuse me—is there something I can do for you?"

He went stiff at the sound of the voice behind him, wondering how he could be so focused on the woman that he had allowed a mortal to walk up on him so easily. He quickly scanned the man who stood behind him. Young, gullible…Gary, the motel's manager. One of his own, a mindless drone, compelled to do his bidding, to protect his secrets, even while remaining blissfully unaware he was doing so. Gary was so loyal he had knocked one of these women unconscious when he caught her snooping. When he had come at the boy's summons, he had thought it was the blond one lying there on the ground. He'd been determined to take her back with him to his island, furious at the whelp for his overreaction. If he had harmed her…

But the blow had been minor, and the victim had been the wrong woman.

Slowly he turned and met Gary's eyes. "You're dreaming, Gary. That's all this is, just a dream. Go back to your bed now, and forget you ever saw me. Forget."

Gary didn't blink. His eyes were fixed and wide. "A dream," he muttered.

"That's it. Just a dream. Forget, Gary. Go to your

bed and forget." He moved his hand in front of the young man's eyes.

Gary turned and shuffled his feet as he moved slowly back toward the motel office, where he entered through a back door, going directly to his rooms. To his bed.

Nodding his satisfaction, the vampire returned his attention to the door, resting his hand against it, feeling for her presence.

There. She was there, on the other side. Asleep, sound asleep in her bed. So sound no dreams wove their spells through her mind.

He moved his hand over the doorknob, felt the locks give way. Then he opened it and stepped slowly inside.

It wasn't the first time he'd seen the strange woman they called Storm. Her hair was soft and pale, cut short, all the better to complement her exquisite face. Her eyes were wide-set and almond-shaped, and her cheekbones sculpted as if by the hand of a loving creator. The name suited her, he thought. He sensed the storm raging inside her, even now. And she had created a maelstrom in him, as well. Closing his eyes, he moved to the bed, stood beside it, willed her to continue to sleep, while he probed and explored the deepest recesses of her mind.

But what he found there startled him so much that he withdrew with a soft gasp. The woman was not one—she was two. Another lived within her even now. Lurking in the hidden depths of her psyche, sleeping, as she was. But strong, and growing stronger.

She stirred. In the room beside this one, someone was awake and moving about. But he could not resist touching her. Just once. He lowered his hand to her hair, closed his eyes as its softness brushed his palm. And then he ran his fingers over her cheek, willing her not to wake.

Her lips parted, and she whispered in her sleep. Words, in his own native tongue, that startled him to his core. *"Iubirea ca moartea e de tare."*

"Love is stronger than death," he whispered. His eyes on her face, he muttered, "Who are you?"

All he saw in her mind, as he probed it ever more deeply, was her intent to come to his island in the morning—bringing her friends along with her.

He couldn't have that. Not by day, and not with Malone. The man was too worthy an adversary to have snooping around his abode.

Fortunately, he had ways of preventing them from visiting in daylight. He would see to it.

He needed to know more about this woman, this

Storm. But to do so, he needed to take her away from the others, her protectors. He needed her alone, far from anyone else.

The movements in the next room grew more lively, and he knew he would be discovered soon if he did not leave. He was not ready for that. Not yet. He hadn't accumulated nearly enough information about these women—about what it was they did. He'd learned only enough to know they were dangerous to him. That all of this—right down to Storm's appearance—could be part of some plot to destroy him. They knew far more about the undead than any mortal should ever know. He had to learn more about them before he made any move.

Beyond that, he didn't want to have to take her by force, harming her friends in the process. To do so would be to incur her hatred, something he wished to avoid. So he must go. But he would solve the mystery of this woman—of her pull on him, and of the sense he couldn't ignore that her soul was being torn slowly apart.

When Max woke in the morning, it was to the sight and sound of a raging storm. High winds, flashes of lightning, cracks of thunder so loud she barely heard the pounding on her door.

She flew out of bed and opened it. Lou, Stormy and Jason surged inside, all of them wet and dripping.

"God, when did this blow up?" Max asked, closing the door against the storm.

"Sunrise," Lou said. He took off his coat and shook it. "It's going to be hell getting out to that island in this."

"Much less finding a boat to get there," Stormy said.

Max hurried into her bathroom, grabbed an armful of towels and brought them back out. She handed one to each of them.

Jason shook his head as he rubbed the rainwater from his face and hair. "We can't. We can't even try it in this storm."

"But, Jay, we have to," Max said. "The girls have been at this maniac's mercy too long already."

He lifted his gaze to hers. "We could end up drowning in the effort, Max. Who's going to get them out of there then?"

Lou lowered his head. "Maybe it'll pass. Maybe if we wait till this afternoon—"

"I don't want to wait on this, Lou."

He met her eyes, and she knew just by looking

into his that he didn't want to wait, either. "It's not safe, Max."

"Not safe for who?" He looked away. "That's what I thought. If it were just you, or you and Jay going out there, you'd do it despite the storm. You know you would." She sighed and put a hand on his arm. "It's sweet that you want to protect us, Lou, but Storm and I are not fragile females in need of a strong man to look out for us. We can do this."

"We don't even have a boat."

"Then we'll go back to that rental place, and this time we won't take no for an answer."

"No." It was Jason who spoke. He faced Max squarely. "Look, Max, I hired you, right? That means you're working for me. It's my sister who's missing, my money paying for all this. It's my call, Max."

She stared at him, blinking. "I can't believe this. You should be pushing harder than any of us to get out there as soon as possible."

He lowered his eyes. "I want the girls back more than you know, Max. But we can't go out there this morning. Not in this. Let's wait it out, see if the storm passes. You've got those visits to make. Call the women, see if you can bump your appointments up a little earlier. Lou and I will split up and go with the two of you, since there's nothing for us to do here. Maybe by the time we get back this will have cleared up."

Max closed her eyes and bit her lip to keep from swearing. Why the hell was Jason so determined? God, could Lou be right about him? Was he keeping something from her?

"He's a vampire, Max," Lou said. "He can't hurt the girls during the day. They'll be safe until we can get out there."

God, it killed Max to have to put off exploring the island until later—to leave those poor girls out there one minute longer than necessary. And her gut instinct told her to find a way to get out there, despite the storm.

Still, she supposed Jason and Lou were right. Waiting for the storm to pass was better than drowning in the effort. And the vampire could do the girls no harm by day. It was a small reassurance but the best she could come up with.

They ate takeout for breakfast, while she phoned the women to change their meeting times. She also phoned Lydia, who told her she'd ordered a replacement pane for the mansion's front door, and that it would likely be installed before Max returned.

The storm kept raging, never relaxing its intensity, right up until she and Lou were in the car, on the road and headed out of town for the first of their scheduled meetings with the survivors of the vampire. The wipers beat frantically against the deluge.

And then they left Endover, and the dark clouds seemed to thin, then vanished entirely. The roads beyond the strange, haunted town were dry, the skies clear and bright.

"Jesus," Lou muttered.

Max just shook her head and tried her damnedest to put a positive spin on the enforced delay. "It'll do Stormy a world of good to get out of that town for the day," she said as she drove her Bug along Route 101 toward Manchester.

"It won't do *us* any harm, either. Though I'm still not sure I like that she's got only Jason for backup."

Max shrugged. "I didn't like it much, either, but she insisted. I think she would have preferred to go alone. But she figured that would make Jason feel excluded and a little crazy, waiting at the motel alone, doing nothing." She swallowed. "Now I'm wondering if she would have been safer on her own. Jason's...I'm beginning to think you might be right. He's got more going on than he's saying."

Lou reached across the space between them to pat her hand where it rested on the seat. "That might be so, but he adores Storm. If she were alone and had one of those episodes, passed out the way she has before—then what? It's better Jay's with her. He knows what's been going on and can get help if he has to. Besides, we all have our phones with us."

"Yeah. And they all miraculously work as soon as we get away from Endover. That storm was centered over the town, too. How freaking powerful must this guy be to be able to control the weather?"

"You don't know that was him, Max."

"Maybe *you* don't. I think he's done something to that town. I think that's why the phones don't work there."

"Bad airwaves as well as bad air, you think?"

She made a face. "Bad jokes must be one of the side effects."

Lou rolled down his window. "I feel better already. I'll bet Stormy does, too, don't you?"

"I hope so. I'm so afraid for her, Lou."

"Me too, hon." He closed his hand around hers, and she was glad he was at her side. "Did you hear from the linguist?"

She nodded. "I e-mailed him again last night, told him it was urgent. His reply came through within the hour, but I didn't get it until this morning. I sneaked in after breakfast, checked the mail while Storm was in the shower."

"And?"

"He said he couldn't be sure, given that what I sent him was spelled phonetically, but he thought it was likely Slavic, possibly Romanian."

"You're shitting me."

She lifted her brows. "You look surprised."

"I honestly expected it to turn out to be gibberish. I don't suppose this guy offered any sort of translation?"

"If it was Romanian, he said it was something like, "'Who lives by the sword, by the sword shall he perish.'"

"That's what she said—when I was getting ready to shoot the wolf?"

"Mmm-hmm."

"And the other? The stuff she whispered when she stroked the critter's neck?"

"'He is not so black as he is painted.'" Max couldn't suppress a shiver as she repeated the translation. "What the hell could this mean, Lou?"

"I don't know. I do not for the life of me know." He sent her a sideways look. "Did you tell Storm about this?"

"Not yet. I'm afraid it's just going to upset her more. But I have to tell her, I guess."

"Yeah," Lou agreed. "You really do."

He kept holding her hand. She let his strength comfort her and wished, as she always did, for more.

Mary Ann Prusinski was a tall woman of perhaps thirty. She arrived at the prearranged meeting spot, a café in Boston, twenty minutes late, and by the time she got there, Stormy was ready to give up and move on. But then she came in, her black hair caught up in a bun behind her head. She wore a suit of muted gray that was so nondescript that Storm guessed she wanted to blend into the woodwork. Nothing about her was noticeable. She could have been a beauty with her huge dark eyes and aristocratic nose. But she wasn't—she was exceedingly, deliberately plain.

"Mary Ann?" Stormy asked, rising as the woman came toward the table where she and Jason sat.

"Yes. You're Ms. Jones?"

"Call me Stormy, everyone does."

The woman didn't acknowledge the invitation but instead glanced nervously at Jason. "Who are you?"

"This is my friend Jason Beck," Stormy said quickly. "His sister is one of the girls who's missing."

"I see."

Jason got to his feet and extended a hand. The woman just shook her head, pulled out the empty chair and sat down. "I'm sorry about your sister," she said. "But I'm afraid I'm not going to be much help. As I told you on the phone, I don't remember anything that happened during the time I was... missing."

"I know," Stormy said. "No one else does, either."

That got the woman's attention. She looked at Stormy sharply. "No one else...there are others?"

"Almost a dozen."

"Not counting my sister and her friend," Jason added.

A waitress came, placing glasses of ice water in front of each of them and handing out menus. She began reciting specials, and Stormy held up a hand. "Give us a minute?"

The waitress nodded and hurried away.

Mary Ann blinked as if in shock. "I...don't understand."

"Neither do we," Stormy said. "All we know is that a lot of women vanished from the face of the earth when they were passing through or near Endover. And all of them showed up again, a few days to a week later, with no memory of where they had been or what had happened to them."

"My God."

"I was hoping you might be able to tell me something that will help us understand what's been going on."

Mary Ann shook her head slowly. "But I don't remember—"

"I know. I know you don't. But there are other things, besides memory, that might give us some clue."

"What kinds of things?"

"Well, I don't know. Was there any physical harm done to you while you were…missing?"

"No. I was in perfect health."

"And what about mentally?"

The woman shot her a look. "I'm not insane, Ms. Jones."

"I know that. I just meant—was there anything different about you, emotionally, mentally? Any habits you developed that you hadn't had before? Fears, phobias, depression?"

The woman blinked…and lowered her head, telling Stormy more surely than words could that she'd hit on something.

"What, Mary Ann? Whatever it is, please…?"

She held up a hand, nodded. "I'm afraid of the dark now. I never was before." She lifted her head. "And there are...dreams."

"Nightmares?" Stormy asked, sliding to the edge of her chair, leaning forward. Around them waitresses carried trays, people sipped coffee and chatted, ice clinked against glassware. Everything was so perfectly normal.

"Not...exactly." The woman shot a look at Jason.

Jason took the hint. "I'm gonna go find the men's room. I'll be back," he said, and he got up from the table and left them alone.

When he was gone, Mary Ann leaned closer. "In the dreams I'm paralyzed. I can't move. And there's a man. And he...does something to me."

Stormy frowned. "Were you sexually assaulted, Mary Ann?"

"No. The doctors found no sign of it, at least. And he doesn't touch me...that way...in the dreams. Not...with his hands, anyway. It's like...he does it with his mind. And he...he bites me."

Stormy had been leaning forward. But the words made her sit up straight. "He drinks from you," she whispered.

Mary Ann nodded hard. "My therapist says that my mind has filled in the missing time with fantasies, stuff I picked up from horror novels or films or pop culture."

"But what do *you* think?"

"I don't know what to think."

Stormy covered the other woman's hand with one of her own. "I'm so sorry, Mary Ann. It must be terrifying for you."

Mary Ann shook her head slowly, lifting her eyes to Stormy's. "No. It's almost...erotic." Her eyes slammed closed quickly, and she jerked her hand away. "God, I'm ashamed to admit that."

"Don't be. It's not your fault."

Mary Ann kept her eyes shut for a moment, and Stormy thought she was battling tears. "Do you think you could draw him? A likeness of him, I mean? Have you ever tried?"

The woman's eyes opened quickly. "How could you know that?"

"You *have* drawn him, then?"

The woman bent to the large handbag that rested on the floor beside her chair. She drew a folder from it and passed it to Stormy with hands that shook almost uncontrollably.

Stormy took the folder and opened it.

The man himself stared at her from the page inside. The pencil drawing seemed to stare at her with an intensity that tied her stomach in knots. Longish, narrow face, full lips, a cleft in his chin, long dark hair. And those deep-set, piercing eyes.

"You don't think he's real?" Mary Ann whispered.

"I don't know." But she *did* know. He *was* real. She'd seen him before—in her mind.

Her head began to swim. She was dizzy and flooded in white noise.

"Ms. Jones?"

Stormy pinched the bridge of her nose, fought the incoming tide. "Can I keep these?" she managed to ask.

"Yes. Yes of course." The woman looked around the café. "God, I feel as if he's here somewhere. Watching."

"It's daylight, Mary Ann. You're safe. But…you should go."

"I should—"

"Go. Now." Stormy leaned back in her chair, pressed both her palms to the sides of her head and closed her eyes tight. Moments later, Jason was there, his hands on her shoulders, tight and hard.

"Hold on, Stormy. Hold on, don't let go." He was pulling her to her feet.

"Is she gone? Mary Ann? Where is…?" Stormy asked.

"She's gone. It's fine."

"Get the drawings," she whispered.

He snatched up the folder, her purse. She thought he threw some bills from his pocket onto the table—a tip for the waitress, since they had never gotten around to ordering anything—and then he was leading her from the café, putting her into his Jeep, buckling her seat belt around her.

"Here," he said as he climbed into the driver's side and reached toward her, holding a cloth-wrapped bundle.

A napkin, she realized, one of the white cloth ones from the café. "Lean forward, bend your head down."

She did. He pressed the bundle to the back of her neck. Cold. It was full of ice. He must have scooped it out of her water glass. She sighed, the breath rushing out of her as the cold hit her nerve endings.

"Any better?"

"I'll let you know."

"Do you want to go back to the motel?"

She reached behind her to hold the bundle, so he could use his hands again. "No," she said. "Let's head to the other meeting."

"But—"

She drew a deep breath. "It's passing. It's passing, it's okay." She met his eyes. "Look. My eyes are still the right color, aren't they?"

"They're the perfect color."

She forced a smile. "And I'm still speaking English. I think the ice worked."

"More likely you're stronger the farther we get away from that place."

"Maybe." She nodded at the keys he held in his hand. "Let's get going. Time's burning, and we need to stop in Salem on the way back."

"Salem? Why?"

"I did some research on the Net yesterday and found a few books that might help me figure out what's going on with me. There's a rare bookstore in Salem, and according to their Web site, they have a couple of them in stock."

He nodded. "All right. But if it happens again…"

"If it happens again, Jay, restrain me if you have to. But don't let me hurt you. Promise me that?"

He nodded, though she wasn't sure he meant it. Then he put the keys into the ignition and started the engine.

They were driving back toward Endover late in the afternoon. Max was already thinking about dinner, her stomach growling, and not for pizza or burgers. "I wonder if it's still storming there," she muttered, voicing her thoughts aloud. "Probably not. It's nearly dark. This trip took a lot longer than I expected. And he doesn't need to keep us off the island after dark."

"Even a natural storm wouldn't be likely to last all day," Lou said.

"Ever the skeptic," she said. "What do you say we eat in a real restaurant tonight?"

"Fine by me. Stormy and Jason will be expecting us back at the motel, though."

"Slow down, I'll call them before we enter the dead zone."

He gave a shiver and told her with his eyes that her new pet name for the town wasn't even a little bit funny to him, but she only shrugged and took out her phone.

Stormy picked up. Her voice was tired, worn.

"Hey, Storm, it's me. You find out anything?"

"Nothing good. What about you?"

"Freakin' creepy stuff. I'll tell you when I see you. Where are you?"

"We'll be back in Endover in another twenty minutes. Why?"

"Why don't we meet at that restaurant on the shore? We passed a billboard for it on the way to the boat rental place the other day, remember? I'm hungry for some real food and in the mood to be waited on. It'll be dark by the time we get there, and we need to decide what to do next."

"Okay. Sure, what the hell. I remember that billboard. The restaurant's outside the Endover town limits, so how bad can it be?"

"You sure you're up for it? You sound a little tired."

"I'm fine. See you in a half hour or less."

Stormy hung up. Max put her phone down and frowned. "She sounds off."

"You think she's losing it again?"

"I don't know. Hell, maybe the restaurant is a bad idea."

"It's a good idea. You need a break, and so does she. Jason and I can handle it if anything happens."

Max told herself it was unreasonable to believe everything would be fine, as long as Lou was with her. Unreasonable and unrealistic. But she felt it anyway, and mostly believed it was true. Even if it was illogical.

She and Lou were closer, so they arrived at the restaurant first. There was no sign of the storm, no rain, no clouds, not even in the distance toward Endover. Then again, it was already dusk.

The restaurant was a large white building, its entire back side mostly made up of glass panes, so that nearly every table in the place looked out over the ocean. There were spotlights set up along the shore that came on once darkness fell, to keep the view alive. It was beautiful.

Lou asked for a table for four, and a hostess in black pants and a crisp white blouse with a black ribbon around its collar led them to a gorgeous table right up against the windows. It relieved Max to no end when she looked the woman in the eyes and saw a real person looking back at her, rather than a tranced-out zombie. She ordered wine, deciding to relax a little. Lou settled for coffee and a large glass of ice water, probably because he wanted to stay sharp. Especially now.

The waitress brought their drinks, left their menus and hurried away.

"This is nice," Max said. "Someday we ought to come back here, just the two of us."

"I don't know if I'm gonna make Endover a regular place on my list of favorite vacation spots, Max."

She shrugged. "No matter. There are lots of nice places overlooking the ocean back in Easton."

He nodded.

"Have you thought any more about that, Lou?"

"About what?"

He looked across the table at her. She sighed. "About coming to work with Stormy and me in Easton. Moving up there for good."

He drew a deep breath. "I can't lie to you, kid. The thought has crossed my mind. I'm just not sure it's the best idea, is all."

"Why not?"

"Honey, we've been over all this."

"No we haven't. You've given me countless reasons—none of them worth a damn, by the way—why we can't be together as a couple. But you've never given me any reasons why we can't work together."

"That's because they're the same reasons."

"Oh." She took a sip of her wine as she thought about that. "So you don't think we could be together that much without...taking our relationship further."

"I didn't say that."

She frowned at him.

He reached for her wineglass and took a big drink. When he set it down again, he nodded. "Okay, I give. You're right, I think if we were together all the time, yeah—something would be bound to happen."

She smiled. "I'm irresistible to you."

"Damn near." He looked away as soon as he said

it, and she knew he was wishing he could pull the words back.

"It wouldn't ruin things, Lou. It would only make things better."

"It would ruin *you*, kid. And I'm not gonna do that."

"Lou, sweetie, don't you get it yet? You can't turn off your heart. You think you have, but you haven't. Denying it doesn't make it go away. And pretending you don't care doesn't make it true."

He looked past her, toward the entrance, but she knew he heard her, saw it in his eyes. Could he actually be listening for a change? Was she finally getting through to him? God, she was almost afraid to think it was even possible.

"There are Stormy and Jason," he said, and standing up, he waved a hand at them.

Max sighed in disappointment. She would have liked more time to pursue the discussion. For the first time, she felt as if she was making progress.

The place had been steadily filling up, but there were still plenty of empty tables around. Stormy spotted them and waved back, but Max thought her smile was forced and her gait heavy. Not her usual bouncing, vibrant steps.

"She's had a hard day," Max muttered, but she

got up, anyway, and gave Stormy a welcoming hug. "Hey, honey. You look wiped out."

"It was a long and interesting day," she said.

Jason pulled out a chair for her, overdoing the chivalrous bit, Max thought, and she sat down. Max returned to her own seat, and Lou waved at the waitress as Jason took his own chair.

The waitress hurried to take Stormy and Jay's drink orders, then went off to fill them.

"So?" Lou asked. "What did you guys find out?"

Stormy drew a deep breath. "The two women had pretty similar things to say. Both have developed a fear of the dark. Both have…disturbing dreams."

"About a man who…drinks from them?" Max asked, lowering her voice to a whisper on the last three words.

Stormy met her eyes, nodded. "Yours, too?"

"Mmm-hmm. One had painted him."

"One of mine sketched him in pencil," Stormy said.

They both reached for their bags at the same time. Max produced a tiny, oval-framed miniature—a portrait of a man with powerful black eyes and long dark hair. She slid it across the table to Stormy, and took the folder in return. Then she opened it and caught her breath.

"Identical," she said.

Stormy nodded, showing the oval miniature to Jason without more than glancing at it herself. Max wondered why. Jay thinned his lips and nodded. Max flipped through the drawings, and Lou leaned over the table to look at them as she did.

"It's uncanny," Stormy said.

"Not so uncanny if he's real," Lou said. "And I think we're well beyond doubting that he is, especially after I got to see him face-to-face." He thumped his forefinger on one of the drawings. "This is the same guy who tried to grab you the other night, Max. This is our vamp."

Max closed her eyes. "Jesus, here we go again."

"Max, maybe it's time we called in some reinforcements," Lou said. "Your sister, Dante, some of their friends…"

She shook her head firmly. "Not until I know for sure what we're dealing with here. Hell, Lou, he came after me. There's every chance he wants to draw them into this—maybe it's some kind of trap for them. Maybe he has some sort of vendetta or something."

"But how the hell would he know you were connected to others of his kind?" Lou asked. Then he lowered his head and answered his own question.

"The break-in. Hell, it happened the first night you were out of the house."

"And the computer was the only thing taken," Max said, nodding. "That seals it. We're not dragging any other vamps into this. He might be a rogue. A killer of his own kind. It wouldn't be the first time a vampire turned on his own."

Jason was sitting there looking from one of them to the other, his eyes grim.

Stormy put a hand on his arm. "That doesn't mean he's done anything to harm Delia. Hell, he let the other women go. He didn't hurt them. There's no reason to believe he would change tactics now."

Max closed the folder and returned it to Stormy, who slid it into the bag at her side. Then Max looked at the bag itself, black with twine handles and a logo on the front. "What's that?" she asked. "You found time to go shopping during all this?"

Stormy nodded. "Just some research materials."

Max reached for the bag, pulled it into her lap and looked inside. Two fat books, hardcover, musty-smelling, with yellowed, rough-edged pages, sat inside. She glanced at the titles. *Case Histories of Demonic Possession* and *Rites of Exorcism: A Guide for the Clergy*. A business card fell out of one, and

Max picked it up and read it. It was for a hypnotist in Salem.

Licking her lips, she tucked the card back into the book, looked up from the bag and saw Stormy's troubled eyes. "Good choices," she said. "We'll read them together."

"Okay."

"But first, let's eat, huh? I'm starved."

Stormy brightened slightly. "Me too." She opened her menu, but Max got the feeling she wasn't really reading it.

16

Max hadn't managed to get Lou into bed with her again since that first night. She'd spent last night in her own lonely motel room, and he hadn't argued with her, though she guessed from the circles under his eyes that he'd been up most of the night. Didn't he realize he would sleep better with her safe in his arms? But no, he preferred to pace the floor, straining his ears to hear any sound of trouble. Maybe stepping outside every now and then to take a look around, make sure her door was still locked. She knew exactly what he was doing—because she was doing much the same, in an effort to watch over Stormy. Hell, maybe they should all just bunk together. Save everyone a lot of time and worry.

Still, he didn't ask. So she got out of the car after dinner and went to her own room, instead of his, all too aware that the earlier storm was long gone. The skies had cleared, except for the occasional lingering finger of cloud, and the wind had died to a gentle ocean breeze. Max had suggested they find a boat and head to the island, despite the added risk of going there by night.

Lou had changed her mind, though, by saying he had a feeling that was just what the vampire wanted them to do.

Hell.

The clock read 12:03 when she heard the sound of a door closing. She'd drifted off and could have kicked herself for it, but she hurried to her own door and opened it just a crack.

Stormy was walking across the parking lot. She wore a pale blue nightgown, filmy and light, and the breeze caught it and sent it waving behind her. She was barefoot. Where the hell was she going? Not to the cars. No, she veered to the side and headed around to the rear of the motel.

Max wasn't dressed. She wore a hockey jersey and panties. Nothing else. She snagged the extra blanket from the foot of the bed, because it was faster than going to the closet for her coat and shoes. Tugging the blanket over her shoulders, she hurried outside to follow. When she passed Lou's door, she almost stopped and called out to him. But she decided to see what the hell was going on first—and kept walking.

Behind the motel, there wasn't much. A Dumpster full of garbage. A thin ribbon of pavement that wound around from the front. And beyond that, a rolling stretch of unmown grass that ended at a patch of spindly trees.

Stormy walked across the field, heading for the trees. Max swallowed hard, giving one last glance back toward the motel, wishing she had alerted Lou. Too late now. If she went back, she would risk losing sight of Stormy. She shrugged the blanket from her shoulders, dropped it in the middle of the grass and then kept walking even as Stormy disappeared into the trees. At least there would be some sign where she had gone, in case she didn't come back, Max thought. She considered calling out to her friend but wasn't sure that would be the best thing to do. Didn't they say you should never startle a sleep-walker awake? Grudgingly, she admitted to herself that she was afraid of just who or what might wake up if she did.

"Hell." Max trudged on. She stepped on pointy twigs and bristly patches every few yards. She stumbled and hopped and fought to avoid the unseen hazards on the forest floor, though it was little use in the dark.

Stormy had no such problems. She walked smoothly, steadily, either intuitively placing her feet in the right spots or simply oblivious to the discomfort of bare feet on the forest floor, and twigs and branches in her face.

Max pushed the branches away as she went and thought she must be the noisiest thing in the woods this night, the way she was crashing through the underbrush. Stormy, on the other hand, didn't seem to be making a sound. Then again, Max thought, she might not hear Stormy over her own ruckus, anyway. Even keeping her friend in sight was becoming a challenge.

And then it wasn't a challenge, it was impossible, because Stormy was gone. Vanished.

Max strained her eyes in the darkness, but she couldn't see her. She hurried forward, racing toward the spot where she'd last sighted Stormy. The woods ended there, suddenly and without warning. Max emerged onto a steep embankment and came to a startled halt. The slope angled sharply downward, dirt, gravel and sand. Hardly any grass grew there. At the bottom there was water, a tiny cove where the ocean lapped at the shore. A small boat sat on the beach off to one side, and a still, pale form lay nearby.

"Stormy!"

Max jerked into motion, starting down the slippery slope. The surface was loose and fell away under her feet. Her legs slid downward, and she leaned back in an effort to keep her balance. In another heartbeat, her hands were grasping the ground behind her, her butt and legs skimming downhill fast, even though she dug her heels in to try to slow her descent. And then she was at the bottom, scrambling to her feet and hurrying to where Stormy lay on the ground.

Her friend's nightgown was wet, the ocean waves rolling in gently, reaching to her legs. Max fell to her knees, grasping Stormy's shoulders. "Storm? Honey? Come on, wake up." She lifted her friend's upper body in her arms and searched her still face. She'd obviously taken a fall. God, had she broken her beautiful neck?

"Stormy? Jesus, talk to me!"

"She's still alive. There's no need to panic."

Max jerked her head up at the sound of the deep male voice coming from very nearby—instantly aware that it didn't belong to Lou or to Jason. And then she saw him, standing on the shore with the waves lapping over his feet and the sea wind lifting his long, black hair from his shoulders. Clouds parted, and the moonlight bathed his face. The same face she'd seen earlier tonight, in the drawings done by his victims.

Instinct told her to back away. She didn't. In fact, she moved closer, rising to her feet to put herself between him and Stormy. "You'll leave here if you know what's good for you," she said.

His brows rose. "Courage? Or foolishness?"

"Probably a little of both. Now, get the hell out of here before the rest of my friends arrive and stake your sorry ass." She was painfully aware she had no weapon. Nothing to use to fight him off.

"Stake me? That's actually rather funny." He stepped closer.

She bent quickly and snatched up the biggest rock within reach.

"Calm down, Maxine Stuart. You have no friends coming, and I think you know that rock in your hands can't harm me."

"I also know it's going to hurt like hell when I cave your skull in with it." She lifted the rock. "Stay back."

He lowered his eyes to Stormy. Then they widened.

Max stole a quick look downward, too, afraid to take her eyes off him for more than an instant. But Stormy's own eyes were open. And they were a deep, dark black that almost seemed to glow in the moonlight.

Her eyes fixed on the man's, the vampire's. She muttered something that sounded like *"Prinţ meu"* as her strange eyes turned to focus on Max and the rock in her hand. And then she shrieked something in that gibberish language she was always speaking, even as she shot into a sitting position, twisted her body and wrapped her arms around Max's legs, toppling her to the ground. She clambered up her, clawing, pounding. All Max could do was try to cover herself with her own arms, but that did little good. Her best friend was beating the hell out of her.

"Tarfa! Şterge-o că-t~i traq us şut in cur!" Stormy ranted.

The man shouted a single word. *"Stai!"* To Max's amazement, Stormy went still, then turned her head slowly toward him, her eyes welling with tears. *"Dragostea cea veche îţi sopteste la ureche."* She reached a hand up to him. *"Prinţ meu."* For a moment he seemed about to take it. But then she passed out, rolling off Max and onto the shore.

"Just what the hell is the meaning of this?" the vampire asked, his voice dangerously quiet, trembling, his eyes moist and focused on Stormy. "What kind of game are the two of you playing?"

"I don't know what you're talking about. She's sick. All I want to do is help her."

"Do you think I believe a word of that?" he demanded. "Where did she learn to speak those words?"

Max blinked. "You mean…you understood her? What did she say?"

He sighed and started to turn away, but Max reached up and gripped his arm. "What did she say?" she cried.

"She called you a bitch. Said to get away before she kicked your ass, to put it bluntly."

Max winced and closed her eyes tightly.

"And then she said, 'Old love will not be forgotten.'" His tone had softened, and his eyes were on Stormy now. "I am not so foolish that I'm not aware this is some kind of a trick," he said.

"I don't really care what you think." Max knelt beside her best friend, leaning over her, touching her face.

"Move aside," he commanded.

"If you think I'm letting you touch her, you can think again, pal."

"You'll never get her back up that hill by yourself." He put a cold, powerful hand on her shoulder. "And if I'd wanted to hurt you, you'd be long dead by now."

She turned to stare up at him. "What have you done with those two girls? Where are Delia and Janie?"

"They're fine. Would you like to see them?"

She was so stunned, she sucked in a breath.

"Come to me on the island. The two of you," he said, nodding at Stormy. "Alone and only by night." He smiled slowly. "I think you've already realized I'll never allow you to reach it by day."

"I knew it…." She looked around her. "This was your doing, wasn't it? Somehow luring Stormy out here in the middle of the night, putting her under some kind of trance—"

"Come to me by night. Bring her to me. When you do, the girls are yours."

"I'll get those girls back, make no mistake about that. But my way, not yours. Never yours."

He shrugged. "Why am I bothering to negotiate

with a mortal? I'll take her with me now. It's not as if you can stop me. *La revedere,* Maxine Stuart."

Max stood between him and Stormy. He reached for her to move aside. "You son of a—"

"Get your hands off her!"

The shout came from halfway up the steep hill, as Lou shot down it. Even as the vampire turned in surprise, Lou was hitting him like a full body rocket. The impact took both of them into the surf, where they tumbled and rolled.

Max shot after them. "Lou, don't. Jesus, look out! He's the—"

The men sprang from the water, crouched, facing each other, knee deep in the froth. Something glinted, and Max saw the knife in Lou's hand.

"You're no match for me, mortal, and I think you know it."

"Maybe not. But I guarantee I'll put a hurting on you that you won't soon forget." Lou lunged forward, swinging the blade.

Max gasped, shocked at the speed of his strike, and the brutality of it, as well. The blade sliced deep, and the vampire jerked backward, clasping his upper arm. Blood swelled, oozing between his fingers, coating his hand and dripping from it.

"Damn you!"

Lou shrugged. "Stick around and finish the fight," he said. "I dare you. You'll bleed out in the process, but what the hell do I care?"

"You know just enough about my kind to be dangerous," the vampire all but growled.

"I know more about your kind than I ever cared to," Lou said. "Your move, pal."

The vamp's eyes narrowed. He nodded once. "You're a worthy adversary—for a mortal. It's going to be a shame to kill you."

"On that we agree."

"See to the one called Storm. I'll want her in good health when I return to take her from you. We'll finish this another time."

Lou tilted his head in acknowledgment. And then the vampire was gone in a blur of speed that seemed to move southward along the shore and then vanish.

Lou turned toward the shore, dragging his legs through the water as he folded the sizable knife and dropped it back into his pocket. Max ran to him, wrapping him in her arms. "God, Lou, he could have killed you."

"Thanks for the vote of confidence." He hugged her back, then set her slightly away from him to look at her, his hand moving her hair off her face. "Jesus, Maxie, what did that bastard do to you?"

She shook her head. "It wasn't him. It was Storm."

He lifted his brows. "Storm did all that?"

All what? she wondered. She knew she hurt pretty thoroughly, over most of her body, but she had no idea what she looked like. "Most of it. Some of it I may have gotten half tumbling down that freaking hill."

He bent over Stormy, gathering her up into his arms. "I feel like I ought to be carrying you back to the motel, too," he said, moving northward along the beach in search of an easier way back up.

Max kept pace right beside him. She saw him notice the little boat, resting on the shore. "That solves one problem," he muttered. "Are you sure you're all right, Max?"

"I'm fine, Lou. Really." She wasn't—in fact, she was hurting more and more as the adrenaline levels in her blood returned to normal and the fight-or-flight impulse faded. She put a hand on his shoulder. "I can't believe you attacked a full-fledged vamp to defend me—for the second time now. You know as well as I do how powerful they are."

He shrugged. "I know their weaknesses, too. The way they feel pain so much more keenly than we do. The way they tend to bleed out when cut."

She nodded. "He'll have to wrap that sucker tighter than tight if he's going to last until dawn."

Lou made a face. "No doubt he'll manage. Then he'll heal with the day sleep, and I'll have to start from square one."

"Not if I have anything to say about it, you won't."

They found a path that wound up a far more gradual slope, back through the woods, and emerged beside, rather than behind, the motel. The entire way, Lou was watching her, eyeing her, worried and protective and angry.

He stopped in front of Stormy's door. Max said, "Wait, I've got a key in my room." She'd left her own door open, so she hurried inside, wincing when the change in her gait brought a fresh stab of pain in her side. Then she grabbed her keys and went back out to open Stormy's door.

Lou carried Stormy in and laid her down on the bed. "Her nightgown's pretty wet," he said.

"I'll get her changed." Max went to Lou, where he stood beside the bed. "You don't have to wait, Lou. I can take it from here."

"Bull. You look like you pissed off a wildcat, honey. You give her the once-over, and then it's your turn."

She smiled slowly, opened her mouth to deliver the obligatory smart-ass comeback. He put a finger to her lips before she could get a word out. "Just do it, Max."

"I'm doing it already."

She went to Stormy's dresser and got out a T-shirt. Then back to the bed, to gently extract the sleeping woman from the wet nightgown. She put the T-shirt on her and lowered her carefully back to the mattress. That done, she got a warm washcloth from the bathroom, and wiped the dirt and sand from Stormy's legs and feet. As she did, she ran her hands over her friend's limbs, feeling for broken bones, hunting for bruises or cuts. She inspected Stormy's head carefully, too, but found no injuries. Finally she drew the covers over her and tucked her in.

"Do you think she's all right?" she asked.

Lou nodded. "She's breathing fine. Her pulse is strong. And if she was physically healthy enough to do all that damage to you, I have no doubt she's all right. It's you I'm concerned about."

"I'm sure it's not as bad as it must look."

"It would have to be pretty bad to be as bad as it looks, kid. Come on."

"Back to your room?"

"That's where the first aid stuff is." He held out a hand.

She took it, noting, as she did, the scratches down her own arms. "Hell, it's worse than I thought."

He nodded, and when she winced on the way to the door, he drew her close to his side, his arm around her. He made sure Stormy's door was locked behind them, then led Max to his room and took her inside.

He took her all the way to the bathroom, then had her sit on the edge of the tub while he turned on the faucets and closed off the drain.

"Am I covered in dirt and sand?"

He shook his head. "No, but you're going to be covered in bruises by morning. A hot soak will ease things a little. Hell, look at your feet." As he said it, he knelt and lifted one of them, shaking his head as he examined the sole, which felt to Maxie as if she had walked over a porcupine.

He lowered her foot again. "Strip down, take a nice soak," he said. "Take your time." He nodded at a plaid flannel robe that hung from the towel rack. "You can put that on when you finish. 'Kay?"

She resigned herself to bathing alone as he left the bathroom. He didn't close the door all the way, though, she noted. Just enough to give her some privacy—unwanted or otherwise.

Maxie peeled off her shirt and panties, stepped into the steaming water and sank down into its heat. It felt good, mostly, though it stung in some places. She leaned back and let the water keep running, so it would rise even higher around her shoulders. When it lapped at her neck, she finally shut it off, but only because it would have run over otherwise. Then she closed her eyes and let the hot water soak her aches and pains away.

Thoughts were chasing their tails in her head. Lou's fearless attack on that vamp. Hell, if that didn't prove he loved her, she didn't know what would. Stormy's possession, or whatever the hell was wrong with her. It seemed to be getting worse. Max had to find a way to help her. The vampire, he was on her mind, too. She'd never seen him before, didn't know his name. But she had drawings of him. Maybe if she sent some copies around—hell, none of the vampires she knew had faxes. What was that bastard doing with two young girls, anyway? And why did he want her and Stormy to come out there…alone?

It was Stormy he wanted. She'd sensed it before, and now he'd admitted it. There had been something palpable and electric between them out there tonight.

But slowly the soothing hot water dissolved her racing thoughts and replaced them with relaxation. She closed her eyes and let the chaos melt away. Stopped thinking and just felt instead. Felt the pain soothing away. Felt the water soaking the grit gently out of her numerous scrapes and scratches. Felt the worry easing from her overworked mind.

Lou waited until he was sure the water must have gone cool before he went to the slightly open door and spoke her name. She didn't answer, so he peered around the door.

She lay in the water, head back against the tub, eyes closed. One arm dangled over the side of the bathtub, smooth skin gleaming and damp, but marred with scratches and bruises that were already growing dark and purple. The ends of her hair were wet against her neck.

"Maxie?" he said, a little louder this time.

Nothing. He would have thought she was faking if he didn't know better. Not that she wouldn't pull a trick like that. She would. Wouldn't even bat a long, thick eyelash first, either. But she wasn't. Not tonight.

Sighing, he walked into the bathroom and told himself not to look at her. He took a big towel from the shelf, held it up and moved toward the tub, willing himself to keep his eyes on her face and nothing else.

It would have worked, too, if he hadn't been human, and male, and in possession of a pulse.

He looked.

She lay on her back in the water like a newborn goddess. Her knees were bent and leaning toward the back of the tub, so his view was of the wet curve of her hip and then that of her waist. Her breasts were tempting beneath the water's surface, her delicate collarbones making him want to touch, to trace. And then her neck. She had a neck to beat all necks. A neck that made a man understand why it was that vampires always went for the jugular. A hell of a lot more than blood pressure, that was for sure.

He moved closer, leaned over her kissable toes and pulled the stopper. The water began to drain, and he waited, not bothering to stop looking now that the damage was done. He figured at this point he could look his fill and do no worse. The problem was, with Maxie, he never got his fill. Not even close.

When the water was gone, and her skin grew goose bumps and her nipples went tight with the chill, he leaned over and laid the towel over her, gathered her closer to tuck it around behind her and scooped her up out of the bathtub. She was dripping wet, and the towel didn't come together very well in the back. He snagged the bathrobe on his way out and tossed it onto the bed. Using one hand, he opened it and then laid her on it.

She opened her eyes a little but didn't move to be of any help. The towel covered her while he slid her hand into the sleeve of the bathrobe. Then he did the same with the other hand, and drew the robe closed over her front. He tied the sash, then tugged the wet towel out from under.

Maxie smiled. "Leave it to you to find a way to get a wet, naked woman out of the tub and into the bed without having to look at or hardly even touch her."

He lifted his brows. "I tried my best, Max, but even I'm not that good."

She blinked at him, looking first confused, then surprised. He didn't give her time to comment or speculate. "I'll get the first aid supplies."

"I'll settle for a morphine drip and a stiff drink."

"Can you make do with aspirin and a beer?"

She nodded. "Sounds like heaven."

He returned to the bathroom. By the time he came

back, she was lying under the covers and the robe was on the floor. She read his face, tugged the covers down in front. "I pilfered one of your T-shirts. The robe was damp, and I was cold."

"That's fine."

"You didn't look like it was fine when you thought I was naked under here."

He smirked and came to sit on the edge of the bed, then handed her two aspirin tablets and glass of water.

She swallowed the pills and set the glass aside. "What else you got?"

He grinned at her. God, Maxie could always make him laugh, no matter the circumstances. Holding up a tube of muscle rub, he said, "It's odor free, but works as well as the smelly kind."

"You travel with muscle rub?" She speared him with her gleaming green eyes. "Is that a prop to convince me you're over the hill?"

"A handful of old injuries. They act up every now and then."

"Yeah? What kind of injuries? You take a bullet in the line of duty?"

He slanted a look at her. "Roll over."

She did. Lou tugged the blankets down to her hips and lifted up the T-shirt. He squeezed some of the liniment onto his palm, rubbed his hands to warm it, then began massaging it into her skin. It was warm and taut, and he loved touching it. Everything in him came alive when he ran his hands over her flesh.

He felt her relaxing into his touch, heard her sigh. "God you've got great hands," she said. "So, you gonna tell me what happened? How you got those old injuries?"

He rubbed at a knot beneath her shoulder blade, then massaged the shoulders themselves. "I was still a rookie, set up in a speed trap on a highway, and a guy went by me doing seventy-five. So I hit the lights and siren and went after him. Pulled him over. Ran the plates. Then I got out and walked up to the driver's door."

"And?"

She was looking over her shoulder at him, her eyes wide.

"Got nailed by a pickup the size of a tank. Felt like it, anyway." He rubbed the small of her back.

She rolled over onto her back so quickly he found himself with his hands on her belly. It was soft, and he liked the feel of his hands there, but he took them away all the same. "Why don't I already know about this stuff, Lou? God, I've known you for— how long now?"

He shrugged. "Years."

"Almost a decade. I thought we were friends."

"We are friends."

"Then why is it I'm just now finding out about major things in your life?"

"Maybe just now is the first time I felt compelled to tell you."

She blinked at him. He stared down at her and read her face. Why now? she wanted to know. She wanted to know if it meant anything, if it was some kind of signal that he was maybe ready to kick this thing up a notch.

Well, he wasn't ready for anything of the sort, but he didn't want to hurt her feelings by telling her not to go there.

"So where's that beer you promised me?" she asked.

He was surprised as all hell. But he got up and went to the cooler on the table across the room, got out two beers, popped the tops and handed one to her. She'd propped up a bunch of pillows and was sitting upright now.

He sat down to sip his beer, then set the can down and reached for the liniment again. He knew this was the lamest, most pathetic, sorry-ass game he'd ever played, because there wasn't a reason on God's earth why she couldn't rub this stuff on her own legs. At least with her back, the need for his assistance was plausible. Barely. But this was purely gratuitous, and he knew she knew it, too.

She would use it against him; he knew she would. But he yanked the covers back, anyway, and when he saw all the scratches, he set the liniment down and picked up the antibiotic ointment instead.

"How badly were you hurt?" she asked.

He used his forefingers to dab ointment on the gouges and cuts, scratches and scrapes. "Broke a femur and three ribs, and dislocated a shoulder."

He stole a look at her eyes. They were wide and fixed on his face. "It's okay, there was no permanent damage. I'm fine now."

"You're lucky it didn't kill you."

"Don't think I don't know it." He shrugged. "Better skip the other stuff on your legs. They're bruised, but that stuff would burn in the cuts and scrapes. Now…" He moved up on the bed, caught her chin in his hand and bent closer to look at her face. He turned her head left, then right. "There are some nasty scratches on your neck."

"Are there?"

He nodded, realizing a little too late how close he was to her face and how intently her eyes were probing his. He cleared his throat and put a little more of the ointment on his fingers, then ran them gently over the smooth skin of her neck.

He was fine until she tipped her head back and closed her eyes, her breath easing out of her lungs in a shuddering sigh.

He didn't realize his hand had gone still until those green eyes opened again and locked onto his.

Then her head lifted from the pillows and she pressed her mouth to his. Briefly, lightly, she kissed him. Then she kissed him again, and again. Taunting, teasing little pecks that only left him wanting more, until finally, unable to resist her, he slid his arms around and underneath her, one at the small of her back, one between her shoulder blades. He drew her to him, and he kissed her fully, deeply. Her arms twined around his neck. Her body arched up against him, and God, everything in him burned for her.

When he finally took a breath and lifted his head away, she whispered, "Don't you dare start giving me a list of reasons why we shouldn't, Lou. You do, and I swear I'll shoot you with your own gun."

He stared down at her, wanting her so badly his entire body strained to get closer.

"It doesn't have to be anything more than this. Just this," she whispered. "Just us, here and now. No future. No past. No demands or expectations or repercussions, I swear."

He knew she meant it. He also knew she was dead wrong.

She straightened and trailed hot kisses across his neck, along his shoulder. And then she said, "For God's sake, Lou, make love to me. Please."

He thought of all the reasons why he shouldn't. But he was way beyond that kind of self-denial. Had been, he figured, since seeing her naked in that bath.

He was almost trembling—both with wanting her so badly for so long and with certainty that he was making the most horrendous mistake of his life—when he cupped her cheek with one hand and drew her mouth back to his again.

He felt her smiling against his mouth. And then her hands were on his chest, fingers wending their way between his body and hers to deftly open the buttons of his shirt. She pushed it open and then her hands were on him, and he was suddenly living in a state of physical bliss.

17

It was happening. She could hardly believe it was happening. His mouth on hers, his hands pushing the T-shirt up. He lay in the bed beside her now, and he stopped kissing her to look at her as he lifted the shirt over her head and tossed it aside. He looked at her the way a child looks at Santa Claus. Awe and wonder in his eyes. His hand moved, the back of it sliding over her neck and collarbones, then lower to her breast, where each knuckle bumped over her and made her close her eyes in pleasure and arch her back to his touch.

He went still, so she opened her eyes again. "Lou?"

He was still staring at her body. But then he looked away. "I can't do this."

"What?"

He rolled away from her, sitting up, feet to the floor on his side of the bed. "I...I've got that muscle rub on my hands."

"That's not a reason.... Lou?"

He was getting up, walking into the bathroom, though he left the door open. His shirt hung open as he leaned against the counter, turned on the faucets and began washing his hands.

She got up, too, knowing damn good and well he was trying to run away from her yet again. She wasn't standing for it. Not this time, dammit.

She strode into the bathroom and stood behind him at the sink. "Don't do this to me, Lou. Not this time...not after...all of that."

He lowered his head, not even meeting her eyes in the mirror.

"I'm doing this for your own good."

"Why don't you let me worry about what's good for me? You stick to worrying about what's good for you. *I'd* be good for you, Lou. So good..."

"Stop."

Swallowing her pride, she dropped the robe from her shoulders. Just let it fall to the floor at her feet.

Then she gripped his arm and tugged him until he turned around. His eyes widened, then fixed on her, before moving up and down her body over and over.

"Jesus, Maxie, what are you doing?"

"I'm doing this for your own good, Lou." She reached for his hands. They were still wet, dripping. She drew them to her breasts and pressed them to her. Then she let go, so she could slide her own hands over him, underneath the shirt that hung open. "God, I love your chest," she said as she let her palms trace every ripple. "And your abs…" Her hands moved lower.

His hands were squeezing her breasts now. Kneading, gently and rhythmically. She wasn't certain he was aware he was moving them. She slid hers to the front of his jeans and opened the button and zipper. He didn't pull free or run away. She felt him tremble under her touch as she drew the zipper down and slid her hand inside.

He was hard, warm to her touch. She let her fingertips dance over the tip of him and heard his breath come stuttering out. She took his measure by wrapping her hand around him, then sliding it down slowly, squeezing as she did.

He made a sound, a deep groan that told her she was on the right track.

Smiling, nearly drunk with the power she felt surging through her—the knowledge that he couldn't say no to her, even if he wanted to—she dropped to her knees, shoving his jeans down as she went, and before he had even an instant to object, she had him in her mouth.

He swore. A long, growling stream of cuss words, and he even backed up a little, but his ass only hit the sink counter. She took him deeper, then let her lips slide all the way to the tip, where she used her tongue before sucking harder and taking him deep again.

She looked upward as she mouthed him. Saw him tip his head back and close his eyes even as his hands buried themselves in her hair. He was shaking harder now. Trying, she thought, to resist the urge to hold her head captive and plow into her throat. Instead, he slid his hands to her shoulders and firmly pushed her away.

Fine. She got to her feet, wrapped her arms around his neck and took his mouth, pulling him away from the sink as she did. His hands moved to her backside, cupping her cheeks, squeezing them, pulling her hard against him. And he pushed her mouth wide open with his tongue, then dug in, licking deep. She thought maybe she'd pushed him past the place where he was capable of turning away, so she used her hold on his neck to support her as she lifted her legs and wrapped her thighs around him.

His hands tightened harder. She wriggled until she felt his hardness nudging at her opening, and then she pushed herself lower, sheathing him, taking him inside. They sank a little as his knees gave, but he caught himself, straightened and moved, carrying her, on him. He pushed her up against a wall and drove up into her, once, twice, again, each time stabbing more deeply. Then he spun her away from the wall and stumbled toward the bed.

Her back hit the mattress, his weight pressing her into it, his hips using the momentum to drive still more deeply. She tipped her hips high, straining to take all he wanted to give her, though he was already stretching her to her limits. She arched. He caught her hips, halting her. "Easy, babe. Easy. I'll hurt you."

She replied by grasping his ass in her hands and tugging, even sinking her nails in a little. "More," she whispered against his ear. "I want all of you." Then she bit his earlobe.

With a deep shudder, he gave her what she asked

for. His hands slid to her knees, and he pushed. She unlinked her ankles from behind his back and let him open her wider. He pushed her knees apart and upward, and he met her eyes.

"Give it to me," she dared him.

He did, driving into her so deeply that she felt the breath leave her lungs in a gust. And then again and again. Harder, each time filling her, stretching her. She whispered his name, moaned and panted as he pushed her higher. He let go of her knees and slid his hands around her, one cupping her buttocks, fingers sliding between its cheeks, exploring and invading her darkest secrets. The other hand slid between them to find her breast, her nipple. He caught it between thumb and forefinger, began tugging and twisting.

"Yes, yes, yes," she whispered as he pushed the flames higher. She lost all sense of what he was doing or how he was doing it. She felt pleasure, delicious naughty stabs of pain mingling with it as he pinched and pulled and drove. And then she was exploding, and she knew he was, too, when he drove into her so hard she felt him in her womb, pulsing into her, holding her to receive him.

She wrapped her arms and legs around him, holding him to her, tightly, desperately, as unbearable pleasure twisted her body into knots. She held on, and so did he; his arms and body were her anchor as her entire being shattered like a dropped mirror and rained down in a deluge of glittering, shining bits that pierced her body and sank deep, and then melted into quicksilver in the warmth that suddenly lived inside her, warmth Lou had put there. Then the parts of herself gathered together again, smooth and shining and better than before. Her body uncoiled. Her arms went from clutching him to simply holding him.

Lou lifted his head, so he could stare down at her face. She thought he was going to kiss her, smiled just a little in expectation. But he didn't. He rolled off her, then gathered her in his arms and maneuvered them both into a more comfortable position in the bed. Then he drew the covers over them both, turned off the light and lay there, holding her, spooning behind her, his arms around her.

"Lou?"

"Hmm?"

"Are you okay with this?"

She felt his breath wafting over her hair. "Go to sleep, hon. We don't need to pick it apart tonight."

"We don't need to pick it apart at all. It was wonderful, Lou. It was a wonderful, amazing, mind-blowing moment. It doesn't have to be anything more."

He snuggled her close to him.

"Would it be better if I went back to my own room?" she asked.

"Don't even think about it."

"But—"

"Maxie, hon, just shut up and go to sleep, okay? Don't worry about what I'm thinking. *I* don't even know what I'm thinking right now. Ask me again in the morning." To soften the words, he pressed a kiss to her shoulder.

"Okay," she said. But she snuggled closer to him. "It's okay, you know. Nothing has to change, Lou."

"Everything's changed, Max."

She closed her eyes tightly, dreading what he would say next. "Was I...I mean, did you...?"

"You were incredible." His arms tightened around her. "You *are* incredible."

And I love you, she added mentally, imagining those words on his lips. *Say it, Lou. Just say it.*

But he didn't. He snuggled her as if he loved her, held her as if she were precious to him, but he didn't say what she was so longing to hear.

"Just get some sleep, hon. We'll figure this out in the morning."

"Then I hope the morning never comes," she whispered. But to her surprise, she did just what he'd suggested. She fell asleep. Deeply, soundly asleep in his strong arms.

When she woke, she was alone in the bed.

She rolled over onto her back, blinking the sleep from her eyes, then winced because even that small movement caused pain. A deep, dull achiness pervaded her body. Her limbs and back hurt.

What hurt more was the uncertainty in her mind. She knew Lou far too well to think he was going to take this easily. He would be a basket case by now. The man thought too much. Well, he could deny it all he wanted, but she knew damn well he'd been as into her last night as she had been into him, and he couldn't take back what had happened between them.

Hell, that would drive him crazier than anything else.

She sat up in the bed and looked around. The bathroom door was open. She smelled fresh soap, shampoo scents lingering on the air, and got to her feet to pad across the floor, stark naked, to take a look. The mirror was still coated with steam and moisture. She ran a palm across it. A damp towel was slung crookedly on the rack.

He'd gotten up early. Must have been damn quiet about it, too. Showered while she slept and then slipped away. Hell, he was probably halfway back to White Plains by now.

Pressing her lips tight, she corrected herself. He wouldn't leave her—not while she was in danger, at least. He would stick around until the case was solved. No longer, though. She had probably sealed her fate by pushing him into something he wasn't ready for last night. No way would he stay with her now. No way.

Tipping her head to one side and rubbing the back of her neck, she walked to the front of the motel room to take a look out the window. Her car wasn't in the parking lot. But Lou would be back. She had no doubt about that. Besides, it wasn't even six-thirty yet. Might as well shower and be ready for the blow he would no doubt deliver when he came back.

She stepped into the tub, yanked the curtain closed but left the door open, and turned the faucets. When the water was flowing just right, she flipped the control lever, switching the flow to the showerhead. Then she let the hot spray massage and soothe her achy muscles.

"Hello? Maxie, you in there?" Stormy's voice came just as Max was wrist deep in shampoo.

"Yep. You bring breakfast?"

"No, Lou's getting it. I saw him on his way out. Thought I'd come get the dirt. So what happened last night?"

Max finished rinsing the suds from her hair, peeked around the curtain and said, "We did it."

"You…" Stormy blinked, then grinned ear to ear. "Son of a gun! About time you nailed that hide to your wall, girl. Good for you."

"Not really." Max ducked under the spray again to finish up.

"You mean it wasn't…?"

"Oh, hell no. The sex part was great. Earth-shatteringly great. It's the repercussions I'm thinking aren't going to be so hot."

"Oh. There are gonna be repercussions?"

Max turned off the water, snatched a towel from the nearby stack and wrapped it around her as she stepped out of the shower. "Oh, yeah. Any minute now he'll be back here. I imagine he's been awake all night figuring out how to explain to me what a huge mistake this was and why it can never happen again."

"If he thought it was a mistake, he wouldn't have done it."

Max was bent over, briskly rubbing her head with

a towel. But she looked up long enough to say, "I didn't exactly give him much choice."

Stormy's brows went up. "What did you do, take him at gunpoint?"

"Not exactly." She slung the towel from her head onto the counter, finger-combed her hair and then strode back into the bedroom. Stormy sat on a comfy chair with her feet propped on the foot of the un-made bed. "I might as well have, though," Max said. She was reaching for Lou's drawer but decided not to keep wearing all his clean T-shirts. "I have to go to my room for some clothes."

"I'll go for you, if you'll do something for me first," Stormy said.

"Name it." She turned from the dresser, but when she saw Stormy's eyes she knew she had more prob-lems to worry about than just Lou's reaction to their night of passion. Stormy was staring at Max's legs, and when Max looked down she saw the bruises that had formed overnight. Her arms didn't look much better, and she knew there were scratch marks on her neck and face.

"Tell me what went on last night, Max. I know damn good and well Lou didn't put those marks there. What the hell happened to you?"

Max rolled her eyes and tried for a casual attitude.

"I thought I saw someone lurking around outside. Went wandering out there like a moron. All alone. Wound up walking right over a drop and rolling all the way to the bottom." She held out her arms, looking from one to the other, shaking her head as if at her own stupidity. "It looks a lot worse than it is."

"If it didn't, you'd be dead."

"It was stupid. Fortunately, Lou saw me slipping away and came out after me. Got me back here and doctored me up."

"Uh-huh."

"That's how we ended up—"

"Max, knock it off."

Max stopped talking. She bit her lip and knew where she'd screwed up her story.

"I woke up bruised to hell and gone, too. And not wearing the same nightie I wore to bed," Stormy said. "Why is that?"

"Okay. Okay, I'll be honest."

"I attacked you."

"No. No. You were actually the one I saw wandering around. I followed you. You fell, same as I did. It was dark, and the drop came up on you kind of suddenly. Lou would have fallen, too, if he hadn't seen me go over first."

Stormy stared at her, as if willing her to reveal the whole truth.

"You were sleepwalking, I think," Max said.

She didn't mention the dark vampire who'd been out there by the shore, maybe waiting for Stormy. She didn't mention wondering if he'd somehow used his powers to lure Stormy out there to him. And above all else, she didn't tell Stormy that she had pummeled her best friend silly last night in what looked a hell of a lot like defense of the vampire.

No way would she tell her that. Not ever.

"You're not telling me everything."

"I am. I mean it, Storm, that's all of it."

Stormy squinted at her, and Max knew she was angry—not so much at her as at the situation. "I hate not being able to remember. I hate that my body seems so willing to walk around doing things without my knowledge or consent. God, it's frustrating."

"I know. But we're gonna get to the bottom of it, hon. Maybe even today." She pointed at the window. "Look, no clouds. Clear skies."

Stormy started to reply but just then Lou came in. He had his arms full. Coffee, pastries. He'd been to the bakery again. He saw Max standing there still wearing a towel, and his eyes slid lower over her body and got all dark with passion again before they leveled on hers.

"I, uh, was just gonna run over to Max's room to get her some clothes," Stormy said. "It'll take me…ten minutes." She looked at her watch. "Good enough? 'Cause it could take me twenty if you—"

"You don't need to—" Max began.

"Make it fifteen," Lou said.

"In that case, I'll take this with me." Stormy grabbed a cup of coffee from Lou, dug into one of the bags he held for a doughnut and hurried from the room.

Here it comes, Max thought. Here comes the big rationalization as to why what happened, happened, and why it must never, ever happen again.

She was nervous and not looking forward to the conversation. "The weather's not bad this morning, is it?"

"No. Clear as a bell."

She nodded. "I wonder if it will turn bad the minute we start for the boat."

"I still have my doubts there's a vamp alive who could control the weather even while he sleeps by day."

"I don't. Last night he all but admitted he caused yesterday's storm."

Lou set the bags down on the table. He faced her, then moved closer, ran a hand through her slightly crazy, still-damp hair and shook his head slowly. "You're looking at me as if you think I'm about to drive a stake through your heart, kid."

"Aren't you?"

"Nope. I give up. You win."

She blinked three times in quick succession. "I win?"

He nodded. "I think we should get married."

Closing her eyes tight, bending her brows, she let that translate in her brain, then focused on him again and said, *"What?"*

"I said I think we shoul—"

"I heard what you said. I'm just not clear on why you said it. Jesus, Lou, how did we get from 'let's just be friends' to 'let's get married'?"

"Well…it's pretty obvious, isn't it?"

"We had sex. I told you, it doesn't have to mean anything."

"But you want it to. And hell, Max, I'm tired of fighting about it. Besides, it's done. The damage is done now, there's no going back. So this is the only solution."

"What planet are you living on?"

He shrugged. "I'm not being old-fashioned, I'm

being practical." He pushed a hand through his hair and paced away from her. "We've gone too far to go back now. The friendship is already ruined, Max. We can't go back to being platonic—not after that."

She tipped her head to one side. "So why can't we just be lovers for a while? What's wrong with that?"

He lifted his brows. "I don't do the 'lovers' thing. I'm too old to be worrying about dating and romance and courtship. And that's where you're going with all this shit, anyway, isn't it? So why not just skip the middle and get on with it? We'll find out soon enough if we can make this work or not."

She could not believe the words were coming from his mouth. Yeah, he was babbling, but damn, he was hurting her with it.

"Besides, I know you pretty well. Well enough to know you're not on any sort of birth control. Suppose last night's idiocy results in—"

She smacked him. Hard. It shocked her as much as it did him, she thought. His head rocked to one side, and her palm stung. A hot, red imprint darkened his cheek.

"Jesus, Maxie, what the hell?"

"Fuck you, Lou."

"I don't—"

"No, you don't, and I guess you never will. But I'll tell you one thing, when you decide what a colossal mistake you've just made, it's gonna be your move. I'm done. I wouldn't come on to you again if you begged me. I'm tired, too—tired of being the only one interested. Tired of being the only one wanting. Tired of being the one rejected, even after the fact. So fuck you. Fuck you to hell and gone."

She stomped to the door and yanked it open. Stormy was standing there with Max's clothes in her hand. Max grabbed them even as she shouldered past her and a second later was slamming her own motel room door so hard the glass in the window rattled.

"Ho-ly shit," Stormy said. She looked at Lou, who stood there as if he were suffering from battle fatigue. "She was expecting you to tell her it would never happen again, Lou, so I can't imagine why she reacted that strongly."

He swallowed. "I didn't tell her it would never happen again. I asked her to marry me."

Stormy frowned. "No way did that reaction come from a woman who finally won the heart of the man she's been nuts about since the tender age of seventeen. How, exactly, did you…uh…pop the question?"

He frowned at her. "I just said it seemed like the logical thing to do, that's all."

"Logical? Logic isn't a real key selling point where matters of the heart are concerned, Lou. Did you tell her you loved her? Couldn't live without her? That you'd been wrong to fight it so hard for so long?"

He was looking at her as if she were speaking Swahili.

"None of the above, huh? So I take it you based your entire proposal on the fact that you'd finally had sex?"

His eyes widened. Clearly it was finally sinking in that Max had told her what had happened between them last night.

"Kind of like a grudging surrender now that the enemy has taken your stronghold?" Stormy asked.

"Jesus, Storm. You know this is private stuff."

She shrugged. "Hey, if you don't want my opinion—"

"I don't."

She sighed, leaning back in her chair, not the least bit inclined to leave now that the conversation was getting interesting. Besides, she had information she needed to wheedle out of Lou, and she thought he was just shaken enough to let a few things slip.

"I hope that doesn't hurt your feelings," he said,

after a moment of what looked like reflection. "I mean, I love you like a kid sister, Storm, but this is personal."

"I totally understand."

He nodded.

"But I'd be derelict in my duty as your friend—and Maxie's—if I didn't tell you, Lou, you probably hurt her pretty bad just now."

"I realize that."

"She's reading it just like I did. You felt she'd defeated you, so you might as well stop fighting."

He lifted his eyebrows, as if maybe he was interested in what she had to say now that she was saying something he didn't know. "You think I wounded her pride?"

She nodded. "You annihilated it. But that's the least of it. You probably also broke her heart."

"Hell."

"If I know Max—and I do, you know—she won't touch you again with a ten-foot pole. Not after this."

He drew a breath, opened his mouth.

"Don't even bother telling me maybe that's for the best. Jesus, Lou, are you really this dense or just clinging to the act out of habit?"

"What?"

She closed her eyes. "When you finally figure out what you want, you're going to have to be the one to go get it. You'll have to go to her—on your knees, I imagine. Possibly with a burnt offering."

He was back to looking confused again.

She rolled her eyes. "Poor Max, after what happened last night, out on the beach—and then this. She must be a basket case."

He frowned at her. "I hadn't even thought of that. It *was* a rough night."

"She's bruised to hell and gone." She lowered her eyes, pressed a hand to her forehead. "God, when I saw her this morning, I couldn't believe…"

"You can't go blaming yourself for that, Storm."

"Of course I can. I'm the one who led her out there."

"But you're not responsible for what you do when you—you know—lose it."

She lifted her head, met his eyes. "If not me, then who?"

He shrugged. "Maybe no one."

Stormy got out of her chair and paced away from him, to keep her face hidden so she wouldn't reveal anything. "Bad enough I led her out there," she said. "I might be able to forgive myself for that. But the rest…"

"Come on, Storm. Max is tough. If you'd been anywhere close to really doing her harm, she'd have fought back."

Oh, God, it was true. Max had lied—she'd thought as much. Read it in her eyes, plain as day. She just hadn't wanted to believe. "She wouldn't fight back—not against me, Lou. She treats me as if I'm made of bone china. She probably just lay there and let me pound her."

"She's fine, Storm. It looks worse than it is."

"That's what she said." She pursed her lips. "Only she said she got that way from a fall. I figured it was me. I just had to know for sure."

Lou swore under his breath.

"Sorry, Lou. I wasn't trying to trick you but…you understand, don't you?"

He sighed, then stomped around for a minute. Finally he found his rapidly cooling coffee. "I guess so," he said at last.

"We have to do something about this. Take some kind of precautions to make sure I can't hurt her again. God, if I did any real damage, I'd never be able to forgive myself."

He nodded. "I'll just have to keep her with me. Make sure she's not out of my sight again."

"Oh, yeah, and you've made *that* a real possibility."

He shot her a look.

"Come on, Lou, you gotta admit, you fucked up. At least when I tear into her I'm out of my mind. You manage to do it in your normal waking state."

"I didn't tear into her."

"You cut her heart right out of her chest. Don't even pretend you don't realize that at this point."

He closed his eyes, and she saw real pain in his face. "I'll fix it."

"You'd better."

18

The knock on her door came as Max was tossing her stuff into a suitcase. She never broke her pace, just called, "Go away."

"Max, it's me," Stormy said. "I'm alone. Let me in."

She stopped packing long enough to turn to the mirror, knuckle her eyes dry. Then she went to the door and checked through the peephole. Not that she thought Stormy would try to trick her, but it didn't hurt to make sure. Then she flipped the lock and unfastened the chain.

Stormy came inside, met her eyes, then hugged her hard. "I'm sorry, honey."

"Hell, don't be. This has been a long time coming."

"I wasn't talking about you and Lou. That game is far from over, anyway." She nodded at the suitcase on the bed. "What are you, forfeiting and going home?"

Max rolled her eyes and sat on the bed. "If you weren't talking about me and Lou, then what are you apologizing for?"

"For beating the hell out of you last night."

"You didn't—"

"Don't bother denying it, Max. I figured out what had happened all by myself, then tricked Lou into confirming it for me. And don't blame him for that. You've got his head spinning so bad he doesn't know which way is up."

Max sighed, hardly knowing which part of that little speech to address first.

"I'm really sorry I hurt you, Max," Stormy said, choosing for her.

"You didn't hurt me. That wasn't you last night. It was someone else."

"Or some*thing* else." She shrugged. "Either way—"

"Don't torture yourself over this, Stormy. It wasn't you. We both know it."

Stormy closed her eyes, lowered her head. When she brought it up again and looked at Max, she said, "So you're leaving?"

Max looked at her suitcase. "I don't know what the hell I'm doing."

"It's not like you to give up. I thought 'never surrender' was your second-most ironclad motto, right after 'trust no one.'"

"Used to be. Hell, Storm, I think I've been deluding myself all this time. Had myself convinced he really loved me, deep down."

"And now you think you were wrong?"

"Now I *know* I was wrong."

"Because he made love to you, and it was awful?"

Max swung her eyes to Stormy's. "It was wonderful. I told you that."

"Right. Then it's because he asked you to marry him?"

"Hell, he didn't *ask*. He just threw it out there, said it was the reasonable thing to do. Acted as if he'd been backed into a corner by a tiger and it was the only escape route."

"And you think he really feels that way?"

"Yeah. I do."

"I disagree. But all that is beside the point, anyway.

You can't just leave, not with Delia and Janie still missing. Jason's counting on you."

She lowered her head. "I know that. And you are, too."

"Don't stay on my account. Hell, getting away from me might be the best move you could make about now."

Maxine frowned. "What are you talking about? Hell, Storm, I assumed if I packed my shit and stomped home, you'd stomp home right beside me. You telling me I'm wrong about that?"

Stormy looked up at the ceiling. "I have to stay here."

"For the girls?"

She brought her gaze level with Max's again, and her eyes were dead serious. "No. I think whatever's wrong with me is somehow linked to this place." She made a face. "Sounds so freakin' stupid, doesn't it? I've never been here before in my life, I don't know anyone here, and yet—"

"No, it doesn't sound stupid. It makes some kind of sense," Max said. "It's worse near the shore, near the ocean. But only here, not so much back in Easton."

Stormy nodded.

"Don't let this freak you, hon, but…that vampire put in an appearance last night. When you first lost it, it almost seemed like you were…trying to protect him."

"Protect him from what?"

"From me."

Stormy frowned hard. "There's no way I could be linked to a vamp. I'm mortal. One hundred percent mortal. I don't even have that Belladonna Antigen in my blood—you said only people with that could become vamps, right?"

"Right. The vamps call them 'The Chosen.' They watch over them, bond with them, though they rarely make contact until and unless they decide to…change them."

"So there's no reason—no possible way there could be any…any bond between me and this crazy vampire. Hell, none of this makes sense." She bit her lip.

"But?"

Stormy looked up.

"I sense a 'but' there. Come on, Storm. Talk to me. What else don't I know?"

Stormy closed her eyes. "I saw his face. Before we ever came here, I saw his face inside my mind. That same face those women drew. How could that be, Max?"

Max got to her feet, turned to her suitcase, started

taking items out of it and returning them to the dresser drawers. "That settles it. I'm not going anywhere until we get to the bottom of this."

Stormy started to argue. "Our mission here is about the girls. That's where you need to focus, not on me and my impending nervous breakdown."

"Don't bother," Max said, before Stormy could get another word out. "I've made up my mind. The thing is, I'm through with the whole cautious approach here. I'm done messing with that egomaniac vamp, and I'm done tiptoeing around this town. We're getting to the bottom of what's wrong with you, and we're getting those girls the hell off that island. Today."

"How?"

Max dropped the last item into a drawer, slammed it closed and turned to face Stormy. "I've got a few ideas."

"What kind of ideas?" Stormy's eyes widened almost before she finished the question. "You're not thinking of going out to that island alone, are you?"

"Of course not," Max said, though she had every intention of doing just that—at the very first opportunity. She couldn't take Stormy out there—that island was no place for her. Max sensed it to her core—besides, that was exactly what the vamp wanted.

Oh, they would try to get out to the island today, but she had no doubt another storm would crop up when they did. Which meant she was going to have to go by night. Without Stormy. And right now, she didn't want Lou going along with her, either.

Time to change the subject. "I was thinking more along the lines of hypnosis."

Stormy tilted her head to one side. "You mean for me."

"Yeah. Don't act like you weren't thinking it, too. I saw that card in your shopping bag with the books the other night."

Sighing, Stormy didn't deny it. "I was talking to a woman in one of the bookstores. She told me this woman, Martha Knoxville, is supposedly very good. Spotless reputation. I was toying with the idea."

"So?"

"Jesus, Max, I'm not sure how comfortable I am with the idea of putting my mind into the hands of a stranger. Someone whose name I picked out of a stack of cards in a bookstore."

"Honey, your mind is in the hands of someone or something you didn't pick at all. And if you *are* linked somehow to this vampire, maybe hypnosis can tell us more about him."

"I don't know." Stormy looked around the room,

almost as if she expected to find someone there, lurking in the shadows. "I'm scared, Max."

Max shrugged. "Hell, if you don't want to do it, never mind. I'll think of something else."

Stormy thought it over. "Suppose I say something I shouldn't while I'm under? I mean, I can't be babbling about vamps to an outsider, Max."

"If that happens, we chalk it up to delusions—mention the recent head injury and go on our way."

"You think she'd buy it?"

"I don't know. What other options do we have?" Max asked.

"We could go to a vampire." Stormy blurted it quickly, probably without thinking it through first. "They can read minds, probe and poke around inside people's heads. Dante could do it. By now maybe Morgan can, as well, and that Sarafina—she must be good at it."

"Sarafina doesn't speak to our side of the…family. Not since my sister stole her precious Dante from her." Max sighed. "Besides, it could be dangerous to bring any of them here."

"We don't *have* to bring them here, or even tell them what's going on. We just go to them. Ask them to take a look around in my belfry, see what sorts of bats they stir up."

Max sighed. "If one of them reads your mind, Storm, they're going to know what's happening here without us having to tell them. And they're going to insist on coming out here to help."

She nodded slowly. "So if this vamp is a dangerous one…"

"I'd be putting my sister, the man she loves and their friends in harm's way," Max said.

Stormy nodded. "Okay. Okay. Let's just call this chick and make me an appointment. Meanwhile, I think we need to at least try to get out to that island, don't you? By day, when it's safe?"

"Great minds think alike," Max said. "But I don't think you should go. It's bad for you."

"I knew that's what you were up to. Don't think for one minute I'm letting you go out there alone, Max."

Max rolled her eyes. "You'd be risking another episode."

"Yeah? Well, do me a favor and be ready this time. Kick my ass, hold me down, and make whoever is looking out through my eyeballs tell you who they are and what they're doing in my body."

Max nodded, but she didn't like it.

"We should bring Lou. Jason, too. Just in case I

go off on you, Max. I don't want to risk hurting you again. Especially not out there."

Shaking her head, Max said, "I was planning to send Lou home to White Plains after breakfast."

Stormy's eyebrows rose in two arches. "You really have given up on him, haven't you? God, Max, what happened? I never thought you'd stop wanting Lou."

"I never wanted him like this. Served up like a goddamn martyr marching bravely to the pyre. Forget it. I'm better than that, and I deserve better than that."

She turned away as she spoke, ducking her friend's perceptive, probing eyes.

"You're right," Stormy said. "You *do* deserve better. It would be a lot easier to walk away and go looking for it if you weren't head over heels in love with the freakin' idiot, though, wouldn't it?"

Max sniffled a little, nodded. "A hell of a lot easier," she agreed.

"He won't leave, you know. You can try to send him home, but he won't leave."

"Probably not. But only because he thinks we're in danger."

"And because he cares."

"Not the way I want him to," Max said. "He cares

like a chivalrous, protective, hero cop cares. Like a favorite uncle—the good kind. Like a father figure. Not like a lover."

"I don't think he knows how he cares. I really don't."

Max shrugged. "I think he knows. I'm the one who's been in denial." Then she got up and gave her head a shake. "Listen to me going on about my love life—or lack thereof—when you're going through all this hell. Where's that card? We need to call and make you that appointment."

Stormy came to her, extracted the card from her pocket and handed it over.

Max reread it. Martha Knoxville, Certified Hypnotherapist.

"She's only an hour away," Stormy said. "What do you think?"

"I think you're taking a road trip. It'll do you good to get out of this town."

"And you good to get away from Lou?"

Max nodded, though she had no intention of accompanying Stormy to the session. She was damn well going to pay that vampire on the island a visit—find out just what the hell it was he wanted from her. She was finished waiting. He wanted her on that damn island? Well, fine. She would go there.

But she wouldn't be unprepared. And she wouldn't drag her best friend into danger. Maybe she could take Stormy away, get her in to see this hypnosis lady, then slip away and come back here without her. Stormy would never forgive her, but it would be worth it to end this thing.

She handed the card back to Stormy. "Call her. See if she has an opening today."

Nodding, Stormy picked up the phone.

Lou didn't know how he'd messed things up as thoroughly as he had. He only knew he hated this new state of affairs. Max was as cold and distant as if he'd kicked her favorite puppy. Not hostile, just… stony.

She and Stormy joined him and Jason at the shore, where he'd walked to check out the little boat. It was a gorgeous day, warm and sunny. No one would suspect a vampire might be lurking nearby. Not with the sun beaming down and the trees all green, budding, blossoming.

"It's not going to work, Lou," Max said. She was close to him. God, everything in him wanted to turn around and pull her against him, kiss her anger away. But for some asinine reason, he resisted the impulse.

Instead he straightened. "The boat's sound. I don't see why—"

"Look."

She was pointing. He turned to look where she was looking and saw a mass of roiling black clouds gathering in the distance. Right before his eyes the sky went darker. Thunder rolled slowly over the sea toward them. The wind picked up.

"He told me last night he would never allow us to come to that island by day. But I have another idea."

"Yeah?"

She nodded. "Storm and I are driving down to Salem this morning."

Lou frowned at her. "What's in Salem?"

"I'm going to see a hypnotist," Stormy said. "See if she can figure out what's going on inside my head these days."

Lou looked out at the ocean. The storm hovered there, as if in waiting. He looked again at the boat and would have sworn the wind whipped up at that precise moment, harder than before. The thunder's dull rumble became a roar.

He almost rolled his eyes but managed to kill the urge before he pissed Max off even more. "Do you really think a hypnotist can help, Storm?"

"It can't possibly hurt," she said. "Besides, Max thinks it's a good idea. And I trust her."

Lou shot a look at Max, but she was deliberately not looking at him. "I do, too. It's just—it seems like a waste of time. We could be here, canvassing more of the locals."

"You *will* be here. Storm and I are going to Salem alone."

Lou felt rebuffed but tried not to show it. "I think your car keys are still in my room," he said. "Walk back with me and I'll get them for you."

He saw the look she shot Stormy, but decided not to try to interpret it, just turned and started toward his room. She caught up with him a few steps later. He glanced sideways at her. "I'm sorry, Max."

"For what, Lou?"

Sighing, knowing damn well he wasn't going to come up with the right answer, he decided it would be better to do this privately. He picked up the pace, not speaking again until they were back at the motel. He opened his door, then held it for her. She went in, and he followed.

"I never meant to hurt you, Max. Hell, that's the last thing in the world I would want to do. You know that, don't you?"

She turned around to face him, looked up at him.

"I know. Look, this isn't your fault. You can't help how you feel. You've been telling me all along that you didn't want that kind of a relationship with me. I should have listened."

Her words registered in his brain as the ones he'd been wanting to hear her say for a long time. And they landed like shards of razor-edged glass. They cut him. Why?

"I knew if we slept together it would change everything. And I didn't want that to happen. But, Max, it was special. It meant something to me, don't think it didn't."

She sighed. "It isn't the sex that's changed things. It's the fact that I finally got the message. And that would have happened, sooner or later, sex or not."

"I don't know what message it is you think I gave you, but—"

She held up a hand. "Look, just give me some time, okay? I've been living with this fantasy so long, I hardly know what to do now that it's gone."

Her voice broke a little on the last few words. It killed him to realize just how deeply he'd hurt her. "What fantasy, Max?"

She lowered her head, shook it slowly. "You don't want to hear that. Not now."

"I do. I really do." He reached out for her, and

when she swayed out of his reach, he felt as if he'd been kicked in the *cojones*. She had never avoided his touch before. Never. Hell, she was usually trying to instigate a touch.

She paced away slowly, oblivious to the fact that he'd even noticed her ducking his hand. "For years I've managed to convince myself that deep down, you were in love with me. That you just hadn't realized it, but that sooner or later you would. And that when you did…" She stopped walking, lifted her head, met his eyes. "It was all so perfect in my mind. We'd be together, work together, spend every night holding each other. We'd be so damn happy…." She seemed to square her shoulders, and her eyes glittered with tears, delivering another blow, this one catching him squarely in the gut and knocking the wind out of him. "It doesn't matter. I was living in a silly bubble of wishful thinking. The bubble's been burst. My feet are firmly planted in reality now. I'll be okay. I just need a little time to adjust to it."

He didn't know what to say. "I never said I didn't want you. In fact, I thought it was probably pretty obvious to you after last night that I did. Do."

"You want me in spite of yourself. You can't be my casual lover, because you're too guilt-ridden, and you can't be my serious lover, either."

"Jesus, Max, I offered to marry you. You can't get much more serious than that!"

"You don't love me. Do you think I want to spend my life with a husband who only married me because I wore him down?" She lowered her eyes, shaking her head. "You were right all along, Lou. We're gonna have to settle for just being friends."

"How are we going to do that when you're this angry with me?" He felt close to panic, and didn't know why.

"I'm not angry with you, Lou. My pride's wounded. I'm embarrassed and kind of sad. But I don't blame you for that, and you can't blame me, either. Hell, I'm bound to be a little sad to see my favorite dream come to an end. But I'll be okay. We'll be okay. Promise."

He lowered his head, not feeling okay at all. About anything.

"You can go back to White Plains if you want. I won't give you any more guilt about it. Grab a bus ticket or whatever. Send me the bill."

"You know better than that, Max."

She held his eyes for a long moment. "Yeah. I guess I do. Well, stick around, then. We'll solve this thing, and then…and then I guess it'll be over."

He felt like an assassin. Like the cruelest, meanest

man in all creation. He felt as if he had done far
worse than kick her favorite puppy.

"I'm going with Storm for the day, Lou. It'll do me
good to put a little space between us. By the time I
get back, I'll be over this. I promise."

He tried to give her a warm smile, because he
didn't know what the hell to say to her to make this
right. She saved him trying by holding out a hand.
"My keys?"

"Oh. Right." He got the keys from the dresser,
handed them to her.

"See you later this afternoon, okay?"

"Okay."

She turned and left the room.

He watched Stormy wave goodbye to Jason and
join Max as she walked toward her car, and a few
seconds later, they were pulling out of the parking
lot and driving out of sight. There was an odd heavi-
ness in Lou's chest. A pulling, aching sensation he'd
never felt before.

He heaved a sigh that did nothing to ease it, then
headed back outside to where Jason stood watching
them go.

"It's the perfect opportunity," Lou said.

Jason looked at him oddly. "Opportunity to do
what?"

"You and I have a job to do, pal. One way or another, we're gonna explore that island today."

All the way down to Salem, Max had been somber. Oh, she made a valiant effort at light conversation, even a few jokes. But she couldn't hide the pain in her eyes. Stormy wanted to fix things, but she knew it wasn't possible. There were only two people who could fix this mess, and she wasn't either one of them.

Max had fallen into another deep brooding silence by the time they neared the town limits, and Stormy wanted to draw her out. "You know, Morgan and Dante could easily be on their way back to the mansion by now."

Max nodded. "I suppose they could."

"Lydia will tell them where we are. And they'll probably call, or even show up here."

"I hope we'll be finished with all this before they do."

If what Max suspected were true, and Storm had picked up some kind of spiritual hitchhiker while she'd been on the other side in her coma, then maybe Morgan could help. She'd been there, too. They'd been beyond the mists together, found their way back together—even though at that point they had never even met.

But Max didn't want other vampires—her friends, much less her sister—involved in this case. Stormy reminded herself that talking to Morgan about any of this would probably result in just that. And if Morgan became involved, her life might be at risk. Okay. So she would save Morgan as a last resort. Maybe if this hypnosis thing failed...

Martha Knoxville lived in a house on a quiet lane in Salem, within walking distance of Salem Village, aka Tourism Central. It sat side by side with other houses like it, tall and rather slender, with a steeply pitched roof, and red shingles, shutters and front door.

To one side, the side toward the short, paved drive-way, there was a second entrance, with a hanging sign that read Office.

That was the entrance Stormy and Max used. It led into what looked for all the world like an ordinary living room, rich with hardwood and done in earth tones. There was a huge aquarium along one wall, with brightly colored fish of many shapes and sizes swimming slowly back and forth. Against another wall stood a man-size fountain, with water cascading down a stone face and collecting in a basin that appeared to be carved out of rock. There were plants everywhere. Large trees in the corners, wispy, hanging baskets on the ceilings. An over-stuffed brown sofa and matching chairs looked so inviting that Stormy wondered if anyone could come in here and resist just sitting down, even for a moment.

"You must be Miss Jones," the woman said. "Or may I call you Tempest?"

Stormy looked up and saw a short, round woman in perhaps her mid-thirties, with a luxurious mass of curling brown hair that reached most of the way down her back. Her eyes were brown, too, sincere and friendly, and her smile was one of the brightest Stormy thought she had ever seen.

"You can call me Storm. Everyone does."

"Storm," the woman said, then she nodded. "Tempest. I get it. That's clever." She offered a hand. "You can call me Martha."

"Good to meet you, Martha." Stormy took her hand. It was warm and soft. "This is my friend Max."

Max took the woman's hand next. "Thanks for seeing us on such short notice."

"Oh, it's not a problem. It's not as if I have a constant stream of clients. Please, sit. Make yourselves comfortable while I get the tea."

"Oh, please, don't go to any trouble," Stormy began. "We're fine."

Martha nodded. "The tea is part of the session. Chamomile and honey. Helps you relax."

"Oh."

Martha hurried from the room, and Stormy sat down on the overstuffed sofa with a sigh. "You really think this is going to work?" she asked.

Max sank into a spot beside her. "I could get hypnotized just watching those fish," she said, nodding toward the aquarium. "Look at the blue one."

Stormy nodded, falling into watching the round, fat fish move slowly through the water, first in one direction, then in another. He was a blue that Stormy would never have believed existed in nature.

Martha returned with a tray bearing three cups of steaming, aromatic tea. She set it on the small coffee table and took a cup. Stormy obediently took one, too, and sipped.

While they sipped, the woman asked, "So why don't you tell me what's been going on with you, Storm? How is it you think hypnosis can help?"

19

"What's wrong with Max?" Jason asked.

He'd joined Lou in his motel room as the storm gathered outside. Lou would have preferred solitude, but he didn't imagine this was any time for wallowing in regrets or wondering what the hell to do next.

"What makes you think something's wrong?" he asked.

"She's acting differently this morning." Jason studied Lou for a second, then said, "So are you, for that matter. You two have a fight?"

"No."

"Misunderstanding, then?"

"It's between us, okay?"

"Sure, fine."

"Actually, it's just as well they took off without us. It gives us a chance to get out to that island without Storm going all haywire."

Jason shook his head. "Bad idea, Lou. Really bad." He looked at the dark, roiling sky. As if on cue thunder rumbled and rolled in. "Not that we could get out there, anyway."

"Look, sooner or later we *have* to check that place out, storm or otherwise. I don't want Max out there, and I know damn good and well she's out of patience. She'll get there come hell or high water. Unless we do it first."

Jason frowned and looked down at his feet.

"Besides," Lou went on, "if we take Storm out there, God only knows what would happen. And you and I both know there's no way those two would let us go without them if they knew what we were up to. So clearly we have to go when they aren't around."

Jason rolled his eyes. "You think Max is pissed at you now, what do you think she'll be if you pull something like this?"

"I never said she was pissed at me."

"She's pissed at someone. I know it's not me. She's spending the day with Storm, despite the fact that

Storm is a threat to her in her condition, so it must not be her. That leaves you."

Ignoring Jason's observations, Lou continued with his train of thought. "This guy's a vamp. He's not going to be any threat to us during daylight hours. So we have to go during the day."

"Yeah, and what about this storm?"

Lou walked to the window, looked up at the sky. "We're just going to have to deal with it."

Jason came to stand beside him, looked out at the same black sky. Even as they stood looking out, fat drops began splatting against the window. Just a few, then a few more. "Jesus, it's like he knows what we're thinking."

"I think maybe he does."

Jason swallowed hard. "I'll ask you once more, Lou. Don't do this. Don't go out there today."

Lou met his eyes, tried to read what was going on behind them. "Sorry, Jason. I have to do this. And not just for your sister and her friend. I gotta do it for Max. I need this thing over with so I can…focus on other things."

Jason nodded, his face grim. "I'll run back to my room. Grab a flashlight, jacket—cell phone, just in case they work out there." He looked at Lou. "There were no life jackets in that boat."

"Not a one," Lou said. "Can you swim?"

Jason nodded, then opened the door. The storm came slashing in at him, and the look he sent back to Lou spoke volumes. No one could swim in this.

Then he left. Lou spent a moment checking his gun, making sure it was loaded and tucked under his clothes, where it would remain dry. He pulled on a coat and dropped a flashlight into the pocket. He carried his jackknife and cell phone. As a final thought, he decided to leave a note for Max.

Those four lines took longer to compose than anything he'd ever written.

Finally he nodded, set the note on the nightstand and pulled on his coat. Then he stepped outside the door and went to Jason's room. Just as he lifted his hand to knock, he swore he heard Jason's voice. As if he were talking to someone.

Frowning, Lou moved to the window beside the door and tried to get a glimpse inside, but the curtains were drawn. A second later, he drew away as he heard Jason approaching the door. It swung open.

Lou pretended he'd been about to knock, all the while looking past Jason into the room beyond him. He didn't see any sign of anyone. The bathroom door was open, and he could see a good portion of the room beyond it. No one in sight there, either.

Jason's coffee cup sat on the stand, right beside the telephone.

Had he made a call, then?

Lou swallowed hard.

"Let's go," Jason said, stepping out and pulling the door closed behind him. He hunched his shoulders against the rain, and together they hustled around behind the motel, across the open field. The wind and rain seemed to ease as they entered the woods. The trees must be breaking more of the storm than he had expected, Lou thought.

They moved fast, all the way through the woods, finally emerging at the top of a steep path on the far side.

As soon as they stepped out of the trees, Lou went still, lifting his head to the sky, swiping a hand through his hair. "It's stopping."

"What?" Jason asked.

"The rain, it's letting up."

Jason looked around, glancing up at the sky. "I think the wind's eased a little, too," he said. "Hell, maybe we can make it out there alive after all."

Lou frowned, first at Jason, then at the sky. The clouds seemed thinner and in the process of break-ing up. What the hell was this?

Swallowing hard, he walked down the path, all

the way to the bottom, and approached the boat. No clouds appeared. No thunder rumbled. No wind blew. He glanced at Jason. "I don't like this."

Jason swallowed. "Maybe he's not in tune to us. Maybe it's just the girls."

"That would make sense if the storm had stopped when they left town. But it didn't. It kept getting stronger. Then it's like…it changed its mind." He glanced at Jason. "Or *he* did."

"Maybe we shouldn't go out there after all," Jason said. "Lou, he's probably got henchmen lining the damned beaches."

Lou patted his side. "I didn't plan to go in there unarmed, Jay." But the look on Jason's face was anything but reassured. He seemed reluctant, but resolved.

Lou felt for him. Then he said, "You know, you're right. It might be risky going out there, even now that the storm has let up. And even during the day. Maybe it would be better to leave someone behind— someone who'd know where to send the cavalry if I should fail to come back."

Jason glanced at him. "You think I'm afraid to go out there, and you're giving me an out. I'm as much a man as you are, Lou."

Lou shrugged—frankly disagreeing, though he

wasn't about to say so. "Look, it's up to you. I'm going. With you or without."

"With," Jason said. "You need me."

"I do?"

"Yeah."

Lou nodded, gave the kid a grudging nod. He saw the fear in Jason's eyes. Hell, it wasn't suspicious behavior. The kid *should* be afraid. He'd never dealt with anything like this before. Still, Lou couldn't shake the feeling that there was more than just fear behind Jason's eyes. There was something else, some knowledge.

Briefly, Lou glanced back at the spot where he'd found Max standing face-to-face with the most powerful vampire she'd ever encountered, defending her friend. He recalled the way she'd looked when he'd gotten her back to the room. It killed him to think of the pain she must have been in.

And he'd caused her even more.

The best thing he could do for Max right now, he thought, was find the missing girls, get them the hell out of that place and take Max back to Maine. He didn't know what the hell would happen after that, how to even begin fixing what he had so thoroughly broken. But he had to start with this.

He grabbed the back end of the boat. Jason helped.

They dragged and pushed it into the water, which meant walking in almost to their knees. Then they climbed aboard, and Lou lowered the motor into the water, while Jason used an oar to push them out a little farther. Lou pulled the rip cord, once, twice— on the third try the thing sputtered to life, and then they were off. And the weather did not change. If anything, it grew clearer.

Almost as if something had decided to let them come. Hell, did it really matter? He had to do this. He owed it to Max.

"Now, Storm, you are deeply, deeply asleep. Relaxed and safe. Comfortable and warm and perfectly safe."

Max thought the woman's voice was so soothing, so mesmerizing, that she might fall into a trance state herself at any moment. She tapped the woman's shoulder, tipped her head slightly.

Frowning, the woman followed her to the far side of the room. Max said, "I have to go. When she wakes, tell her—"

"I don't think that's a good idea, Max," Martha said, keeping her voice low.

"But...she'll be all right. It's important that I—"

"She's frightened. We have no idea what the

session might reveal. It could be very traumatic for her." Max frowned, sending a look back at Stormy, who sat, relaxed, her eyes closed, on the sofa. "Your friend needs you, Maxine," Martha went on. "Besides, this won't take long."

As if to punctuate her words, Stormy whispered, "Max?" and lifted a hand, grasping at air.

"She needs you," Martha repeated.

Swallowing hard, Max returned to the sofa, closed her hand around Stormy's and sat down beside her. Stormy relaxed again, a sigh escaping her lips.

"You're safe, Storm," Martha said, returning to her former position in the chair facing Stormy. "You're safe. Max is here, and I'm here, and nothing can harm you. Understand?"

"Yes," Stormy said. "Safe." Her hand closed more tightly around Max's.

"I wish to speak now to the other. The being inside this body who is not Tempest Jones. Are you there?"

Nothing. Stormy sat on the sofa, head leaning against the back of it, eyes closed, her breathing deep and even.

"Please, talk to me. I wish to speak to the other."

Stormy's head snapped up. Her eyes flashed open. Her lips parted, and she spewed forth a stream of words that might as well have been Babylonian for all Max could make of them. Romanian? Jesus.

"Lasă-mă în pace!"

Max saw Martha jump a little, saw her blink in surprise. "Look at her eyes," Max whispered. "I told you they would change color."

Martha nodded, patting Max's hand as if to calm her. Her voice remained placid, though she was obviously startled. "You'll have to speak in English, my friend."

The person—it wasn't Stormy, Max couldn't think of it as Stormy—nodded slowly, seemed to think, then spoke. "Leave me alone."

"I will. Soon. But first you need to tell me who you are."

"I am she. She is me."

"You are Storm?"

"I am."

"Then who is the other woman inside you? The one with the blue eyes, the one who speaks English?"

"She is me. We are one."

"She doesn't know you."

"She doesn't remember. I am from before."

"From before?"

The person nodded. Amazing how different she

looked from the Stormy that she knew and loved, Max thought.

"Why do you attack Storm's friends?" Martha asked, slowly, patiently. "After all, if you are Storm, then they are your friends, too."

"I protect my own."

"I see." Martha's voice remained calm, soothing. "And they are a threat to something of your own?"

The person nodded again, slowly and totally un-Storm-like.

"Can you tell me what?"

"Him. *Prinţ meu.*" The eyes fell closed. "I'm so weak here. Take me back to the ocean."

"First, tell me your name."

"I'm sick. *Sunt bolnav.*"

"Please, just your name. Then you can return."

The eyes opened slightly, the black color changing slowly, growing lighter. "Names mean nothing. I've had so many. Now, my name is Tempest. Once I was called Mina, and before that I was Elisabeta. But it doesn't matter. We are one and the same."

Her eyes closed again, then slowly opened, and when they did, they were bright, clear sapphire-blue. "Storm," she said in her own voice. "My name is Storm."

Martha nodded slowly. Max couldn't take her eyes

off her best friend. She was herself again, looking relaxed, normal. "Storm, tell me how you feel when you're near the ocean in Endover."

She smiled. "It's like coming home."

"Is that because you've lived in a place like it before? In your childhood, perhaps?"

"No. We moved to White Plains from Iowa when I was a little girl."

"And how do you feel when you experience the… the blackouts you've been having?"

Stormy's body stiffened a little. "It's as if I've been asleep and dreamed it all. Only in the dream, it wasn't me. It was someone else, doing things I would never do. And then, when I wake, I find out it was me who did them."

"So you can see the things you do, in these dreams?"

Her head lowered a bit as she nodded. "Sometimes. It makes me feel even more guilty."

"It's not your fault, Storm."

"It feels as if it is."

"When you do see these things, in the dreams, who is doing them?"

Stormy's brows creased. "A woman."

"And what does she look like?"

"She's beautiful. Skin like cream, wild golden hair, ebony eyes."

"Do you know her?"

Stormy shook her head, then stopped in midmotion. "It feels as if I should. She's very familiar to me. Like when you run into someone you haven't seen in a long time and you know you know them, but you can't place them, or when you see your doctor's receptionist in the grocery store and don't recognize her out of context."

"I see."

"I wish I could remember her."

"I think you will, when you're ready. Storm, I want you to relax just a bit more deeply with me now. I'm going to count you down, all right? I'm going to take you a little bit deeper."

Jason settled onto the bench seat and snapped the oar back into its spot—there were holders mounted to the inside of the boat, one on each side. Lou sat on a smaller seat in the rear and used the handle on the motor to steer the boat away from the motel.

"So where do you suppose this boat came from?" Jason asked.

"I don't know. I suspect it's Gary's, but that's just a hunch."

"Gary? The motel manager?"

Lou nodded as he guided the boat around a bend in the shoreline. He spotted the lighthouse ahead and aimed toward it. When they got a little closer, the island appeared on the horizon. "There it is." The island rose from the sea, a dark shadow against the lighter sky, swathed in mist.

Jason looked out over the bow, his back to Lou. "Are you sure you want to do this?"

"Gotta do it. You want your sister back, don't you?" And he wanted Max back. The thought whispered through Lou's mind like an errant breeze. He didn't even try to analyze it.

"I'd do anything—*will* do anything—I have to, to get Delia back," Jason said. He turned to glance back at Lou. "You would, too, wouldn't you? If it were Max?"

"I would."

"Then you understand."

Lou frowned a little, wondering what he was getting at, but then Jason faced front again and said, "So how we gonna do this?"

"I think I see a roof. On the far side of the island, see it?"

Jason nodded. Trees blocked the structure, but peaks and gables were coming into view.

He said, "Why don't we beach it on this side, so we can't be seen from the house. Just in case."

"Good idea." Lou slowed the boat as they drew closer, guiding them around to the west end, where their arrival would be concealed from the house. Then he cut the motor and grabbed the oars, rowing the rest of the way.

Near shore, they both jumped out and dragged the boat up onto the pebbly beach. Lou had landed it near a clump of scraggly brush, and they wedged the boat into its cover as far as possible, to keep it concealed.

Then Lou straightened and looked around. The island was dense with pines, large, old trees that towered high and kept the ground swathed in shadow. Pine cones littered the ground, along with a thick blanket of browning needles. The scent was amazing. Max would love this place, he thought as he started walking. She would absolutely love it.

He and Jason picked their way beneath the giant pines. Birds were singing, flitting among the trees, startling him every time they took off. He kept walking, eventually finding the place where the trees ended and the house stood, glaring down at him as if in silent anger. It was built of huge rough-hewn blocks of white granite, with rounded turrets at the corners, flanking the giant arch-topped wooden entry doors. It looked like a church, Lou thought. Or a castle.

"Doesn't look like getting inside will be easy," Jason said.

"Getting inside won't be any trouble at all." Both men spun around, because the voice came from behind them.

Chief Fieldner and two other men stood with weapons drawn, trained on Lou, every one of them. Lou reacted instantly, years of training kicking in without thought, and clocked the closest thug in the jaw, grabbed his arm, twisted it behind his back and took his gun. In the space of a heartbeat Lou had the guy in front of him as a human shield and was holding his gun on the others.

"You two, drop your weapons, or your friend here is history." They stared at him, then at one another.

"Do it!" Lou barked, moving the barrel toward his hostage's head.

They looked at Jason. Jason nodded at them. "You'd better do what he says."

Each man dropped his firearm on the ground. Lou shot Jason a look. "Get the guns, Jay."

With a nod, Jason scrambled to gather up the guns.

He tucked two into his waistband, kept the other in his hand. Then he hurried to stand beside Lou.

"You'll be sorry for this," Fieldner said. "You were supposed to bring the women out here, not the man!" he shouted at Jason.

Lou's alarm bells went off, and he swung his gaze and his gun around toward Jason—only to find the gun Jason held pointed right dead center at his forehead.

"I told you on the phone, I couldn't stop him from coming," Jason said. "But it won't matter. The women will come. If he's out here, they'll come."

"Jesus, Jason, just what the hell do you think you're doing?"

"Put the gun down, Lou. I told you, I'll do whatever it takes to get my sister back. Unfortunately, that includes hurting you."

"Me, yeah. I get that. But Maxie? And Storm?"

"I'm sorry, Lou. Just put the gun down."

Lou hesitated.

"Don't make me shoot you." Jason thumbed the hammer back on the revolver.

It was a goddamn .44. A .44-caliber round would blow the back of his head off on the way out, Lou thought. There was no chance he would survive if Jason fired, and then Max would be at his mercy.

Trusting a friend who didn't deserve her trust. He had to stay alive. For her. For Max.

He dropped the weapon he'd taken from the man he held, and the man jerked himself free.

"Your own gun, too," Jason said. "I know you brought one."

Nodding, Lou took his gun out carefully and dropped it on the ground. "Don't do this, Jason. He's not just going to let Delia go just because you do what he says."

"He's gonna kill her if I don't."

"How do you know he won't kill her either way?" Lou took a step toward Jason, but no more. Someone smashed him in the head from behind with something hard. He dropped to his knees, and they hit him again.

Lou went down and stayed down. No point getting back up, not against four of them. He lay there, clinging to consciousness, but pretending to be long past it.

But he heard the impact of fist on flesh, heard Jason grunt and swear.

"You stupid fool! You were told not to bring him here." Fieldner was doing the talking, but it was the other two beating the hell out of Jason.

"I tried to stop him—I called to tell you—"

"Bull. You went back on your word!" Another thud, another grunt, and then Jason was on the damp ground not far from where Lou lay.

"Enough," Chief Fieldner commanded. Lou peered through mostly closed eyes and saw the police chief standing near Jason. "We'll have to make the best of it. Having Mr. Malone here might work to our advantage. Take him inside."

"What about this one?" one thug asked, looking down at Jason.

"He's going to have to go back. Tell the women Malone's being held here, lead them back to rescue him."

Lou opened his eyes. He fixed Jason with a glare that told him in no uncertain terms not to *dare* follow those orders.

The chief went on. "It'll have to look like he fought us, tried to save his companion." He nodded at his two henchmen. "Make it convincing. Just not so much that he can't make it back to the mainland." He shrugged. "Then again, if you do, you can always take him back yourselves."

They smiled, actually smiled, and closed in around Jason, who curled in more tightly around himself before the first boot landed. When they finished, Jason was lying still in the dirt. They grabbed Lou's arms and began dragging him toward the house.

Martha proceeded to guide Stormy into a deeper state of hypnosis. Then she told her that she, Storm, was in control and the other part of her psyche must not take over again. She gave the other permission to speak to Stormy and told it to listen as well, and again reaffirmed that Stormy was in control. Then, slowly, she brought Stormy back out of the trance state, telling her to remember everything they had discussed, even the things said by the other, and to awake feeling refreshed, in control and safe.

By the looks of things, Stormy did.

Martha poured fresh tea, this time a cinnamon-and-spice blend she said would lend energy. She instructed Stormy to eat some of the cookies she'd brought in, whether she wanted them or not.

"So? What do you make of all this?" Max asked. It had been killing her to keep quiet and watch for so long, without speaking or injecting thoughts or opinions. Killing her, too, that her plan to slip away and head out to the island alone had backfired. But there was still time. "Is it a case of possession?"

"If it is," Martha said, "it's by someone who is convinced she really is a part of Storm." She looked at Stormy. "Do you remember the parts of the conversation when I was speaking to the other?"

Stormy frowned, and then her brows rose. "I do. I remember all of it."

"And what did you sense from her when she was speaking to me?"

"Honesty. Sincerity and a kind of...almost a desperation."

"Then she really does believe what she's saying," Max said.

"Either that, or what she's saying is really true," Martha put in.

"How could it be true?"

Martha sipped her tea, set the cup on the saucer thoughtfully and met Stormy's eyes. "What I have to say to you is purely theoretical. You must know that, and understand that no one can be certain about what happens to us in the spiritual realms. My opinion is no more valid than anyone else's. It's one possibility, out of many. All right?"

Stormy nodded. "All right."

"All right. I believe that each of us has...a spiritual self. A higher self, if you will. I think that when we pass on from our lifetime, the person we have been, the soul, leaves the physical world and goes into the spiritual realm, where, if all goes well, it merges with the higher self. Are you with me so far?"

Max was nodding. Not sure she agreed, but as a theory, it wasn't bad.

Stormy just stared at Martha, rapt.

"So the higher self is made up of each person we've been in each and every lifetime. And the higher self generates a new soul, made up of the combined experiences of all the old ones, to be born into each new lifetime."

"If you buy into the theory that we live more than once," Max said.

"Yes. Now, you're familiar with the idea of ghosts—of souls that refuse or are for some reason unable to move on and remain in the physical world instead."

Max nodded. Stormy said, "You think this is a ghost?"

"Not exactly," Martha said. "I think most souls do move on, leave the physical realm and go on to the other side. But I think once there, some might be unable or unwilling to merge with the higher self. So they remain an individual, even though the higher self generates a new soul, that is reborn and living a new lifetime. Do you understand?"

"I understand," Max said. "Not sure if I buy it, but I understand."

"Storm?"

Stormy nodded but still didn't speak.

"Now," Martha said, "before we began, you told me that when you were in the coma, you left your body. You spoke of the experience of being lost. Even meeting someone else you had never met before, but whom you met later in real life. And she remembered this meeting, too."

"Yes," Stormy said. "If she hadn't, I'm not sure I would believe it was anything more than a hallucination."

"Too often we mistrust our own senses," Martha said. "Suppose that while you were there, wandering, a soul that had failed to merge with its higher self saw you and somehow attached itself to you, so that when you returned to your body, there were two souls, rather than one."

"I think we're getting a little far-fetched here," Max said, reaching for her tea, shaking her head.

"But, Max, that's exactly how it feels," Stormy said, her voice louder, her face more animated, than it had been before. "Who is this other soul? Why did she want to come back with me?"

"I can't say for sure, Storm. She kept telling me

she was you. I think there's a possibility—and mind you, only a possibility—that she might be part of you. Another soul that was generated by your higher self."

Stormy frowned, puzzled, but Max saw where this was going. "You think this *other* is one of Storm's previous incarnations?"

"I think it's one possibility she ought to consider."

Stormy closed her eyes. "It's not fair. I just want to get rid of her. How can I do that? What does she want from me?"

"Now, that's the relevant question. What does she want? Why did she return? It may be that she left unfinished business in her own time. It may be that there is something here, in the physical realm, that she wants and can only claim by being here herself." Martha slid a hand over Stormy's. "I believe I have opened the lines of communication for you. I tried. If it worked, then you'll be able to find out. Talk to her, listen to her, feel what she feels, and maybe you'll come to understand."

"And if I can't?"

Martha lowered her eyes. "I don't know."

"Wait a minute," Max demanded. "Are you telling me there's no way to get rid of this…this intruder, this interloper? What about an exorcism? Could that work?"

"It might. Or it might end up banishing the wrong soul."

Stormy shivered visibly at those words.

"Then what the hell are we supposed to do?"

"Max, don't raise your voice. She's doing the best she can," Stormy said.

Max rolled her eyes and paced away. "I'm sorry, Martha. I'm just worried about my friend."

"I don't blame you. You know, I've long suspected that what I've just explained to you is the cause of many cases of multiple-personality disorder. I believe older souls may step in to protect a younger one who's experiencing severe trauma, to save them, and it works, but ends in the creation of many individuals inhabiting one body. Whether that's true or not, the symptoms are much the same, and so the treatment could be, as well."

"And what treatment would that be?" Max asked.

"There are two schools of thought on that. In one, therapists lead the patient through guided meditations in which they imagine finding and killing the other parts. I seriously doubt this is the best course. Other psychiatrists have had great success with merging the individual personalities into the whole, which I feel could be a far healthier solution."

"You're telling me she's stuck with this thing? You want her to…to *adopt* it?" Max shook her head. "I say we go with option one. Kill the goddamn thing and get rid of it."

"No." Stormy rose to her feet as she said it. "No, I don't want to do that. Not yet, anyway."

"Stormy, are you out of your freaking mind?"

"Maybe." Stormy met Max's eyes and smiled a shaky smile. "But I need to know who she is, why she came back, and what she wants from me."

"Storm, I hate like hell to bring this up, but this bitch attacked Lou. She attacked *me*. She's dangerous."

"She's a part of me. And I think Martha let her know that you and Lou are friends, and mean her no harm. I don't think she'll become violent again."

"I agree," Martha said. "And there's also what she said about the sea. Meaning Endover." She sighed. "I don't want to frighten you with gossip, but it's not the first whisper of strange goings-on I've heard in relation to that place. Still…she's stronger near it, weaker farther inland. You can use that to remain in control."

Stormy nodded. "Thank you, Martha. You've given me a lot to think about."

"Yes, thanks," Max said, though even to her own ears it sounded less than sincere. Frankly, she'd been happier to believe this was some foreigner, a ghost or even a demon. To think it was some long-lost part of Stormy's own higher self—that was just too much. And it was tough to reconcile her love for Stormy with her hatred for this other. If it were a part of her, how could Max feel both those things?

In the car on the ride back, Stormy was silent.

Finally Max had to break the tension. "Honey, I adore you. You know that. If this is the way you want to handle this thing, then I'm with you."

"I feel like I'm letting you down. Betraying you, even. Embracing your sworn enemy."

"Next time she comes around, I'll try to make friends."

Stormy laid her head back on the seat and closed her eyes. Max glanced sideways and saw tears squeezing out onto her lashes.

"I don't have to take you back there, you know," Max said. "If this other is stronger there, maybe the best thing would be for you to go in the opposite direction."

Stormy shook her head. "I have to go back. I'm not going to find the answers anywhere else." She offered Max a weak smile. "Besides, we still have Delia and Janie to rescue. It's okay, Max. Really, it's okay."

"It's not. But it will be. I promise, Storm, I'm gonna find some way to make this okay." She drove on in silence for a long moment. Then she said, "You know, Storm, it's entirely possible Martha is dead wrong about all of this. Even she admitted as much."

"I know. It just...it feels true. Everything she said put a knot in my belly that told me it was true."

Max nodded. "I guess we have to trust your instincts. Hell, this doesn't impact anyone as much as it does you. It's your life, your body, your soul."

"My higher self." She sighed.

"Should we go back, then?" Max asked.

"Lunch, then back," Stormy said. "I'm starved for the first time in days. It's a good sign, don't you think?"

"I'm hungry, too," Max said, though she was worried about the time. She had to get to that island today.

"You're always hungry, Max."

There was a glimmer of the old light in Stormy's

tired eyes. It did Max's heart good to see it there. Then Stormy took her hand.

"I'm sorry, honey. I'm so sorry. You're in crisis, and I ought to be there for you, helping you through it, and instead I've developed a crisis of my own to contend with." She shook her head. "And you're there for me, even though your heart is breaking over Lou."

"And you're there for me, too."

"I want to be."

"You are, hon," Max told her. "Just being here with me is a big help, you know that. Besides, what more can you do? Lou and me—that boat's been torpedoed. It's a lost cause."

"Don't give up on him just yet, Max."

Max glanced at her friend and lied through her teeth, to Stormy and to herself. "I already have."

Then she drove them to an out-of-the-way diner for a quick lunch before heading the car back toward the cursed little town of Endover. And the farther they drove, the more urgently she felt the need to get back there. She hadn't reached any conclusions about how to reclaim her friendship with Lou, how to deal with the heartbreak of realizing he would never love her the way she wanted him to. But she had to see him, to be with him. The need was almost crippling, and growing with every mile.

20

"I cannot freakin' believe this!"

Max got out of the car, which was nose down in a ditch, and surveyed the blown-out front tire. "This is great. Just great."

"It's no big deal, hon. We can fix it."

Max sighed, nodded and trudged to the trunk for the jack and the spare, but as soon as she gripped the spare tire, she realized that it was flat, too. "Hell, Storm. We are so screwed."

Stormy came up beside her, thumped the spare with a fist and made a face. "Not screwed, exactly. We still have the cell phones."

"We have reception?"

Stormy yanked a phone from her pocket and looked at the panel. "Yep. Three bars. Almost full power."

"That's odd, isn't it? We usually lose it by the time we get this close to Endover."

"Hey, who am I to turn up my nose at small favors? Maybe somebody's looking out for us."

That, Max thought, was what she was afraid of. "I'm worried about Lou. I've got this bad feeling, Storm, and I just can't shake it."

"Lou's fine. And we'll get this tire changed and get back there in no time. We just need to call a garage or something. I don't suppose you know a number?"

"I think there's an auto-club card in the glove compartment," Max said, then zipped around the car to get in and dig it out. She found the card and took it back to Stormy, who dialed the number, pushed buttons to negotiate her way through the menu and then entered the membership number from the card.

Then she looked up from the phone. "Your membership has expired. Would you like to renew?"

"Will it get me a tow truck?"

"You want me to ask the computerized voice?

'Cause all she's giving me so far is one for yes or two for no."

Rolling her eyes, Max said, "One for yes." Then she dug a credit card from her purse and read off the numbers while Storm punched them in.

Finally they got to a real live human being, only to be told it would be an hour before a tow truck could get to them.

Stormy disconnected and pocketed the phone. "An hour. Hell, Max, maybe you should lock yourself in the car."

"For what?"

"Look around, Max."

Max did. They were on a deserted stretch of highway—well, off it, to be more precise. Another car hadn't passed since the tire had blown and they'd gone skidding across the pavement and into the ditch. The road stretched like a black ribbon, unwinding over hills, around curves and vanishing into the trees in the distance. They'd come to rest off the shoulder, nose partway into a ditch where water trickled in a thin stream along the bottom. It could have been worse. A grassy bank rose up for twenty yards on either side, ending at a tree line of pines. It was as if they were in a tunnel with a pavement floor and a blue-sky ceiling.

She looked at Stormy again, then let her mouth fall open in surprise. "You think I'm afraid to be alone with you?"

"Aren't you?"

"No!"

"You should be. Jesus, Max, what if *she* comes back?"

"She…oh, hell, Storm. You're in control now, if what Martha did worked."

"What if it didn't?"

It killed her to see her friend so worried about what she might do. "I told you, I'll make friends."

"Don't joke, Max. This isn't funny."

"All right, all right. Look, if your eyes so much as start to change color, I'll get into the car and lock you out, okay?"

"Promise?"

"Promise," Max said. "Otherwise I might be forced to kick your scrawny ass, and I don't want to do that."

Stormy picked up on the teasing in her eyes, and sent it right back. "You couldn't if you tried."

"Oh, please. I'd wipe you all over the pavement." Max playfully shoved Stormy's shoulder.

"Yeah, you would, if you had a dozen friends for backup." Stormy shoved back. They got into a pushing match, started laughing, and wound up tripping back and falling into the ditch, arms around each other. When they got untangled, they sat there in the damp grass, catching their breath as their laughter slowly died.

"You'd never hurt me, Stormy. Not really. Come on, deep down, you know that."

Stormy sighed, and Max thought she didn't agree. How awful it must be to doubt yourself that way.

"I wish we could get back," Stormy said, looking at her watch as she got to her feet and brushed the twigs and dirt from her jeans.

"Me too. I was tough on Lou, I think. Made him feel bad."

"He deserves to feel bad after that episode. For crying out loud, how could he go that far with you and still not acknowledge his feelings?"

"He did acknowledge his feelings. They just turned out not to be the feelings I was hoping for."

"Bullshit."

Max sighed. "I was kind of mean to him. He didn't deserve that."

"He deserves my size eight in his butt."

"Well, yeah. Maybe a little." Max sighed. "How long has it been since we called?"

"Twenty minutes. You really that eager to get back to him, Max?"

She nodded. "I've gotta make things right with him. If I let last night ruin our friendship, then I'm just proving he was right all along."

"That's probably why you're having all these feelings of dread," Stormy reasoned. "Guilt. Just a big pile of guilt."

"I hope so," Max whispered. She looked at the position of the sun in the sky. "I just want to get back to Lou and find out for sure."

As it turned out, though, she wasn't getting back to Lou anytime soon. The tow truck took closer to an hour and a half, and then all it did was haul them to the nearest garage, close to forty miles in the opposite direction, where they waited two more hours for their tire to be changed. During that time, Max tried three times to call Lou, both on his cell and in the motel room, but there was no answer at either number. She tried Jay, too, and got no better results.

Finally, just as she was waiting for the mechanic to run her credit card, she tried the motel office.

Gary answered.

"Hey, Gary. This is Max Stuart. Room three."

"I know who you are," he said. His tone was dull, lifeless—but then, so was he, most of the time.

"I was wondering, have you seen Lou Malone or Jason Beck? I've been trying to get them on the phone, but they don't answer."

"No. Haven't seen them."

"Um, is Jason's car in the lot? It's a Jeep Wrangler. Light brown. Kind of caramel co—"

"Yep, it's out there."

"Well, where could they be?" By now Stormy had come over and was staring at her, looking worried. She covered the receiver. "Jay's Jeep is there, but the guys aren't answering the phone."

"How would I know?" Gary answered.

Max thinned her lips. "Could you go check the rooms, see if they're in there?"

The kid sighed so heavily she was surprised she didn't feel the breeze hitting her ear, but he said, "Just a minute, then," and set the phone down. She heard heavy footfalls, heard the door bang, wondered if he were really checking on the guys or just making sound effects for her benefit.

Minutes ticked by. Eventually she heard the door again, the footsteps again. Then, "They aren't in their rooms, but that goddamn kid is back here. I can't have him lurking around outside the rooms. It's bad for business."

"Yeah, almost as bad as night stalkers who try to kidnap your guests, I'll bet."

"Huh?"

"Just leave him alone. I'll be there in an hour. Let the kid wait, okay?"

"Whatever." He hung up the phone, and Max felt like bashing him in the head with it.

The mechanic was back with her card and a receipt. "Sign here," he said.

She scribbled her name as fast as she could, tore off her copy and headed for her car. Stormy was on her heels. "You really think something's wrong, don't you, Max?"

Max nodded. "I *know* something's wrong. And goddammit, it's getting dark."

Lou lost his grip on consciousness at some point while being dragged into the house. He regained it some time later, all at once coming wide awake with a surge of adrenaline between the space of one heartbeat and the next. He found himself in a locked room in what had to be a basement. No windows, just concrete floor and walls. He looked at his watch, shocked when he realized that the entire day had passed. No way had he been out that long due to the beating those thugs had delivered. He suspected a more supernatural cause. The room had only one door—a steel door without a pane of glass in it. It opened outward, so the hinges were completely out of reach on the other side. The doorknob wouldn't budge, but he messed with it enough to know where the lock was engaged—just below the knob. No dead bolt, or at least he thought not.

He pulled up a pant leg and took out the small, snub-nosed .38 he had hidden there in a pancake-style calf holster. It was the same gun he'd been insisting Stormy keep with her when she had to be alone—although since her attack on Max, he'd decided it might be better to keep firearms out of her reach. They'd never spotted it. Hell, they must think they were dealing with someone who'd never tangled with criminals before. Much less vamps. He knew better than to show up under-armed.

He took off his shirt, wadded it up as tightly as he could, buried the gun barrel in the fabric and rested it against the door. Without hesitation he pulled the trigger.

Even muffled, the shot was deafening.

And yet it did its job. The door swung slowly open, its lock blown to bits. Lou shook the shirt open and put it on, despite that the bullet had ripped through several folds, creating a holey pattern. He kept the gun in one hand, not sure if it would be better to conceal it in case he were caught. Then he decided if he were caught, he would damn well shoot his way out of here. He had to get to Max before she came charging to the rescue. The thought of her walking into the trap of a goddamn rogue vamp as powerful as this one was too frightening to contemplate.

He crept out of his cell, pulling the door closed behind him, so it would take a few extra moments for anyone to realize he had escaped. Then he crept through a basement that was like a labyrinth, with corridors that twisted, turned and branched off. He passed several rooms with closed doors. He thought the place was deliberately designed to confuse. Freaking Magellan could get lost down here, he thought.

He wandered for a very long time, eventually finding a staircase that led upward and following it. At the top was an ordinary-looking door, and when he tried the knob, he found it unlocked.

Listening intently for any sounds, he opened the door, back to the wall, peering around it, gun first, before he crept through and into pure opulence. The house was lush—he couldn't think of another word for it. He stepped onto deep carpet. The walls were covered in velveteen paper, the windows draped in multiple layers of jewel-toned fabrics over black, which blocked the glass.

"The windowpanes are tinted," a man's voice said. "But one can never be too careful."

Lou whirled to see the vamp standing in the middle of the room. Behind him, the two teenage girls stood docile and frightened, their hands bound behind them. "It's okay," Lou told them. "I'm here to get you out." He nodded to the vampire. "It's time to let these girls go, don't you think?"

"And you are going to use that weapon to force me? I think you know that gun will do me no harm."

"I think you know we've covered all this."

He lifted his dark eyebrows. "I'm impressed by your courage, Malone. Tell me, how is it you've come to know as much as you do about the Undead?"

"I get around."

"And just how much *do* you know about my kind?"

"Enough to know you're not the animals some make you out to be. At least, not all of you. As for you personally, I think you're the scum of the earth."

The vampire smiled slowly. "And why is that, when you barely know me?"

"What did you want with those two girls? They're children, for crying out loud." As he asked the question, he tried to gauge the girls' well-being without shifting his gaze from the vampire for more than a second at a time. They were clean, groomed. Dressed, apparently, in their own clothes. He didn't see any outward signs of injury—only fear.

"What do you think I wanted with them? Hmm? Use your imagination, Malone." He smiled slowly as he watched Lou's face, had to know exactly what Lou was thinking, and seemed to enjoy letting him think it before he went on. "Fortunately for them, my...tastes do not run to children. Or I'd have drained them and left their bodies like dry shells on the shore."

Lou blinked. "Now *you're* lying."

"Am I?"

Lou nodded. "You've kidnapped a lot of women, but they always turn up again. Alive and unharmed."

He shrugged. "I don't have to kill in order to feed, Malone. Do not mistake that for an inability to do so. I kill when I want to. When I need to. I have no remorse for it when I do. Just as I will have no remorse if I have to kill you."

"Just what the hell do you want from me?" Lou demanded.

"From you? Nothing. It's the women I want."

"Find another font to assuage your sick appetite, pal. You're not getting close enough to smell them."

He nodded slowly. "I do not wish to feed from them. The fiery-haired one—she is the one who is the real expert on my kind, yes?"

"I know as much as she does."

"Gallant, the way you try to protect her." He smiled slowly. "You love her." Then his brows rose. "Oh, you deny it, do you? Even to yourself? It baffles me how you mortals waste what precious little time you have on such trivial matters as self-deception and fear."

"Let the girls go. You don't need them anymore, you have me."

"Yes, but I want the women. Both of them."

Lou felt a fissure of anger open up in his soul. It felt as if hot lava were bubbling out of it. "What do you want with them?"

"Oooh, you can imagine so many things, I see it in your eyes." He smiled again. "There's something puzzling about the one you call Storm. Something about her that I must understand for my own peace of mind. She...intrigues me." He sighed. "I grew so impatient waiting for Jason to bring her to me that I broke my own rules, I risked discovery, to go after her myself. You should have just let me take her, you know. It would have been easier on us all."

"And what do you want with Max?"

He shrugged. "From your woman, I want only information. For the most part. And, well, maybe just a taste. Just a sip. It's not as if you can stop me."

Lou fired the gun dead-on at the vamp's heart. But the man moved so fast it seemed he vanished, then appeared again behind Lou.

Lou spun, hit him with all his might, using the gun to send him sailing across the room. He hit hard, and the vamp grunted in pain. Then Lou lunged at the girls, yanking the ropes free that bound their hands. "There's a boat hidden," he whispered. "Walk counterclockwise around the island about fifty yards. It's near the shore, in the bushes. Get the hell out of here. And if you see my friends, warn them that they're walking into a trap. Go!"

The girls didn't hesitate, they ran. The vampire lunged again, and Lou turned to take him on, knowing he had very little hope of defeating one of the Undead. Especially one as powerful as this one.

But he held out, fighting with everything in him to give the girls time to escape. Praying there were no longer any thugs outside to grab them again.

He ducked a blow, then delivered one. Then he took one full on to the center of his chest, and it hit him so hard he thought it stopped his heart, even as he slammed backward into the wall, cracking the plaster.

"You are a worthy opponent," the vamp said, standing over him as Lou pulled himself to his feet for more. "It's going to be a shame—it really is. But I thank you for the amusement." He shook his head slowly, sadly; then with a great sigh, he flung up a hand and barked a single command. "Sleep!"

Lou blacked out instantly.

By the time the tire was repaired and they were on their way, Max was petrified with worry about Lou. What the hell could have happened to him? She drove as fast as the little Bug would go all the way back to Endover and skidded to a halt in the motel parking lot.

There, in front of Lou's motel room door, little

Sid stood uneasily, shifting his weight from one foot to the other.

Max jumped out of the car and ran to him. She dropped to her knees, gripped his shoulders. "Sid. Do you know what's happened? Where is Lou?"

"I don't know."

She looked around frantically, but there was no sign of either Lou or Jason, so she turned her attention back to the boy. "Did you have something you wanted to tell us, Sid?"

The boy met her eyes. "Something to tell Lou."

She nodded and fought for patience. "I don't know where he is, Sid. I'm very worried about him, and I promise, I'm going to go find him very, very soon. But first, why don't you tell me what it is you came to tell him? That way I can tell him for you when I find him."

He pursed his lips and seemed to think it over.

Max decided to help things along by digging a twenty out of her pocket and handing it to him. "And I'll pay you for him, too," she added.

The boy smiled and took the money. "I came to tell him about the other one. Jay-man."

"Jason?"

"Yeah. He's hurt. Pretty bad, I think."

By now Stormy was standing beside her. Max

shot her friend a look of alarm and saw Stormy's eyes widen with concern. "Where is he, Sid? Do you know where he is, so we can go help him?"

Sid nodded. He pointed behind the motel. "By the water. I go down there sometimes to look for seashells. He started to walk back here, but then he fell down. He didn't get up again."

Max blinked, not sure how the hell he knew as much as he did, and not wanting to take the time to ask. "You go home now, okay, Sid? I want you to stay in your house tonight."

"I will. Mom says I have to go to bed early. 'Cause tomorrow we're going away."

The visit to the private school—right. She'd nearly forgotten. "That's great, honey. You get home now, so you won't be late."

"Okay." He turned and ran to his bike, got on and started off.

"Sid?" she called after him. He looked back, and she said, "Thank you for your help."

His smile was quick and bright, and then he pedaled away.

When he was out of sight, she and Stormy exchanged glances. "We need to get inside Lou's room," Max said. "If he didn't take his guns with him, we should."

Stormy nodded and stood back as Max kicked the door open, too impatient to wait for a key. The two raced into the room and began tossing it in search of Lou's guns. But Max paused when she saw the note lying on the telephone stand.

It was written in Lou's hand, and it was addressed to her.

Max,
I'm heading out to the island, even though I know it's going to piss you off. I figure I've screwed things up royally with you and me. And I've been kicking myself ever since. I just hope I get the chance to make things right again. Love,
Lou.

She swallowed hard. "He went out there," she whispered to Stormy, her fingers trembling as they traced the word *love*.

"Let's go find Jason, see what he knows." Stormy put a hand on her arm when she didn't respond. "He'll be all right, Max."

"He damn well better be," Max said. She shoved the note into her pocket, and the two left the room. They ran together into the woods behind the motel, far from the glow of the parking-lot lights and neon sign. They found the path and raced down it to the shore. The little boat that had been there the night before was long gone. And Jason lay still on the ground.

They fell to their knees on either side of him. "God, he's bruised to hell and gone."

"And for once, I know it wasn't me," Stormy said. She touched his face. "Jason. Jay, honey?"

Max ran to the water's edge, scooped up a handful and brought it back to splash him in the face. "Dammit, Jason, wake up!"

His eyes flickered. Then opened.

"Where is Lou?" she asked, voicing the top question on her mind. Even though she was sorely afraid she already knew the answer.

"I—I—I…"

"If he says I don't know—" she muttered.

"Island."

Jesus, that was even worse. "He's on the island? With that insane vampire?"

"Captured."

"Let's get him to the room," Stormy said.

"*You* get him to the room. I'm going after Lou." Max rose, fully intending to do just that. But there was no boat. She spun to Jason again. "You were on the island with him?"

He nodded weakly.

"How the hell did you get back here, Jason? How did you manage to get away and leave him behind, and all without a boat?"

Jason opened his eyes. "They…brought me back. Dumped me here."

"They? Who?"

"The vampire's thugs. Locals, I think. And Fieldner." He closed his eyes; one was purpling and swollen, and his lip was split. "Don't go, Max. It's a trap."

She stomped across the beach. "They're gonna think it's a fuckin' trap when I get my hands on them—"

"Max."

Stormy rose from Jason's side and went to her. "Max!"

"What!" She hadn't meant to snap, but dammit, she had to get to Lou.

"Help me get Jay to the room. We'll get a boat and go right back out. Okay?"

Jason was already trying to get to his feet. Max turned toward him, to help him up, but then she heard something. Splashing. Voices in the water.

She turned and saw the boat moving slowly closer.

Her heart jumped. "Lou?" she whispered, straining her eyes.

But no. It was a woman in the boat, her long blond hair blowing in the breeze behind her. No. Two women. Two…girls.

"Delia!" Jason cried. He went staggering into the surf, and probably would have drowned if Max and Storm hadn't lunged after him, gripping his arms on either side.

"Jason!" Delia clambered out of the boat, into the water, and slogged toward him. The other girl was in the process of doing the same, so Max let go of Jason and went to grab the vessel before they let it float away. She tugged it to the shore as the happy reunion went down in the surf. Jason and the two girls dragged one another out of the water. Delia was hugging Jason and sobbing. Jason was crying openly, as well, and had one arm around the other girl, Janie.

"God, Jason, what happened to you?"

"There will be time for that later," Stormy said, and she said it firmly. "Are either of you girls hurt?"

"No. No, he didn't hurt us," Janie said. "He said as long as Jason did as he was told, we would be set free."

"As long as Jason did as he was told," Max repeated, turning to pin Jason to the ground with a glare that should have set him on fire.

Janie nodded hard. "There's another man out there—your friend. They were fighting, and he knocked the guy down and untied us. Told us to run, told us where the boat was, and to tell his friends not to come—that it's a trap."

"We didn't know how to start the motor," Delia said. "We had to row the whole way. I thought for sure that strange man would come after us. I think he was through with us, or he would have." She stared at her brother. "He's not human. I don't think he's human, Jay."

"I know." He hugged her close, his eyes meeting Max's.

Max marched up to him, gripped his arm and jerked him away from his sister. She nodded to Stormy who got the message without a word. She took the girls a few steps away and continued questioning them to give Max a moment with Jason.

Max held his arm hard. "You betrayed us."

"He said he'd kill her."

"You led Lou out there like a goddamn sacrificial bull."

"No, Max. He's the one who insisted we go out there. I tried to stop him."

"Why?"

He lowered his eyes. "Because you're the ones this guy wants. You and Storm. Not Lou." He paused, swallowed, caught his breath. "They took him captive and then beat me up to make it look good, and dumped me back here. I'm supposed to tell you where Lou is, so you'll go out there after him."

She nodded. "So can I trust you at all anymore, Jason?"

"I'm sorry, Max. He said he'd kill my sister. I was only trying to keep her alive."

She thought about her own sister, the lengths she had gone to, trying to protect her. Finally she nodded. "Will you do something for me? Can I trust you to do something for me, Jason?"

"Anything. Jesus, if I can make this up—"

"You can't." She dragged a pen from her jacket pocket and wrote a telephone number on the back of Jason's hand. "I want you to take these two girls directly to your Jeep, get in and drive out of here. Don't stop to take your stuff or check out or pay your motel bill. Nothing. Just go straight to the car and drive the hell out of here."

He nodded.

"I'll bring your stuff later, if I survive this. The second you're out of range of Endover and picking up a signal on your cell phone, you call this number. You tell whoever answers that you are calling for Max, and that she's in trouble. And then you tell them where I've gone. Warn them it might be a trap. Tell them there's a rogue vamp on that island and that he has Lou. Understand?"

He nodded.

"Do you swear to me on your sister's life that you'll do this exactly as I've told you?"

"I swear. I will, Max. But I wish you wouldn't go out there. Come with me. When your help arrives, then we'll all—"

She shook her head. "I love him. I can't leave him out there alone. I'm going. And a freaking army of rogue vamps couldn't stop me."

Stormy led the two girls back over to Jason. "Get him up there to his Jeep, and get out of this town," she said.

"We will."

"Good. Go." Stormy turned to Max. "Don't even think about telling me to stay behind. I'm going with you. Are you ready?"

Max nodded. "You realize we're walking right into it, right?"

"Yeah," Stormy said. "I picked up on that part of the conversation."

"So there's no point being sneaky. We may as well march right up to the front door."

"I wish we had some of that goddamn vamp-tranquilizer that Stiles jerk used on your brother-in-law," Stormy said.

"Remind me to stock up." *If we survive this,* she thought.

They got into the boat and Max yanked the rip cord until the motor came to life. It wasn't long before the island came into view, and then lights. Torches, she realized slowly, marking a lighted, fiery path all the way along the shoreline, leading the way to the house.

"Guess he really rolled out the red carpet," Stormy said.

"Yeah, let's just hope it's not blood-red."

They killed the motor, beached the boat and got out, and Max rubbed her arms against the chill that came only partly from the early spring night and the fresh, salty breeze that wafted in from the ocean. She started along the path.

And then she heard a sound. A man's voice, crying out in pain.

Lou's voice.

"Goddammit!" She stopped walking, grabbed a torch and ran. And she knew damn good and well that her best friend was right beside her. "What the hell did I do, Stormy?"

"What do you mean? You didn't do anything. He came out here on his own!"

"I wasn't here. I took off, left him alone, brushed him off because he hurt my feelings. Burst my little fantasy bubble. Didn't feel the way I wanted him to feel. I left in a huff, and he did just what he always does. He tried to fix everything for me. He came charging out here thinking he'd have the vamp on ice and the girls safe and sound by the time I got back, and then I'd forgive him for the rest."

She paused at a fork in the trail, held her torch out in front of her, peering in each direction.

"He didn't come out here because of you," Stormy said.

"Of course he did. If it wasn't for me, he'd be on a fishing boat, sucking down a beer and telling cop stories with his friends."

Even Stormy couldn't argue with that.

The gut-wrenching cry came again, and, a moment later, another sound. A voice, deep and rich. Not loud in a normal way, but so full it carried all over the island, as if it were aided by a loudspeaker or megaphone. And yet Max had the feeling it wasn't.

"Miss Stuart, don't keep us waiting much longer. I don't want to have to keep hurting your beloved, but I will if you delay."

Max clenched her hands into fists at her sides and released a feral shriek that split the night.

She heard the vampire's laughter then, echoing like that of a god, through the trees and reverberating on the very air.

Clutching her torch in her fist, she began running, racing for all she was worth, until finally the house rose into view, palatial and elegant. She lunged up the steps and pounded on the door.

It opened. Just swung slowly inward, as if by itself. She sprang inside and shouted, "Where the hell are you, you sick bastard!"

"Shall I provide more sound effects for you to follow?"

"That's it. I'm done." She lunged at the nearest window and swung her torch, painting the beautiful, lush draperies in strokes of pure fire. Then she moved to the next window, and the next.

"You don't know who you're messing with, do you? But you're about to find out. And then you can burn in hell, you son of a bitch. Starting right now."

21

Lou heard Maxie's challenge, and saw the bastard's face change from malicious and amused to afraid.

Goddamn, that woman was something.

His woman. That was what the vamp had called her. And he'd liked the sound of it. God, he'd been an idiot.

The vampire set the cattle prod down on the table with his other "tools" and, turning, sniffed the air. "She dares…"

"She dares anything," Lou said. "And if you hurt her, I'll make you suffer like you've never suffered in your life."

The vampire slanted a look at Lou. "If you had

any inkling of how I have suffered, you might realize how difficult that will be." Then he was gone.

Lou tugged at the chains that held his arms to the wall in a rough approximation of a crucifixion. But it was no use. The bastard had jolted him with enough electricity to reduce his muscles to jelly. He was still shaking with it, feeling the ghostly aftershocks zapping his nerve endings. And even at full strength, he couldn't have hoped to snap chains like these.

In a moment, the vampire was back, and he was dragging Max with one hand and Stormy with the other. He held each by one arm, and when he let them go, they stumbled to the floor.

"You're both fortunate I managed to douse those flames. If you'd burned my home, I'd have seen to it you burned with it. And your friend here, as well."

Max lifted her head, spotted him and then shot to her feet. "Lou!" She ran to him, her arms snapping around his neck, her mouth pressing to his face, his neck, her hands threading in his hair.

Damn his body for reacting to her touch, even in this sorry state, Lou thought. Who the hell had he ever thought he was kidding, anyway?

Eventually she backed off a little, and her beautiful green eyes slid over his face and then down his body. His ragged, torn shirt hung in tatters, hiding very little from her probing eyes. And then those green eyes narrowed, turned deadly dangerous as she spun to face the vampire.

"You hurt him. You low-life scum. You *dare* to hurt him? Do you even know who I am?"

"I fully expected to be asking you that question by now. Do you know who *I* am?" He shrugged. "It is of little consequence. I did your friend no permanent damage, Miss Stuart. And finding out who you are—and more precisely, what you know and how you know it—is only a small part of the reason I brought you here." As he said that, his gaze slid toward Stormy. But he dragged it back to Max again. "You are some sort of a…detective. An expert on my kind. How is that?"

"Why do you want to know?"

He smiled slowly, walked to his table and picked up the long metal rod. Turning slowly with it, he took a step toward Lou, and Lou felt himself tense up in expectation.

Max stepped bodily in front of him. "I get the message. I'm here to answer questions, and if I don't do so fast enough to suit you, Lou gets hurt. You're smart, I'll give you that."

He nodded, seeming surprised when Stormy walked right up to him and gently took the prod from his hand. She put it on the table. He spoke to Max, but his eyes were on Stormy. "I pride myself on finding others' weaknesses. Scanning your mind was not easy."

"I've been taught how to guard my thoughts from the Undead."

He nodded, impressed. "And what about you, little one? Do you guard your thoughts, as well?"

Stormy met his eyes. Hers were smoky and distant, as if she were walking in some kind of a daze. "I wouldn't know which thoughts to guard these days. Some of them are mine. Others are…someone else's." She couldn't seem to break the grip of the vampire's eyes on hers. Max wondered if she even wanted to.

He frowned at her, searching her face intently. Then Max went to Stormy, took her arm and led her to a chair in the corner, easing her into it. "Just rest here, babe. Okay?"

Stormy nodded. "Something's off, Maxie. Something's…" She closed her eyes, pressed her hands to her head.

"It's okay. Just take it easy. Get a handle on it. I've got this."

Max returned her attention to the vampire, but Lou noticed the way his gaze kept shifting to Stormy. He also noticed the way she sat there, almost in a stupor. He wondered if the vamp had done something to her before bringing her in here. Drugged her or something. Or if this was another of her spells. He worried about her.

"What did you find when you scanned my thoughts, vampire?" Max asked.

The vampire jerked his attention back to her. "I found that this man is the most important person in your life. That you would die for him without a second thought. You love him?"

"Madly," she admitted. "So much so that I'll tell you whatever you want to know—but I'll ask for one concession first." The vampire lifted a brow. She went on. "Take him down from there."

The vampire glanced Lou's way. "He's too resourceful, and far too fearless."

"He's right, Max. He cuts me loose, I'm going to find a way to hurt his ass. You ought to take Stormy and get the hell out of here. Leave me to it."

She closed her eyes slowly. "I couldn't leave you behind, Lou."

"Storm's on the edge and she's teetering, Max."

Max looked at Stormy. Stormy lowered her hands, opened her eyes, met Max's, then Lou's. "We aren't leaving you, Lou. I'll be all right."

Max nodded. "Then I guess I'll make this fast." She looked at the vamp again. "My twin sister is a vampire. Her name is Morgan de Silva. She's married now, to the vampire Dante. Do any of those names mean anything to you?"

He shook his head slowly.

"Dante was sired by his great-aunt, a very old Gypsy vampiress named Sarafina."

"Aah. This name I know. Sarafina has a...reputation."

"Lou and I saved Dante's life last year. Sarafina would tear anyone to ribbons who threatened to hurt either one of us." Lou knew that was a lie. Sarafina didn't even like them. But it was a good bluff. "And she'd have plenty of help," Max went on. "Trust me."

The vampire smiled slowly. "You are not going to intimidate me with threats, Maxine. Don't waste your time." He shrugged. "Besides, I can see you're lying. In fact, Sarafina doesn't even like you all that much."

"Wouldn't matter. She owes me."

He still didn't seem impressed. "So being related to one of us is why you know so much about us."

"No," she said. "Not entirely. Are you familiar with the DPI?"

He frowned, looked over at Stormy again, as if checking on her before returning his gaze to Max's. "I've heard of them. The government agency devoted to the research and elimination of the Undead. They're defunct now, yes?"

"A gang of vampires burned their headquarters to the ground and killed most of the agents a little more than five years ago. I was a curious teenager and lived near the site. After the fire I wandered onto the grounds and found a CD full of information—files on vampires they had studied, tests they had done and so on. It read like a horror novel. But it was real." She shrugged. "I've been studying the subject ever since."

The vampire lifted his brows. "If any of them survived and know about the files—"

"Several of them survived. Frank W. Stiles being the most dangerous of the bunch. And he does know. He's targeted me, my sister, her friends." She lifted her chin and stepped closer to him. "He shot my friend Stormy in the head and tried to frame Lou for the crime. She spent a week in a coma, and we didn't know if she would live or die. We, all three of us, have risked our lives to protect our vampiric loved ones from the likes of Frank Stiles and the vampire hunters. The last thing we ever expected was to be repaid like this. With torture and trickery. But then again, I guess there are bad apples in every group, aren't there, Mr....." There she paused. "What's your name, anyway?"

He smiled slowly. "So you can send your army of preternatural protectors after me?"

"Oh, they're already on the way. Those children you abducted made their way back to shore." She looked at her watch. "It's been more than an hour now. I sent them out of town with instructions to call my sister, and I'm sure they made that call long before now. Your time is extremely limited, my friend. So if there is anything more you need to know from me, you'd better ask fast."

His face went utterly blank.

"I'm not bluffing. So get to the point. What is it you want to know?"

"I want to know about Gilgamesh."

"The first vampire. Why?"

He reached for the cattle prod.

"Nu! Stai!" Stormy cried. She surged to her feet. Her face was fierce, and her eyes had changed color. They were gleaming onyx jewels now.

Though she didn't want to, Max gripped the vampire's arm. "Don't hurt her. She's got no idea what she's doing. Look at her eyes."

He did, and then he couldn't seem to take his eyes from hers. "What's wrong with her?" he asked, his voice a whisper now.

"We don't know. It's some sort of possession. That's not Stormy right now, it's…it's someone else. When she comes back to herself, she might not even remember what she did or said in this other state. She gets violent when she's like this. If she attacks you, please, don't hurt her. It's not her fault."

He glanced at Max as if she were insane. Then at Stormy again. Her eyes were fixated on his and filling with tears.

He lifted a hand. "Relax, little one."

"Let them go," she whispered. *"Vă rog."*

He glanced toward Max, then Lou. "Tell me what you know of Gilgamesh."

"I ask you again, why?"

"Because he was the first. Because he sought power over life and death. Power he gained. Power I need."

"So you intend to kill him?"

"Don't judge me. You'd do the same to bring this one back," he said with a nod toward Lou, "if you were in my position."

She frowned. "You want to bring someone…*back?* From where? From the dead?"

"Dead is dead," Stormy muttered. Then she screamed it. "Dead is dead! Dead is dead! Dead is dead!" She kept shrieking the words over and over as she launched herself at the vampire, her fists pounding him, hands clenching into claw shapes and scratching at him.

He went down onto his back under the force of her assault, and a set of keys flew from his pocket. To his credit, he was trying not to hurt her but simply to fend off her assault without causing her any injury. To that end, he gripped her wrists and held them in his hands.

Lou didn't have any clue what to expect next, but suddenly Stormy wasn't fighting the vampire anymore. She was kissing him. Lying atop his prone body, legs straddling him, body pressing close. She murmured things against his mouth. *"Unde-i dragoste e si ceartă.* This love is sweet torment, *prinţ meu.* My prince."

Max scrambled after the keys and quickly went over to Lou, while the vamp was so distracted he couldn't possibly pay attention to her. She didn't know what the hell was going on with Stormy, why she—or maybe the being possessing her—was making out with the vamp, but he was clearly swept up in it.

Dammit, he'd better not try to bite her!

She quickly unsnapped the manacles at Lou's wrists, at just about the same time the vampire groaned deep in his throat, closed his arms around Stormy, and began returning her kisses with a fervor that bordered on desperation.

"Stormy!" Max ran to her, gripped her shoulders, pulled her head away from the creature's lips.

The vampire stopped kissing her, moving her rather gently off him. He got to his feet, his chest heaving, his eyes gleaming and fixed on Stormy. She sat there on the floor. He looked bemused, puzzled. "Who *are* you?"

"*Prin depãrtare dragostea se uitã.* How is it you have forgotten me, of all people, my love?"

He narrowed his eyes on her, got to his feet and took a single, bemused step closer.

"*Sunt rãtããt,*" she whispered. "I'm so lost. I need you. *Am nevoie de ajutorul vostru.*" She pushed her hand backward through her hair, blinked her eyes clear and frowned in confusion.

"Tell me who you are," he said. And his voice was hoarse, almost choked with what sounded like emotion.

Stormy seemed puzzled as she looked from one of them to the other. When she spoke again, her voice was her own. "My name is Tempest Jones," she said. "But my friends call me Stormy. Who are you?"

She was back—she was herself again.

And Lou was back, too, and this time, he was holding the cattle prod.

"Back away from her, pal."

The vampire looked at him, his eyes widening. Then he shot an angry look at Stormy. "At least you used a pleasant blade to drive into my back."

"What are you talking about?"

"You kissed me. You're telling me it wasn't just a diversionary tactic?" He shook his head. "I'm ashamed I let myself believe, even for a moment—"

"I kissed you?" She shot a look at Max. "I *kissed* him?"

"Yeah, sort of."

Stormy lifted fingers to her lips, and her eyes met his. "I did. I…why did I do that?"

The vamp reached down to help Stormy to her feet, but Lou jabbed him with the prod and sent a jolt through him that dropped him to his knees.

"No, don't!" Stormy shouted. And to everyone's surprise she went to him, then seemed to stop herself just short of reaching down to help him and instead stood there, staring in confusion.

The vampire knelt there, palms to the floor, shaking.

"Come on, Max. Storm. Let's get the hell out of here." Stormy turned slowly toward Lou.

"No!" The vampire rose to his feet, shaking off the effects of the jolt, and before Lou knew what was happening, he had grabbed Stormy from behind, jerked her to the front of him, her back pressed to his body, his face dangerously near her throat. "You're not going anywhere."

"Jesus, just tell us what you want!" Max cried. "Don't hurt her. I swear to you, she wasn't trying to trick you. She's been having these episodes for days now. I swear."

"I want Gilgamesh. I want to know how to find him. And then I want to know all there is to know about this…Storm."

"I can't just tell you how to find a vampire so you can hunt him down to steal his power."

He bent his head then, opened his mouth and closed it over Stormy's neck. Lou gasped and lunged forward, but the vampire only turned to keep Stormy between them. Stormy let her head fall backward against him, closed her eyes, opened her mouth and gasped as if in pain or pleasure—it was impossible to tell which. She lifted her hands to his head, threaded her fingers into his hair.

The vampire lifted his head. His eyes gleamed with bloodlust and passion. Two small wounds remained in Stormy's neck. She opened her eyes, and they were swirling and changing. She cupped the vampire's head, moving her hand slowly, caressing him. She didn't try to get free. If anything, she leaned into him even more closely.

He frowned but otherwise ignored her touch. "Shall I drain her, or will you tell me before your friends arrive to destroy what I have worked so hard to build here?"

"It's your own lust for power that destroyed your kingdom, my love," Stormy whispered. "Just like before."

He scowled at her, pulled her around to face him. "What are you doing?"

She muttered. "Do you not know me? Do you no longer love me?"

"Stop it!" he cried. He flung an arm toward her just as Max dove at her and took the brunt of the invisible force that wafted with that arm. It caught her off guard, and she slammed backward into the wall.

Lou lunged at the bastard. "You brutal son of a—"

And then he was locked in combat with the powerful creature. They spun, fought, slammed each other bodily into walls and furniture. Lou smashed into the wall, and something heavy fell from a shelf and cracked as it landed atop Max's head.

The two men froze. The vampire looked stricken and lunged forward, but Lou shoved him aside and went to Max himself.

"Are you truly the heartless bastard you seem?" Stormy cried.

The prince turned to the woman called Stormy, even as Malone gathered his own woman into his arms. Blood trickled down her forehead. Jesus, had he killed her?

"Can't you see it's over?" Stormy asked him. "The others are drawing near. You'll soon be dust if you don't get out of here."

"How do you know they're near?"

She scowled at him. "Are you so blinded by hate that you can't sense them? Open your mind! Let these two go. You have no use for them."

"I have plenty of use for them. As hostages." He turned away from her, striding across the room toward Lou, only to be stopped by the small hand on his shoulder.

"I know you," she whispered. "You're not this being you pretend to be. You're a great leader, a prince. You are Vlad Dracul. Dracula. Prince of my heart."

He stopped there—stopped dead in his tracks. "What did you call me?"

He turned slowly, staring at her eyes with their constantly changing colors. "How can you know to call me that name?"

She pressed her hands to either side of her head, and tears sprang into her eyes. "I don't know. Jesus, I don't know. I only know...you. Somehow, I know you. Please, Vlad..."

He moved closer to her, slowly. She didn't back away. She looked past him once, then said, for his ears alone, "Take me as hostage, if you must have one. Leave them. Let them be."

"Do you know what you're asking?" He caressed her with his eyes. "I will not let you go until it pleases me to do so. And if I find out you have been attempting to trick me with this—"

"It's not a trick. Maybe...maybe you're the only one who can help me to find out what it is."

He held out a hand. She lifted hers, and it trembled,

but she placed it into his. And then he whirled her
into his arms and carried her out of the castle.

Max lay on the floor with her head pounding like
a bass drum, but she managed to open her eyes. Lou
was holding her against his chest, her face buried
in his neck, his in her hair. He rocked her gently,
and she felt wetness and thought it might be tears.
"I've been such an idiot," he whispered. "God,
Max, don't die on me. Not now. Don't do it, don't
go. I love you. I've loved you the whole goddamn
time. I was just too stubborn and too damn scared
to admit it. I was so afraid I'd mess up your life. So
afraid I'd end up losing you in the end. The way I
lost my wife…and my little boy. Baby, I couldn't
stand it. I couldn't. I didn't want to risk that again,
but lemme tell you something, Mad Max. You're
worth it. You're worth any risk. Every risk."

His hand was at her wrist, and she thought he
might be feeling for a pulse. There must be one.
She was certainly alive, but he wasn't finding it, and
she thought maybe that was a good thing. "I'll do
anything, Jesus, anything. Just don't take her from
me. God, what was I doing? Thinking I could keep
from tying myself to her, when I've been tied to her

all along in every way that matters? I love her. I've always loved her."

Hell, now she knew she was alive. And if he couldn't feel her pulse, he must be the one near death, because it was pounding.

"Lou?"

He loosened his arms a little, just enough to let her body relax away from his so he could look at her face. "Max, baby, you're alive."

"Yeah. So far, yeah. You had some doubt?"

"I couldn't feel a pulse. Jesus, Max."

"I'm here. I'm fine. I think you panicked."

He shook his head, doubting it. "How long have you been awake?"

"Long enough to—where's Stormy?"

Lou shot a look across the room. "No," he whispered. "Goddammit, no!" He got up, helping Max to her feet as he did.

Then there was the sound of doors breaking to smithereens, the whisk of movement.

Morgan and Dante appeared, looking furious and ready for battle.

Morgan surged across the room and swept her twin sister into her arms. Dante came forward, clapping Lou on the shoulder.

"You look like hell, my friend," Dante said.

Lou shook his head. "Yeah, well he got his share, too."

"Who? The vampire? Vlad Dracul?"

Lou and Max looked at each other, then at Dante. "What do you mean, Vlad Dracul? He wasn't…"

"He was," Morgan said. "It's all over the preternatural world that he's been living out here—set himself up like a king and had an entire town under the control of his mind. No one's had the nerve to bother him—no one saw it as overly urgent to stop him, since he wasn't killing his victims."

"When we got home and Lydia told us you were in Endover, we came immediately. We were nearly here when your friend Jason phoned." Dante looked at Lou in awe. "You held your own against Prince Vlad. The one and only Dracula."

"And I'll have to again, by the looks of things," Lou said. "The bastard kidnapped Stormy."

"We have to go after him!" Max shouted.

"We will. We will." He touched her hair, the wound there. "You need this stitched up."

"Take care of her," Dante said. "We'll get on his trail and contact you when he beds down for the day sleep. You can catch up with us then. All right?"

Lou nodded.

Max shook her head. "I can't just let them go."

"You aren't," Morgan said softly. "I swear to you, as your sister, we'll stay on their trail, Max. I promise." She sighed softly. "I owe her, you know. Storm and I—we have a bond now. I won't let harm come to her."

Max lowered her eyes. "Okay."

Lou scooped her up in his arms and carried her back down the stairs and out of the mansion. He moved all the way to the beach, finding the boat Stormy and Max had brought out here. Gently, he lowered Max into it and sped as rapidly as he could back to the mainland.

On the shore, he spotted Gary, who helped him pull the boat in and seemed worried when he saw Max. "Hell, what happened?"

Gary looked different, Lou noticed. His eyes weren't as clouded as before. Both his face and his wit seemed sharper.

"She had an accident. Out on the island," Lou explained.

"The island?" Gary looked past them. "Well, what was she doing out there? No one goes out there. There's nothing there but woods and weeds." Then he frowned. "What…what's burning?"

Maxie lifted her head and stared out toward the island. The flames were rising into the night, licking at the very stars, it seemed. Morgan and Dante had finished the job she had begun. The place would be nothing but smoldering ash by sunrise.

"Where can he be taking her?" she whispered to Lou. "Where could he be going with Stormy?"

"Max, listen to me. You said the language she was speaking…was Romanian."

Max looked into his eyes, silent for a long, searching moment. Then she said, "You don't think— you don't think there could be some sort of… connection."

"Did you see the way she was kissing him? And he wasn't putting those words into her head, Max. He was dumbfounded, accusing her of tricks. So if it wasn't him, what the hell was it?"

Max swallowed hard, recalling the theory Martha had suggested. Some kind of past-life explanation for Stormy's odd behavior and symptoms.

"We'll find them," Lou told her. "I promise. I owe you that." He carried her up the hill to the motel, brought her into his room and dropped her onto the bed. He vanished into the bathroom, for a towel, then stepped outside and returned with the towel full of ice from the machine. "Press this to your head."

She lifted it to her head, leaned back on the bed and watched as Lou yanked a duffel out from under his bed and began stuffing everything he'd brought into it. It took him all of five minutes.

"Can you walk?"

She nodded, and he took her hand and tugged her to her feet, leading her out of his room and into hers. She reached for her suitcase, but he wouldn't let her. "Just sit and keep that ice on your head. I'll get it."

She thinned her lips. "I'm not hurt that badly." It was a lie. Her vision kept blurring, and she was dizzy as hell. She had a concussion, at the least.

"You are, or else you would be with your sister chasing after Storm," he said.

Damn him, he knew her too well.

He paused in stuffing her belongings into her suitcase, looked her in the face. "I thought you were dead, you realize that? I thought it was over out there."

"I'm not dead."

"I know." He stopped packing to lean closer, cupped her face in his hands. "Max, I'm sorry about the way I acted after we—I didn't mean any of it the way you took it."

"Didn't you?"

He stared into her eyes. "This isn't easy for me, you know."

"I know."

Nodding, he stuffed the rest of her things into her bag, closed it and took her hand, drawing her to her feet again. He led her out to Stormy's room and told her to wait there, by the door. Then he ran across the parking lot to her car, flung the bags into the trunk and drove the Bug over to park it in front of where Max stood waiting. He opened the door to Stormy's room and led her inside, again insisting she sit and hold the ice to her head while he gathered up Stormy's things, shoving them into her overnight bag. He spoke as he packed.

"I want to tell you something, and I don't want you to respond right away. All right?"

She nodded.

"When we made love—and that's what it was, Maxie. Don't even think it was anything less. When we made love, and I was lying there, holding you and thinking about what had to happen next, I wasn't feeling defeated or conquered or painted into a corner. I was feeling…mostly…relieved."

"You were?"

He nodded, and paused with Stormy's hairbrush in his hand, staring down for a moment at the yellow hairs, reflecting the light he'd flicked on when he'd entered the room. "I don't think Storm is in any danger from that vampire," he said.

Max blinked at the total change of subject. "What makes you think that?"

"Because when he looks at her...there's something in his eyes."

"He doesn't even know her."

"Even so, that look—it reminds me of the way I feel when I look at you."

She lifted her gaze to his. But he just gripped her hand and tugged her to her feet again, leading her out of the room. He tossed the bag into the car on the way, then took her into Jason's room. She knew the drill by now and sat down in the chair. Lou looked in the closet, yanked out Jay's coat, then skimmed the room for the handful of things Jason had acquired while in this town.

"My ice is melting."

"Hold on a little longer. I got off the subject. Where was I?"

"You were relieved after we made love."

"Yeah. I was relieved. Mostly because I was so tired of resisting you. Tired of saying no, tired of trying to keep my feelings under control so you wouldn't see them."

She frowned. He wasn't looking at her. He finished checking dresser drawers and moved into the bathroom, returning with a handful of items he dropped onto the coat.

"Why didn't you want me to know?"

He rolled the coat up, toiletries and all.

She got to her feet before he could pick it up. "Lou, could you stop bustling for a minute and look at me?"

He did. He looked at her, and he looked tormented. "I'm so fucking scared I'll screw this up. I tried to make marriage work once, Maxie. I tried, and I failed, and I ended up bleeding, and so did she. I lost her. I tried to be a father to my kid, and I lost him, too. If I hurt you that way, I don't think I could live with myself."

"I'm not gonna let you hurt me, Lou. And you're sure as hell not gonna lose me."

He ran his hands through her hair. Nodded once, and seemed to square his shoulders. "Okay, then. Here it is, straight up. I love you. I am goddamn head over heels for you, Max. I think I have been for just about always."

"You have?"

"Hell, yes. How could I not be?" He took the melting-ice-filled towel and moved it away, so he could look at the cut on her head. "I was relieved after we made love, because I figured I could stop fighting it.

Just—for some reason I was still denying how I felt. Force of habit. Fear of failure. I don't know. So I told you we might as well get married and made it sound like I was taking a plea-bargain deal from a D.A. who was about to fry my ass. That wasn't what I was doing, though."

"No?"

"Max, it took scaring me half to death to prove it to me out there. But it finally came clear. You and me, we're already partners. We work together. We play together. When the shit hits the fan in my life, the only thing I want to do is call you, or come over and tell you about it. Ditto when something good happens. And I think it's the same for you."

She nodded. "It's always been."

"You're my best friend," he told her. "But it goes way deeper. 'Cause the thought of you with another man makes me want to do murder, kid. When we first hooked up with Jason, I was…I thought he… Jesus, Max, I wanted to beat him senseless. You're mine."

"I've always been yours. Just waiting for you to decide you wanted me to be."

"I've always wanted you to be. I just didn't realize what was right under my nose. I want to be your partner in the business, Maxie. I want to move up there to Maine and buy a fishing boat and take you out on the ocean for weekends and holidays. I want to have the right to be jealous and possessive and overprotective of you—and I want the whole world to know I have that right. Because I love you like nobody ever loved anybody. *Ever.* And that's why I want you to marry me, Max."

She slid her arms around his neck, stood on tiptoe and kissed his mouth slowly. "You know how long I've waited for you to wake up and smell the doughnuts, Malone?"

"Too long. I'm sorry, babe. I'm not gonna make you wait for anything ever again. Promise. I'll marry you right now—as soon we can drive to a justice of the peace, if you want."

She shook her head sadly. "I can't get married without my best friend standing beside me, Lou."

"Then we'd better get busy tracking her down. Because, frankly, I don't think I want to wait much longer." He slid an arm around her, picked up the bundle from the bed and led her out to the car. Then he opened the passenger door, and when she got in, he leaned over, buckled her seat belt around her and lingered just long enough to press his mouth to hers.

It was going to take some getting used to, having

him be the one seducing her for a change. She thought she liked it.

Lou straightened away, his eyes dancing over her face as if he were looking at heaven; then he closed her door, flung Jason's rolled-up coat into the back seat and went around the car to get behind the wheel. He started the engine and drove onto the road, away from the town of Endover. As they passed through town, the sun was rising. People were stepping out of their houses, looking around, blinking in the light like moles too long underground. Their eyes were clear and sharp, if still a bit squinty.

"God, I'm glad to leave that place behind," Max said as they drove on. "But I think the thrall that held it is already fading."

"I think so, too. It felt different when we came back from the island. Lighter. And Gary seemed more normal, too."

"We faced down Dracula," Max said, looking sideways at Lou. "I can't believe this was the very first official case of our new agency. Dracula. The biggest, baddest of all the big bads."

"And we lived to tell the tale," he said. "Doesn't bode well for a quiet, peaceful future, does it?"

She sent him an alarmed look.

He smiled. "Honey, don't worry. It's you I want.

Not peace and quiet. But lively, lovely Mad Max Stuart." He smiled slowly then. "Mad Max Malone. Hell, that's got a sweet ring to it."

"I've always thought so," she said, and she leaned across the car to kiss his neck, then rested her head, hair still damp from the towel, on his shoulder. "I adore you, Lou."

"It's mutual, kid."

"Where are we going?"

"We're going to find a doc to stitch up your head. And then we're going to find Stormy. After that, it doesn't matter. Because wherever we go, we'll be going together. For as long as I live, Max. That's a promise."

"I'm going to hold you to it," she told him.

"I'm counting on it."

Epilogue

Stormy sat in the sailboat, her hands bound together, watching as the man she believed to be Dracula himself manned the sailboat with the skill of a seasoned sailor. He aimed for the dark horizon as the night wind billowed in the sails and sent them skimming over the ocean at dizzying speeds, farther and farther away from everything she had ever known....

And toward something she both anticipated and feared. Something strangely enticing, oddly familiar, and yet terrifying, all at once. Something that both drew and repelled her.

Just like the man himself.

Dracula.

He looked back at her, his long black hair whipping in the wind. He looked at her as warily as if she were one of those vampire hunters she'd heard Max talking about.

She said, "You can untie me, you know."

"I don't trust you not to try to escape. And if you do, you'll drown, Tempest."

Tempest. Somehow the name wasn't so unpleasant when it came from his lips, in his voice. She couldn't take her eyes off him, couldn't stop feeling his mouth on her, his teeth—God, her neck tingled and came alive at the mere memory. "I promise I won't try to escape. I couldn't swim all the way to shore from here, anyway. And I know you aren't going to hurt me."

"Don't be so sure of that, little one."

He leaned down, and she lifted her bound wrists to him. He drew out a blade and held her hand in one of his, while he used the other to slice the ropes cleanly. Then he held it a moment longer.

"What you are feeling," he whispered close to her ear, "has an explanation."

"Does it?"

He nodded, lifting his black eyes and locking them with hers. "I drank from you. It was foolish of me. I should not have done it. All for the sake of making a

point, shocking your friends. But I am sometimes…
impulsive."

"It wasn't like I thought it would be."

"No. And it creates a…an attraction. That is why
your blood heats when you meet my eyes, little one.
It will pass."

She held his eyes with hers. She said, "I don't
think so."

"No?"

Shaking her head side to side, she whispered, "No.
Because I was feeling…what I am feeling…long before you so much as touched me. Maybe…before I
even met you. Maybe…maybe far, far longer than
that."

He narrowed his eyes on her. "What do you mean
by that?"

She drew a breath, eyelids lowered. "I don't know.
I don't know, Vlad."

He stared at her for a long, long time as they sailed
on. "The sun will be up soon. I will be forced to seek
shelter. I hope you won't mind resting through the
day with your body bound to that of a dead man."

The thought made her shudder with fear. And with
something else. Something that felt like desire.

* * * * *

MILLS & BOON®
Book Club

Free Book!

Get your free books now at
www.millsandboon.co.uk/freebookoffer

Or fill in the form below and post it back to us

THE MILLS & BOON® BOOK CLUB™—HERE'S HOW IT WORKS: Accepting your free books places you under no obligation to buy anything. You may keep the books and return the despatch note marked 'Cancel'. If we do not hear from you, about a month later we'll send you 3 brand-new stories from the Nocturne™ series, two priced at £4.99 and a third, larger version priced at £6.99 each. There is no extra charge for post and packaging. You may cancel at any time, otherwise we will send you 4 stories a month which you may purchase or return to us—the choice is yours. *Terms and prices subject to change without notice. Offer valid in UK only. Applicants must be 18 or over. Offer expires 28th February 2012. **For full terms and conditions, please go to www.millsandboon.co.uk/termsandconditions**

Mrs/Miss/Ms/Mr (please circle) _____

First Name _____

Surname _____

Address _____

_____

_____ Postcode _____

E-mail _____

Send this completed page to: Mills & Boon Book Club, Free Book Offer, FREEPOST NAT 10298, Richmond, Surrey, TW9 1BR

Find out more at
www.millsandboon.co.uk/freebookoffer

Visit us Online

0611/T1ZEE